# THE
# WANDERING
# FIRE

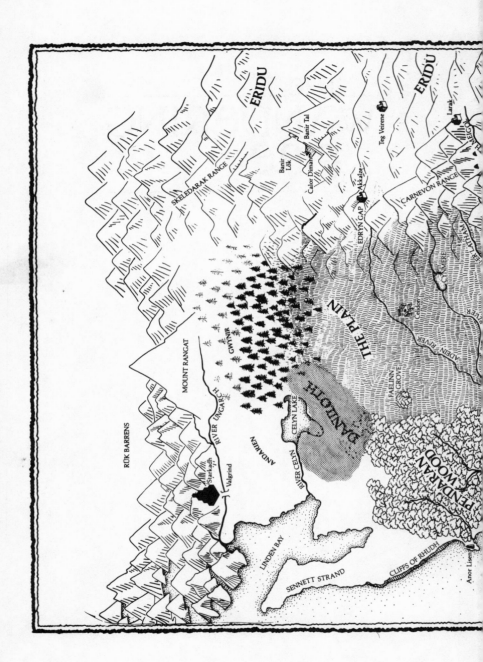

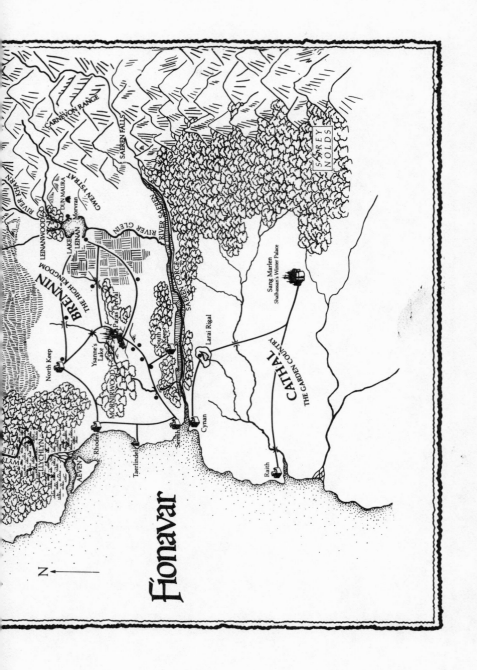

ALSO BY GUY GAVRIEL KAY

*The Summer Tree*

# THE WANDERING FIRE

Guy
Gavriel
Kay

## THE FIONAVAR TAPESTRY
### Book Two

ARBOR HOUSE
NEW YORK

SF

Library of Congress Cataloging in Publication Data
Kay, Guy Gavriel.
   The wandering fire.

   (The Fionavar tapestry ; bk. 2)
   I. Title.   II. Series: Kay, Guy Gavriel. Fionavar
tapestry (New York, N.Y.) ; bk. 2.
PR9199.3.K39W3   1986        813'.54        85-26722
ISBN: 0-87795-785-1

*The Wandering Fire* is dedicated to my wife,
LAURA,
who came with me to find it.

# ACKNOWLEDGMENTS

This second book of the Tapestry was written on the farm of our friends, Marge and Antonios Katsipis, near the town of Whakatane, New Zealand. The shaping of my own world was immeasurably aided by the warmth with which the two of them, and their son, Iakomi, welcomed us to theirs.

# CONTENTS

# THE CHARACTERS

*The Five:*

KIMBERLY FORD, Seer of Brennin
KEVIN LAINE
JENNIFER LOWELL
DAVE MARTYNIUK ("Davor")
PAUL SCHAFER, Lord of the Summer Tree ("Pwyll
  Twiceborn")

*In Brennin:*

AILERON, High King of Brennin
DIARMUID, his brother

LOREN SILVERCLOAK, First Mage of Brennin
MATT SÖREN, his source, once King of the Dwarves
TEYRNON, a mage
BARAK, his source

JAELLE, High Priestess of the Goddess
AUDIART, her second in command, in the province of
  Gwen Ystrat
LEILA, a young priestess

COLL, lieutenant to Diarmuid
CARDE
ERRON
TEGID      the men of South Keep, members of
ROTHE      Diarmuid's band
AVERREN

GORLAES, the Chancellor of Brennin
MABON, Duke of Rhoden
NIAVIN, Duke of Seresh
CEREDUR, Warden of the North Marches

VAE, a woman in Paras Derval
FINN, her son
SHAHAR, her husband
BRENDEL, a lord of the lios alfar, from Daniloth
BROCK, a Dwarf, from Banir Tal

*In Cathal:*

SHALHASSAN, Supreme Lord of Cathal
SHARRA, his daughter and heir ("the Dark Rose")
BASHRAI, Captain of the Honor Guard (eidolath)

*On the Plain:*

IVOR, Chieftain of the third tribe of the Dalrei
LEITH, his wife
LEVON
CORDELIANE ("LIANE") } his children
TABOR

TORC, a Rider of the third tribe

GEREINT, shaman of the third tribe

*In Daniloth:*

RA-TENNIEL, King of the lios alfar
GALEN
LYDAN
LEYSE } lords and ladies of the lios alfar
HEILYN
ENROTH

*The Powers:*

THE WEAVER at the Loom

MÖRNIR of the Thunder
DANA, the Mother
CERNAN of the Beasts
CEINWEN of the Bow, the HUNTRESS
MACHA }
NEMAIN } goddesses of war

OWEIN, Leader of the Wild Hunt

*The Dark:*

RAKOTH MAUGRIM the UNRAVELLER

GALADAN, Wolflord of the andain, his lieutenant
METRAN, once First Mage of Brennin, now allied with
   the Dark
AVAIA, the Black Swan
BLÖD, a Dwarf, servant to Rakoth
KAEN, brother to Blöd, ruling the Dwarves in Banir
   Lök

*From the Past:*

IORWETH FOUNDER, first High King of Brennin

CONARY, High King during the Bael Rangat
COLAN, his son, High King after him ("the Beloved")
AMAIRGEN WHITEBRANCH, first of the mages
LISEN of the Wood, a deiena, source and wife to
   Amairgen

REVOR, ancestral hero of the Dalrei, first Lord (Aven)
   of the Plain

# PART 1

## The Warrior

# Chapter 1

**W**inter was coming. Last night's snow hadn't melted and the bare trees were laced with it. Toronto woke that morning to see itself cloaked and made over in white, and it was only November.

Cutting across Nathan Philips Square in front of the twin curves of the City Hall, Dave Martyniuk walked as carefully as he could and wished he'd worn boots. As he maneuvered toward the restaurant entrance on the far side, he saw with some surprise that the other three were already waiting.

"Dave," said sharp-eyed Kevin Laine. "A new suit! When did this happen?"

"Hi, everyone," Dave said. "I got it last week. Can't wear the same corduroy jackets all year, can I?"

"A deep truth," said Kevin, grinning. He was wearing jeans and a sheepskin jacket. And boots. Having finished the obligatory apprenticeship with a law firm that Dave had just begun, Kevin was now immersed in the equally tedious if less formal six-month Bar Admission course. "If that is a three-piece suit," he added, "my image of you is going to be irrevocably shattered."

Wordlessly, Dave unbuttoned his overcoat to reveal the shattering navy vest beneath.

"Angels and ministers of grace defend us!" Kevin exclaimed, crossing himself with the wrong hand while making the sign against evil with the other. Paul Schafer laughed. "Actually," Kevin said, "it looks very nice. Why didn't you buy it in your size?"

"Oh, Kev, give him a break!" Kim Ford said. "It *is* nice,

3

Dave, and it fits perfectly. Kevin's feeling scruffy and jealous."

"I am not," Kevin protested. "I am simply giving my buddy a hard time. If I can't tease Dave, who can I tease?"

"It's okay," said Dave. "I'm tough, I can take it." But what he was remembering in that moment was the face of Kevin Laine the spring before, in a room in the Park Plaza Hotel. The face, and the flat, harshly mastered voice in which he'd spoken, looking down at the wreckage of a woman on the floor:

*"To this I will make reply although he be a god and it mean my death."*

You gave some latitude, Dave was thinking, to someone who'd sworn an oath like that, even if his style was more than occasionally jarring. You gave latitude because what Kevin had done that evening was give voice, and not for the only time, to the mute rage in one's own heart.

"All right," said Kim Ford softly, and Dave knew that she was responding to his thought and not his flippant words. Which would have been unsettling, were she not who she was, with her white hair, the green bracelet on her wrist, and the red ring on her finger that had blazed to bring them home. "Let's go in," Kim said. "We've things to talk about."

Paul Schafer, the Twiceborn, had already turned to lead them through the door.

How many shadings, Kevin was thinking, are there to helplessness? He remembered the feeling from the year before, watching Paul twist inward on himself in the months after Rachel Kincaid had died. A bad time, that was. But Paul had come out of it, had gone so far in three nights on the Summer Tree in Fionavar that he was beyond understanding in the most important ways. He was healed, though, and Kevin held to that as a gift from Fionavar, some recompense for what had been done to Jennifer by the god named Rakoth Maugrim, the Unraveller. Though recompense was hardly the word; there was no true compensation to be found in this or any other world, only the hope of retribution, a flame so faint, despite what he had sworn, it scarcely burned. What were any of them against a god? Even Kim, with her Sight, even Paul, even Dave, who had changed among the Dalrei on the Plain and had found a horn in Pendaran Wood.

And who was he, Kevin Laine, to swear an oath of revenge? It all seemed so pathetic, so ridiculous, especially here, eating fillet of sole in the Mackenzie King Dining Room, amid the clink of cutlery and the lunchtime talk of lawyers and civil servants.

"Well?" said Paul, in a tone that made their setting instantly irrelevant. He was looking at Kim. "Have you seen anything?"

"Stop that," she said. "Stop pushing. If anything happens I'll tell you. Do you want it in writing?"

"Easy, Kim," Kevin said. "You have to understand how ignorant we feel. You're our only link."

"Well, I'm not linked to anything now, and that's all there is to it. There's a place I have to find and I can't control my dreaming. It's in this world, that's all I know, and I can't go anywhere or do anything until I find it. Do you think I'm enjoying this any more than you three are?"

"Can't you send us back?" Dave asked, unwisely.

"I am not a goddamned subway system!" Kim snapped. "I got us out because the Baelrath was somehow unleashed. I can't do it on command."

"Which means we're stuck here," Kevin said.

"Unless Loren comes for us," Dave amended.

Paul was shaking his head. "He won't."

"Why?" Dave asked.

"Loren's playing hands-off, I think. He set things in motion, but he's leaving it up to us, now, and some of the others."

Kim was nodding. "He put a thread in the loom," she murmured, "but he won't weave this tapestry." She and Paul exchanged a glance.

"But why?" Dave persisted. Kevin could hear the big man's frustration. "He needs us—or at least Kim and Paul. Why won't he come for us?"

"Because of Jennifer," said Paul quietly. After a moment

he went on. "He thinks we've suffered enough. He won't impose any more."

Kevin cleared his throat. "As I understand it, though, whatever happens in Fionavar is going to be reflected here and in the other worlds too, wherever they are. Isn't that true?"

"It is," said Kim calmly. "It is true. Not immediately, perhaps, but if Rakoth takes dominion in Fionavar he takes dominion everywhere. There is only one Tapestry."

"Even so," said Paul, "we have to do it on our own. Loren won't demand it. If the four of us want to go back, we'll have to find a way ourselves."

"The four of us?" Kevin said. So much helplessness. He looked at Kim.

There were tears in her eyes. "I don't know," she whispered. "I just don't know. She won't see the three of you. She never goes out of the house. She talks to me about work and the weather, and the news, and she's, she—"

"She's going ahead with it," Paul Schafer said.

Kimberly nodded.

Golden, she had been, Kevin remembered, from inside the sorrow.

"All right," said Paul. "It's my turn now."

Arrow of the God.

She'd had a peephole placed in the door so she could see who was knocking. She was home most of the day, except for afternoon walks in the park nearby. There were often people at the door: deliveries, the gas man, registered mail. For a while at the beginning there had been, fatuously, flowers. She'd thought Kevin was smarter than that. She didn't care whether or not that was a fair judgment. She'd had a fight with Kim about it, when her roommate had come home one evening to find roses in the garbage can.

"Don't you have any idea how he's feeling? Don't you care?" Kimberly had shouted.

Answer: no, and no.

How could she come to such a human thing as caring, any more? Numberless, the unbridged chasms between where she now was, and the four of them, and everyone else. To everything there yet clung the odor of the swan. She saw the world through the filtered unlight of Starkadh. What voice, what eyes seen through that green distortion, could efface the power of Rakoth, who had shoveled through her mind and body as if she, who had once been loved and whole, were so much slag?

She knew she was sane, did not know why.

One thing only pulled her forward into some future tense. Not a good thing, nor could it have been, but it was real, and random, and hers. She would not be gainsaid.

And so, when Kim had first told the other three, and they had come in July to argue with her, she had stood up and left the room. Nor had she seen Kevin or Dave or Paul since that day.

She would bear this child, the child of Rakoth Maugrim. She intended to die giving birth.

She would not have let him in, except that she saw that he was alone, and this was sufficiently unexpected to cause her to open the door.

Paul Schafer said, "I have a story to tell. Will you listen?"

It was cold on the porch. After a moment she stepped aside and he entered. She closed the door and walked into the living room. He hung up his coat in the hall closet and followed her.

She had taken the rocking chair. He sat down on the couch and looked at her, tall and fair, still graceful though no longer slim, seven months heavy with the child. Her head was high, her wide-set green eyes uncompromising.

"I walked away from you last time, and I will again, Paul. I will not be moved on this."

"I said, a story," he murmured.

"Then tell it."

So he told her for the first time about the grey dog on the wall of Paras Derval and the fathomless sorrow in its eyes; he told her about his second night on the Summer Tree, when

Galadan, whom she also knew, had come for him, and how the dog had appeared again, and of the battle fought here in the Mörnirwood. He told her about being bound on the Tree of the God, and seeing the red moon rise and the grey dog drive the wolf from the wood.

He told her of Dana. And Mörnir. The powers shown forth that night in answer to the Darkness in the north. His voice was deeper than she remembered; there were echoes in it.

He said, "We are not in this alone. He may break us into fragments in the end, but he will not be unresisted, and whatever you may have seen or endured in that place you must understand that he cannot shape the pattern exactly to his desire. Or else you would not be here."

She listened, almost against her will. His words brought back words of her own, spoken in Starkadh itself: *You will have nothing of me that you do not take,* she had said. But that was before. Before he had set about taking everything— until Kim had pulled her out.

She lifted her head a little. "Yes," Paul said, his eyes never leaving her face. "Do you understand? He is stronger than any of us, stronger even than the God who sent me back. He is stronger than you, Jennifer; it is not worth saying except for this: he cannot take away what you are."

"I know this," said Jennifer Lowell. "It is why I will bear his child."

He sat back. "Then you become his servant."

"No. You listen to me now, Paul, because you don't know everything either. When he left me . . . after, he gave me to a Dwarf. Blöd was his name. I was a reward, a toy, but he said something to the Dwarf: he said I was to be killed, *and that there was a reason.*" There was cold resolution in her voice. "I will bear this child because I am alive when he wished me dead—the child is random, it is outside his purposes."

He was silent a long time. Then, "But so are you, in and of yourself."

Her laugh was a brutal sound. "And how am I, in and of myself, to answer him? I am going to have a son, Paul, and he will be my answer."

He shook his head. "There is too much evil in this, and only to prove a point already proven."

"Nonetheless," said Jennifer.

After a moment his mouth crooked sideways. "I won't press you on it, then. I came for you, not him. Kim's already dreamt his name, anyhow."

Her eyes flashed. "Paul, understand me. I would do what I am doing whatever Kim said. Whatever she happened to dream. And I will name him as I choose!"

He was smiling, improbably. "Stick around and do that then. Stay with us, Jen. We need you back." Only when he spoke did she realize what she'd said. He'd tricked her, she decided, had goaded her quite deliberately into something unintended. But she couldn't, for some reason, feel angry. Had this first tenuous spar he'd thrown across to her been a little firmer she might, in fact, have smiled.

Paul stood up. "There is an exhibition of Japanese prints at the Art Gallery. Would you like to see it with me?"

For a long time she rocked in the chair, looking up at him. He was dark-haired, slight, still frail-seeming, though not so much as last spring.

"What was the dog's name?" she asked.

"I don't know. I wish I did."

After another moment she rose, put on her coat, and took her first careful step on the first bridge.

Dark seed of a dark god, Paul was thinking, as he tried to simulate an interest in nineteenth-century prints from Kyoto and Osaka. Cranes, twisted trees, elegant ladies with long pins in their hair.

The lady beside him wasn't talking a great deal, but she was there in the gallery, and it was not a small grace. He remembered the crumpled figure she had been seven months before, when Kim had brought them desperately from Fionavar with the wild, blazing power of the Baelrath.

This was Kim's power, he knew: the Warstone and the dreams in which she walked at night, white-haired as Ysanne had been, two souls within her, and knowledge of two worlds. It had to be a difficult thing. *The price of power,* he

9

remembered Ailell the High King telling him, the night they played their game of ta'bael. The night that had been overture to the three nights that became his own hard, hardest thing. The gateway to whatever he now was, Lord of the Summer Tree.

Whatever he now was. They had moved into the twentieth century now: more cranes, long, narrow mountain scenes, low boats riding on wide rivers.

"The themes don't change much," Jennifer said.

"Not much."

He had been sent back, he was Mörnir's response, but he had no ring with which to burn, no dreams down which to track the secrets of the Tapestry, not even a horn such as Dave had found, no skylore like Loren, or crown like Aileron; not even—though he felt a chill at the thought—a child within him like the woman at his side.

And yet. There had been ravens at his shoulder in the branches of the Tree: Thought and Memory were their names. There had been a figure in the clearing, hard to see, but he had seen horns on its head and seen it bow to him. There had been the white mist rising up through him to the sky in which a red moon sailed on new moon night. There had been rain. And then the God.

And there was still the God. At night, sometimes, he could feel the tacit presence, immense, in the rush and slide of his blood, the muffled thunder of his human heart.

Was he a symbol only? A manifestation of what he had been telling Jennifer: the presence of opposition to the workings of the Unraveller? There were worse roles, he supposed. It gave him a part to play in what was to come, but something within—and there was a god within him—said that there was more. *No man shall be Lord of the Summer Tree who has not twice been born,* Jaelle had said to him in the sanctuary.

He was more than symbol. The waiting to learn what, and how, seemed to be part of the price.

Almost at the end now. They stopped in front of a large print of a river scene: boats being poled along, others unloading at a crowded dock; there were woods on the far side of the stream, snow-capped mountains beyond. It was badly hung, though; he could see people behind them reflected in the glass, two students, the sleepy guard. And then Paul saw the blurred reflection in the doorway of a wolf.

Turning quickly on a taken breath he met the eyes of Galadan.

The Wolflord was in his true shape, and hearing Jennifer gasp Paul knew that she, too, remembered that scarred, elegant force of power with the silver in his dark hair.

Grabbing Jennifer's hand, Paul wheeled and began to move quickly back through the exhibition. He looked over his shoulder: Galadan was following, a sardonic smile on his face. He wasn't hurrying.

They rounded a corner. Mumbling a swift prayer, Paul pushed on the bar of a door marked EMERGENCY EXIT ONLY. He heard a guard shout behind him, but no alarm sounded. They found themselves in a service corridor. Without saying a word, they clattered down the hallway. Behind them Paul heard the guard shout again as the door opened a second time.

The corridor forked. Paul pushed open another door and hurried Jennifer through. She stumbled and he had to hold her up.

"I can't run, Paul!"

He cursed inwardly. They were as far from the exit as they could be. The door had taken them out into the largest room in the gallery, Henry Moore's permanent sculpture exhibit. It was the pride of the Art Gallery of Ontario, the room that placed it on the artistic map of the world.

And it was the room in which, it seemed, they were going to die.

He helped Jennifer move farther away from the door. They passed several huge pieces, a madonna and child, a nude, an abstract shape.

"Wait here," he said, and sat her down on the broad base of one of the sculptures. There was no one else in the room—not on a weekday morning in November.

It figures, he thought. And turned. The Wolflord walked through the same door they had used. For the second time he and Galadan faced each other in a place where time seemed to hang suspended.

Jennifer whispered his name. Without taking his eyes from Galadan he heard her say, in a voice shockingly cold, "It is too soon, Paul. Whatever you are, you must find it now. If not, I will curse you as I die."

And still reeling from that, he saw Galadan raise a long slender finger to a red weal on his temple. "This one," said the Lord of the andain, "I lay at the root of your Tree."

"You are lucky," Paul said, "to be alive to lay it anywhere."

"Perhaps," the other said, and smiled again, "but no more fortunate than you have been until now. Both of you." There was, though Paul had not seen it come, a knife in his hand. He remembered that knife. Galadan moved a few steps closer. No one, Paul knew, was going to enter the room.

And then he knew something more. There was a deep stirring, as of the sea, within him, and he moved forward himself, away from Jennifer, and said, "Would you battle the Twiceborn of Mörnir?"

And the Wolflord replied, "For nothing else am I here, though I will kill the girl when you are dead. Remember who I am: the children of gods have knelt to wash my feet. You are nothing yet, Pwyll Twiceborn, and will be twice dead before I let you come into your force."

Paul shook his head. There was a tide running in his blood. He heard himself say, as if from far off, "Your father bowed to me, Galadan. Will you not do so, *son of Cernan?*" And he felt a rush of power to see the other hesitate.

But only for a moment. Then the Wolflord, who had been a force of might and a Lord of the mighty for past a thousand years, laughed aloud and, raising his hand again, plunged the room into utter darkness.

"What son have you ever known to follow his father's path?" he said. "There is no dog to guard you now, *and I can see in the dark!*"

The surging of power stopped within Paul.

In its place came something else, a quiet, a space as of a pool within a wood, and he knew this, instinctively, to be the true access to what he now was and would be. From within this calm he moved back to Jennifer and said to her, "Be easy, but hold fast to me." As he felt her grip his hand and rise to stand beside him, he spoke once more to the Wolflord, and his voice had changed.

"Slave of Maugrim," he said, "I cannot defeat you yet, nor can I see you in the dark. We will meet again, and the third time pays for all, as well you know. But I will not tarry for you in this place."

And on the words he felt himself dropping into the still, deep place, the pool within, which uttermost need had found. Down and down he went, and, holding tight to Jennifer, he took them both away through the remembered cold, the interstices of time, the space between the Weaver's worlds, back to Fionavar.

# Chapter 2

Vae heard the knocking at the door. Since Shahar had been sent north she often heard sounds in the house at night, and she had taught herself to ignore them, mostly.

But the hammering on the shop entrance below was not to be ignored as being born of winter solitude or wartime fears. It was real, and urgent, and she didn't want to know who it was.

Her son was in the hallway outside her room, though; he had already pulled on trousers and the warm vest she had made him when the snows began. He looked sleepy and young, but he always looked young to her.

"Shall I go see?" he said bravely.

"Wait," Vae said. She rose, herself, and pulled on a woolen robe over her night attire. It was cold in the house, and long past the middle of the night. Her man was away, and she was alone in the chill of winter with a fourteen-year-old child and a rapping, more and more insistent, at her door.

Vae lit a candle and followed Finn down the stairs.

"Wait," she said again in the shop, and lit two more candles, despite the waste. One did not open the door on a winter night without some light by which to see who came. When the candles had caught, she saw that Finn had taken the iron rod from the upstairs fire. She nodded, and he opened the door.

In the drifted snow outside stood two strangers, a man, and a tall woman he supported with an arm about her shoulders. Finn lowered his weapon; they were unarmed. Coming nearer, and holding her candle high, Vae saw two things: that the woman wasn't a stranger after all, and that she was far gone with child.

"From the ta'kiena?" said Vae. "The third time."

The woman nodded. Her eyes turned to Finn and then back to his mother. "He is still here," she said. "I am glad."

Finn said nothing; he was so young it could break Vae's heart. The man in the doorway stirred. "We need help," he said. "We are fleeing the Wolflord from our world. I am Pwyll, this is Jennifer. We crossed here last spring with Loren."

Vae nodded, wishing Shahar were there instead of in the windy cold of North Keep with his grandfather's spear. He was a craftsman, not a soldier; what did her husband know of war?

"Come in," she said, and stepped back. Finn closed and bolted the door behind them. "I am Vae. My man is away. What help can I offer you?"

"The crossing brought me early to my time," the woman called Jennifer said, and Vae saw from her face that it was true.

"Make a fire," she said to Finn. "In my room upstairs." She turned to the man. "You help him. Boil water on the fire. Finn will show you where the clean linen is. Quickly, both of you."

They left, taking the stairs two at a time.

Alone in the candlelit shop, among the unspun wool and the finished craftings, she and the other woman gazed at each other.

"Why me?" said Vae.

The other's eyes were clouded with pain. "Because," she said, "I need a mother who knows how to love her child."

Vae had been fast asleep only moments before; the woman in the room with her was so fair she might have been a creature from the dreamworld, save for her eyes.

"I don't understand," said Vae.

"I will have to leave him," the woman said. "Could you give your heart to another son when Finn takes the Longest Road?"

In daylight she might have struck or cursed anyone who

said so flatly the thing that twisted through her like a blade. But this was night and half a dream, and the other woman was crying.

Vae was a simple woman, a worker in wool and cloth with her man. She had a son who for no reason she could understand had been called three times to the Road when the children played the prophecy game, the ta'kiena, and then a fourth time before the Mountain went up to signal war. And now there was this.

"Yes," said Vae, simply. "I could love another child. It is a son?"

Jennifer wiped away her tears. "It is," she said. "But there is more. He will be of andain, and I don't know what that will mean."

Vae felt her hands trembling. Child of a god and a mortal. It meant many things, most of them forgotten. She took a deep breath. "Very well," she said.

"One thing more," the golden woman said.

Vae closed her eyes. "Tell me, then."

She kept them closed for a long time after the father's name was spoken. Then, with more courage than she would have ever guessed she had, Vae opened her eyes and said, "He will need to be loved a great deal. I will try." Watching the other woman weep after that, she felt pity break over her in waves.

At length Jennifer collected herself, only to be racked by a visible spasm of pain.

"We had best go up," said Vae. "This will not be an easy thing. Can you manage the stairs?"

Jennifer nodded her head. Vae put an arm around her, and they moved together to the stairway. Jennifer stopped.

"If you had had a second son," she whispered, "what name would he have had?"

The dreamworld, it was. "Darien," she said. "For my father."

It was not an easy thing, but neither was it a long one. He was small, of course, more than two months early, but not as small as she had expected. He was placed on her breast for a moment, afterward. Looking down for the first time upon her son, Jennifer wept, in love and in sorrow for all the worlds, all the battlegrounds, for he was beautiful.

Blinded, she closed her eyes. Then, once only, and formally, that it should be done and known to be done, she said, "His name is Darien. He has been named by his mother." Saying so, she laid her head back upon the pillows and gave her son to Vae.

Taking him, Vae was astonished how easily love came to her again. There were tears in her own eyes as she cradled him. She blamed their blurring and the shifting candlelight for the moment—no more than that—when his very blue eyes seemed red.

It was still dark when Paul went out into the streets, and snow was falling. Drifts were piling up in the lanes of Paras Derval and against the shops and houses. He passed the remembered signboard on the Black Boar. The inn was dark and shuttered, the sign creaked in the pre-dawn wind. No one else was abroad in the white streets.

He continued, east to the edge of the town and then—though the going became harder—north up the slope of the palace hill. There were lights on in the castle, beacons of warmth amid the wind and blowing snow.

Paul Schafer felt a deep desire to go to those beacons, to sit down with friends—Loren, Matt, Diarmuid, Coll, even Aileron, the stern, bearded High King—and learn their tidings even as he shared the burden of what he had just witnessed.

He resisted the lure. The child was Jennifer's thread in this weaving, and she was owed this much: he would not take that thread away by spreading word throughout the land of a son born that day to Rakoth Maugrim.

Darien, she had named him. Paul thought of Kim saying, *I know his name.* He shook his head. This child was something so unpredictable, so truly random, it numbed the mind: what would be the powers of this newest of the andain, and where, oh, where, would his allegiance fall? Had Jennifer brought forth this day not merely a lieutenant but an heir to the Dark?

Both women had cried, the one who had given birth and the one who would raise him. Both women, but not the child, not this fair blue-eyed child of two worlds.

Did the andain cry? Paul reached down toward the still place, the source of the power that had brought them here, for an answer but was not surprised to find nothing there.

Pushing through the last swirling mound of snow he reached his destination, drew a breath to steady himself, and pulled on the chain outside the arched doorway.

He heard a bell ring deep within the domed Temple of the Mother; then there was silence again. He stood in the darkness a long time before the great doors swung open and the glow of candlelight spun out a little way into the snow-bound night. He moved sideways and forward to see and be seen.

"No farther!" a woman said. "I have a blade."

He kept his composure. "I'm sure you do," he said. "But you also have eyes, I hope, and should know who I am, for I have been here before."

There were two of them, a young girl with the candle and an older woman beside her. Others, with more light, were coming forward as well.

The girl moved nearer, raising her light so that his face was fully lit by the flame.

"By Dana of the Moon!" the older woman breathed.

"Yes," said Paul. "Now quickly, please, summon your Priestess. I have little time and must speak with her." He made to enter the vestibule.

"Hold!" the woman said again. "There is a price of blood all men must pay to enter here."

But for this he had no tolerance.

Stepping quickly forward, he grabbed her wrist and twisted. A knife clattered on the marble floor. Still holding the grey-robed woman in front of him Paul snapped, "Bring the Priestess, now!" None of them moved; behind him the wind whistled through the open door.

"Let her go," the young girl said calmly. He turned to her; she looked to be no more than thirteen. "She means no harm," the girl went on. "She doesn't know that you bled the last time you were here, Twiceborn."

He had forgotten: Jaelle's fingers along his cheek as he lay helplessly. His glance narrowed on this preternaturally self-possessed child. He released the other priestess.

"Shiel," the girl said to her, still tranquilly, "we should summon the High Priestess."

"No need," a colder voice said, and walking between the torches, clad as ever in white, Jaelle came to stand facing him. She was barefoot on the cold floor, he saw, and her long red hair was twisted down her back in untended spirals.

"Sorry to wake you," he said.

"Speak," she replied. "And carefully. You have assaulted one of my priestesses."

He could not afford to lose his temper. This was going to be difficult enough as it was.

"I am sorry," he lied. "And I am here to speak. We should be alone, Jaelle."

A moment longer she regarded him, then turned. "Bring him to my chambers," she said.

"Priestess! The blood, he must—"

"Shiel, be silent for once!" Jaelle snapped in a wholly unusual revealing of strain.

"I told her," the young one said mildly. "He bled the last time he was here."

Jaelle hadn't wanted to be reminded. She went the long way around, so he would have to pass the dome and see the axe.

The bed he remembered. He had awakened here on a morning of rain. It was neatly made. Proprieties, he thought wryly—and some well-trained servants.

"Very well," she said.

"News first, please. Is there war?" he asked.

She walked over to the table, turned, and faced him, resting her hands behind her on the polished surface. "No. The winter came early and hard. Not even svart alfar march well in snow. The wolves have been a problem, and we are short of food, but there have been no battles yet."

"So you heard Kim's warning?" *Don't attack, he's waiting in Starkadh!* Kimberly had screamed, as they passed into the crossing.

Jaelle hesitated. "I heard it. yes."

"No one else?"

"I was tapping the avarlith for her."

"I remember. It was unexpected." She made an impatient movement. "They listened to you then?"

"Eventually." This time she gave nothing away. He could guess, though, what had happened, knowing the deep mistrust the men in the Great Hall that morning would have had for the High Priestess.

"What now?" was all he said.

"We wait for spring. Aileron takes council with everyone who will talk to him, but everyone waits for spring. Where is the Seer?" Some urgency there.

"Waiting also. For a dream."

"Why are you here?" she asked.

Smile fading, then, with no levity at all, he told her: Arrow of Mörnir to Priestess of the Mother. Everything. Softly he gave her the name of the child and, more softly yet, who the father was.

She didn't move during the telling of it or after; no indication anywhere in her of the impact. He had to admire her self-control. Then she asked again, but in a different voice, "Why are you here?"

And he said, "Because you made Jennifer a guest-friend last spring." She hadn't been ready for that—this time it showed in her face. A triumph for him of sorts, but the moment was too high by far for petty score-keeping in the power game. He went on, to take away the sting, "Loren would mistrust the wildness of this too much, but I thought you could deal with it. We need you."

"You trust me with this?

His turn to gesture impatiently. "Oh, Jaelle, don't exaggerate your own malevolence. You aren't happy with the power balance here, any fool can see that. But only a very great fool would confuse that with where you stand in this war. You serve the Goddess who sent up that moon, Jaelle. I am least likely of all men to forget it."

She seemed very young in that moment. There was a woman beneath the white robe, a person, not merely an icon; he'd made the mistake of trying to tell her that once, in this very room, with the rain falling outside.

"What do you need?" she said.

His tone was crisp. "A watch on the child. Complete secrecy, of course, which is another reason I came to you."

"I will have to tell the Mormae in Gwen Ystrat."

"I thought as much." He rose, began pacing as he spoke. "It is all the same, I gather, within the Mormae?"

She nodded. "It is all the same, within any level of the Priesthood, but it will be kept to the inner circle."

"All right," he said, and stopped his pacing very close to her. "But you have a problem then."

"What?"

"This!" And reaching past her, he pulled open an inner door and grabbed the listener beyond, pulling her into the room so that she sprawled on the carpeted floor.

"Leila!" Jaelle exclaimed.

The girl adjusted her grey robe and rose to her feet. There was a hint of apprehension in her eyes, but only a hint, Paul saw, and she held her head very high, facing the two of them.

"You may owe a death for this." Jaelle's tone was glacial.

Leila said hardily, "Are we to discuss it with a man here?"

Jaelle hesitated, but only for a second. "We are," she replied, and Paul was startled by a sudden change in her tone. "Leila," the High Priestess said gently, "you must not lecture me, I am not Shiel or Marline. You have worn grey for ten days only, and you must understand your place."

It was too soft for Paul's liking. "The hell with that! What was she doing there? What did she hear?"

"I heard it all," Leila said.

Jaelle was astonishingly calm. "I believe it," she said. "Now tell me why."

"Because of Finn," said Leila. "Because I could tell he came from Finn."

"Ah," said Jaelle slowly. She walked toward the child then and, after a moment, stroked a long finger down her cheek in an unsettling caress. "Of course."

"I'm lost," said Paul.

They both turned to him. "You shouldn't be," Jaelle said,

in complete control again. "Did Jennifer not tell you about the ta'kiena?"

"Yes, but—"

"And why she wanted to bear her child in Vae's house? Finn's mother's house?"

"Oh." It clicked. He looked at slim, fair-haired Leila. "This one?" he asked.

The girl answered him herself. "I called Finn to the Road. Three times, and then another. I am tuned to him until he goes."

There was a silence. "All right, Leila," Jaelle said. "Leave us now. You have done what you had to do. Never breathe a word."

"I don't think I could," said Leila, in a small voice. "For Finn. There is an ocean inside me sometimes. I think it would overrun me if I tried." She turned and left the room, closing the door softly behind her.

Looking at the Priestess in the light of the tall candles, Paul realized that he had never seen pity in her eyes before.

"You will do nothing?" he murmured.

Jaelle nodded her head, still looking at the door through which the girl had gone. "Anyone else I would have killed, believe me."

"But not this one?"

"Not this one."

"Why?"

She turned to him. "Leave me this secret," she said softly. "There are some mysteries best not known, Pwyll. Even for you." It was the first time she had spoken his name. Their eyes met, and this time it was Paul who looked away. Her scorn he could master, but this look in her eyes evoked access to a power older and deeper, even, than the one he had touched on the Tree.

He cleared his throat. "We should be gone by morning."

"I know," said Jaelle. "I will send in a moment to have her brought here."

"If I could do it myself," he said, "I would not ask this of you. I know it will drain the earthroot, the avarlith."

She shook her head; the candlelight made highlights in her

22

hair. "You did a deep thing to bring her here by yourself. The Weaver alone knows how."

"Well, I certainly don't," he said. An admission.

They were silent. It was very still in the sanctuary, in her room.

"Darien," she said.

He drew a breath. "I know. Are you afraid?"

"Yes," she said. "And you?"

"Very much."

They looked at each other across the carpeted space that lay between, a distance impossibly far.

"We had better get moving," he said finally.

She raised her arm and pulled a cord nearby. Somewhere a bell rang. When they came in response she gave swift, careful orders, and it seemed very soon when the priestesses returned, bearing Jennifer.

After that it took little time. They went into the dome and the man was blindfolded. She took the blood from herself, which surprised some of them; then she reached east to Gwen Ystrat, found Audiart first, then the others. They were made aware, manifested acceptance, then traveled down together, touched Dun Maura, and felt the earthroot flow through them all.

"Good-bye," she heard him say, as it changed for her, in the way it always had—the way that had marked her even as a child—into a streaming as of moonlight through her body. She channeled it, gave thanks, and then spun the avarlith forth to send them home.

After, she was too weary to do anything but sleep.

In the house by the green where the ta'kiena had been chanted, Vae held her new child in her arms by the fire. The grey-robed priestesses had brought milk and swaddling clothes and promised other things. Finn had already put together a makeshift crib for Darien.

She had let him hold his brother for a moment, her heart swelling to see the brightness in his eyes. It might even keep him here, she thought; perhaps this awesome thing was so powerful it might overmaster the call that Finn had heard. It might.

And another thought she had: whatever the father might be, and she laid a curse upon his name, a child learned love from being loved, and they would give him all the love he needed, she and Finn—and Shahar when he came home. How could one not love a child so calm and fair, with eyes so blue—blue as Ginserat's wardstones, she thought, then remembered they were broken.

# Chapter 3

**P**aul, on lookout up the road, whistled the all-clear. Dave grabbed the post for support and hurdled the fence, cursing softly as he sank ankle deep in spring mud.

"Okay," he said. "The girls."

Kevin helped Jen first and then Kim to balance themselves on the stiff wire for Dave to swing them up and over. They had been worried that the fence might be electrically charged, but Kevin's checking earlier had established that it wasn't.

"Car coming!" Paul cried sharply.

They flattened themselves on the cold, mucky ground till the headlights went by. Then Kevin rose and he too vaulted over the fence. This part was easy, but the ground was pressure-sensitive farther in, they knew, and an alarm would sound in the guards' underground room when they walked that far.

Paul jogged up and neatly cleared the fence. He and Kevin exchanged a glance. Despite the immensity of what they were about to do, Kevin felt a surge of exhilaration. It was a joy to be *doing* something again.

"All right," he said, low and in control. "Jen, you're with me. Prepare to be sexy as hell. Dave and Paul—you know what to do?" They nodded. He turned to Kim. "All set, sweetheart. Do your thing. And—"

He stopped. Kim had removed her gloves. The Baelrath on her right hand was very bright; it seemed like a thing alive. Kim raised it overhead.

"May all the powers of the dead forgive me for this," she

said and let the light carry her foward past the crumbling Heelstone to Stonehenge.

On a night at the beginning of spring she had taken the second step at last. It had been so long in coming she had begun to despair, but how did one command a dream to show itself? Ysanne had never taught her. Nor had the Seer's gift of so much else offered this one thing to her. Dreamer of the dream, she now was, but there was much waiting involved and never, ever, had Kimberly been called a patient person.

Over and over though the summer of their return and the long winter that followed—and was not over yet, though April had come—she had seen the same image tumble through her nights, but she knew it now. She had known this first step on the road to the Warrior since a night in Paras Derval. The jumbled stones and the wind over the grass were as famliar as anything had ever been to her, and she knew where they were.

It was the time that had confused her, or it would have been easy despite the blurring of the vision in those first dreams when she was young in power: she had seen it not as it now was, but as it had been three thousand years ago.

Stonehenge. Where a King lay buried, a giant in his day, but small, small, beside the one whose secret name he held sacrosanct beyond the walls of death.

Sacrosanct except now, at last, from her. As ever, the nature of this power overwhelmed her with sorrow: not even the dead might have rest from her, it seemed, from Kimberly Ford with the Baelrath on her hand.

Stonehenge, she knew. The starting point. The hidden Book of Gortyn she had found under the cottage by the lake, and in it she had found—easily, because Ysanne was within her—the words that would raise the guardian dead from his long resting place.

But she had needed one thing more, for the dead man had been mighty and would not give up this secret easily: she had needed to know the other place, the next one, the last. The place of summoning.

And then, on a night in April, she did.

It would have misled her again, this long-sought image, had not she been prepared for the trick that time might play. The Seers walked in their dreams along loops spun invisibly in the Weaver's threading through the Loom, and they had to be prepared to see the inexplicable.

But this she was ready for, this image of an island, small and green, in a lake calm as glass under a just-risen crescent moon. A scene of such surpassing peacefulness that she would have wept a year ago to know the havoc she would wreak when she came.

Not even a year ago, not so much even. But she had changed, and though there was sorrow within her—deep as a stone and as permanent—there was too much need, and the delay had been too long to allow her the luxury of tears.

She rose from her bed. The Warstone flickered with a muted, presaging light. It was going to blaze soon, she knew. She would carry fire on her hand. She saw by the kitchen clock that it was four in the morning. She also saw Jennifer sitting at the table, and the kettle was coming to a boil.

"You cried out," her roommate said. "I thought something was happening."

Kim took one of the other chairs. She tightened her robe about her. It was chilly in the house, and this traveling always left her cold. "It did," she said, wearily.

"You know what you have to do?"

She nodded.

"Is it all right?"

She shrugged. Too hard to explain. She had an understanding, of late, as to why Ysanne had withdrawn in solitude to her lake. There were two lights in the room: one on the ceiling and the other on her hand. "We'd better call the guys," she said.

"I already have. They'll be here soon."

Kim glanced sharply at her. "What did I say in my sleep?"

Jennifer's eyes were kind again; they had been since Darien was born. "You cried out for forgiveness," she said. *She would drag the dead from their rest and the undead to their doom.*

"Fat chance," said Kimberly.

The doorbell rang. In a moment they were standing all around her, anxious, disheveled, half asleep. She looked up. They were waiting, but the waiting was over; she had seen an island and a lake like glass.

"Who's coming with me to England?" she asked, with brittle, false brightness in her voice.

All of them went. Even Dave, who'd had to virtually quit his articling job to get away on twenty-four hours' notice. A year ago he'd carried a packet of Evidence notes into Fionavar with him, so determined was he to succeed in the law. He'd changed so much; they all had. After seeing Rangat throw up that unholy hand, how could anything else seem other than insubstantial?

Yet what could be more insubstantial than a dream? And it was a dream that had the five of them hurtling overseas on a 747 to London and, in a Renault rented at Heathrow and driven erratically and at speed by Kevin Laine, to Amesbury beside Stonehenge.

Kevin was in a fired-up mood. Released at last from the waiting, from months of pretending to take an interest in the tax, real estate, and civil-procedure courses that preceded his call to the Bar, he gunned the car through a roundabout, ignored Dave's spluttering, and skidded to a stop in front of an ancient hotel and tavern called, of course, the New Inn.

He and Dave handled the baggage—none of them had more than carry-ons—while Paul registered. On the way in they passed the entrance to the bar—crowded at lunchtime—and he caught a glimpse of a cute, freckled barmaid.

"Do you know," he told Dave, as they waited for Paul to arrange for the rooms, "I can't remember the last time I was laid?"

Dave, who couldn't either, with greater justification, grunted. "Get your mind out of your pants, for once."

It *was* frivolous, Kevin supposed. But he wasn't a monk and couldn't ever pretend to be. Diarmuid would understand, he thought, though he wondered if even that dissolute

Prince would comprehend just how far the act of love carried Kevin, or what he truly sought in its pursuit. Unlikely in the extreme, Kevin reflected, since he himself didn't really know.

Paul had the keys to two adjacent rooms. Leaving Kimberly, at her own insistence, alone in one of the rooms, the four others drove the mile west to join the tour buses and pocket cameras by the monument. Once there, even with the daytime tackiness, Kevin sobered. There was work to be done, to prepare for what would happen that night.

Dave had asked on the plane. It had been very late, the movie over, lights dimmed. Jennifer and Paul had been asleep when the big man had come over to where Kevin and Kim were sitting, awake but not speaking. Kim hadn't spoken the whole time, lost in some troubled country born of dream.

"What are we going to do there?" Dave had asked her diffidently, as if fearing to intrude.

And the white-haired girl beside him had roused herself to say, "You four will have to do whatever it takes, to give me enough time."

"For what?" Dave had said.

Kevin, too, had turned his head to look at Kim as she replied, far too matter-of-factly, "To raise a King from the dead and make him surrender a name. After that I'll be on my own."

Kevin had looked past her then, out the window, and seen stars beyond the wing; they were flying very high over deep waters.

"What time is it?" Dave asked for the fifth time, fighting a case of nerves.

"After eleven," said Paul, continuing to fidget with a spoon. They were in the saloon bar of the hotel; he, Dave, and Jen at the table, Kevin, unbelievably, chatting up the waitress over by the bar. Or not, actually, unbelievably; he'd known Kevin Laine a long time.

"When the hell is she coming down?" Dave had an edge in

his voice, a real one, and Paul could feel anxiety building in himself as well. It was going to be a very different place at night, he knew, with the crowds of the afternoon gone. Under stars, Stonehenge would move back in time a long way. There was a power here still, he could feel it, and he knew it would be made manifest at night.

"Does everyone know what they have to do?" he repeated.

"Yes, Paul," said Jennifer, surprisingly calm. They'd worked out their plans over dinner after returning from the monument. Kim hadn't left her room, not since they'd arrived.

Kevin strolled back to the table, with a full pint of beer.

"Are you drinking?" Dave said sharply.

"Don't be an idiot. While you two have been sitting here doing nothing, I've gotten the names of two of the guards out there. Len is the big bearded one, and there's another named Dougal, Kate says."

Dave and Paul were silent.

"Nicely done," said Jennifer. She smiled slightly.

"Okay," said Kim, *"let's go."* She was standing by the table in a bomber jacket and scarf. Her eyes were a little wild below the locks of white hair and her face was deathly pale. A single vertical line creased her forehead. She held up her hands; she was wearing gloves.

"It started to glow five minutes ago," she said.

And so she had come to the place and it was time indeed, here, now, to manifest herself, to show forth the Baelrath in a crimson blaze of power. It was the Warstone, found, not made, and very wild, but there was a war now, and the ring was coming into its force, carrying her with it past the high shrouded stones, the fallen one, and the tilting one, to the highest lintel stone. Beside which she stopped.

There was shouting behind her. Very far behind her. It was time. Raising her hand before her face Kimberly cried out in a cold voice, far from what she sounded like when allowed to be only herself, only Kim, and said into stillness, the waiting calm of that place, words of power upon power to summon its dead from beyond the walls of Night.

*"Damae Pendragon! Sed Baelrath riden log verenth. Pendragon rabenna, nisei damae!"*

There was no moon yet. Between the ancient stones, the Baelrath glowed brighter than any star. It lit the giant teeth of rock luridly. There was nothing subtle or mild, nothing beautiful about this force. She had come to coerce, by the power she bore and the secret she knew. She had come to summon.

And then, by the rising of a wind where none had been before, she knew she had.

Leaning forward into it, holding the Baelrath before her, she saw, in the very center of the monument, a figure standing on the altar stone. He was tall and shadowed, wrapped in mist as in a shroud, only half incarnated in the half-light of star and stone. She fought the weight of him, the drag; he had been so long dead and she had made him rise.

No space for sorrow here, and weakness shown might break the summoning. She said:

"Uther Pendragon, attend me, for I command your will!"

"Command me not, I am a King!" His voice was high, stretched taut on a wire of centuries, but imperious still.

No space for mercy. None at all. She hardened her heart. "You are dead," she said coldly, in the cold wind. "And given over to the stone I bear."

"Why should this be so?"

The wind was rising. "For Ygraine deceived, and a son falsely engendered." The old, old telling.

Uther drew himself to his fullest height, and he was very tall above his tomb. "Has he not proven great beyond all measure?"

And thus: "Even so," said Kimberly, and there was a soreness in her now that no hardening could stay. "And I would call him by the name you guard."

The dead King spread his hands to the watching stars. "Has he not suffered enough?" the father cried in a voice that overrode the wind.

To this there was no decent reply, and so she said, "I have no time, Uther, and he is needed. By the burning of my stone I compel you—*what is the name?*"

She could see the sternness of his face, and steeled her own

31

that he might read no irresolution there. He was fighting her; she could feel the earth pulling him away, and down.

"Do you know the place?" Uther Pendragon asked.

"I know."

And in his eyes, as if through mist or smoke, she saw that he knew this was so, and with the Baelrath would master him. Her very soul was turning over with the pain of it. So much steel she could not be, it seemed.

He said, "He was young when it happened, the incest, and the rest of it. He was afraid, because of the prophecy. Can they not have pity? Is there none?"

What was she that the proud Kings of the dead should beseech her so? "The name!" said Kimberly into the keening of the wind, and she raised the ring above her head to master him.

And, mastered, he told her, and it seemed as if stars were falling everywhere, and she had brought them tumbling down from heaven with what she was.

She was sheer red, she was wild, the night could not hold her. She could rise, even now, to come down as red moonlight might fall, but not here. In another place.

It was high. High enough to have once been an island in a lake like glass. Then the waters had receded all over Somerset, leaving a plain where waters had been, and a seven-ridged hill high above that plain. But when a place has been an island the memory of water lingers, and of water magic, no matter how far away the sea may be, or how long ago it fell away.

And so it was with Glastonbury Tor, which had been called Avalon in its day and had seen three queens row a dying king to its shore.

So much of the filtered legends had been close to true, but the rest was so far off it carried its own grief with it. Kim looked around the summit of the Tor and saw the thin moon rise in the east above the long plain. The Baelrath was beginning to fade even as she watched, and with it the power that had carried her here.

There was a thing to do while it yet burned, and raising the ring she turned, a beacon in the night, back to face

Stonehenge, so many miles away. She reached out as she had done once before, though it was easier now, she was very strong tonight, and she found the four of them, gathered them together, Kevin and Paul, Jennifer and Dave, and before the Warstone faded, she sent them to Fionavar with the last red wildness Stonehenge had engendered.

Then the light she bore became only a ring on her finger, and it was dark on the windy summit of the Tor.

There was enough moonlight for her to make out the chapel that had been erected there some seven hundred years ago. She was shivering, now, and not only with cold. The burning ring had lifted her, given her resolution beyond her ordinary reach. Now she was Kimberly Ford only, or it seemed that way, and she felt daunted here on this ancient mound that yet gave scent of sea wind here in the midst of Somerset.

She was about to do something terrible, to set once more in motion the workings of a curse so old it made the wind seem young.

There had been a mountain though, in the northland of Fionavar, and once it had held a god prisoner. Then there had been a detonation so vast it could only mean one thing, and Rakoth the Unraveller had been no longer bound. There was so much power coming down on them, and if Fionavar was lost then all the worlds would fall to Maugrim, and the Tapestry be torn and twisted on the Worldloom past redress.

She thought of Jennifer in Starkadh.

She thought of Ysanne.

With the ring quiescent on her hand, no power in her but the name she knew, terrible and merciless, she drew upon her need for strength in that high dark place and spoke in her own voice the one word that the Warrior needs must answer to:

*"Childslayer!"*

Then she closed her eyes, for the Tor, the whole Somerset Plain, seemed to be shaking with an agonized convulsion. There was a sound: wind, sorrow, lost music. He had been young and afraid, the dead father had said—and the dead spoke truth or lay silent—Merlin's prophecy had tolled a knell for the shining of the dream, and so he had ordered the children slain. Oh, how could one not weep? All the children, so that his incestuous, marring, foretold seed might not live to break the bright dream. Little more than a child himself he had been, but a thread had been entrusted to his name, and thus a world, and when the babies died . . .

When the babies died the Weaver had marked him down for a long unwinding doom. A cycle of war and expiation under many names, and in many worlds, that redress be made for the children and for love.

Kim opened her eyes and saw the low, thin moon. She saw the stars of spring hang brightly overhead, and she was not wrong in thinking they were brighter than they had been before.

Then she turned and, in the celestial light, saw that she was not alone in that high enchanted place.

He was no longer young. How could he have been young after so many wars? His beard was dark, though flecked with grey, and his eyes not yet fixed in time. She thought she saw stars in them. He leaned upon a sword, his hands wrapped around the hilt as if it were the only certain thing in the wide night, and then he said in a voice so gentle and so weary it found her heart, "I was Arthur here, my lady, was I not?"

"Yes," she whispered.

"I have carried other names elsewhere."

"I know." She swallowed. "This is your true name, though, your first."

"Not the other?"

*Oh, what was she?* "Not that. I will never tell it, or speak it again. I give you an oath."

Slowly he straightened. "Others will, though, as others have before."

"I cannot do anything to alter that. I only summoned because of our need."

He nodded. "There is war here?"

"In Fionavar."

At that he drew himself up: not so tall as his father had been, yet majesty lay about him like a cloak, and he lifted his head into the rising wind as if hearing a distant horn.

"Is this the last battle, then?"

"If we lose, it will be."

On the words, he seemed to coalesce, as if acceptance ended his passage from wherever he had been. There were no longer stars in the depths of his eyes; they were brown, and kind, and of the broad, tilled earth.

"Very well," said Arthur.

And that mild affirmation was what, finally, broke Kimberly. She dropped to her knees and lowered her face to weep.

A moment later she felt herself lifted, effortlessly, and wrapped in an embrace so encompassing she felt, on that lonely elevation, as if she had come home after long voyaging. She laid her head on his broad chest, felt the strong beating of his heart, and took comfort even as she grieved.

After a time he stepped back. She wiped away her tears and saw, without surprise, that the Baelrath was aglow again. She was aware, for the first time, of how weary she felt, with so much power channeling itself through her. She shook her head: no time, none at all, to be weak. She looked at him.

"Have I your forgiveness?"

"You never needed it," Arthur said. "Not half as much as I need all of yours."

"You were young."

"They were babies," he said quietly. And then, after a pause, "Are they there yet, the two of them?"

And the hurting in his voice laid bare for her, for the first time, the true nature of how he had been cursed. She should have known, it had been there to see. *For the children and for love.*

"I don't know," she said, with difficulty.

"They always are," he said, "because I had the babies killed."

There was no answer to make, and she didn't trust her voice in any case. Instead she took him by the hand, and holding high the Baelrath once again with the last strength she had, she crossed with Arthur Pendragon, the Warrior Condemned, to Fionavar and war.

# PART II
## Owein

# Chapter 4

Ruana essayed the thin chant, having only Iraima to aid him. He had scant hope it would carry as far as it had to go, but there was nothing else he could think of to do. So he lay in the dark, listening to the others dying around him, and he chanted the warnsong and the savesong over and over again. Iraima helped when she could, but she was very weak.

In the morning their captors found that Taieri had died, and he was taken out and devoured. After, the ones outside burned his bones for warmth against the bitter cold. Ruana choked on the smoke that drifted from the pyre. It had been placed in front of the cave, to make breathing harder for them. He heard Iraima coughing. They would not be killed directly, he knew, for fear of the bloodcurse, but they had been without food in the caves a long time now, and breathing the smoke of their brothers and sisters. Ruana wondered, abstractly, what it would be like to feel hate or rage. Closing his eyes, he chanted the kanior once for Taieri, knowing it was not being done in proper accordance with the rites, and asking forgiveness for this. Then he began the other two again in cycle, the warnsong and the savesong, over and over. Iraima joined in with him awhile, and Ikatere as well, but mostly Ruana sang alone.

They climbed up to Atronel over the green grass, and the high ones of all three Marks were there before Ra-Tenniel.

Only Brendel was away south, in Paras Derval, so Heilyn represented the Kestrel. Galen and Lydan, the twins, stood forth for the Brein Mark, and fairest Leyse for the Swan, and she was clad in white as the Swan Mark always were, for memory of Lauriel. Enroth, who was eldest since Laien Spearchild had gone to his song, was there as well—Markless and of all Marks, as were the Eldest and the King alone.

Ra-Tenniel made the throne glow brightly blue, and fierce Galen smiled, though it could be seen that her brother frowned.

Leyse offered a flower to the King. "From by Celyn," she murmured. "There is a fair grove there, of silver and red sylvain."

"I would go with you to see them," Ra-Tenniel replied.

Leyse smiled, elusive. "Are we to open the sky tonight, Brightest Lord?"

He accepted the deflection. This time Lydan smiled.

"We are," said Ra-Tenniel. "Na-Enroth?"

"It is woven," the Eldest affirmed. "We will try to draw him forth from Starkadh."

"And if we do?" Lydan asked.

"Then we go to war," Ra-Tenniel replied. "But if we wait, or if the Dark One waits as he seems purposed to do, then our allies may be dead of this winter before Maugrim comes after us."

Heilyn spoke for the first time. "He has made the winter then? This is known?"

"It is known," Enroth replied. "And another thing is known. The Baelrath blazed two nights ago. Not in Fionavar, but it was on fire."

They stirred at that. "The Seer?" Lyse ventured. "In her world?"

"So it would seem," Enroth said. "Something new is threading across the Loom."

"Or something very old," Ra-Tenniel amended, and the Eldest bowed his head.

"Then why do we wait?" Galen cried. Her rich singer's voice carried to the others on the slopes of Atronel. A murmur like a note of music came to the six of them by the throne.

"We do not, once we are agreed," Ra-Tenniel replied. "Is it not bitterest irony that we who are named for Light should have been forced to cloak our land in shadow for this thousand years? Why should Daniloth be named the Shadowland? Would you not see the stars bright over Atronel, and send forth our own light in answer back to them?"

The music of agreement and desire was all about them on the mound. It carried even careful Lydan, and he, too, let his eyes reach crystal as Ra-Tenniel made the throne shine full bright, and, speaking the words necessary, he undid the spell Lathen Mistweaver had woven after the Bael Rangat. And the lios alfar, the Children of Light, sang then with one voice of praise to see the stars undimmed overhead, and to know that all over the northland of Fionavar the shining of Daniloth would illuminate the night for the first time in a thousand years.

It exposed them, of course, which was the gallant purpose of what they did. They made themselves a lure, the most tantalizing lure there could ever be, to draw Rakoth Maugrim down from Starkadh.

All night they stayed awake. No one would sleep, not with the stars to see, and then the waxing moon. And not with their borders open to the north, where they knew the Unraveller would be upon his towers among the Ice, seeing their taunting, iridescent glow. They sang in praise of the light, that their clear voices might reach him, too, and clearest of them all sang Ra-Tenniel, Lord of the lios alfar.

In the morning they put back the Mistweaver's shadowing. Those sent to keep watch by the borders returned to Atronel to report that a mighty storm was howling southward over the bleak, empty Plain.

Light is swifter than wind. In the country south of Rienna the Dalrei saw the glow above Daniloth as soon as it went up. The newest storm would take some time to reach them.

Which is not to say it wasn't cold enough on watch by the

gates where Navon of the third tribe took his turn on guard. Being a Rider among the Dalrei was still a glorious thing for one who had seen his animal so recently, but there were less pleasant aspects to it for a fourteen-year-old, staring out into the white night for wolves while the wind tore at his eltor cloak, seeking the thin bones underneath.

While word of the light far in the northwest ran wild through the clustered camps, Navon concentrated on his watch. He had slipped up on his first hunt as a Rider; his attempt at a flashy kill had been one of the failures that led Levon dan Ivor to risk his life trying Revor's Kill. Trying and succeeding. And though the hunt leader of the third tribe had never said a word to him, Navon had striven ever since to erase the memory of his folly.

The more so, because every member of the third tribe felt an added pride and responsibility after what had happened at Celidon when the snows began and the wolves had begun to kill the eltor. Navon remembered his first sickening sight of slaughtered grace in the land between the Adein and Celidon itself, mockingly near to the mid-Plain stones. For whereas the Dalrei might kill fifteen or twenty of the flying beasts on one hunt and only by adherance to their stern Law, that day the joined Riders of the third and eighth tribes had ridden over a swell of rising land, to see two hundred eltor lying in the snow, their blood shockingly red on the white drifts of the Plain.

It was the snow that had undone them. For the eltor, so fast over the grass that men spoke of a swift of eltor, not a herd, had hooves ill-adapted to the deep piled snow. They foundered in it, their fluid grace turning to ungainly, awkward motion—and they had become easy prey for the wolves.

Always in autumn the eltor went south to leave the snow behind, always the Dalrei followed them to this milder country on the fringes of the grazing lands of Brennin. But this year the snow had come early, and savagely, trapping the animals in the north. And then the wolves had come.

The Dalrei cursed, turning faces of grief and rage to the north. But curses had done no good, nor had they stayed the next bad thing, for the winds had carried the killing snow all the way south to Brennin. Which meant there was no safe place for the eltor anywhere on the Plain.

And so Dhira of the first tribe had issued a Grand Summoning to Celidon of all nine chieftains and their shamans and advisers. And venerable Dhira had risen up—everyone knew the story by now—and asked, "Why does Cernan of the Beasts allow this slaughter?"

And only one man of that company had stood to make reply.

"Because," Ivor of the third tribe had said, "he cannot stop it. Maugrim is stronger than he, and I will name him now by his name, and say Rakoth."

His voice had grown stronger to quell the murmuring that came at the never-spoken name.

"We must name him and know him for what he is, for no longer is he a presence of nightmare or memory. He is real, he is here now, and we must go to war against him for our people and our land, ourselves and with our allies, or there will be no generations after us to ride with the eltor on the wide Plain. We will be slaves to Starkadh, toys for svart alfar. Each man in this Gathering must swear by the stones of Celidon, by this heart of our Plain, that he will not live to see that sunless day. There is no Revor here with us, but we are the sons of Revor, and the heirs to his pride and to the High King's gift of the Plain. Men of the Dalrei, shall we prove worthy of that gift and that pride?"

Navon shivered in the dark as the remembered words ran through his mind. Everyone knew of the roar that had followed Ivor's speech, exploding outward from Celidon as if it might run all the white leagues north, through Gwynir and Andarien, to shake the very walls of Starkadh.

And everyone knew what had followed when mild, wise Tulger of the eighth tribe had risen in his turn to say, simply, "Not since Revor have the nine tribes had one Lord, one Father. Should we have an Aven now?"

"Yes!" the Gathering had cried. (Everyone knew.)

"Who shall that be?"

And in this fashion had Ivor dan Banor of the third tribe

become the first Aven of all the Plain in a thousand years, his name exploding in its turn from the holy place.

They all showed it, Navon thought, pulling his cloak more tightly about him against the keening wind. All of the third tribe partook of both the glory and the responsibility, and Ivor had made sure they had no special status in the distribution of labors.

Celidon would be safe, he'd decided. No wolves would enter there as yet, risking the deep, ancient power that bound the circle of the standing stones or the House that stood inside them.

The eltor were the first priority for now. The animals had finally made their way south to the country by the River Latham, and thither the tribes would follow them; the hunters would circle the gathered swifts—though the name was a mockery in snow—and the camps would be on constant alert against attack.

And so it had come to be. Twice had the wolves ventured to attack one of the protected swifts, and twice had the racing auberei gotten word to the nearest camp in time to beat back the marauders.

Even now, Navon thought, pacing from north to south along the wooden outer wall, even now Levon, the Aven's son, was out there in the bitter cold on night duty around the large swift near the camp of the third tribe. And with him was the one who had become Navon's own hero— though he would have blushed and denied it had the thought been attributed to him by anyone. Still, no man in any tribe, not even Levon himself, had killed as many wolves or ridden so many nights of guard as had Torc dan Sorcha. He had been called "the Outcast" once, Navon remembered, shaking his head in what he thought was an adult disbelief. Not any longer. The silent deadliness of Torc was a byword now among the tribes.

His tribe had more than its share of heroes these days, and Navon was determined not to let them down. He peered keenly into the dark south, a fourteen-year-old sentinel, and not the youngest either.

But youngest or not, he was first to see and hear the lone auberei come galloping up, and it was Navon who raised the alarm, while the auberei went on to the next camp without pausing to rest his horse.

It was, evidently, a major attack.

A very major attack, Torc realized, as he saw the dark, fluid shapes of the wolves bear down on the huge swift that the third and seventh tribes were guarding together. Or trying to guard, he amended inwardly, racing to Levon's side for the hunt leader's orders. This was going to be bad; the wolves were in force this time. In the growing chaos he rose up in his saddle and scanned the swift: the four lead eltor were still roped and held, an ugly thing but necessary, for if this enormous, mingled swift were to take flight then chaos would become hopelessness. As long as the leaders stayed, the swift would hold together, and the eltor were horned and could fight.

And they *were* fighting, he saw, as the lead edge of the wolf attack reached them. It was an unholy scene: wolf snarls, the high-pitched cries of the eltor, the lurid, weaving torches the Riders bore in the darkness, and then eltor blood on the snow again.

Rage threatened to choke Torc's breathing. Forcing himself to stay calm, he saw that the right front edge of the swift was undermanned, and the wolves were racing around for it.

Levon saw it too. "Doraid!" he shouted to the hunt leader of the seventh. "Take half your men for the near flank!"

Doraid hesitated. "No," he said, "I have another idea. Why don't we—"

At which point he found himself pulled from his horse and hurtling into the snow. Torc didn't stop to see where he fell. "Riders of the seventh," he screamed over the noise of the battle, *"follow me!"*

Tabor dan Ivor, bearing a torch for his brother, saw that the hunters of the seventh did indeed follow. His heart swelled, even amid the carnage, to see how the reputation of Torc dan Sorcha enforced obedience. No man on the Plain had a more defiant hatred of the Dark than the black-clad

Rider of the third tribe, whose only concession to the winter winds was an eltor vest over his bare chest. His aura was such now that the hunters of another tribe would follow him without a question asked.

Torc beat the wolves to the flank, barely. He and the Riders of the seventh smashed, swords scything, into the wolf pack. They cut it in two and wheeled swiftly to knife back the other way.

"Cechtar," Levon said, cool as ever. "Take twenty men around the other way. Guard the lead eltor on that side."

"Done!" Cechtar cried, flamboyant as always, and raced off over the powdered snow with a group of Riders at his heels.

Rising as high as he could in the saddle, Tabor almost fell, but he balanced himself and, turning to Levon, said, "The auberei got through. I see torches coming from the camp!"

"Good," said Levon grimly, looking the other way. "We are going to need them all."

Wheeling his horse to follow his brother's glance, Tabor saw them too, and his heart clenched like a fist.

There were urgach coming up from the south.

The savage creatures were mounted on beasts such as Tabor had never seen—huge six-legged steeds, as monstrous as their riders, with a viciously curved horn protruding from their heads.

"We seem to have a fight here," said Levon, almost to himself. And then, turning to Tabor with a smile, he said, "Come, my brother, it is our turn."

And the two sons of Ivor, the one tall and fair, the other young yet, nut-brown and wiry, hurled their horses forward toward the advancing line of the urgach.

Try as he could, Tabor couldn't keep up, and Levon soon outdistanced him. He did not ride alone though, for angling to intercept his path, low on his flying horse, came a Rider in black leggings and an eltor vest.

Together Levon and Torc raced directly toward the wide line of the urgach. There are too many, Tabor thought, trying furiously to catch up. He was closer than anyone else, and so saw what happened best of all. Thirty paces from the advancing urgach, Levon and Torc, without a word spoken, suddenly wheeled their horses at right angles, and racing across the line of the huge, six-legged steeds, fired three arrows each at dazzling speed.

Six of the urgach fell.

Tabor, however, was in no position to cheer. Churning fiercely forward in Torc and Levon's wake he suddenly found himself galloping with only a torch in his hand right at the line of monsters.

He heard Levon scream his name, not very helpfully. Swallowing a fifteen-year-old's yelp of apprehension, Tabor angled his horse for a gap in the onrushing line. An urgach, hairy and huge, changed course to intercept him.

"Cernan!" Tabor cried and hurled the torch even as he swung himself under the belly of his horse. He heard the whistle of a sword where his head had been, a guttural roar of pain as the flung torch struck hair and flesh, and then he was through the line and riding away from the fight over the wide sweeping beauty of the white Plain under a waxing moon and all the stars.

Not for long. He checked his horse and turned it, reaching for the small sword slung from his saddle. There was no need—none of the urgach had come after him. Instead they smashed viciously into the terrified eltor and then, hewing and carving the screaming animals like so much meat, they swung, en masse, and hit the left side contingent of Dalrei with a brutal force. There were reinforcements coming— Tabor could see the torches streaming toward them from the camps in the distance—but they were not going to be enough, he thought despairingly, not against the urgach.

Levon and Torc were speeding to attack again, he saw, but the urgach were deep within the mass of Riders, their gigantic swords wreaking havoc among the hunters while the wolves, unimpeded, ran wild through the eltor.

He heard hoofbeats behind him. Sword raised, he spun his horse frantically. And a glad cry escaped his throat.

*"Come on, little brother!"* someone shouted, and then

Dave Martyniuk thundered by, an axe of Brennin held high, a golden Prince racing beside him and thirty men behind.

Thus did the warriors of Brennin come to the aid of the Dalrei, led by Prince Diarmuid and by the one called Davor, huge and fell, wrapped in battle fury like a red halo under the waxing moon.

Tabor saw them crash in their turn, these trained soldiers of Diarmuid's band, into the nearest wolf pack, and he saw their swords descend in silver sweeps and rise again, dark with blood. Then they hit the massed phalanx of the urgach with Torc and Levon, and brave Cechtar beside, and over the squeals of the dying eltor, the snarl of wolves, Tabor heard, rising above the torchlit carnage, the voice of Davor cry, "Revor!" once and again, and he was young in the tidal wave of his relief and pride.

Then, suddenly, he was young no more, nor was he only a fifteen-year-old newly called Rider of the Dalrei.

From his vantage point behind the battle scene and on a slope above it Tabor saw, off to the east, a dark mass approaching very fast, and he realized that the Dalrei were not the only ones to be receiving reinforcements. And if he could see the urgach at such a distance, then there were very many, there were too many, and so.

And so it was time.

*Beloved.* He formed the thought in his mind.

*I am here,* he heard instantly. *I am always here. Would you ride?*

*I think we must,* Tabor sent reply. *It is time for us, bright one.*

*We have ridden before.*

He remembered, would always remember. *But not to battle. We will have to kill.*

A new note in the mind voice: *I was made for war. And to fly. Summon me.*

Made for war. It was true, and a grief, but the urgach were nearer now, and so.

And so in his mind Tabor spoke her name. *Imraith-Nimphais,* he called, on a cresting of love, and he dismounted from his horse, for on the words she was in the sky above him, more glorious than anything on earth, the creature of his dreaming.

She landed. Her horn was luminous, a silver such as the silver of the moon, though her coat was deep red as had been the moon that gave her life. And where she walked, the snow showed no imprint of her hooves, so lightly did she move.

It had been a long time. His heart full as with light, he raised a hand and she lowered her head, the single horn grazing him like a caress, that he might in turn caress her head.

*Only each other,* he heard, and he sent back affirmation and acceptance. Then: *Shall we fly?* she asked.

He could feel the straining desire run through her, and then through himself, and he said aloud, *"Let us fly, and kill, my darling."*

And Tabor dan Ivor mounted himself upon the flying creature of his vigil, the double-edged gift of Dana that was to bear him, young as they both were, into the sky and away from the world of men. And Imraith-Nimphais did so. She left the ground for the cold wide heavens, carrying the Rider who alone of all creatures had dreamt her name, and to the men below they were as an unleashed comet between the stars and the Plain.

Then Tabor said within, *You see?*

And: *I do,* she replied.

He turned her to where the urgach were riding to the battlefield, and they came down upon them like a killing light. She changed as they sped down, and with her shining horn she killed once, and once more, and many, many times again under the guidance of his hand. And the urgach fled before them and they pursued, slaying, and the wolves broke and fled also, southward away, and the Dalrei and the men of Brennin cheered, amazed and exultant to see the shining thing from heaven come to their aid.

She heard them not, nor did he. They pursued, killing, until her horn was sticky and clotted with blood and there were no more of the loathsome creatures of the Dark to slay.

And finally, trembling with weariness and the shock of

aftermath, they came down in a white place far from blood and Tabor cleaned her horn with snow. After, they stood close together in the wide silence of the night.

*Only each other,* she sent.

*Only each other at the last,* he replied. Then she flew off, glittering, and as dawn broke over the mountains he began the long walk back to the camps of men.

# Chapter 5

"The first battle is always the worst," Carde said, moving his horse toward Kevin so no one else would hear.

The words were meant to be reassuring, and Kevin managed a gesture of acknowledgment, but he was not prone to be dishonest with himself and he knew that the shock of battle, though real, was not his deepest problem.

Nor was it envy of Dave Martyniuk, though honesty compelled admission that this was also a part of his mood now, just after it had all ended, with the electrifying appearance of the winged, shining creature in the sky. Dave had been extraordinary, almost terrifying. Wielding the huge axe Matt Sören had found for him in the Paras Derval armory, he had roared into battle, outpacing even Diarmuid and wreaking violent havoc among the wolves while screaming at the top of his lungs. The big man had even gone one-on-one with one of the enormous, fanged brutes they called urgach. And he had killed it too; blocking a vicious sword thrust, he had launched a backhanded sweep of the axe that had half severed the creature's head and sent it tumbling from the back of its giant steed. Then Dave had killed the six-legged horned beast as well.

And Kevin? Quick, sharp Kevin Laine had been his torchbearer at the time. Oh, they'd given him a sword to fight with, but what did he know about fighting wolves with a sword on horseback? Staying on the plunging horse was challenge enough in the screaming inferno of that fight. And when he had gained enough space to realize how utterly useless he was, Kevin had swallowed his pride, sheathed the sword, and grabbed a burning torch to give Dave light enough by which to kill. He hadn't been too good at that, either, and twice had been nearly felled himself by Dave's whirling axe.

They had won, though, this first real battle of the war, and something magnificent had been revealed in the sky. Kevin clung to the splendor of that image of the winged unicorn and tried to lift himself enough to share the triumph of the moment.

Yet it seemed that someone else wasn't happy; there was a confrontation taking place. He and Carde edged their horses closer to the knot of men surrounding a husky brown-haired Rider and Torc, Dave's friend, whom Kevin remembered from their last days in Paras Derval.

"And if you ever do so again," the brown-haired man was saying loudly, "I will cripple you and stake you out in the Plain with honey on your eyes to draw the aigen!"

Torc, impassive on his dark grey horse, made no reply, and the other man's blustered threat fell fatuously into the silence. Dave was grinning. He was sitting his horse between Torc and Levon, the other Rider Kevin remembered from their last time.

It was Levon who spoke, quietly but with immense authority. "Doraid, be done. And hear me: you were given a direct command in battle, and you chose that moment to discuss strategies. If Torc had not done what I asked *you* to do, the wolves would have turned the flank of the swift. Do you wish to explain your action here or before the Aven and the leader of your tribe?"

Doraid turned to him furiously. "Since when does the third tribe command the seventh?"

"It does not," Levon replied with equanimity. "But I command this guard, and you were there when that command was given me."

"Ah, yes!" Doraid sneered. "The precious son of the Aven. He is to be obeyed, and—"

"One moment!" a familiarly inflected voice snapped, and Doraid stopped in mid-word. "Do I understand what happened here?" Diarmuid continued, moving into the ring of Riders. "Did this man refuse a direct order? And is he complaining about it now?" The tone was acid.

"He did," Torc spoke for the first time. "And he is. You do understand correctly, my lord Prince."

Kevin had a blinding attack of déjà vu: an innyard to the south, a farmer crying, "Mörnir guard you, young Prince!" And then something else.

"Coll," Diarmuid said.

"No!" Kevin screamed and launched himself in a flat dive from his horse. He hit his friend, Diarmuid's big lieutenant, with a tackle that sent them both flying to land with a double crunch in the snow among the stamping horses of the Dalrei.

He was about a half second too late. There was another man lying in the snow, not far away: Doraid, with Coll's arrow buried deep in his chest.

"Oh, hell," Kevin said, sick at heart. "Oh, bloody hell."

Nor was he eased to hear a chuckle beside him. "Nicely done," Coll said softly, not at all discomfited. "You almost broke my nose again."

"God. Coll, I'm sorry."

"No matter." He chuckled again. "I was half expecting you, in fact. I remember you don't like his justice."

No one was even looking at them. His wild leap seemed to have been utterly pointless. From where he lay on the ground, he saw two men face each other in the ring of torches.

"There were enough Dalrei dead tonight without adding another," Levon said evenly.

Diarmuid's voice was cool. "There will be enough dead in this war without our risking more by allowing what this man did."

"It was a matter then for us, for the Aven, to decide."

"Not so," Diarmuid replied. For the first time he raised his voice. "Let me remind you all, and better now than later, of how things are. When Revor was given the Plain for himself and his heirs, he swore an oath of loyalty to Colan. Let it not be forgotten. Ivor dan Banor, Aven of the Dalrei, holds that title in the same way that Revor himself did: under the High King of Brennin, who is Aileron dan Ailell, and to whom you swore an oath of your own, Levon!"

Levon's color was high, but his eyes never wavered. "I do

not forget it," he said. "Justice is still not served by arrows at night on a battlefield."

"Not so," Diarmuid said a second time. "There is seldom time in war to serve it any other way. What," he asked softly, "does the Law of the Dalrei invoke for what Doraid did this night?"

It was Torc who answered. "Death," he said clearly. "He is right, Levon."

Still on the ground with Coll, Kevin realized that Diarmuid, pupil, once, of Loren Silvercloak, had known exactly that. And after a moment he saw Levon nod his head.

"I know he is," he said. "I am my father's son, though, and I cannot order a death so easily. Will you forgive me, my lord Prince?"

For reply, Diarmuid swung down from his horse and walked over to Levon's. With a formal gesture he served as footman to help the other dismount, and then the two of them, both young, both fair, embraced, as the Dalrei and the men of Brennin shouted their approval.

"I feel like an idiot!" Kevin said to Coll. He helped the other man to his feet.

"We all feel that way sometimes," said the big man sympathetically. "Especially around Diar. Let's go get drunk, friend. The Riders make a lethal drink!"

They did. And there was a great deal of it. It didn't really lift his mood, though, nor did Diarmuid's indulgent response to his precipitate action earlier.

"I didn't know you liked Coll so much!" the Prince had said, triggering a round of laughter in the huge wooden house in which most of them had gathered.

Kevin faked a laugh; he couldn't think of a reply. He had never felt superfluous before, but more and more it was beginning to look as if he was. He noticed Dave—Davor they called him here—huddled with Levon, Torc, and a number of other Dalrei, including a teenage kid, all arms and legs and disordered hair who, he'd been given to understand, had ridden the unicorn that flew. He saw Diarmuid rise up and make his way through a giggling cluster of women to join the group. He thought about doing the same, knowing they would welcome him, but it seemed pointless somehow. He had nothing to contribute.

"More sachen?" a soft voice said in his ear. He tilted his head to see a pretty brown-haired girl holding a stone beaker. Coll winked surreptitiously and shifted a little bit away on the bench, making room.

Oh, well. "Okay," Kevin said. He smiled. "Are you joining me?"

Neatly she slipped in beside him. "For a little while," she said. "I'm supposed to be serving. I'll have to get up if my mother comes. My name is Liane dal Ivor."

He wasn't really in the mood, but she was bright and sharp and carried the ball herself much of the time. With an effort, wanting at least to be polite, Kevin did a little half-hearted flirting.

Later, her mother did appear, surveying the scene with a hostess's eye, and Liane scrambled off with a surprising oath to serve some more beakers of sachen. A little later the conclave at the far end broke up and Dave came over.

"We're leaving early in the morning," he said tersely. "Levon wants to see Kim in Paras Derval."

"She wasn't there yet," Kevin protested.

"Gereint says she will be," the other replied, and without amplification strode off into the night, buttoning his coat against the cold.

Kevin glanced at Coll. They shrugged. At least the sachen was good; saved the evening from being a total write-off.

Much later, something else did as well. He hadn't been in his bed very long, was just feeling the heavy covers warming up, when the door opened and a slim figure bearing a candle slipped inside.

"If you ask me for a breaker of sachen," Liane said, "I'll break it over your head. I hope you're warm in there." She placed the flame on the low table beside the bed and undressed. He saw her for a moment in the light; then she was under the blankets beside him.

"I like candles," she said.

It was the last thing either of them said for a long time.

And again, despite everything, the curving act of love took him away with it, so far that the colors of the light seemed to change. Before the flame burnt out he saw her bend back above him like a bow, in her own transcending arc, and he would have spoken then if he could.

Later it was dark and she said, "Fear not. We went so deep because we are near to Gwen Ystrat. The old stories are true after all."

He shook his head. He had to travel a long way back to do that much, and farther still to speak. "Everywhere," he said. "This deep."

She stiffened. He hadn't meant it to wound. How to explain? But Liane stroked his forehead and in a different voice whispered, "So you carry Dun Maura within yourself?" Then she called him, as he thought, drifting, by another name. He wanted to ask. There were questions, but the tide was going out and he was far along with it, much too far.

In the morning when Erron woke him with a shake and a grin, she was, naturally, gone. Nor did he see her before they rode off, the thirty men of Diarmuid's band, he and Dave, with Levon and Torc alongside.

For Dave the journey northeast to the upper reaches of the Latham had promised reunion and in the end had offered both that and revenge. From the moment he'd understood that the man Diarmuid was to bring back was Gereint of the third tribe, his heart had begun racing with anticipation. There was no way they could have kept him from joining that party of the Prince's men. Loren wanted Gereint for some reason having to do with figuring out the winter, he gathered. That didn't matter so much to him; what mattered was that soon he would be among the Dalrei again.

The roads had been cleared east as far as Lake Leinan, but the going became harder as they turned north the next morning. Diarmuid had hoped to make the camps before sundown, but it was slow going among the drifts and into the teeth of the bitter wind that blew unobstructed down from the Plain. They had given Dave and Kevin wonderfully warm woven coats in Paras Derval. Lightweight, too—they knew how to work with wool and cloth here, that much was obvious. Without the coats they would have frozen. Even with them, when the sun went down, the going became very bad, and Dave had no idea how far away they were from the camps.

Then all thoughts of cold had disappeared, for they had seen torches moving in the night, heard the screams of dying animals and the shouts of men in battle.

Dave hadn't waited for anyone else. He'd kicked his big stallion forward and charged up over a mound of snow, to see a battlefield spread out before him, and, astride a horse between him and the melee, a fifteen-year-old boy he remembered.

Diarmuid, the elegant Prince, had caught up with him as they galloped past Tabor down the slope, but Dave was scarcely aware of anyone else as he plunged into the closest pack of wolves, hewing on either side, aiming straight for the closest urgach, with a memory of deaths by Llewenmere to drive him on.

He remembered little else, as battle fury overtook him. Kevin Laine had been beside him with a torch for light at one point and they told him afterward that he had slain an urgach and its mount by himself. The six-legged horned beasts were called slaug, they told him. But that was after.

After Tabor, astonishingly, had appeared in the sky overhead, riding a lethal winged creature with a horn of its own that shone and killed.

After the moment when the wolves had fled and the slaug had borne the urgach away in flight, and he had dismounted to stand facing his brothers again. A great deal had been made whole then as he felt Torc's hard grip on his arm and then Levon's embrace.

There had been an interlude of some tension when Diarmuid had had a Dalrei slain for insubordination and then faced Levon down in a confrontation, but that, too, had ended all right. Kevin Laine, for no reason Dave could grasp, had tried to interfere, but no one else seemed to have taken much notice of it.

Then they had ridden back to the camp and to Ivor, who had a new title now but was still the same stocky, greying man he remembered, with the same deep-set eyes in a weather-beaten face. Ivor said, to lift Dave even higher, "Welcome home, Davor. A bright thread in darkness spins you back."

There had been sachen after, and good food by the fires, and many remembered faces. Including Liane's.

"How many times am I going to have to dance an urgach kill of yours?" she asked, bright-eyed, pert, her mouth soft on his cheek where she'd kissed him on tiptoe before moving off.

Tabor had come in quite a while later, and he'd wanted to embrace the boy but something in Tabor's face stopped him. It stopped all of them, even his father. It was then that Ivor had gestured Dave over to join a meeting around a smaller fire off to the side of the room.

With Dave, there were seven people there, and Diarmuid, carrying his own beaker, made a slightly disheveled eighth a moment later. Dave wasn't sure what he thought of this Prince; he'd been rather more impressed with Aileron, the older brother who was now High King. Diarmuid seemed altogether too suave for Dave's taste; on the other hand, there had been nothing soft about the pace he'd set on the ride, or the control he'd asserted in the matter of the Dalrei he'd ordered killed. Ivor, Dave noticed, hadn't brought the issue up either.

And Diarmuid, despite the drinking, seemed very much in command as he concisely outlined the wish of the High King and his First Mage that Gereint the shaman ride back with him to Paras Derval. There to join with the mages in seeking the source of the winter that was slowly grinding them all down under its malevolent heel.

"For it *is* malevolent," the Prince added quietly from where he'd crouched in front of blind Gereint. "The lios have confirmed what we've all guessed. We would like to leave tomorrow—if it suits the shaman, and all of you."

Ivor nodded an acknowledgment of the courteous proviso. No one spoke, though; they waited for Gereint.

Dave had still not gotten over the uneasiness he felt in the presence of this wrinkled ancient whose hollowed eye sockets seemed, nonetheless, to see into the souls of men and down the dark avenues of time. Cernan, god of the wild things, had spoken to Gereint, Dave remembered—and had called Tabor to his fast, to the animal they had seen in the sky. That thought led him to Ceinwen, and the stag in Faelin Grove. And this was his own dark avenue.

He turned from it to hear Gereint say, "We are going to need the Seer as well."

"She hasn't come yet," Diarmuid said.

Everyone looked at Dave. "She was bringing someone," he said. "She sent us ahead."

"Who was she bringing?" the man called Tulger asked from beside Ivor.

But a rare discretion led Dave to murmur, "I think that's for her to say, not me." Ivor, he saw, nodded his agreement.

Gereint smiled thinly. "True," the shaman said. "Although I know, and they have arrived by now. They were in Paras Derval before you left." This was exactly what drove Dave crazy about Gereint.

Diarmuid didn't seem bothered. "With Loren, probably," he murmured, smiling as if at a jest. Dave didn't get the joke. "Will you come then?" the Prince continued, addressing the shaman.

"Not to Paras Derval," Gereint replied placidly. "It is too far for my old bones."

"Well, surely—" Diarmuid began.

"I will meet you," Gereint went on, ignoring him, "in Gwen Ystrat. I will leave tomorrow for the Temple in Morvran. You will all be coming there."

This time even Diarmuid looked discomfited. "Why?" he asked.

"Which way did the wolves fly?" the shaman asked, turning unnervingly to where Torc sat.

"South," the dark man said, and they were silent. There was a burst of laughter from the largest fire. Dave glanced over involuntarily and saw, with a sudden chill, that Liane was sitting next to Kevin, and the two of them were whispering in each other's ears. His vision blurred. Goddamn that flashy skirt-chaser! Why did the slick, carefree Kevin Laines always have to be around to spoil things? Inwardly seething, Dave forced himself to turn back to the conclave.

"You will all be there," Gereint was repeating. "And Gwen Ystrat is the best place for what we will have to do."

Diarmuid stared at the blind shaman for a long moment. Then: "All right," he said. "I will tell my brother. Is there anything else?"

"One thing." It was Levon. "Dave, you have your horn."

The horn from Pendaran. With the note that was the sound of Light itself. "I do," Dave said. It was looped across his body.

"Good," said Levon. "Then if the Seer is in Paras Derval I would like to ride back with you. There is something I'd like to try before we go to Gwen Ystrat."

Ivor stirred at that, and turned to his elder son. "It is rash," he said slowly. "You know it is."

"I don't know," Levon replied. "I know we have been given Owein's Horn. Why else if not to use?" This was reasonable enough on its own terms to silence his father. It happened, however, to be quite wrong.

"What exactly are we talking about?" the Prince asked.

"Owein," Levon said tensely. There was a brightness in his face. "I want to wake the Sleepers and set free the Wild Hunt!"

It held them, if only for a moment.

"What fun!" said Diarmuid, but Dave could see a gleam in his eye, answering Levon's.

Only Gereint laughed, a low, unsettling sound. "What fun," the shaman repeated, chuckling to himself as he rocked back and forth.

It was just afterward that they noticed that Tabor had fainted.

He'd revived by morning and come out, pale but cheerful, to bid them good-bye. Dave would have stayed with the

Dalrei if he could, but they needed him for the horn, it seemed, and Levon and Torc were coming with them, so it was all right. And they'd be meeting again soon in Gwen Ystrat. Morvran was the place Gereint had named.

He was thinking about Gereint's laughter as they set off south again to meet the road to Paras Derval where it began to the west of Lake Leinan. In any normal weather, Levon said, they would have cut across the grazing lands of north Brennin, but not with the ice and snow of this unnatural season.

Kevin was riding, uncharacteristically subdued, with a couple of Diarmuid's men, including the one he'd so asininely jumped the night before. That was fine by Dave; he wanted nothing to do with the other man. If people wanted to call it jealousy, let them. He didn't care enough to explain. He wasn't about to confide in anyone that he'd renounced the girl himself—to Green Ceinwen in the wood. Nor was he about to recount what the goddess had replied.

*She's Torc's*, he'd said.

*Has she no other choice?* Ceinwen had answered, and laughed before she disappeared.

That part was Dave's own business.

For now, though, he had catching up to do with the men he called his brothers, ever since a ritual in Pendaran Wood. Eventually the catching up took them to the moment in the muddy fields around Stonehenge where Kevin had been explaining to the guards in French and mangled English what he and Jennifer were doing necking in forbidden territory. It had been a remarkably effective performance, and it had lasted precisely until the moment when the four of them had felt the sudden shock of power gathering them together and hurling them into the cold, dark crossing between worlds.

# Chapter 6

It was, Jennifer realized, as the now-familiar cold of the crossing receded, the same room as the first time. Not the same as her second crossing, though, when she and Paul had come through so hard they had both fallen to their knees in the snow-drifted streets of the town.

It had been there, while Paul, still dazed, had struggled to his feet under the swinging sign of the Black Boar, that she had felt the first pangs of premature labor. And with these, as she grasped where he had somehow taken them, she had had a sudden memory of a woman crying in the shop doorway by the green, and her way had seemed very clear.

So they had come to Vae's house and Darien had been born, after which a great deal seemed to change within her. Since Starkadh she had become a creature of jarring angles and dislocated responses. The world, her own world, was tinted balefully, and the possibility of ever one day crossing back to ordinary human interaction seemed a laughable, hopeless abstraction. She had been carved open by Maugrim; what healing was there anywhere for that?

Then Paul had come and said what he had said, had opened with his tone, as much as anything, the glimmering of a path. However much Rakoth might be, he was not all, not everything; he had not been able to stop Kim from coming for her.

And he could not stop her child from being born.

Or so she thought until, with a lurch of terror, she had seen Galadan in their own world. And she had heard him say that she would die, which meant the child.

So she had said to Paul that she would curse him if he failed. How had she said such a thing? From where had that come?

It seemed another person, another woman entirely, and perhaps it was. For since the child had been born and named and sent out into the worlds of the Weaver to be her own response to what had been done to her, her one random weft of thread laid across the warp—since then, Jennifer had been astonished at how mild everything was.

No angles or jarrings any more. Nothing seemed to hurt; it was all too far away. She had found herself capable of dealing with others, of surprising acts of gentleness. There were no storm winds any more; no sunshine either. She moved in slow motion, it sometimes seemed, through a landscape of grey, with grey clouds overhead; at times, but only at times, the memory of color, of vibrancy, would come to her like the low surge of a distant sea.

And all this was fine. It was not health; she was wise enough to understand that much, but it was infinitely better than what had been before. If she could not be happy and whole, at least she could be . . . mild.

The gentleness was an unexpected gift, a compensation of sorts for love, which had been mangled in Starkadh, and for desire, which had died.

Being touched was a difficult thing—not a sharp, hurting problem, but difficult, and when it happened she could feel herself twisting inwardly, a small fragile person who had once been Jennifer Lowell and golden. Even the dissembling at Stonehenge earlier that night, where she and Kevin had deceived the guards into believing that they were Gallic lovers seeking the pagan blessing of the stones—even then it had been difficult to feel his mouth on hers before the guards came. And impossible not to let him sense this, for it was hard to hide things from Kevin. But how, from this mild grey country in which she moved, did one tell a former lover, and the kindest of them all, that he had lain with her in Starkadh, obscene and distorted, black blood dripping from his severed hand to burn her flesh? How to explain that there was no going back past that, or forward from that place?

She had let him hold her, had simulated embarrassed dismay when the guards had come up to them, and had smiled and pouted mutely, as instructed, while Kevin launched into his frantic, incoherent explanation.

Then she had felt the gathering and the cold, as Kim took hold of them, and now they were in this room, their first room in Paras Derval, and it was night again.

The tapestry was the same and the torches were blazing this time, so they could make it out properly: the dazzlingly crafted depiction of Iorweth the Founder in the Godwood, before the Summer Tree. Jennifer, Kevin, and Dave glanced at it, then all three of them looked, instinctively, at Paul.

Scarcely pausing to acknowledge the tapestry, he moved quickly to the unguarded doorway. There had been a guard the last time, Jennifer remembered, and Matt Sören had thrown a knife.

This time, Paul stepped into the corridor and called softly. There was a noisy clatter of weaponry, and a moment later a terrified boy, in gear a size too large for him, came forward down the corridor with a bow drawn none too steadily.

"I know you," said Paul, ignoring the bow. "You're Tarn. You were the King's page. Do you remember me?"

The bow was lowered. "I do, my lord. From the ta'bael game. You are . . ." There was awe in the boy's face.

"I am Pwyll, yes," Schafer said simply. "Are you a guard now, Tarn?"

"Yes, my lord. I am too old to be a page."

"So I see. Is the High King in the palace tonight?"

"Yes, my lord. Shall I—"

"Why don't you lead us to him," Paul said. It was Kevin who heard, and remembered hearing before, the crisp tone in Schafer's voice. There had been an undeniable tension between Paul and Aileron when last they had met. Apparently it still existed.

They followed the boy through a web of corridors and down one drafty flight of stone stairs before they came at length to a pair of doors that only Paul remembered.

Tarn knocked and withdrew; after a startled glance, a tall guard admitted them.

The room had changed, Paul saw. The gorgeous wall

hangings had been taken down, and in their place had been hung a sequence of maps and charts. Gone too were the deep armchairs he remembered; in their place were a number of hard wooden seats and a long bench.

The chessboard with its exquisitely carved pieces was nowhere to be seen. Instead, a huge table stood in the middle of the room and on it lay an enormous map of Fionavar. Bent over the map, his back to the door, stood a man of average height, simply dressed in brown, with a fur vest over his shirt against the cold.

"Who is it, Shain?" the man said, not pausing in his scrutiny of the map.

"If you turn around you can see for yourself," Paul Schafer said before the guard could make reply.

And, very fast, Aileron did turn, almost before Paul's voice died away. His eyes above the beard blazed with an intensity three of them remembered.

"Mörnir be praised!" the High King exclaimed, taking a few quick steps toward them. Then he stopped and his face changed. He looked from one to another. "Where is she?" cried Aileron dan Ailell. *"Where is my Seer?"*

"She's coming," Kevin said, moving forward. "She's bringing someone with her."

"Who?" Aileron snapped.

Kevin looked at Paul, who shook his head. "She'll tell you herself, if she succeeds. I think it is hers to tell, Aileron."

The King glared at Paul as if minded to pursue it further, but then his face softened. "Very well," he said. "So long as she is coming. I have . . . very great need of her." After a moment a wry tone came into his voice. "I am bad at this, am I not? You deserve a fairer greeting, all of you. And is this Jennifer?"

He came to stand before her. She remembered his brother and their first meeting. This one, austere and self-contained, did not call her a peach, nor did he bend to kiss her hand. Instead, he said awkwardly, "You have suffered in our cause, and I am sorry for it. Are you well now?"

"Well enough," she said. "I'm here."

His eyes searched hers. "Why?" Aileron asked.

A good question and one nobody had asked her, not even

Kim. There was an answer, but she wasn't about to give it now to this abrasive young King of Brennin. "I've come this far," she said levelly, meeting his look with her own light green eyes. "I'll stay the course."

Men better versed in dealing with women had broken off a stare when faced with Jennifer's gaze. Aileron turned away. "Good," he said, walking back to the map on the table. "You can help. You will have to tell us everything you remember of Starkadh."

"Hey!" Dave Martyniuk said. "That's not fair. She was badly hurt there. She's trying to forget!"

"We need to know," Aileron said. Men, he could outface.

"And you don't care how you find out?" Kevin asked, a dangerous quality in his voice.

"Not really," the King replied. "Not in this war."

The silence was broken by Jennifer. "It's all right," she said. "I'll tell what I can remember. But not to you"—she indicated the King—"or any of the rest of you either, I'm afraid. I'll talk about it to Loren and Matt. No one else."


The mage had grown older since last they had seen him. There was more white among the grey of his beard and hair, deeper lines in his face. His eyes were the same as ever, though: commanding and compassionate at the same time. And Matt Sören hadn't changed at all, not even the Dwarf's twisted grimace that passed for a smile.

They all recognized it for what it was, though, and after the brittleness of Aileron the greeting they received from mage and source marked, for all of them, their true return to Fionavar. When Matt took her hand between his own two calloused ones, Jennifer cried.

"We never knew," Loren Silvercloak said, a roughness in his voice. "We didn't know if she pulled you out. And only Jaelle heard the last warning about Starkadh. It saved many lives. We would have attacked."

"And then the winter came," Aileron said. "And there was no hope of attack or anything. We've been unable to do anything at all."

"We can offer wine to our guests," the Dwarf said tartly.

"Shain, find some cups and serve anyone who wants it," Aileron said absently. "We need Kim badly," he went on. "We have to find out how Maugrim is controlling the winter—it was not a thing he could ever do before. The lios have confirmed that."

"He's making it worse?" Paul asked soberly.

There was a silence. Loren broke it. "You don't understand," he said softly. "He is making it. He has twisted the seasons utterly. These snows have been here for nine months, Pwyll. In six nights it will be Midsummer's Eve."

They looked out the window. There was ice on the glass. It was snowing again, and a bitter wind was howling about the walls. Even with two fires blazing in the room and torches everywhere, it was very cold.

"Oh, God!" said Dave abruptly. "What's happening to the Dalrei?"

"They are gathered near the Latham," Loren said. "The tribes and the eltor."

"Just in that corner?" Dave exclaimed. "The whole Plain is theirs!"

"Not now," Aileron said, and there was helpless anger in his voice. "Not while this winter lasts."

"Can we stop it?" Kevin asked.

"Not until we know how he is doing it," Loren replied.

"And so you want Kim?" Paul said. He had walked away from the others to stand by the window.

"And someone else. I want to bring Gereint here, Ivor's shaman. To see if all of us together can break through the screen of ice and snow to find their source. If we do not," the mage said, "we may lose this war before it begins. And we must not lose this war."

Aileron said nothing. It was all in his eyes.

"All right," said Jennifer carefully. "Kim's on her way, I think. I hope. In the meantime, I guess I have some things to tell Loren and Matt."

"Now?" Kevin asked.

"Why not?" She smiled, though not an easy smile. "I'll just take some of that wine, Shain. If nobody minds."

She and the mage and his source withdrew into an inner chamber. The others looked at each other.

"Where's Diarmuid?" Kevin said suddenly.

"Where do you think?" Aileron replied.

About half an hour earlier, shortly after Matt and Loren had left for the palace, Zervan of Seresh had lain in his bed in the mages' quarters, not sleeping.

He had no real duties left: he had built up the front-room fire to a level that should last the night, and he knew that if Brock returned before the other two, he'd build it up again for them.

It was never a hard life being servant to the mages. He had been with them now for twenty years, ever since they had told him he was not cut from mage cloth himself. It hadn't been a surprise; he'd sensed it very early. But he had liked all three of them—even, though it was a bitter memory, Metran, who had been clever before he had been old, before he turned out to be a traitor. He had liked Paras Derval too, the energy of the town, the nearness of the palace. It was nice being at the center of things.

When Teyrnon had asked him, Zervan had been pleased to stay on and serve the mages.

Over twenty years the original liking had grown to something akin to love. The four of them who were left, Loren and Teyrnon, Matt and Barak, were the nearest to family that Zervan had, and he worried over them all with a fussy, compulsive eye for detail.

He had been briefly ruffled when Brock of Banir Tal had come to live with them a year before. But although the new Dwarf was obviously of high rank among his people, he was unobtrusive and undemanding, and Zervan quite approved of his manifest devotion to Matt Sören. Zervan had always thought Matt drove himself too hard, and it was good to have Brock around in support, sharing the same view.

It was from Brock that Zervan had come to understand the source of Matt's occasional descents into deep moodiness and a silence that was marked even in one of taciturn nature. It was clear now to Zervan: Matt Sören, who had been King under Banir Lök, was silent and grim when he was fighting off the ceaseless pull of Calor Diman, the Crystal Lake. All Dwarf Kings, Brock had explained, spent a full moon night beside that lake between the twin mountains. If they survived what they saw, and were still sane, they could claim the Diamond Crown. And never, Brock said, never would they be free of the tidal pull of Calor Diman. It was this tide, Zervan understood, that so often pulled Loren's source awake at night, around the time of the full moon, to pace his room with a measured tread, back and forth, unsleeping until dawn.

But tonight it was Zervan himself who could not sleep. Matt was in the palace with Loren. Brock, tactfully, had excused himself to go off to the Black Boar. He often did something like that, to leave mage and source alone. Zervan, alone in the house, was awake because, twice now, he had heard a sound from outside his window.

The third time Zervan swung out of bed, dressed himself, and went to take a look. Passing through the front room, he threw a few more pieces of wood on each of the fires and then took a stout stick to carry with him. Opening the door, he went out into the street.

It was bitterly cold. His breath frosted, and even through gloves he could feel his fingertips chilling. Only the wind greeted him, and the unnatural snow. He walked around the side of the house toward the back where the bedrooms were and from where he thought he'd heard a sound.

A cat, he thought, crunching through the snow between the house and the one next door. I probably heard a cat. There were no footprints in the snow ahead of him. Somewhat reassured, he rounded the corner at the back of the house.

He had time to see what it was, to feel his mind grapple with the impossibility, and to know why there were no footsteps in the snow.

He had no time to shout or scream or give any kind of warning at all.

A long finger reached out. It touched him and he died.

After the numbing wind and icy, treacherous streets, the heat of the Black Boar struck Kevin like an inferno. The tavern was packed with shouting, perspiring people. There were at least four huge fires blazing and a myriad of torches set high in the walls.

It was almost exactly as he remembered it: the dense, enveloping smoke, the smell of meat broiling over the cooking fires, and the steady, punishing level of noise. As the three of them pushed their way through the door, Kevin realized that the Boar seemed even more crowded than it was because most of the patrons were squeezed together in a wide circle around a cleared area in the middle of the tavern. The tables had been lifted from their trestles and overturned and benches had been stacked away to open a space.

With Dave serving as a massive battering ram, Kevin and Paul pushed through behind him toward the front of the crowd near the door. When they got there, amid jostling elbows and spilling beer, Kevin saw that there was a burly redheaded man in a ring formed by the crowd. The man was carrying a smaller figure seated on his shoulders.

Facing them, roaring belligerent defiance that somehow could be heard over the din, was that vast human mountain Tegid of Rhoden, and on his shoulders, laughing, was Diarmuid, Prince of Brennin.

Beginning to laugh himself, Kevin could see wagers flying all through the crowd as the two pairs warily circled each other. Even in wartime! he thought, looking at the Prince. People were standing on tables for a better view; others had gone upstairs to look down on the battle. Kevin spotted Carde and Erron, each with a fistful of wagers, standing on the bar. Beside them, after a second, he recognized Brock, the Dwarf who had brought them word of treachery in Eridu. He was older than Matt, with a lighter-colored beard, and he was laughing aloud, which Matt Sören very seldom did. All eyes were on the combatants; not a soul had yet recognized the three of them.

"Yield, North Keep intruders!" Tegid roared. Abruptly, Kevin realized something.

"They're Aileron's men!" he shouted to Dave and Paul as

Tegid launched himself in a stumbling, lurching run toward the other two.

The big man opposing him sidestepped neatly and Diarmuid, whooping with laughter, barely managed to dodge the grasp of the other rider, who was trying to pull him to the ground. Tegid terminated his run by crashing into a table on the far side of the ring, wreaking ruin among the spectators and almost unseating his rider.

Slowly he turned, breathing stertorously. Diarmuid lowered his head and spoke a series of instructions into the ear of his unstable mount. This time they advanced more cautiously, Tegid waddling wide-footed for balance on the rush-strewn floor.

"You drunken whale!" the opposing rider taunted him.

Tegid stopped his careful advance and eyed him with red-faced ire. Then, sucking air into the bellows of his lungs, he screamed, "Beer!" at a deafening volume. Immediately a girl dashed forward with two foaming pints and Diarmuid and Tegid each drained one in a long pull.

"Twelve!" Carde and Erron shouted together from the bar top. The match had obviously been going on for some time. Diarmuid tossed his tankard back to the serving girl while Tegid hurled his over his shoulder; a patron ducked quickly and tipped over the table on which he and four other men were standing. Had been standing.

It was too much for Kevin Laine.

A moment later the North Keep duo were quite inexcusably thrown to the ground by an attack from behind. It hadn't been subtle; they'd been simply run over. As the howls and screams rose to unprecedented levels, Kevin, mounted firmly on Dave's broad shoulders, turned to the pair from the Boar.

"Have at you!" he cried.

But Tegid had other ideas. With a howl of joy, he rushed, open-armed, toward Dave, grabbed him in a titanic bear hug, and, quite unable to do anything so complex as stop, toppled the four of them to the floor in a tangled, sodden heap.

Once down, he commenced buffeting both of them with

fierce blows intended to signify affection and pleasure, Kevin doubted not, but formidable enough to make the room spin for him. He was laughing breathlessly and trying to ward off Tegid's exuberance when he heard Diarmuid whisper in his ear.

"Neatly done, friend Kevin." The Prince was not even slightly impaired. "I would have hated to lose. But down here on the floor we have a problem."

"What?" The tone had affected Kevin.

"I was keeping an eye on someone by the door for the last hour, perched up on Tegid. A stranger, I'm afraid. It wasn't concerning me much because I rather hoped he'd report we were ill prepared for war."

"What kind of stranger?"

"I was hoping to find out later. But if you're here, it changes things. I don't want him reporting that Kim and Paul are back."

"Kim isn't. Paul's here."

"Where?" said the Prince sharply.

"By the door."

There were a lot of people surrounding them by then: Carde and Erron, Coll, quite a few women. By the time they fought through to the doorway it was too late to do anything.

Paul watched the fight with a certain bemusement. It seemed that nothing, really, could induce in Diarmuid a sense of responsibility. And yet the Prince was more than a wastrel; he had proved it too many times in the short while they'd been here in the spring for the issue to still be in doubt.

In the spring. Spring a year ago, actually, if midsummer was approaching; it was on that, and on the meaning of this savage, inflicted winter, that Paul was reflecting. In particular, on something he had noticed on the icy walk from palace to tavern.

So he was preoccupied with implications and abstractions even amid the pandemonium. With only half an eye he saw Kevin mount up on Dave's shoulders and the two of them charge forward to down the North Keep pair from behind.

The roar that followed got his attention and he grinned, taking in the scene. Funny, manic Kevin Laine, in his own way quite as irrepressible as Diarmuid was, and as full of life.

His grin became a laugh as he saw Tegid rumble forward to gather Dave in a vast embrace, and then he winced as all four of them came crashing down.

Thus occupied, thus preoccupied, he didn't even see the figure, cloaked and hooded—even in the broiling heat of the Boar—that was picking its way to his side.

Someone else did, though. Someone who had seen Kevin and Dave and had guessed Paul might be there. And just as the cloaked figure came abreast of him, someone interposed herself.

"Hold it, sister! This one is mine first," said brown-haired Tiene. "You can have the others for your bed, wherever it is, but he is mine, upstairs, tonight."

Paul turned to see the slight, pretty girl whose tears had driven him from lovemaking into the night a year ago and, from that starry night, after he'd heard a song he hadn't been meant to hear, to the Summer Tree.

And it was because he'd been on the Tree and had survived, because the God had sent him back, that the one in the cloak—who was indeed a woman, though not sister to any mortal—had been coming to kill him where he stood.

Until the foolish, interfering girl had stepped between. A hand came out from within the cloak and touched Tiene with one long finger. No more than that, but the girl gasped as an icy, numbing pain shot into her arm where she'd been touched. She felt herself falling, and as she fell, she reached out with her other arm, where the cold had not yet penetrated, and pulled the hood from the other's face.

It was a human face, but only just. Skin so white it was almost blue; one sensed it would be freezing to the touch. She had no hair at all and her eyes were the color of moon on ice, glacial ice, and cold enough to bring winter into the heart of those who looked at them.

But not Paul. He met her glance and saw her retreat momentarily before a thing she read in his own depths. Around them, unbelievably, no one seemed to have noticed anything, not even Tiene's fall. People were falling all over the tavern that night.

But only one man heard a raven speak, and it was Paul. *Thought, Memory.* Those were the names, he knew, and they had been there, both of them, in the Tree at the end when the Goddess came and then the God.

And in the moment when the apparition before him recovered herself and moved to strike at him as she had Tiene, Paul heard the ravens and he chanted the words given to him, and they were these:

> *"White the mist that rose through me,*
> *Whiter than land of your dwelling.*
> *It is your name that will bind thee,*
> *Your name is mine for the telling."*

He stopped. Around the two of them, powers of the first world and so of all worlds, the careening pandemonium continued. No one paid them the slightest mind. Paul's voice had been pitched low, but he saw each word cut into her. Then, as low as before, but driving every syllable, for this was as old and as deep a magic as any there was, he said, "I am Lord of the Summer Tree, there is no secret to my name, no binding there." She had time, she could have moved to touch him and her touch could freeze the heart, but his words held her. Her ice eyes locked on his, and she heard him say, "You are far from the Barrens and from your power. Curse him who sent you here and be gone, Ice Queen, *for I name thee now by thy name, and call thee Fordaetha of Rük!"*

There came a scream that was not a scream, from a throat human and yet not. It rose like a wounded thing, took monstrous flight of its own, and stopped all other sounds in the Black Boar quite utterly.

By the time the last wailing vibration had died away into the terrified stillness, there was only an empty cloak on the floor in front of Paul. His face was pale with strain and weariness, and his eyes gave testimony to having seen a great evil.

Kevin and Diarmuid, with Dave and the others close

behind, came rushing up as the tavern exploded into frightened, questioning life. None of them spoke; they looked at Paul.

Who was crouched beside a girl on the floor. She was blue already from her head to her feet, in the grip of an icy death that had been meant for him.

At length he rose. The Prince's men had cleared a space for them. Now, at a nod from Diarmuid, two of them lifted the dead girl and bore her out into the night, which was cold but not so cold as she.

Paul said, "Fruits of winter, my lord Prince. Have you heard tell of the Queen of Rük?"

Diarmuid's face showed no trace of anything but concentration. "Fordaetha, yes. The legends have her the oldest force in Fionavar."

"One of them." They all turned to look at the grim face of the Dwarf, Brock. "One of the oldest powers," the Dwarf continued. "Pwyll, how came Fordaetha down from the Barrens?"

"With the ice that came down," Paul replied and said again, bitterly, "Fruits of winter."

"You killed her, Paul?" It was Kevin and there was a difficult emotion vivid in his face.

*Power*, Paul was thinking, remembering the old King whose place he'd taken on the Tree. He said only, "Not killed. I named her with an invocation, and it drove her back. She will not take any shape for a long time now, nor leave the Barrens for longer yet, but she is not dead and she serves Maugrim. Had we been farther north, I couldn't have dealt with her. I wouldn't have had a chance." He was very weary.

"Why do they serve him?" he heard Dave Martyniuk say, a longing to comprehend incarnate in his voice.

He knew the answer to this question, too; he had seen it in her eyes. "He promised her Ice. Ice this far south—so much of a winter world for her to rule."

"Under him," Brock said softly. "To rule under him."

"Oh, yes," Paul agreed. He thought of Kaen and Blöd, the brothers who had led the Dwarves to serve Maugrim as well. He could see the same thought in Brock's face. "It will all be under him, and for always. We cannot lose this war."

Only Kevin, who knew him best, heard the desperation in Paul's voice. He watched, they all did, as Schafer turned and walked to the doorway. He paused there, long enough to remove his coat and drop it on the floor. He had only an open-necked shirt on underneath.

"There's another thing," Paul said. "I don't need a jacket. The winter doesn't touch me. For what that's worth."

"Why?" It was Kevin who asked, for all of them.

Schafer stepped into the snow before turning to reply through the open door, "Because I tasted it on the Tree, along with all the other shapes of death."

The door swung shut behind him, cutting off the wind and the blowing snow. They stood there in the bright, noisy tavern, and there was warmth all around them, and good companionship. Nor were there many things more dear in any world.

At about the time Paul was leaving the tavern, Loren Silvercloak and his source were making their way home to the mages' quarters in the town. Neither of them was immune to the cold, and though the snow had stopped the wind had not and in places there were drifts piled as high as the Dwarf's chest. Overhead the summer stars shone brightly down on a winter world, but neither of them looked up, nor did they speak.

They had heard the same story, so they shared the same emotions: rage at what had been done to the woman they had just left in the palace; pity for the hurt they could not heal; and love, in both of them, for beauty that had proven itself defiant in the darkest place. There was something beyond all these in Matt Sören as well, for it had been a Dwarf, Blöd, who had marred her when Maugrim was done.

They did not know of Darien.

At length they reached their quarters. Teyrnon and Barak were elsewhere and Brock was out, with Diarmuid, probably, so they had the large space to themselves. As a matter of deliberate policy they were sleeping in town each night, to reassure the people of Paras Derval that the high ones of the realm were not hiding behind palace walls. Zervan had built the fires up before he went to bed, so it was blessedly warm, and the mage walked over to stand before the largest hearth in the front room, as the Dwarf poured two glasses of an amber-colored liquor.

" 'Usheen to warm the heart,' " Matt quoted as he gave Loren his drink.

"Mine is cold tonight," the tall mage said. He took a sip and made a wry face. "Bitter warmth."

"It will do you good." The Dwarf dropped into a low chair and began pulling off his boots.

"Should we reach for Teyrnon?"

"To say what?" Matt raised his head.

"The one thing we learned."

They looked at each other in silence.

"The Black Swan told Metran that the cauldron was theirs and he was to go to the place of spiraling," Jennifer had said, white and rigidly controlled as she went back in words to the woodcutter's clearing where Avaia had come for her. This was the one thing.

"What will he do there with the dead?" Matt Sören asked now. Hatred deep as a cavern lay in the query.

The mage's face was bleak. "I don't know," he said. "I don't know anything, it seems. Except that we cannot go after him until we break the winter, and we cannot break the winter."

"We will," said the Dwarf. "We will break it because we must. You will do this, there is no doubt in me."

The mage smiled then, softening the harsh lines of his face. "Aren't you tired," he asked, "after forty years of supporting me like this?"

"No," said Matt Sören simply. And after a moment, he smiled as well, the crooked twist of his mouth.

Loren drained the usheen, making a face again. "Very well," he said. "I want to reach for Teyrnon before we sleep. He should know that Metran has the Cauldron of Khath Meigol and has gone with it . . . to Cader Sedat."

He said it as prosaically as he could, but even in the

speaking of the island's name they both felt a chill, nor could any of their order not do so. Amairgen Whitebranch, first of the mages, had died in that place a thousand years ago.

Matt braced and Loren closed. They found Teyrnon through Barak, a day's ride off with the soldiers in North Keep. They conveyed what had happened and shared among the four of them doubts that would not go outside the Council of the Mages.

Then they broke the link. "All right?" Silvercloak asked his source after a moment.

"Easy," Matt replied. "It will help me sleep."

At which point there came a heavy knocking at the door. It wouldn't be Brock; he had the key. One glance, only, they exchanged, premonitory, for they were what they were, and had been so for a long time. Then they went, together, to open the front door.

In the night outside, with stars bright behind him and a half-moon, stood a bearded man, broad-shouldered, not tall, time spun far into his eyes, and a woman unconscious in his arms.

It was very still. Loren had a sense that the stars, too, were motionless, and the late-risen moon. Then the man said, in a voice rich and low, "She is only weary, I think. She named this house to me before she fainted away. Are you Loren Silvercloak? Matt Sören?"

They were proud men, the mage and his source, and numbered among the great of Fionavar. But it was with a humbled, grateful awe that they knelt then in their open doorway, both of them, before Arthur Pendragon and the one who had summoned him, and they were kneeling to the woman no less than to the man.

Another knock on another door. In her room in the palace, Jennifer was alone and not asleep. She turned from contemplating the fire; the long robe they had given her brushed the deep carpets of the floor. She had bathed and washed her hair, then combed it out before the mirror, staring at her own strange face, at the green eyes that had seen what they had seen. She had been standing before the fire a long time, how long she knew not, when the tapping came.

And with it, a voice: "Never fear me," she heard through the door. "You have no greater friend."

A voice like a chiming of bells, sound at the edge of song. She opened the door to see Brendel of the lios alfar. From a long way off she was moved to see his bright, slender grace.

"Come in," she said. "But it is past time for tears."

She closed the door behind him, marveling at how the flames of the fire, the candle by her bed, seemed to flicker and dance the more vividly with his presence in the room. The Children of Light, the lios were; their very name meant light, and it spoke to them and was answered in their being.

And the Darkest One hated them with a hate so absolute it made all else seem small beside. It was a measure of evil, she thought, who of all mortals needed no such measure, that it could so profoundly hate the creature that stood before her, eyes dry, now, and shading to amber even as she watched.

"There are graces in this King," Brendel said. "Though one would not have thought so. He sent word to my chambers that you were here."

She had been told, by Kevin, of what Brendel had done: how he had followed Galadan and his wolves, and sworn an oath in the Great Hall. She said, 'You have no cause to reproach yourself for me. You did, I have heard, more than anyone could have done."

"It was not enough. What can I say to you?"

She shook her head. "You gave me joy as well. My last memory of true delight is of falling asleep hearing the lios sing."

"Can we not give you that once more, now that you are with us again?"

"I do not know if I can receive it, Brendel. I am not . . . whole." It was easier, somehow, for her than for him. There was a long silence in which she suffered his eyes to hold hers. He did not probe within, although she knew he could, just as Loren had not used a Searching on her. None of them would intrude, and so she could hide Darien, and would.

"Will you unsay that?" he asked, the music in him deep and offering pain.

"Shall I lie to you?"

He turned and went to the window. Even the clothing he wore seemed woven of many colors that shifted as he moved. The starlight from outside lit his silvery hair and glinted within it. How could she so deny one who could have stars caught in his hair?

And how could she not? *I will take all*, Rakoth had said, and had come too near to doing so.

Brendel turned. His eyes were golden; it seemed his truest color. He said, "I have waited here a long time, by Ra-Tenniel's desire and my own. His, that I might give our counsel to this young King and learn what the men of Brennin purpose; mine, to see you here and alive, that I might offer you and ask one thing."

"Which is?" She was very tall, fairer even than she had been, marked by sorrow and shadow and given something thereby.

"That you come with me to Daniloth to be made whole again. If it can be done, it will be there."

She looked at him as if from a great height or a great depth—it was distance either way. She said, "No," and saw pain flare like fire in his eyes. She said, "I am better as I am. Paul brought me this far, he and another thing. Leave it rest. I am here, and not unhappy, and I am afraid to try for more light lest it mean more dark."

There was no answer he could make; she had meant that to be so. He touched her cheek before he left, and she endured the touch, grieving that such a thing should not bring joy, but it did not, and what could she do or say?

The lios alfar spoke from the doorway, the music almost gone from his voice. "There is vengeance then," said Brendel of the Kestrel Mark. "There is only that and always that." He closed the door softly behind him.

Oaths, she thought, turning slowly to the fire again. Kevin, Brendel, she wondered who else would swear revenge for her. She wondered if it would ever mean anything to her.

Even as she stood thus, in the grey country of muting and shadow, Loren and Matt were opening their door to see two figures in the snow with the stars and moon behind.

One last doorway, late of a bitter night. Few people left abroad in the icy streets. The Boar had long since closed, Kevin and Dave making their way to the South Keep barracks with Diarmuid and his men. In that pre-dawn hour when the north seemed closer and the wind wilder yet, the guards held close to their stations, bent over the small fires they were allowed. Nothing would attack, nothing could; it was clear to all of them that this wind and snow, this winter of malign intent, was attack enough. It was cold enough to kill, and it had; and it was growing colder yet.

Only one man felt it not. In shirt sleeves and blue jeans, Paul Schafer walked alone through the lanes and alleyways of the town. The wind moved his hair but did not trouble him, and his head was high when he faced the north.

He was walking almost aimlessly, more to be in the night than anything else, to confirm this strange immunity and to deal with the distance it imposed between him and everyone else. The very great distance.

How could it be otherwise for one who had tasted of death on the Summer Tree? Had he expected to be another one of the band? An equal friend to Carde and Coll, to Kevin even? He was the Twiceborn, he had seen the ravens, heard them speak, heard Dana in the wood, and felt Mörnir within him. He was the Arrow of the God, the Spear. He was Lord of the Summer Tree.

And he was achingly unaware of how to tap into whatever any of that meant. He had been forced to flee from Galadan, did not even understand *how* he had crossed with Jennifer. Had needed to beg Jaelle to send them back, and knew she would hold that over him in their scarcely begun colloquy of Goddess and God. Even tonight he had been blind to Fordaetha's approach; Tiene's death had been the only thing that gave him time to hear the ravens speak. And even that—he had not summoned them, knew not whence they came or how to bring them back.

He felt like a child. A defiant child walking in winter without his coat. And there was too much at stake, there was absolutely everything.

A child, he thought again, and gradually became aware that his steps had not been aimless after all. He was in the street leading to the green. He was standing before a door he remembered. The shop was on the ground level; the dwelling place above. He looked up. There were no lights, of course; it was very late. They would be asleep, Vae and Finn, and Darien.

He turned to go, then froze, cold for the first time that night, as moonlight showed him something.

Moving forward, he pushed on the open door of the shop. It swung wide, creaking on loose hinges. Inside, there were still the shelves of cloth and wool, and crafted fabrics across the way. But there was snow in the aisle and piled against the counters. There was ice on the stairs as he went up in the dark. The furniture was all in place, all as he remembered, but the house was deserted.

He heard a sound and wheeled, terror gripping him. He saw what had made the noise. In the wind that blew through a broken window, an empty cradle rocked slowly back and forth.

# Chapter 7

Early the next morning, the army of Cathal crossed the River Saeren, into the High Kingdom. Their leader allowed himself a certain amount of satisfaction. It had been well planned, exquisitely timed, in fact. They had arrived at Cynan by night, quietly, and then sent word across the river in the morning only half an hour before the specially built barges had carried them across to Seresh.

He had counted on the main road to Paras Derval being kept clear of snow, and it was. In the biting cold and under a brilliant blue sky, they set off over a white landscape for the capital. The messenger to the new High King could only be a couple of hours ahead of them; Aileron was going to have no time to organize anything at all.

And this, of course, was the point. There had been word back and forth across Saeren, barges between Seresh and Cynan, coded lights across the river farther east—the court of Brennin knew that soldiers from Cathal were coming, but now how many or when.

They were going to look shabby and badly prepared when this glittering force, twenty-five hundred strong, galloped up from the southwest. And not just the horsemen, either. What would the northmen say when they saw two hundred of the legendary war chariots of Cathal sweep up to the gates of Paras Derval? And in the first of them, pulled by four magnificent stallions from Faille, would be not a war leader or mere captain of the eidolath, the honor guard, but Shalhassan himself, Supreme Lord of Sang Marlen, of Larai Rigal, of the nine provinces of the Garden Country.

Let young Aileron deal with that, if he could.

Nor was this trivial display. Shalhassan had ruled a country shaped by intrigue far too long to indulge in mere flamboyance. There was a cold will guiding every step of this maneuver, a controlling purpose to the speed he demanded from his charioteer, and a reason for the splendor of his own appearance, from the pleated, scented beard to the fur cloak he wore, artfully slit to allow access to his curved, bejeweled sword.

One thousand years ago Angirad had led men from the south to war against the Unraveller, and they had marched and ridden under the moon and oak banner of Brennin, under Conary and then Colan. But there had been no real Cathal then, no flag of flower and sword, just the nine fractious provinces. It was only on his return, covered with the glory of having been at Andarien and Gwynir, at the last desperate battle before the Valgrind Bridge, and then at the binding under Rangat, that Angirad was able to show forth the wardstone they had given him and make a realm, to build a fortress in the south and then the summer palace by the lake at Larai Rigal.

But he had done these things. No longer was the south a nest of feuding principalities. It was Cathal, the Garden Country, and it was no subservient realm to Brennin, however Iorweth's heirs might style themselves. Four wars in as many hundred years had made that clear. If Brennin had its Tree, the boast went in the south, Larai Rigal had its ten thousand.

And it also had a real ruler, a man who had sat the Ivory Throne for twenty-five years now, subtle, inscrutable, imperious, no stranger to battle, for he had fought in the last war with Brennin thirty years ago—when this boy-king Aileron was not yet alive. To Ailell he might possibly have deferred, but not to the son, scarce one year out of exile to wear the Oak Crown.

Battles are won en route, Shalhassan of Cathal thought. A worthy thought: he raised his hand in a certain way, and a moment later Raziel galloped up, uneasy on a horse at speed, and the Supreme Lord of Cathal made him write it down. Ahead, the five members of the honor guard that had been thrown hastily together by the shocked Duke of Seresh whipped their horses to stay ahead of the chariots. He thought about passing them but decided otherwise. It would be more satisfying, to the certain degree he allowed such things to satisfy him, to arrive in Paras Derval nipping at the heels of their honor guard as if putting them to flight.

It was, he decided, well. In Sang Marlen, Galienth would monitor the decisions of his daughter. It was appropriate for her to begin to practice the statecraft she had been learning since her brother died. He was not going to have another heir. Escapades such as the one of the previous spring, when she had outraced his envoys to Paras Derval, could no longer be countenanced. He had never, in fact, received a wholly or even moderately satisfactory account of that affair. Not that he really expected one, given with whom he was dealing. Her mother had been exactly the same. He shook his head. It was time for Sharra to be wed, but every time he raised the point she evaded him. Until the last encounter, when she had smiled her falsely deferential smile (he knew it; it had been her mother's once) and murmured into her dish of chilled m'rae that if he but raised the question one more time she would wed indeed . . . and choose Venassar of Gath for her mate.

Only decades of skill had kept him from rising from his couch to let the entire court and the eidolath view his discomfiture. Worse, even, than the prospect of that semi-sentient, gangling excuse for a man beside Sharra on the throne was the thought of vulpine Bragon of Gath, his father, standing behind them.

He had turned the subject to how she should deal with the taxes while he was away. The unprecedented winter, freezing even the lake at Larai Rigal and laying waste T'Varen's gardens, had wreaked its toll everywhere, he explained, and she would have to walk a fine line of judgment between compassion and indulgence. She listened, all outward show of attentiveness, but he saw her smile behind downcast eyes. He never smiled; it gave too much away. On the other hand he had never been beautiful, and Sharra was, exceedingly. With her it was a tool, a weapon even, he knew, as he fought again to keep royal composure.

He had to work at it even now, racing to Paras Derval,

remembering his impossible child's superior smile. There was a thought here, he told himself, and in a moment he had made it abstract enough. He raised his half-closed palm again, and moment later Raziel bounced up alongside, gratifyingly unhappy, to record it. After which Shalhassan put his mind from his daughter, looked at the angle of the afternoon sun, and decided they were getting close. He drew himself up straight, shook loose his heavy cloak, combed out his forked beard, and prepared to sweep the horsemen and the war chariots of Cathal, dazzling and crisp of line, into the chaotic capital of his unprepared allies. Then they would see what they would see.

About a league from Paras Derval, everything started to go completely wrong.

First of all, the road was blocked. As the advance guard slowed and his charioteer gradually did the same, Shalhassan peered ahead, his eyes squinting in the glare of sun on snow. By the time they all stopped, the horses stamping and snorting in the cold, he was cursing inwardly with an intensity not even hinted at by his outer equanimity.

There were a score of soldiers mounted before them, clad neatly in brown and gold, weapons presented toward him with high ceremoniousness. A horn blew, sweet and clear, from behind their ranks, and the soldiers turned sharply to line the sides of the wide road, making way for six children, dressed alike in red, brilliant against the snow. Two of them approached past the Seresh honor guard and, unruffled by the movements of his horses, brought to Shalhassan of Cathal flowers of Brennin for welcome.

His face grave, he accepted them. *How did they have flowers in this winter?* Then he turned to see a tapestry being held high on poles by the other four children, and in front of him was raised high a work of sheerest art in a gesture befitting royalty: on this open road, exposed to the elements, they held up for him a woven scene from the Bael Rangat. In evanescent shades, a pinnacle of the weaver's art, Shalhassen saw the battle of Valgrind Bridge. And not just any part of the battle, but the one moment, sung and celebrated in Cathal ever since, when Angirad, first of all men in that glittering host, had set foot on the bridge over Ungarch to lead the way across to Starkadh.

It was a double honor they were doing him. As he lowered his gaze, moved despite all his striving, Shalhassan saw a figure walk beneath the tapestry to stand in the road before him, and he knew that the honor was triple and that he had miscalculated badly.

In a cloak of purest white, falling in thickly furred splendor from shoulder to white boots, stood Diarmuid, the King's brother and heir. *The wastrel*, Shalhassan thought, struggling to fight the immediate overwhelming impression of effortless elegance. Diarmuid wore white gloves as well, and a white fur hat on his golden hair, and the only color on this brilliant Prince of Snow was a red djena feather in his hat—and the red was exactly the shade the children wore.

It was a tableau of such studied magnificence that no man alive could miss the import, and no man present, of either country, would fail to tell of it.

The Prince moved a finger, no more, and there rang out over the wide snow-covered vista the exquisitely played, heart-stirring sounds of the renabael—the battle summons of the lios alfar, crafted so long ago by Ra-Termaine, greatest of their lords, greatest of their music weavers.

And then the white Prince gestured again, and again it was no more than a finger's movement, and as the music stopped, its echoes falling away in the cold, still air, the player of that music came forward, more graceful even than the Prince, and for the first time in his days Shalhassan of Cathal, quite unbelieving, saw one of the lios alfar.

The Prince bowed. The lios bowed. Over their heads Angirad stood in blood up to his knees and claimed the Valgrind Bridge in the name of Light.

Shalhassan of Cathal stepped down into the road from his carriage and bowed in his turn.

The five guards from Seresh had gone on ahead, doubtless relieved to be thus superseded. For the last league of the approach to Paras Derval, the army of Cathal was led by an honor guard of the men of Prince Diarmuid, precise and formidable; on one side of Shalhassan's chariot walked the Prince himself, and on the other was Na-Brendel, Highest of the Kestrel Mark from Daniloth.

Nor did they go faster than a walking pace, for as they drew nearer the capital, a huge crowd of cheering people lined the roadway, even among the drifted snow, and Shalhassan was forced to nod and wave in measured, dignified response.

Then, at the outskirts of the town itself, the soldiers were waiting. For the entire twisting, ascending route to the square before the palace, the foot soldiers, archers and horsemen of Paras Derval, each one turned smartly out in uniform, stood at equal intervals.

As they came into the square itself, densely packed around its outer edges with still more cheering people, the procession halted again and Prince Diarmuid presented to him, with flawless formality, the First Mage of Brennin and his source, with another Dwarf beside him whom the Prince named as Brock of Banir Tal; the High Priestess of Dana—and she, too, was dazzling in white and crowned in red as well, the thick red fall of her hair; and finally to one of whom he had heard tell, a young man, dark of hair, slim and not tall, whom the Prince named soberly as Pwyll Twiceborn, Lord of the Summer Tree.

And Shalhassan could hear the crowd's response even as he met the blue-grey eyes of this young man from another world who was the chosen of the God.

Without another word spoken, these five joined the Prince and the lios alfar. Dismounting because there was no room to sweep up in a chariot, Shalhassan walked forward to the gates of the palace to meet Aileron the High King. Who had done this, all of this, on perhaps two hours' warning.

He had been briefed by Sharra in Sang Marlen, given an idea of what to expect. But it was only an idea and not enough, for as Aileron stepped forward to meet him partway, Shalhassan, who had been shown what Brennin could do if it chose, saw what Brennin chose.

Under the unkempt dark hair, the eyes of the High King

were fierce and appraising. His stern, bearded face—not so boyish as he'd thought it would be—was fully as impassive as Shalhassan's own, and as unsmiling. He was clad in shades of brown and dun, and carelessly: his boots stained, his trousers well-worn. He wore a simple shirt and over it a short warm vest, quite unadorned. And at his side was no blade of ceremony but a long-hilted fighting sword.

Bareheaded he came forward, and the two Kings faced each other. Shalhassan could hear the roaring of the crowd and in it he heard something never offered him in twenty-five years on his own throne, and he understood then what the people of Brennin understood: the man standing before him was a warrior King, no more and certainly not less.

He had been manipulated, he knew, but he also knew how much control underlay such a thing. The dazzle of the younger brother was balanced here, and more, by the willed austerity of the older one who was King. And Shalhassan of Cathal realized in that moment, standing between the fair brother and the dark, that he was not going to lead this war after all.

Aileron had not spoken a word.

Kings did not bow to each other, but Shalhassan was not a small-minded man. There was a common enemy and an awesome one. What he had been shown had been meant not just to put him in his place but to reassure, and this, too, he grasped, and was reassured.

Abandoning on the instant every stratagem he'd envisaged for this day, Shalhassan said, "High King of Brennin, the army and chariots of Cathal are here, and yours. And so, too, is such counsel as you should seek of me. We are honored by the welcome you have offered us and stirred by your reminder of the deeds of our ancestors, both of Brennin and Cathal."

He had not even the mild pleasure of reading relief or surprise in the other's dark eyes. Only the most uninflected acceptance, as if there had been no doubt, ever, of what he would say.

What Aileron replied was, "I thank you. Eighteen of your chariots have unbalanced wheels, and we will need another thousand men, at least."

He had seen the numbers at Seresh and here in Paras Derval, knew of the garrisons at Rhoden and North Keep. Without missing a beat, Shalhassan said, "There will be two thousand more before the moon is new." Just under three weeks; it could be done, but Sharra would have to move. And the chariot master was going to be whipped.

Aileron smiled. "It is well." He stepped forward, then, the younger King to the older, as was proper, and embraced Shalhassan with a soldier's grip as the two armies and the populace thundered approval.

Aileron stepped back, his eyes now bright. He raised his arms for silence and, when he had it, lifted his clear dry voice into the frosty air. "People of Paras Derval! As you can see, Shalhassan of Cathal has come himself to us with twenty-five hundred men and has promised us two thousand more. Shall we make them welcome among us? Shall we house them and feed them?"

The shouted agreement that followed did not mask the real problem and, obscurely moved, Shalhassan decided it was time for a gesture of his own, that the northerners not mistake the true grandeur of Cathal. He raised one hand, his thumb ring glinting in the brilliant sunshine, and when he, too, had silence, said, "We thank you in our turn, High King. Shelter we will need, so far from our gardens, but the people of Cathal will feed the soldiers of Cathal and as many of the folk of Brennin as our winter granaries allow."

Let the northern King find words to engender an ovation that equaled *that*, Shalhassan thought triumphantly from behind his expressionless face. He turned to Aileron. "My daughter will arrange for the provisions and the new soldiers, both."

Aileron nodded; the roaring of the crowd had not yet stopped. Cutting through it, Shalhassan heard a lightly mocking voice.

"A wager?" said Diarmuid.

Shalhassan caught an unguarded flash of anger in the narrowed eyes of the young King before turning to face the Prince.

"Of what sort?" he asked repressively.

Diarmuid smiled. "I have no doubt at all that both provisions and soldiers will soon be among us, but I have no doubt either that it will be the formidable Galienth, or perhaps Bragon of Gath, who arranges for them. It will certainly not be your daughter."

"And why," Shalhassan said softly, concealing an inward wince at the mention of Bragon, "are you of this view?"

"Because Sharra's with your army," the Prince replied with easy certitude.

It was going to be a pleasure, and one he would allow himself, to tame this overconfident Prince. And he could; if only because his own apprehensions of such a thing had led him to have the army checked twice on the way from Seresh to Paras Derval for a wayward Princess in disguise. He knew his daughter well enough to have watched for it. She was not in the army.

"What have you to wager?" the Supreme Lord of Sang Marlen asked, very softly so as not to frighten his prey.

"My cloak for yours," the other replied promptly. His blue eyes were dancing with mischief. The white was the better cloak and they both knew it. Shalhassan said so. "Perhaps," Diarmuid replied, "but I don't expect to lose."

A very great pleasure to tame him. "A wager," said Shalhassan as the nobility about them murmured. "Bashrai," he said and his new Captain of the Guard stepped sharply forward. He missed the old one, remembering how Devorsh had died. Well, Sharra, back, in Sang Marlen, would make some recompense for that now. "Order the men to step forward in groups of fifty," he commanded.

"And to remove their headgear," Diarmuid added.

"Yes, and that," Shalhassan confirmed. Bashrai turned crisply again to execute orders.

"This is utter frivolity," Aileron snapped, his eyes cold on his brother.

"We can use some," a musical voice interposed. Brendel of the lios alfar smiled infectiously. His eyes were golden, Shalhassan noted with a thrill and, just in time, caught the corners of his mouth curving upward.

Word of the wager had spread through the crowd by now

and a laughing, anticipatory sound filled the square. They could see scribbled wagers passing from hand to hand. Only the red-haired Priestess and the grim High King seemed impervious to the lifting mood.

It didn't take long. Bashrai was pleasingly efficient, and in a short while the entire army of Cathal had stepped bareheaded past the palace gates where the two Kings stood. Diarmuid's men were checking them, and carefully, but Shalhassan had checked as carefully himself.

Sharra was not in the ranks.

Shalhassan turned slowly to the white-clad Prince. Diarmuid had managed to maintain his smile. "The horses, I wonder?" he tried. Shalhassan merely raised his eyebrows in a movement his court knew very well, and Diarmuid, with a gracious gesture and a laugh, slipped out of his rich cloak in the cold. He was in red underneath to match his feather and the children.

"The hat too?" he offered, holding them both out to be claimed.

Shalhassan gestured to Bashrai, but as the Captain, smiling on behalf of his King, stepped forward, Shalhassan heard an all-too-familiar voice cry out, "Take it not, Bashrai! The people of Cathal claim only wagers they have fairly won!"

Rather too late it came clear to him. There had been an honor guard of five, hastily assembled at dawn in Seresh. One of them now walked forward from where they had gathered on the near side of the square. Walked forward and, pulling off a close-fitting cap, let tumble free to her waist the shining black hair for which she was renowned.

"Sorry, Father," said Sharra, the Dark Rose of Cathal.

The crowd erupted in shouting and laughter at this unexpected twist. Even some of the Cathalian soldiers were cheering idiotically. Their King bestowed a wintry glance upon his sole remaining child. How, he thought, could she thus lightly bring him so much shame in a foreign land?

When she spoke again, though, it was not to him. "I thought I'd do it myself this time," she said to Diarmuid, not with any degree of warmth. The Prince's expression was hard to read. Without pausing, however, Sharra turned to his brother and said, "My lord King, I am sorry to have to report a certain laxity among your troops, both of Seresh and here. I should not have been able to join this guard, however chaotic the morning was. And I should certainly have been discovered as we came into Paras Derval. It is not my place to advise you, but I must report the facts." Her voice was guileless and very clear; it reached every corner of the square.

In the stony heart of Shalhassan a bonfire burst into warming flame. Splendid woman! A Queen to be, and worthy of her realm! She had turned a moment of acute embarrassment for him into a worse one for Brennin and a triumph for herself and for Cathal.

He moved to consolidate the gain. "Alas!" cried Shalhassan. "My daughter, it seems has the advantage over us all. If a wager has been won today, it has been won by her." And with Bashrai quick to aid, he doffed his own cloak, ignoring the bite of wind, and walked over to lay it at his daughter's feet.

Precisely in step beside him, neither before nor behind, was Diarmuid of Brennin. Together they knelt, and when they rose the two great cloaks, the dark one and the white, lay in the snow before her and the thronged square echoed to her name.

Shalhassan made his eyes as kind as he could, that she might know he was, for the moment, pleased. She was not looking at him.

"I thought I had saved you a cloak," she said to Diarmuid.

"You did. How should I better use it than as a gift?" There was something very strange in his eyes.

"Is gallantry adequate compensation for incompetence?" Sharra queried sweetly. "You are responsible for the south, are you not?"

"As my brother's expression should tell you," he agreed gravely.

"Has he not cause to be displeased?" Sharra asked, pressing her advantage.

"Perhaps," the Prince replied, almost absently. There was a silence: *something very strange.* And then just before he spoke again it flashed maliciously in his blue eyes and, a pit yawning before them, father and daughter both saw a hilarity he could no longer hold in check.

"Averren," said Diarmuid. All eyes turned to where another figure detached itself from the four remaining riders from Seresh. This one, too, removed a cap, revealing short copper-colored hair. "Report," said Diarmuid, his voice carefully neutral.

"Yes, my lord. When word came that the army of Cathal was moving west, I sent word to you from South Keep, as instructed. Also as instructed, I went west myself to Seresh and crossed yesterday evening to Cynan. I waited there until the army arrived and then, in Cathalian colors, I sought out the Princess. I saw her bribe a bargeman to take her across that night and I did the same."

"Wasting my money," said the Prince. There was utter silence in the square. "Go on."

Averren cleared his throat. "I wanted to find out the going rate, my lord. Er . . . in Seresh I picked up her trail without difficulty. I almost lost her this morning, but ah . . . followed your surmise, my lord Prince, and found her in the colors of Seresh waiting with the guards. I spoke with Duke Niavin and later with the other three guards, and we simply rode with her in front of the army all day, my lord. As instructed."

After silence, sound. Sound of a name cried on rising note after rising note to reach a crescendo so high it bade fair to break through the vaults of sky above and earth below, that Mörnir and Dana both might hear how Brennin loved its brilliant laughing Prince.

Shalhassan, calculating furiously, salvaged one meager crumb of nurture from the ashes of the afternoon: they had known all along, but if that was bad it was a comprehensible thing and better that it had been done this way than in two hours, utterly without warning. That was—would have been—simply too formidable.

Then he chanced to see Aileron's face, and even as he mentally added another score to Diarmuid's tally for the day, he felt his one crumb turn to ash as well. It was abundantly clear from the High King's expression—*Aileron hadn't known any of this.*

Diarmuid was looking at Sharra, his own expression benign. "I told you the cloak was a gift, not a wager lost."

Her color high, she asked, "Why did you do it that way? Why pretend not to know?"

And laughing suddenly, Diarmuid replied, "Utter frivolity," in a passable imitation of his brother. Then, laughing still, he turned to face the black expression, very close to a killing look, in the High King's eyes. It was perhaps more than he had expected. Slowly the laughter faded from his eyes. At least it was gone, Shalhassan thought wryly, though he himself had not wiped it away. The cheering was still going on.

Aileron said, "You knew all along." It was not a question.

"Yes," said Diarmuid simply. "We do things differently. You had your charts and plans."

"You didn't tell me, though."

Diarmuid's eyes were wide and there was a questing in them and, if one knew what to look for, a long desire. Of all the people in that square, only Kevin Laine, watching from among the crowd, had seen that look before, and he was too far away this time. The Prince's voice was even, if very low, as he said, "How else would you have ever known? How else would you have been able to put your planning to the test? I expected you to succeed, brother. We had it both ways."

A long silence. Too long, as Aileron's heavy-lidded gaze remained bleakly on his brother's face. The cheering had run itself down. A moment passed. Another. A stir of cold, cold wind.

"Brightly woven, Diar," Aileron said. And then dazzled them all with the warmth of his smile.

They began to move inside. *Both ways,* Shalhassan was thinking bemusedly. They knew all along *and* they had prepared in two hours. What sort of men were these two sons of Ailell?

"Be grateful," came a voice at his side. "They are ours." He turned and received a golden wink from a lios alfar and a

grin from Brock, the Dwarf next to him. Before he knew
what he was doing, Shalhassan smiled.

Paul had wanted to waylay the Priestess immediately, but she
was ahead of him in the procession and turned to the left as
soon as she passed through the great doors of the palace, and
he lost sight of her in the crowded entranceway. Then, as he
fought to get free and follow, Kevin came up and he had to
stop.

"He was brilliant, wasn't he?" Kevin grinned.

"Diarmuid? Yes, very." Paul rose on tiptoe to try to see
over the people milling about them. There was a banquet
being readied; servants and courtiers jostled each other as
they crisscrossed the vestibule. He saw Gorlaes, the handsome Chancellor, taking charge of the party from Cathal,
which now included, unexpectedly, a Princess.

"You're not listening," Kevin said.

"Oh. What?" Paul drew a breath. "Sorry. Try me again."
He managed a smile.

Kevin gave him a searching glance. "You okay? After last
night?"

"I'm fine. I walked a lot. What were you saying?"

Again Kevin hesitated, though with a different, more
vulnerable expression. "Just that Diarmuid's riding off
within the hour to fetch this shaman from the Dalrei. Dave's
going and I am too. Do you want to come?"

And how did one explain how dearly one wanted to
come? To come and savor, even amid war, the richness of
companionship and the laughter that the Prince and Kevin
both knew how to engender. How explain, even if he had
the time?

"Can't, Kev. I've too much to do here."

"Umm. Right. Can I help?"

"Not yet. Maybe later."

"Fine," Kevin said, feigning a casualness. "We'll be back
in three or four days."

Paul saw red hair through an archway. "Good," he said to

his closest friend. "Take care." There should have been more, he thought, but he couldn't be everything; he wasn't even sure what, exactly, he could be.

He squeezed Kevin on the shoulder and moved off quickly to intercept Jaelle, cutting through the eddying crowd. He didn't look back; Kevin's expression, he knew, would have forced him to stop and explain, and he didn't feel up to explaining how deeply fear lay upon him.

Halfway across the floor he saw, with a shock, that Jennifer was with the Priestess. Schooling his features, he came up to them.

"I need you both," he said.

Jaelle fixed him with her cool regard. "It will have to wait."

Something in the voice. "No, it won't," Paul said. And gripping her right arm very hard and Jennifer's more gently, he propelled them both, smiling fatuously for the crowd, across the entrance foyer, down a branching hallway, and then, almost without breaking stride, into the first room they came to.

It was, thankfully, empty of people. There were a number of musical instruments laid out on the two tables and on the window seat. A spinet stood in the middle of the room and, beside it, what appeared to be a harp laid on its side, mounted into brackets and with free-standing legs.

He closed the door.

Both women regarded him. At any other time he might have paused to appreciate the order of beauty in the room with him, but neither pair of green eyes was less than cold at the moment, and the darker ones flashed with anger. He had bruised Jaelle, he knew, but she wasn't about to let him see that. Instead, she snapped, "You had best explain yourself."

It was a bit much.

"*Where is he?*" said Paul, hurling the question like a blade.

And found himself nonplused and weaponless when, after a blank instant, both women smiled and exchanged an indulgent glance.

"You were frightened," Jaelle said flatly.

He didn't deny it. "Where?" he repeated.

It was Jennifer who answered. "He's all right, Paul. Jaelle was just telling me. When did you find out?"

"Last night. I went to the house." *The cradle rocking in the icy wind . . . in the empty house.*

"I would rather you checked with me or with Jaelle before doing that sort of thing," Jennifer said mildly.

He felt the explosion coming, moved ruthlessly to curb it, and succeeded, barely. Neither woman appeared quite so smug as they looked at him. He said, paying out the words carefully, "There seems to be a misconception here. I don't know if either of you are capable of grasping this trenchant point, but we are not talking about some cuddly infant with spittle on his chin; we are dealing with the son of Rakoth Maugrim *and I must know where he is!*" He felt his voice crack with the strain of keeping it from rising to a shout.

Jaelle had paled, but again it was Jennifer who answered, hardily. "There is no misconception, Paul. I am unlikely to forget who his father is."

It was like cold water in the face; he felt his anger being sluiced away, leaving behind a residue of sorrow and deep pain.

"I know that," he said after a difficult moment. "I'm sorry. I was frightened last night. The house was the second thing."

"What was the first?" Jaelle asked, not harshly this time.

"Fordaetha of Rük."

With some distant satisfaction he saw her hands begin to tremble. "Here?" she whispered. "So far south?" She put her hands in the pockets of her gown.

"She was," he said quietly. "I drove her back. But not before she killed. I spoke to Loren this morning. Their servant is dead: Zervan. And so is a girl from the tavern." He turned to Jennifer. "An ancient power of winter was in Paras Derval. She tried to kill me as well and . . . failed. But there is a great deal of evil about. I must know where Darien is, Jennifer." She was shaking her head. He pushed on. "Listen to me, please! He cannot be only yours now, Jen. He can't. There is too much at stake, and we don't even know what he is!"

"He is to be random," she replied calmly, standing very tall, golden among the instruments of music. "He is not to be used, Paul."

So much dark in this, and where were his ravens now? It was a hard, a savage thing, but it had to be said, and so:

"That isn't really the issue. The issue is whether or not he has to be stopped."

In the silence that followed they could hear the tread of feet outside in the corridor and the continuing buzz of the crowd not far away. There was a window open. So as not to have to look any more at what his words had done to Jennifer, Paul walked over to it. Even on the main level of the palace they were quite high up. Below, to the south and east, a party of thirty men or so were just leaving Paras Derval. Diarmuid's band. With Kevin, who might in fact have understood, if Paul had known clearly what he wanted to explain.

Behind him Jaelle cleared her throat and spoke with unwonted diffidence. "There is no sign yet of that last, Pwyll," she said. "Both Vae and her son say so and we have been watching. I am not so foolish as you take me for."

He turned. "I don't take you for foolish at all," he said. He held the look, longer perhaps than necessary, before turning reluctantly to the other woman.

Jennifer had been looking pale a long time, it was almost a year since she'd had a healthy tan, but never had he seen her as white as now she was. For a disoriented instant he thought of Fordaetha. But this was a mortal woman, and one to whom unimaginable damage had been done. Against the white of her skin, the high cheekbones stood out unnaturally. He wondered if she was going to faint. She closed her eyes; opened them. "He told the Dwarf I was to die. Told him there was a reason." Her voice was an aching rasp.

"I know," Paul said, as gently as he could. "You explained to me."

"What reason could there be for killing me if . . . if not because of a child?" How did one comfort a soul to whom this had been done? "What reason, Paul? Could there be another?"

"I don't know," he whispered. "You're probably right, Jen. Please stop."

She tried; wiped at her tears with both hands. Jaelle walked forward with a square of silk and gave it to her awkwardly. Jennifer looked up again. "But if I'm right . . . if he was afraid of a child, then . . . shouldn't Darien be *good?*"

So much yearning in the question, so much of her soul. Kevin would lie, Paul thought. Everyone he knew would lie.

Paul Schafer said, very low, "Good, or a rival, Jen. We can't know which, and so I must know where he is."

Somewhere on the road Diarmuid and his men were galloping. They would wield swords and axes in this war, shoot arrows, throw spears. They would be brave or cowardly, kill or die, bonded to each other and to all other men.

He would do otherwise. He would walk alone in darkness to find his own last battle. He who had come back would say the cold truths and the bitter, and make a wounded woman cry as though whatever was left of her heart was breaking even now.

Two women. There were bright, disregarded tears on Jaelle's cheeks as well. She said, "They have gone to the lake. Ysanne's lake. The cottage was empty, so we sent them there."

"Why?"

"He is of the andain, Pwyll. I was telling Jennifer before you came: they do not age as we do. He is only seven months old, but he looks like a five-year-old child. And is growing faster now."

Jennifer's sobs were easing. He walked over to the bench where she was and sat down beside her. With a real hesitation, he took her hand and raised it to his lips.

He said, "There is no one I have known so fine as you. Any wound I deal to you is more deeply bestowed upon myself; you must believe this to be true. I did not choose to be what I have become. I am not even sure what that is."

He could sense her listening.

He said, "You are weeping for fear you have done wrong, or set loose an evil. I will say only that we cannot know. It is just as possible that Darien will be our last, our deepest hope of light. And let us remember"—he looked up and saw that Jaelle had come nearer—"let all three of us remember that Kim dreamt his name and so he has a place. He is in the Tapestry."

She had stopped crying. Her hand remained in his, and he did not let it go. She looked up after a moment. "Tell me," she said to Jaelle, "how are you watching him?"

The Priestess looked uncomfortable. "Leila," she said.

"The young one?" Paul asked, not comprehending. "The one who spied on us?"

Jaelle nodded. She walked over to the horizontally mounted harp and plucked two strings before answering. "She is tuned to the brother," she whispered. "Exactly how, I don't understand, but she *sees* Finn and he is almost always with Darien. We take them food once a week as well."

His throat was dry again with fear. "What about an attack? Can't they just take him?"

"Why should they be attacked," Jaelle replied, lightly touching the instrument, "a mother and two children? Who knows they are even there?"

He drew a breath. It felt like such naked, undefended folly. "Wolves?" he pursued. "Galadan's wolves?"

Jaelle shook her head. "They never go there," she said. "They never have. There is a power by that lake warding them."

"What power?" he asked.

"I don't know. I truly don't. No one in Gwen Ystrat knows."

"Kim does, I'll bet," said Jennifer.

They were silent for a long time, listening to the Priestess at the harp. The notes followed one another at random, the way a child might play.

Eventually there came a knocking.

"Yes?" said Paul.

The door opened, and Brendel stepped inside. "I heard the music," he said. "I was looking for you." His gaze was on Jennifer. "Someone is here. I think you should come." He said nothing more. His eyes were dark.

They all rose. Jennifer wiped her face; she pushed back her hair and straightened her shoulders. Very like a queen, she looked, to Paul. Side by side, he and Jaelle followed her from the room. The lios alfar came after and closed the door.

Kim was edgy and afraid. They had been planning to bring Arthur to Aileron in the morning, but then Brock had discovered Zervan's frozen body in the snow. And before they could even react, let alone properly grieve, tidings had come of Shalhassan's imminent arrival from Seresh, and palace and town both had exploded into frenzied activity.

Frenzied, but controlled. Loren and Matt and Brock, grim-faced, all three of them, hurried off, and so Kim and Arthur, alone in the mages' quarters, went upstairs and watched the preparations from a second-floor window. It was clear, both to her untrained glance and to his profoundly expert one, that there was a guiding purpose to the chaos below. She saw people she recognized rushing or riding past: Gorlaes, Coll, Brock again; Kevin, racing around the corner with a banner in his hand; even the unmistakable figure of Brendel, the lios alfar. She pointed them out to the man beside her, keeping her tone as level and uninflected as she could manage.

It was hard, though. Hard because she had next to no idea what to expect when the Cathalians had been greeted and it came time to bring Arthur Pendragon to Aileron, the High King of Brennin. Through three seasons she had waited—fall, winter, and the winterlike spring—for the dream that would allow her to summon this man who stood, contained and observant, by her side. She had known in the deepest way she now knew things that it was a necessary summoning, or she would not have had the courage or the coldness to walk the path she'd trod the night before, through a darkness lit only by the flame she bore.

Ysanne had dreamt it too, she remembered, which was reassuring, but she remembered another thing that was not. *It is to be my war,* Aileron had said. At the very beginning, their first conversation, before he was King even, before she was his Seer. He had limped to the fire as Tyrth, the crippled servant, and walked back as a Prince who would kill to claim a crown. And what, she wondered anxiously, what would this young, proud, intolerant King do or say when faced with the Warrior she had brought? A Warrior who had been a King himself, who had fought in so many battles against so many different shapes of Darkness, who had come back from his island, from his stars, with his sword and his destiny, to fight in this war Aileron claimed as his own.

It was not going to be an easy thing. Past the summoning, she had not yet seen, nor could she do so now. Rakoth unchained in Fionavar demanded response; for this reason if for no other, she knew, had she been given fire to carry on her hand. It was the Warstone she bore, and the Warrior she had brought. For what, and to what end, she knew not. All she knew was that she had tapped a power from beyond the walls of Night, and that there was a grief at the heart of it.

"There is a woman in the first group," he said in the resonant voice. She looked. The Cathalians had arrived. Diarmuid's men, dressed formally for the first time she had ever seen, had replaced the guard from Seresh. Then she looked again. The first group was that guard from Seresh, and one of them, incredibly, she knew.

"Sharra!" she breathed. "Again! Oh, my God." She turned from staring at the disguised Princess she had be-friended a year ago to glancing with astonishment at the man beside her, who had noticed a disguise in one of so many riders in such a tumultuous throng.

He looked over at her, the wide-set dark eyes gentle. "It is my responsibility," said Arthur Pendragon, "to see such things."

Midafternoon, it was. The breath of men and horses showed as puffs of smoke in the cold. The sun, high in a clear blue sky, glittered on the snow. Midafternoon, and at the window Kimberly thought again, looking in his eyes, of stars.

She recognized the tall guard who opened the door: he had escorted her to Ysanne's lake the last time she went. She saw, from his eyes, that he knew her as well. Then his face changed as he took in the man who stood quietly beside her.

"Hello, Shain," she said, before he could speak. "Is Loren here?"

"Yes, and the lios alfar, my lady."

"Good. Are you going to let me in?"

He jumped backward with an alacrity that would have been amusing were she in any state to be amused. They feared her, as once they had feared Ysanne. It wasn't funny now, though, not even ironic; this was no place or time for such shadings.

Drawing a deep breath, Kim pushed back her hood and shook out her white hair, and they walked in. She saw Loren first and received a quick nod of encouragement—one that did not mask his own tension. She saw Brendel, the silver-haired lios alfar, and Matt, with Brock, the other Dwarf, and Gorlaes the Chancellor.

Then she turned to Aileron.

He hadn't changed, unless it were simply to become more, in a year's time, of what he had already been. He stood in front of a large table that was spread with a huge map of Fionavar. His hands were clasped behind his back, his feet balanced wide apart, and his deep-set, remembered eyes bored into her. She knew him, though: she was his Seer, his only one.

Now she read relief in his face.

"Hello," she said calmly. "I'm told you got my last warning."

"We did. Welcome back," Aileron said. And then, after a pause, "They have been walking on tiptoe around me this past half hour, Loren and Matt. Will you tell me why this is and whom you have brought with you?"

Brendel knew already; she could see the wonder silver in his eyes. She said, raising her voice to make it clear and decisive, as a Seer's should be, "I have used the Baelrath as Ysanne dreamt long ago. Aileron, High King, beside me stands Arthur Pendragon, the Warrior of the old tales, come to make one with our cause."

The lofty words rose and then fell into silence, like waves breaking around the King's rock-still face. Any of the others in this room would have done it better, she thought, painfully aware that the man beside her had not bowed. Nor could he be expected to, not to any living man, but Aileron was young and newly King, and—"

"My grandfather," said Aileron dan Ailell dan Art, "was named for you, and have I a son one day he too will be." As the men in the room and the one woman gasped with astonishment, the High King's face broke into a joyful smile. "No visitation, not even of Colan or Conary, could be more bright, my lord Arthur. Oh, brightly woven, Kimberly!" He squeezed her shoulder hard as he strode past and embraced fiercely, as a brother, the man she had brought.

Arthur returned the gesture, and when Aileron stepped back, the Warrior's own eyes showed, for the first time, a glint of amusement. "They led me to understand," he said, "that you might not entirely welcome my presence."

"I am served," said Aileron, with a heavy emphasis, "by advisers of limited capacities. It is a sad truth that—"

"Hold it!" Kim exclaimed. "That's not fair, Aileron. That's . . . not fair." She stopped because she couldn't think of what else to say, and because he was laughing at her.

"I know," Aileron said. "I know it isn't." He controlled himself, then said in a very different voice, "I don't even want to know what it is you had to go through to bring us this man, though I was taught as a boy by Loren and I think I can hazard a guess. You are both full welcome here. You could not be otherwise."

"Truly spoken," said Loren Silvercloak. "My lord Arthur, you have never fought in Fionavar before?"

"No," the deep voice replied. "Nor against Rakoth himself, though I have seen the shadows of his shadow many times."

"And defeated them," Aileron said.

"I never know," Arthur replied quietly.

"What do you mean?" Kim asked in a whisper.

"I die before the end." He said it quite matter-of-factly. "I think it best you understand that now. I will not be here for the ending—it is a part of what has been laid upon me."

There was silence, then Aileron spoke again. "All I have

been taught tells me that if Fionavar falls then all other worlds fall as well, and not long after—to the shadows of the shadow, as you say." Kim understood: he was moving away from emotion to something more abstract.

Arthur nodded gravely. "So it is told in Avalon," he said, "and among the summer stars."

"And so say the lios alfar," Loren added. They turned to look at Brendel and noticed for the first time that he had gone. Something stirred in Kimberly, the faintest, barely discernible anticipation, far too late, of the one thing she could not have known.

Na-Brendel of the Kestrel Mark had the same sense of belated awareness, but more strongly, because the lios alfar had traditions and memories that went deeper and farther back then did those of the Seers. Ysanne once, and Kimberly now, might walk into the future, or dream some threads of it, but the lios lived long enough to know the past and were often wise enough to understand it. Nor was Brendel, Highest of the Kestrel, least among them in age or understanding.

And once, a year ago in a wood east of Paras Derval, a sense of a chord half heard had come to him, as it came now again, more strongly. With sorrow and wonder both, he followed the sound of a harp to another door and, opening it, bade all three of them come back with him, one for the God, one for the Goddess, and one in the name of the children, and for bitterest love.

Nor was he wrong, nor Kimberly. And as he entered the King's room with Pwyll and the women, Brendel saw from the mage's suddenly rigid face that he, too, understood. Loren and his source and Brock of Banir Tal were standing with Kim by the window. Aileron and Arthur, with Gorlaes, stood over the spread-out map.

The King and the Chancellor turned as they came in. Arthur did not. But Brendel saw him lift his head quickly as if scenting or hearing a thing to which the rest were oblivious, and he saw that Arthur's hands, resting on the tabletop, had gone suddenly white.

106

"We have been granted aid beyond measure," he said to the three he had brought. "This is Arthur Pendragon, whom Kimberly has summoned for us. My lord Arthur, I would present to you—"

He got no further. Brendel had lived long and seen a very great deal in his days and had shared more through the memories of the Elders of Daniloth. But nothing, ever, could touch the thing he saw in the Warrior's eyes as Arthur turned. Before that glance he felt his voice fail; there were no words one could say, no pity deep enough to touch, to even nearly touch.

Kim saw them too, the eyes of the one she'd summoned from a vanished island, from the summer stars. To war, she'd thought, because there was need. But understanding in that instant the fullness of the curse that had been laid on him, Kim felt her heart turn over and over as if tumbling down a chasm. A chasm of grief, of deepest love, deeply returned, most deeply betrayed, saddest story of all the long tales told. She turned to the second one. Oh, Jen, she thought. Oh, Jennifer.

*"Oh, Guinevere,"* said Arthur. *"Oh, my very dear."*

All unexpecting had she walked the long corridors and up the stone stairwell. The stone of the walls in its muted shadings matched the serenity of grey she had built inside. It would be all right or, if not, it was not meant to be. There was a hope that Darien might be what she'd so deeply wanted him to be, back in the days when things reached deeply into her. There was a chance; there were people aware of it. She had done what she could, and it was as much as she could.

She entered the room and smiled to see Kim and to see that she seemed to have brought the one she'd waited for. Then Brendel spoke his name and Arthur slowly turned and she saw his eyes and heard him name her by the other name, and there was fire, light, memory, so much love, and desire: an explosion in her breast.

*Then another memory, another explosion.* Rangat's fire climbing to block out her sight of heaven, and the hand, the severed hand, the blood black, as his fortress was, green light, and red his eyes had been, Rakoth's, in Starkadh.

And here as well. They were. And, oh, too brutally between. She had only to cross to the table where Arthur stood. By whom she was loved, even still, and would be sheltered. But the Unraveller lay between.

She could not come, not ever, to such perfect love, nor had she, the first time, or in any of the after times. Not for this reason, though. It had never been Fionavar before. Shadows of the shadow there had been, and the other sword of Light, the other one, brightest, bitterest love. But never Rakoth before. She could not pass, not through that flame, not past the burning of that blood on her body, not over; oh, she could not rise over the Dark and what it had done to her.

Not even to the shore that Arthur was.

She needed grey. No fire or blood, no colors of desire, access to love. She said, and her voice was very clear, "I cannot cross. It is better so. I have been maimed but will not, at least, betray. He is not here. There is no third. The gods speed your blade in battle, and grant you final rest."

There were so many falling stars in his eyes, so many fallen. She wondered if any were left in the sky.

"And you," he said after a long time. "Grant you rest."

So many fallen stars, so many falling still.

She turned and left the room.

# Chapter 8

She had no one to blame but herself, of course; Shalhassan had made that very clear. If the heir to the throne of Cathal chose to come to a place of war, she would have to conduct herself in a manner befitting royalty. There was also the matter of saving face as best one could after the disaster of yesterday.

So all morning and into the afternoon Sharra found herself sitting around a table in the High King's antechamber as the tedious business of planning the disposition and provisioning of troops was conducted. Her father was there, and Aileron, cool and efficient. Bashrai and Shain, the Captains of the Guard, stood by to register orders and relay them through runners stationed just outside the room.

The other man, the one she watched most closely, was a figure from the shadowy realm of childhood stories. She remembered Marlen her brother pretending to be the Warrior when he was ten years old, pretending to pull the King Spear from the mountainside. And now Marlen was five years dead and beside her stood Arthur Pendragon, giving counsel in a deep, clear voice, favoring her with a glance and a gentle smile now and again. But his eyes didn't smile; she had never seen eyes like his, not even those of Brendel, the lios alfar.

It continued through the afternoon. They ate over the map and the innumerable charts Aileron had prepared. It was necessary, she understood, but it seemed pointless, somehow, at the same time. There was not going to be a true war while the winter lasted. Rakoth was making this winter-in-summer, but they didn't know how and so they couldn't do anything to stop it. The Unraveller didn't need to risk battle, he wasn't going to. He was going to freeze them to death, or starve them, when the stored food ran out. Already it had begun: the elderly and the children, first victims always, were starting to die in Cathal and Brennin and on the Plain.

Against that brutal reality, what good were abstract plans to use chariots as barricades if Paras Derval were attacked?

She didn't say it, though. She was quiet and listened and, about midafternoon, had been silent so long they forgot about her, and she made her escape and went in search of Kim.

It was Gorlaes, the omniscient Chancellor, who directed her. She went to get a cloak from her chambers and noticed that the white one had already been trimmed to her size. Expressionlessly she put it on and, climbing all the stairs, came out on a turret, high above everything else. Kim was standing there, in furred cloak and gloves but unhooded, her startling white hair whipping into her eyes. To the north, a long line of clouds lay along the horizon and a north wind was blowing.

"Storm coming," Sharra said, leaning on the parapet beside the other woman.

"Among other things." Kim managed a smile but her eyes were red.

"Tell me," Sharra said. And listened as it came out like a pent-up flood. The dream. The dead King and the undead son. The children slain and Jennifer shattered in Starkadh. The one thing unforeseen: Guinevere. Love betrayed. Grief at the heart of it, the heart of everything.

Cold in the high wind they stood when the story ended. Cold and silent, facing the bitter north. Neither wept; it was wind that laid freezing tears on their cheeks. The sun slid low in the west. Ahead of them the clouds were thick on the horizon.

"Is he here?" Sharra asked. "The other one? The third?"

"I don't know. She said he wasn't."

"Where is she now?"

"In the Temple, with Jaelle."

Silence again, save for the wind. As it happened, though for very different reasons, the thoughts of both of them were away to the east and north where a fair-haired Prince was riding at the head of thirty men.

A short while later the sun was lost in trees behind Mörnirwood and the cold became too great. They went inside.

Three hours later they were back on that tower with the King and half the court, it seemed. It was full dark and savagely cold, but no one noticed, now.

Away to the north, very, very far, a luminous pearly light was being cast into the sky.

"What is it?" someone asked.

"Daniloth," Loren Silvercloak replied softly. Brendel was standing beside him, his eyes the color of the light.

"They are trying it," the lios breathed. "Not for a thousand years has Daniloth been unsheathed. There are no shadows on the Land of Light tonight. They will be looking at the stars later when they fade the shining. There will be starlight above Atronel."

It was almost a song, so beautiful was his voice, so laden with yearning. Every one of them looked at that cast glow and, wondering, understood that it had been like that every night before Maugrim had come, and the Bael Rangat, before Lathen had woven the mist to change Daniloth into the Shadowland.

"Why?" Sharra asked. "Why are they doing it?"

Again it was Loren who replied. "For us. They are trying to draw him down from Starkadh to divert his power from the winter's shaping. The lios alfar are offering themselves so that we might have an end to the cold."

"An ending to it for them as well, surely?" Gorlaes protested.

Never taking his eyes from the light in the north, Na-Brendel answered him. "There is no snow in Daniloth. The sylvain are blooming now as they do each midsummer, and there is green grass on Atronel."

They watched, picturing it, heartened despite the knife of wind by that lifted glow that meant courage and gallantry, a play of light in heaven at the very door of the Dark.

Watching it, Kim was distracted by a sound, very thin, almost a drift of static in her mind. More that than music, and coming, so far as she could tell, from the east. She lifted her hand; the Baelrath was quiescent, which was a blessing. She was coming to fear its fire. She pushed the whisper of sound away from her—it was not hard—and turned her whole being to the light of Daniloth, trying to draw strength and some easing of guilt and sorrow. It was less than forty-eight hours since she had stood at Stonehenge and she was weary, through and through, with so much yet to be done.

Beginning, it seemed, immediately.

When they returned to the Great Hall, a woman in grey was there waiting for them. Grey, as in the grey robes of the priestesses, and it was Jaelle, striding past the Kings, who spoke to her.

"Aline, what is it?"

The woman in grey sank to the floor in a deep curtsy before Jaelle; then she offered a perfunctory version to Aileron. Turning back to the High Priestess, she spoke carefully, as from memory.

"I am to convey to you the obeisance on the Mormae and Audiart's apologies. She sent this in person because it was thought the men here would greater appreciate urgency if we did not use the link."

Jaelle remained very still. There was a forbidding chill in her face. "What urgency?" she asked, velvet danger sheathed in her voice.

Aline flushed. I wouldn't be in her shoes for anything, Kim thought suddenly.

"Again, Audiart's apologies, High One," Aline murmured. "It is as Warden of Gwen Ystrat, not as Second of the Mormae, that she sent me. I was told to say this to you."

Imperceptibly, almost, Jaelle relaxed. "Very well—" she began but was interrupted before she could finish.

"If you are sent by my Warden, you should be speaking to me," Aileron said, and his own voice was fully as cold as Jaelle's had been. The High Priestess stood immobile and impassive. No help there, Kim thought. She felt briefly sorry for Aline, a pawn in a complex game. Only briefly, though; in some ways pawns had it easy.

Aline decided; she sank down into a proper curtsy before the King. Rising, she said, "We have need of you, High King. Audiart requests you to remember how seldom we ask aid and that you therefore consider our plight with compassion."

"To the point!" the High King growled. Shalhassan, just behind him, was taking it all in avidly. It was no time for anything but control.

Again Aline glanced at Jaelle and again found no assistance. She licked her lips. Then, "Wolves," she said. "Larger than any of us have ever seen. There are thousands of them, High King, in the wood north of Lake Leinan, and they are raiding at night among the farms. The farms of your people, my lord King."

"Morvran?" said Jaelle sharply. "What about us?"

Aline shook her head. "They have been seen near the town but not yet in the Temple grounds, High One. If they had been, I am to say, then—"

"Then the Mormae would have linked to tell me. Audiart," Jaelle murmured, "is cleverness itself." She tossed her head, and the red hair rippled down her back like a river.

Aileron's eyes were bright in the torchlight. "She wants me to come and clean them out for her? What says the High Priestess?"

Jaelle didn't even look at him. "This," she said, "is your Warden, not my Second, Aileron."

There was a silence, and then a polite cough and Paul Schafer walked forward toward Audiart's messenger.

"One moment," he said. "Aileron, you spoke of cleaning out the wolves. It may be more than that." He paused. "Aline, is Galadan in Leinanwood?"

The priestess had fear in her eyes. "We never thought of that. I do not know."

And so it was time. That was a cue for her, if anything was. Kim schooled her face and, as she did, Aileron's glance swung over to find her.

Would she ever be used to this? Had Ysanne ever grown

accustomed to this shuttling back and forth on the timeloom? Only last night, restless and heartsick for Jennifer, she had fallen into half sleep and a blurred, insubstantial dream of a hunt in a wood, in some wood, somewhere, and a rushing thunder over the ground.

She met the King's glance. "Something is there," she said, keeping her voice crisp. "Or someone. I have seen a hunt."

Aileron smiled. He turned to Shalhassan and to Arthur beside him. "Shall we three hunt wolves of the Dark in Gwen Ystrat?"

The dour King of Cathal nodded.

"It will be good to have an enemy to kill just now," Arthur said.

He meant more, Kim knew, than Aileron heard, but she had no space for sorrow because something else from her dream had slotted into place with the High King's words.

"It will be more than a hunt," she murmured. It was never necesssary for a Seer to speak loudly. "I'll be coming, and Loren, and Jaelle, if she will."

"Why?" It was Paul, challenging, bearing his own burdens.

"I dreamt the blind one," she explained. "Gereint of the Dalrei will be going to Morvran tomorrow."

There was a murmur at that. It was, she supposed, unsettling for people to hear such things. Not much she could do, or cared at the moment to do, about it. She was very weary, and it wasn't about to get easier.

"We'll leave tomorrow then, as well," Aileron said decisively.

Loren was looking at her.

She shook her head, then pushed her hair back from her face. "No," she said, too tired to be diplomatic. "Wait for Diarmuid."

It wasn't going to get any easier at all, not for a long time, maybe not ever.

It was passing away from him. He had seen it coming long ago, in some ways he had willed it to come, but it was still a hard thing for Loren Silvercloak to see his burdens passing to others. The harder, because he could read in them the toll exacted by their new responsibilities. It was manifest in Kim, just as her power was manifest: a Seer with the Baelrath and the gift of another's soul, she must be staggering under the weight of it.

Today was a day of preparations. Five hundred men, half from Cathal and half from Brennin, were to ride for Gwen Ystrat as soon as Diarmuid returned. They were waiting because Kim had said to wait. Once it might have been the mages who offered such decisive counsel, but it was passing from them. He had set the thing in motion when he brought the five of them, and he was wise enough, for all Matt's reproachful glances, to let it move without his interference, insofar as that was possible. And he was compassionate enough to pity them: Kim, and Paul who bore the weight of the name Twiceborn, with all such a thing implied, but who had not been able to tap into his power yet. It was there, any fool could see, it might be greater than any of them could fathom, but as of now it was latent only. Enough to set him painfully apart, not enough to give him compensation or direction.

And then there was Jennifer, and for her he could weep. No compensation, or even dream of it, for her, no chance to act, only the pain, so many shadings of it. He had seen it from the first—so long ago, it seemed—before they crossed, when he had read a message in her beauty and a dark future in her eyes. He had taken her anyhow, had told himself he had no choice; nor was that merely sophistry—such, at least, Rangat's exploding had made clear.

Which did not take away the sorrow. He understood her beauty now, they all did, and they knew her oldest name. *Oh, Guinevere,* Arthur had said, and was any fate more harsh in any world than that of the two of them? And the third.

He passed the day alone in untranquil thought. Matt and Brock were at the armories, giving the benefit of their expertise in weapons to the two Captains of the Guard. Teyrnon, whose pragmatic good sense would have been of some help, was in North Keep. They would reach for him that night; he and Barak, too, would have their place in Gwen Ystrat.

If ever any mage, any worker in the skylore, could be said to have a place so near Dun Maura. The tall mage shook his head and threw another log on the fire. He was cold, and not just from the winter. How had it come to be that there were only two mages left in Brennin? There could never be more than seven; so Amairgen had decreed when first he formed the Council. But two, only two, and at such a time? It was passing from them, it seemed, in more ways than one.

Two mages only in Brennin to go to war against Maugrim; but there were three mages in Fionavar, and the third had put himself in league with the Dark. He was on Cader Sedat, that enchanted island, long since made unholy. He was there, and he had the Cauldron of Khath Meigol and so could bring the newly dead back to life.

Whatever else might pass from them, that one was his. His and Matt's. *We will have our battle in the end,* he had said to the Dwarf.

If the winter ever ended. Metran.

Night came, and with it another storm worse than any yet. Wind howled and whistled down the Plain into the High Kingdom, carrying a wall of snow. It buried farms and farmhouses. It blanketed the woods. It hid the moon, and in the inhuman darkness figures of dread seemed to be moving within the storm and the howling of wind was the sound of their laughter.

Darien lay in bed listening to it. He'd thought at first it was another nightmare but then knew he was awake. Frightened, though. He pulled the covers up over his head to try and muffle the voices he heard in the wind.

They were calling. Calling him to come and play outside in the wild dark dancing of the storm. To join them in this battering of wind and snow. But he was only a little boy, and afraid, and he would die if he went outside. Even though the storm wasn't so bad where they were.

Finn had explained about that. How even though Darien's

real mother couldn't be there with them she was protecting him all the time, and she made the winter easier around his bed because she loved him. They all loved him; Vae his mother and even Shahar his father, who had been home from war only once before they had come to the lake. He had lifted Darien up in the air and made him laugh. Then he had said Dari would soon be bigger than Finn and laughed, himself, though not the funny laugh.

Finn was his brother and he loved Dari most of all and he was the most wonderful person in the world and knew everything besides.

It was Finn who had explained what Father had meant when Dari came crying to him after, because there was something wrong about him being bigger than Finn. Soon, Father had said.

Finn had dressed him in his coat and boots and carried him out for a walk. Dari liked it more than anything when they did that. Finn would throw Dari in the snow, but only where it was new and soft, and then fall in himself so they both got all white, rolling about, and Dari would laugh so hard he got the hiccups.

This time, though, Finn had been serious. Sometimes he was serious and made Dari listen to him. He said that Dari was different from other little boys. That he was special because his real mother was special, and so he was going to be bigger and stronger and smarter than all the other boys. Even Finn, Finn said. And what that meant, Finn said, was that Dari had to be better, too, he had to be kinder and gentler and braver, so he would deserve what his real mother had given him.

He had to try to love everything, Finn said, except the Dark.

The Dark was what was causing the storm outside, Dari knew. And most of the time he hated it like Finn said. He tried to do it all the time, to be just like Finn was, but sometimes he heard the voices, and though mostly they frightened him, sometimes they didn't. Sometimes he thought it might be nice to go with them.

Except that would mean leaving Finn, and he would never

do that. He got out of bed and put on his knitted slippers. He pulled back the curtain and paddled over, past where his mother slept, to the far wall where Finn's bed was.

Finn was awake. "What took you so long?" he whispered. "Come in, little brother, we'll keep each other warm." With a sigh of pleasure, Dari kicked off the slippers and crawled in beside Finn, who moved over, leaving Dari the warm part where he'd lain.

"There are voices," he said to Finn.

His brother didn't say anything. Just put an arm around Dari and held him close. The voices weren't as loud here, when he was beside Finn. As he drifted to sleep, Dari heard Finn murmur into his ear, "I love you, little one."

Dari loved him back. When he fell asleep he dreamed again, and in his dream he was trying to tell that to the ghostly figures calling from the wind.

# Chapter 9

In the afternoon after the storm—a day so clear and bright it was almost a mockery—came Diarmuid, Prince of Brennin, back to Paras Derval. With certain others he was brought to the High King's antechamber, where a number of people waited for him, and in that place he was presented by Aileron, his brother, to Arthur Pendragon.

And nothing happened.

Paul Schafer, standing next to Kim, had seen her pale when Diarmuid came into the room. Now, as the Prince bowed formally to Arthur and the Warrior accepted it with an unruffled mien, he heard her draw a shaky breath and murmur, from the heart, "Oh, thank God."

A look passed between her and Loren, who was on the far side of the room, and in the mage's countenance Paul read the same relief. It took him a moment, but he put it together.

"You thought he was the third one?" he said. "Third angle of the triangle?"

She nodded, still pale. "I was afraid. Don't know why now. Don't know why I was so sure."

"Is that why you wanted us to wait?"

She looked at him, grey eyes under white hair. "I thought it was. I knew we had to wait before going to the hunt. Now I don't know why."

"Because," came a voice, "you are a true and loyal friend and didn't want me to miss the fun."

"Oh, Kev!" She wheeled and gave him a very un-Seerlike hug. "I missed you!"

"Good," said Kevin brightly.

"Me too," Paul added.

"Also good," Kevin murmured, less flippantly.

Kim stepped back. "You feeling unappreciated, sailor?"

He gave her a half smile. "A bit superfluous. And now Dave's fighting an urge to bisect me with his axe."

"Nothing new there," Paul said dryly.

"What now?" Kim asked.

"I slept with the wrong girl."

Paul laughed. "Not the first time."

"It isn't funny," Kevin said. "I had no idea he liked her, and anyhow, she came to me. The Dalrei women are like that. They call the shots with anyone they like until they decide to marry."

"Have you explained to Dave?" Kim asked. She would have made a joke but Kevin did look unhappy. There was more to this, she decided.

"He's a hard man to explain things to. Hard for me, anyway. I've asked Levon. It was his sister." Kevin indicated someone with a sideways nod of his head.

*And that, of course, was it.*

Kim turned to the handsome, fair-haired Rider standing just behind them. There had been a reason for waiting for this party, and it wasn't Diarmuid or Kevin. It was this man.

"I have explained," Levon said. "And will do so again, as often as necessary." He smiled; then his expression grew sober and he said to Kim, "Seer, I asked if we might talk, a long time ago."

She remembered. The last morning, before the Baelrath had blazed and her head had exploded with Jennifer's screams and she had taken them away.

She looked at her hand. The ring was pulsing; only a very little, but it was alive again.

"All right," she said, almost curtly. "You too, Paul. Kev, will you bring Loren and Matt?"

"And Davor," Levon said. "Diarmuid too. He knows."

"My room. Let's go." She walked out, leaving them to follow her. Her and the Baelrath.

*"The flame will wake from sleep,*
*The Kings the horn will call,*
*But though they answer from the deep,*
*You may never hold in thrall*
*Those who ride from Owein's Keep*
*With a child before them all."*

Levon's voice faded away. In the silence Kim became aware, annoyingly, of the same faint static she'd heard two nights ago; again it was from the east. Gwen Ystrat, she decided. She was getting herself tuned in to whatever sendings the priestesses were throwing back and forth out there. It was a nuisance and she pushed it from her mind. She had enough to worry about, starting with all these men in her bedroom. A frustrated woman's dream, she thought, unable to find it amusing.

They were waiting for her. She kept silent and let them wait. After a moment it was Levon who resumed—it was his idea, after all. He said, "I learned that verse from Gereint as a boy. I remembered it last spring when Davor found the horn. Then we located the tree and the rock. And so we know where Owein and the Sleepers are." He couldn't keep the excitement from his voice. "We have the horn that calls them and . . . and it is my guess that the Baelrath roused is the flame that wakes them."

"It would fit," said Diarmuid. He had kicked off his boots and was lying on her bed. "The Warstone is wild, too. Loren?"

The mage, by exercise of seniority, had claimed the armchair by the window. He lit his pipe methodically and drew deeply upon it before answering.

"It fits," he said at length. "I will be honest and say I do not know what it forms."

The quiet admission sobered them. "Kim?" Diarmuid asked, taking charge from where he lay sprawled across her bed.

She was minded to give them a hard time, still, but was too proud to be petty. "I haven't seen it," she murmured. "Nothing of this at all."

"Are you sure?" Paul Schafer asked from by the door,

where he stood with Matt Sören. "You were waiting for Levon, weren't you?"

He was awfully clever, that one. He was her friend, though, and he hadn't given away her first apprehension about Diarmuid. Kim nodded, and half smiled. "I sensed he was coming. And I guessed, from before, what he wanted to ask. I don't think we can conclude much from that."

"Not much," Diarmuid concurred. "We still have a decision to make."

"We?" It was Kevin Laine. "Kim's ring, Dave's horn. Their choice, wouldn't you say?"

Levon said, "They aren't really theirs. Only—"

"Anyone planning to take them away and use them?" Kevin asked laconically. "Anyone going to force them?" he continued, driving the point home. There was a silence. Another friend, Kim thought.

There was an awkward cough. "Well," said Dave, "I'm not about to go against what gets decided here, but I'd like to know a little more about what we're dealing with. If I've got the horn that calls these . . . ah, Sleepers, I'd prefer to know who they are."

He was looking self-consciously at Loren. They all turned to the mage. The sun was behind him, making it hard to see his face. When he spoke, it was almost as a disembodied voice.

"It would be altogether better," he said, from between the setting sun and the smoke, "if I could give a fair answer to Dave's question. I cannot. Owein and the Wild Hunt were laid to rest an infinitely long time ago. Hundreds and hundreds of years before Iorweth came from oversea, or the Dalrei crossed the mountains from the east, or even men pushed into green Cathal from the far lands in the southeast.

"Even the lios alfar were scarcely known in the land when the Hunt became the Sleepers. Brendel has told me, and Laien Spearchild before him, that the lios have only shadowy legends of what the Wild Hunt was before it slept."

"Was there anyone here?" Kevin murmured.

"Indeed," Loren replied. "For someone put them under that stone. Tell me, Levon, was it a very great rock?"

Levon nodded without a word.

Loren waited.

"The Paraiko!" Diarmuid said, who had been student to the mage when he was young. His voice was soft; there was wonder in it.

"The Paraiko," Loren repeated. "The Giants. They were here, and the Wild Hunt rode the night sky. It was a very different world, or so the legends of the lios tell. Shadowy kings on shadowy horses that could ride between the stars and between the Weaver's worlds."

"And the child?" Kim asked this time. It was the question that was gnawing at her. *A child before them all.*

"I wish I knew," Loren said. "No one does, I'm afraid."

"What else *do* we know?" Diarmuid asked mildly.

"It is told," came a deep voice from the door, "that they moved the moon."

"What?" Levon exclaimed.

"So it is said," Matt repeated, "Under Banir Lök and Banir Tal. It is our only legend of the Hunt. They wanted greater light by which to ride, and so they moved the moon."

There was a silence.

"It *is* closer here," Kevin said wonderingly. "We noticed it was larger."

"It is," Loren agreed soberly. "The tales may be true. Most of the Dwarf tales are."

"How were they ever put under the stone?" Paul asked.

"That is the deepest question of all," Loren murmured. "The lios say it was Connla, Lord of the Paraiko, and it is not impossible for one who made the Cauldron of Khath Meigol and so half mastered death to have done so."

"It would have been a mighty clash," Levon said softly.

"It would have been," Loren agreed, "but the lios alfar say another thing in their legends." He paused. His face was quite lost in the glare of the sun. "They say there was no clash. That Owein and the Hunt asked Connla to bind them, but they do not know why."

Kim heard a sound, or thought she did, as of quick wings flying. She looked to the door.

And heard Paul Schafer say, in a voice that sounded scraped up from his heart, "I know." His expression had gone distant and estranged but when he continued, his voice was clear. "They lost the child. The ninth one. They were eight kings and a child. Then they made a mistake and lost the child, and in grief and as penance they asked the Paraiko to bind them under the stone with whatsoever bonds they chose and whatsoever method of release."

He stopped abruptly and passed a hand before his eyes. Then he leaned back for support against the wall.

"How do you know this?" Levon asked in amazement.

Paul fixed the Dalrei with those fathomless, almost inhuman eyes, "I know a fair bit about half-death," he said.

No one dared break the silence. They waited for Paul. At length he said, in a tone more nearly his own, "I'm sorry. It . . . catches me unawares, and I'm thrown by it. Levon, I—"

The Dalrei shook his head. "No matter. Truly not. It is a wonder, and not a gift, I know, but earned. I am grateful beyond words that you are here, but I do not envy you."

Which, Kim thought, was about it. She said, "Is there more, Paul? Do we wake them?"

He looked at her, more himself with each passing second. It was as if an earthquake had shaken the room and passed. Or a roll of very great thunder.

"There is no more," he said, "if you mean do I know anything more. But, for what it's worth, I did see something just before we left the other room."

Too clever by half, she thought. But he had paused and was leaving it for her. "You don't miss much, do you?" she murmured. He made no reply. She drew a breath and said, "It's true. The Baelrath glowed for a moment when Levon came up to me. In the moment when I understood what he had come for. I can tell you that, for what, as Paul says, it's worth."

"Something, surely," Levon said earnestly. "It is as I have been saying: why else have we been given the horn, shown the cave? Why, if not to wake them? And now the stone is telling us!"

"Wild to wild," Loren murmured. "They may be calling

each other, Levon, but not for any purpose of ours. This is the wildest magic. And it is in the verse: we will never hold them. Owein and the Hunt were powerful enough to move the moon and capricious enough to do it for their pleasure. Let us not think they will tamely serve our needs and as tamely go away."

Another silence. Something was nagging at the back of Kim's mind, something she knew she should be remembering, but this had become a chronic condition of late, and the thought could not be forced.

It was, surprisingly, Dave Martyniuk who broke the stillness. Awkward as ever in such a situation, the big man said, "This may be very dumb, I don't know . . . but it occurred to me that if Kim's ring is being called, then maybe Owein is ready to be released and we've been given the means to do it. Do we have the right to deny them, regardless of whether we know what they'll do? I mean, doesn't that make us jailers, or something?"

Loren Silvercloak rose as if pulled upward. Away from the angled light, they could see his eyes fixed on Dave. "That," said the mage, "is not even remotely a foolish thing to say. It is the deepest truth yet spoken here." Dave flushed bright red as the mage went on. "It is in the truest nature of things, at the very heart of the Tapestry: the wild magic is meant to be free, whether or not it serves any purpose of ours."

"So we do it?" Kevin asked. And turned to Kim again.

In the end, as in the beginning, it came back to her because she wore the ring. Something nagging still, but they were waiting and what Dave had said was true. She knew that much.

"All right," she said, and on the words the Baelrath blazed like a beacon with red desire.

"When?" Paul asked. In the tinted light they were all on their feet.

"Now, of course," said Diarmuid. "Tonight. We'd best get moving, it's a white ride."

They had lost Matt and Loren and picked up the other Dalrei, Torc, and Diarmuid's lieutenant, Coll.

The mage had volunteered to stay behind and inform the two Kings of what was happening. Torc, Kevin was given to understand, had been there when the horn and the cave were found; he had a place in this weaving. Kevin wasn't about to question it, seeing as he himself had no real place at all. Coll was with Diarmuid because he always was.

Kevin rode beside Paul for the early going, as Diarmuid led them northeast through a gentle valley. It was curious, but the cold seemed milder here, the wind less chill. And when they came around a ridge of hills he saw a lake, small, like a jewel in a setting of white-clad slopes—and the water of the lake wasn't frozen.

"A wind shelter, you think?" he said to Paul.

"More than that. That's Ysanne's lake. Where the water spirit is. The one Kim saw."

"Think that's doing it?"

"Maybe." But by then Paul wasn't really with him any more. He had slowed his mount and was looking down at a small cottage by the lake. They were skirting it, passing by on a high ridge, but Kevin could see two boys come out to gaze at the party of riders passing by. Impulsively, Kevin waved and the older one waved back. He seemed to bend, speaking to his brother, and after a moment the little fellow raised a hand to them.

Kevin grinned and turned to say something to Paul, but what he saw in Schafer's rigid features erased the easy smile from his own. They resumed riding a moment later, moving quickly to catch the others. Paul was silent, his face clenched and rigid. He didn't offer anything, and this time Kevin didn't ask. He wasn't sure if he could deal with another rejection.

He caught up to Coll and rode the rest of the way beside him. It was colder when they came to the north end of the valley, and dark by the time they crossed the High Road from Rhoden to North Keep. He was carrying a torch by then, something which seemed, of late, to be his lot. The main illumination, though, more even than the low moon shining through clouds on their right, was the increasing brilliance of the red light cast by the ring Kim wore. *Wild to wild*, Kevin remembered.

And so, led by the Baelrath, they came at length to Pendaran Wood. There were powers there, aware of them, drawn by their presence and by the power of the ring. There were powers beyond these as well: the goddess whose gift had come to more than she had meant, and her brother, god of beasts and the wood. Above these also, Mörnir waited, and Dana, too, knew why the Warstone burned. Very far to the north, in his seat amid the Ice, the Unraveller was still a moment and wondered, though not clearly knowing what, or why.

And far, far above all of this, outside of time, the shuttle of the Worldloom slowed and then was still, and the Weaver, too, watched to see what would come back into the Tapestry.

Kimberly went forward, then, to the edging of Pendaran Wood, led by the flame on her hand. The company waited behind her, silent and afraid. She went without guidance, as if it had all been done before, to the place where a giant tree had been split by lightning so long ago not even the lios alfar had known the night of that storm. And she stood in the fork of that tree, wild magic on her hand, and wilder magic asleep behind the great rock Connla of the Paraiko had put there, and now, at the time of doing it, there was no fear in her heart, not even any wonder. She was tuned to it, to the wildness, to the ancient power, and it was very great. She waited for the moon to clear a drift of cloud. There were stars overhead, summer stars above the snow. The Baelrath was brighter than any of them, brighter than the moon the Hunt had moved so long ago. She drew a breath of gathering, felt the heart of things come over into her. She raised her hand, that the wandering fire might shine through the broken tree. She said:

"Owein, wake! It is a night to ride. Will you not wake to hunt among the stars?"

They had to close their eyes, all of them, at the pulse of red the words unleashed. They heard a sound like a hillside falling, and then there was stillness.

"It's all right," Kim said. "Come, Dave. Your turn now." And they opened their eyes to see a gaping cave where Connla's rock had been, and moonlight shining on the grass before the cave. The Baelrath was muted; it gleamed softly, a red against the snow, but not a flame.

It was by moonlight, silver and known, that they saw Dave stride, with long slow steps, more graceful than he knew in that moment, to stand by Kim and then, as she stepped back, to stand alone in the fork of the tree.

"The fire wakes them," they heard her say. "The horn calls, Dave. You must set them free."

Without a word the big man tilted back his head. He spread his legs wide for balance in the snow. Then, lifting Owein's Horn so that it glinted under the moon, he set it to his lips and with all the power of his lungs he sent forth the sound of Light.

No man there, nor the woman, ever forgot that sound for the length of their days. It was night, and so the sound they heard was that of moonlight and starlight falling on new snow by a deep wood. On and on it went, as Dave hurled the notes aloft to claim the earth and sky and be his own challenge to the Dark. On and on he blew, until it seemed his lungs must crack, his braced legs buckle, his heart break for the beauty vouchsafed him, and the great fragility of it.

When the sound stopped, the world was a different place, all of the worlds were, and the Weaver's hands moved to reclaim a long-still weft of thread for the web of the Tapestry.

In the space before the cave were seven shadowy figures, and each of them bore a crown and rode a shadowy horse, and the outline of each was blurred as through smoke.

And then there was an eighth as the seven kings made way, and from the Cave of the Sleepers came Owein at last after so long a sleep. And where the hue of the kings and of their shadowy horses was a dark grey hue, that of Owein was light grey shading to silver, and the color of his shadowy horse was black, and he was taller than any of them and his crown gleamed more brightly. And set in it were stones red like the red of the Baelrath, and a red stone was set as well in the hilt of his drawn sword.

He came forward, past the seven kings, and his horse did not touch the ground as it moved, nor did the grey horses of the kings. And Owein raised his sword in salute to Dave and again to Kim, who wore the fire. Then he lifted his head to look beyond those two, and he scanned the company behind them. A moment he did so, and they saw his brow grow dark, and then the great black horse reared high on its legs, and Owein cried in a voice that was the voice of the storm winds, "*Where is the child?*"

And the grey horses of the kings reared high as well, and the kings lifted their own voices and cried, "*The child! The child!*" in a chorus like moaning winds; and the company was afraid.

It was Kimberly who spoke while in her heart she was naming herself a fool: for this, this was the thing she had been trying to think of all afternoon and through the ride to this place of power.

"Owein," she said, "we came here to free you. We did not know what more you needed done."

He whipped his horse, and with a cry it rose into the air above her, its teeth bared, its hooves striking toward her head. She fell to the ground. He loomed above her, wrathful and wild, and she heard him cry a second time, "*Where is the child?*"

And then the world shifted again. It shifted in a way none of them, not one, neither mortal nor forest power nor watching god, had foreknown.

From the fringe of trees not far from her a figure walked calmly forward.

"Do not frighten her. I am here," said Finn.

And so he came to the Longest Road.

From first waking in the morning after the storm he had been uneasy. His heart would begin to race inexplicably, and there would be a dampness on his palms. He wondered if he was ill.

Restless, he dressed Dari in his boots and coat and the hat their mother had made in a blue that came near to the blue of Dari's eyes. Then he took his little brother for a walk in the wood around the lake.

Snow was everywhere, soft and clear, weighing the

branches of the bare trees, piling in the paths. Dari loved it. Finn lifted him high, and the little one shook down a white powder from the branches he could reach. He laughed aloud and Finn lifted him up to do it again. Usually Dari's laughter picked up his own mood, but not today. He was too unsettled. Perhaps it was the memory of the night before: Dari seemed to have forgotten the voices calling him, but Finn could not. It was happening more often of late. He had told their mother, the first time. She had trembled and turned pale and then had wept all night. He had not told her of any of the other times Dari had come into his bed to whisper, "There are voices."

With his long strides he carried Dari farther into the grove, farther than they usually went—close to the place where their copse of trees thickened and then merged with the dark of Mörnirwood. It began to feel colder, and he knew they were leaving the valley. He wondered if Dari's voices would be louder and more alluring away from the lake.

They turned back. He began to play with his brother, tossing Dari into snowbanks and piling in after him. Dari was not as light or as easy to throw around as he used to be. But his whoops of delight were still those of a child and infectious, and Finn began to enjoy himself after all.

They had tumbled and rolled a good distance from the path when they came to one of the strange places. Amid the piled snow that lay deep on the forest floor, Finn spotted a flash of color; so he took Dari by the hand and clumped over through the snow.

In a tiny patch of improbably green grass there were a score of flowers growing. Looking up, Finn saw a clear space overhead where the sun could shine through the trees. And looking back at the flowers he saw they were all known to him—narcissus and corandiel—except for one. They had seen these green places before, he and Dari, and had gathered flowers to bring home to Vae, though never all of them. Now Dari went to pluck a few, knowing how much his mother liked receiving gifts.

"Not that one," Finn said. "Leave that one." He wasn't

sure why, but something told him it should be left, and Dari, as always, obeyed. They took a handful of corandiel, with a yellow narcissus for color, and went back home. Vae put the flowers in water on the table and then tucked Dari into bed for his nap.

They left behind them in the wood, growing in the strange place, that one blue-green flower with red at its center like blood.

He was still restless, very much on edge. In the afternoon he went walking again, this time toward the lake. The grey waters chopped frigidly against the flat stone where he always stood. They were cold, the waters of the lake, but not frozen. All the other lakes, he knew, were frozen. This was a protected place. He liked to think the story he told Dari was true: that Dari's mother was guarding them. She had been, he remembered, like a queen, even with her pain. And after Dari was born and they came to carry her away, she had made them put her down beside Finn. He would never forget. She had stroked Finn's hair with her long fingers; then, pulling his head close, had whispered, so no one else would hear, "Take care of him for me. As long as you can."

As long as you can. And on the thought, as if she had been waiting, annoyingly, for her cue, Leila was in his mind.

*What do you want?* he sent, letting her see he was irritated. In the beginning, after the last ta'kiena, when they discovered that she could do this, it had been a secret pleasure to communicate in silence and across the distances. But lately, Leila had changed. It had to do, Finn knew, with her passage from girl to woman; but knowing this didn't make him any more comfortable with the images she sent him from the Temple. They kept him awake at night; it was almost as if Leila enjoyed doing so. She was younger than he by more than a year, but never, ever, had he felt older than Leila.

All he could do was let her know when he was displeased, and not answer back when she began to send thoughts of greater intimacy than he could deal with. After a while, if he did this, she would always go away. He'd feel sorry, then.

He was in a bad mood today, though, and so, when he became aware of her, the question he sent was sharp and unaccommodating.

*Do you feel it?* Leila asked, and his heart skipped a beat, because for the first time ever he sensed a fear in her.

Fear in others made him strong, so as to reassure. He sent, *I'm uneasy, a little. What is it?*

And then his life began to end. For Leila sent, *Oh, Finn, Finn, Finn*, and with it an image.

Of the ta'kiena on the green, when she had chosen him.

So that was it. For a moment he quailed and could not hide it from her, but the moment passed. Looking out at the lake, he drew a deep breath and realized that his uneasiness had gone. He was deeply calm. He had had a long time to accept this thing and had been a long time waiting.

*It's all right*, he sent to Leila, a little surprised to realize that she was crying. *We knew this was going to come.*

*I'm not ready*, Leila said in his mind.

That was a bit funny: she wasn't being asked to do anything. But she went on, *I'm not ready to say good-bye, Finn. I'm going to be all alone when you go.*

*You'll have everyone in the sanctuary.*

She sent nothing back. He supposed he'd missed something, or not understood. No help for it now. And there was someone else who was going to miss him more.

*Leila*, he sent. *Take care of Darien.*

*How?* she whispered in his mind.

*I don't know. But he's going to be frightened when I go, and . . . he hears voices in the storms, Leila.*

She was silent, in a different way. The sun slipped behind a cloud and he felt the wind. It was time to move. He didn't know how he knew that, or even where he was to go, but it was the day, and coming on toward the hour.

*Good-bye*, he sent.

*The Weaver grant you Light*, he heard her say in his mind.

And she was gone. Walking back to the cottage, he already had enough of a sense of where he was about to go to know that her last wish was unlikely to be granted.

Long ago he had decided he would not tell his mother

when the time came. It would smash her as a hammer smashes a lock, and there was no need for any of them to live through that. He went back in and kissed her lightly on the cheek where she sat weaving by the fire.

She smiled up at him. "Another vest for you, my growing son. And brown to match your hair this time."

"Thank you," he said. There was a catch in his throat. She was small and would be alone, with his father away at war. What could he do, though; what was in him to deny what had been laid down? These were dark times, maybe the very darkest times of all. He had been marked. His legs would walk even if his heart and courage stayed behind. It was better, he knew, to have the heart and soul go too, to make the offering run deeper and be true. He was beginning to know a number of unexpected things. He was already traveling.

"Where's Dari?" he asked. A silly question. "Can I wake him?"

Vae smiled indulgently. "You want to play? All right, he's slept enough, I suppose."

"I'm not asleep," Dari said drowsily, from behind his curtain. "I heard you come in."

This, Finn knew, was going to be the hardest thing. He could not weep. He had to leave Dari an image of strength, clean and unblurred. It was the last guarding he could do.

He drew the curtains, saw his little brother's sleepy eyes. "Come," he said. "Let's dress you quick and go weave a pattern in the snow."

"A flower?" Dari said. "Like the one we saw?"

"Like the one we saw."

They hadn't been outside for very long. A part of him cried inwardly that it wasn't enough, he needed more time. Dari needed more. But the horsemen were there, eight of them, and the part of him that was traveling knew that this was the beginning, and even that the number was right.

Even as he looked, Dari holding him tightly by the hand, one of the riders lifted an arm and waved to him. Slowly Finn raised his free hand and signaled an acceptance. Dari was looking up at him, an uncertainty in his face. Finn knelt down beside him.

"Wave, little one. Those are men of the High King, and they're saying hello to us."

Still shy, Dari lifted a small mittened hand in a tentative wave. Finn had to look away for a moment.

Then, to the brother who was all his joy, he said calmly, "I want to run and catch up with them a moment, little one. I have a thing to ask. You wait and see if you can start the flower by yourself."

He rose then and began to walk away so his brother wouldn't see his face because the tears were falling now. He couldn't even say "I love you" at the end, because Dari was old enough to sense something wrong. He had said it so often, though, had meant it so much. Surely it had been enough in the little time he'd had. Surely it would be enough?

When Vae looked out a while later she saw that her older son was gone. Dari had done a thing of wonder, though: he had traced a perfect flower in the snow, all alone.

She had her own courage, and she knew what had come. She tried to do all her weeping first before going out in the yard to tell her little one how beautiful his newest flower was, and that it was time to come in and eat.

What broke her in the end was to see that Dari, moving quietly in the snow, was tracing his flower neatly with a thin branch in the growing dark while tears were pouring down his face without surcease.

In the twilight he followed them, and then by moonlight and their torches. He even got a little ahead, at first, cutting through the valley, while they took the higher ridges. Even when they passed him, torches, and a red flame on his right, they did not hurry; he was not far behind. Somehow he knew he could have kept up, even if they had been making speed. He was traveling. It was the day, the night, and nearly, now, the hour.

And then it was all three. There was no fear in him; as he'd moved farther and farther from the cottage his sorrow, too, had faded. He was passing from the circles of men into another place. It was only with an effort, as they neared the Wood, that he remembered to ask the Weaver to hold fast on the Loom to the thread of the woman, Vae, and the child, Darien. An effort, but he did it, and then, with that as the last thing, he felt himself cut loose as the fire blazed to let the horn sound and he saw and knew the kings.

He heard Owein cry out for him, *"Where is the child?"* He saw the woman of the flame fall down before Cargail's hooves. He remembered Owein's voice, and knew his tone to be fear and unease. They had been so long asleep in their cave. Who would lead them back into the starlit sky?

Who, indeed?

"Do not frighten her," he said. "I am here." And walking forward from the trees he came past Owein, into the circle of the seven mounted kings. He heard them cry out for joy and then begin to chant Connla's verse that had become the ta'kiena, the children's game, so long afterward. He felt his body changing, his eyes. He knew he looked like smoke. Turning to the cave, he spoke in a voice he knew would sound like wind. "Iselen," he said, and saw his white, white horse come forth. He mounted and, without a backward glance, he led Owein and the Hunt back into the sky.

It came together, Paul thought, still twisting inside with the dazzle and the hurt. The two verses had come to the same place: the children's game and the one about Owein. He looked around and saw, by the moonlight, that Kim was still on her knees in the snow, so he went and, kneeling, gathered her to his chest.

"He was only a boy," she wept. "Why do I cause so much sorrow?"

"Not you," he murmured, stroking her white hair. "He was called long ago. We couldn't know."

"I *should* have known. There had to be a child. It was in the verse."

He never stopped stroking her hair. "Oh, Kim, we can

reproach ourselves fairly for so many things. Be easy on the ones that are not fair. I don't think we were meant to know."

What long premeditating will, Paul thought, down all the years, had been farseeing enough to shape this night? Softly he spoke, to frame it:

> *"When the wandering fire*
> *Strikes the heart of stone*
> *Will you follow?*
> *Will you leave your home?*
> *Will you leave your life?*
> *Will you take the Longest Road?"*

The ta'kiena had become skewed over the long years. It wasn't four different children to four different fates. The wandering fire was the ring Kim wore. The stone was the rock it had smashed. And all questions led to the Road that Finn had taken now.

Kim lifted her head and regarded him with grey eyes, so like his own. "And you?" she asked. "Are you all right?"

To anyone else he might have dissembled, but she was kindred in some way, set apart as he was, though not for the same thing.

"No," said Paul. "I'm too frightened to even weep."

She read it in him. He saw her face change, to mirror his own. "Oh," she said. "Darien."

Even Diarmuid was silent on the long ride home. The sky had cleared and the moon, nearing full, was very bright, and high. They didn't need the torches. Kevin rode next to Kim, with Paul on her other side.

Glancing at her, and then at Paul, Kevin felt his own sense of grievance slipping away. It was true that he had less to offer here, demonstrably less than his marked, troubled friends, but neither did he have to carry what, so manifestly, they did. Kim's ring was no light, transfiguring gift. It could be no easy thing to have set in motion what had happened to that boy. How could a human child have become, even as they watched, a thing of mist, diffused enough to take to the night sky and disappear among the stars? The verses, he understood, something to do with both verses coming to-gether. He wasn't sure, for once, if he wanted to know more.

Paul, though, Paul didn't have a choice. He did know more, and he couldn't hide the fact, nor the strain of wres-tling with it. No, Kevin decided, he wouldn't begrudge them their roles this once, or regret his own insignificance in what had happened.

The wind was behind them, which made things easier, and then, when they dipped down toward the valley around the lake again, he felt it grow milder and less chill.

They were skirting the farmhouse again, retracing their path. Looking down, he saw there was a light, still, in the window, though it was very late, and then he heard Paul call his name.

The two of them stopped on the trail. Ahead, the others kept moving and then disappeared around a bend in the hill slope.

They looked at each other a moment, then Paul said, "I should have told you before. Jennifer's child is down there. He's the young one we saw earlier. It was his older brother . . . so to speak . . . whom we just watched go with the Hunt."

Kevin kept his voice level. "What do we know about the child?"

"Very little. He's growing very fast. Obviously. All the andain do, Jaelle says. No sign yet of any . . . tendencies." Paul drew a breath and let it out. "Finn, the older one, was watching over him, and so were the priestesses, through a girl who was mind-linked to Finn. Now he's gone and there is only the mother, and it'll be a bad night down there."

Kevin nodded. "You're going down?"

"I think I'd better. I need you to lie, though. Say I've gone to Mörnirwood, back to the Tree, for reasons of my own. You can tell Jaelle and Jennifer the truth—in fact, you'd better, because they'll know from the girl that Finn's gone."

"You're not coming east, then? To the hunt?"

Paul shook his head. "I'd better stay. I don't know what I can do, but I'd better stay."

Kevin was silent. Then, "I'd say be careful, but that doesn't mean much here, I'm afraid."

"Not much," Paul agreed. "But I'll try."

They looked at each other. "I'll take care of what you wanted," Kevin said. He hesitated. "Thanks for telling me."

Paul smiled thinly. He said, "Who else?" After a moment, leaning sideways on their horses, the two men embraced.

"Adios, amigo," said Kevin and, turning, kicked his mount to a trot that carried him around the bend.

Paul watched him go. He remained motionless for a long time after, his eyes fixed on the curve in the trail past which Kevin had disappeared. The road was not only bending now, it was forking, and very sharply. He wondered when he'd see his friend again. Gwen Ystrat was a long way. Among many other things, it might be that Galadan was there. Galadan, who he'd sworn would be his when they met for the third time. If they did.

But he had another task now, less filled with menace but as dark, notwithstanding that. He turned his thoughts from bright Kevin and from the Lord of the andain to one who was also of the andain and might yet prove greater than their Lord, for good or ill.

Picking his way carefully down the slope, he circled the farmyard by the light of the moon and the glow of the lamp in the window. There was a path leading up to the gate.

And there was something blocking the path.

Anyone else might have been paralyzed with fear, but Paul felt a different thing, though not any the less intense. *How many twists for the heart*, he thought, *are gathered in this one night?* And thinking so, he dismounted and stood on the path facing the grey dog.

A year and more had passed, but the moon was bright and he could see the scars. Scars earned under the Summer Tree while Paul lay bound and helpless before Galadan, who had come to claim his life. And had been denied by the dog who stood now in the path that led to Darien.

There was a difficulty in Paul's throat. He took a step forward. "Bright the hour," he said and sank to his knees in the snow.

For a moment he wasn't sure, but then the great dog came forward and suffered him to place his arms about its neck. Low in its throat it growled, and Paul heard an acceptance, as of like to like.

He leaned back to look. The eyes were the same as they had been when first he'd seen them on the wall, but he was equal to them now; he was deep enough to absorb their sorrow, and then he saw something more.

"You have been guarding him," he said. "I might have known you would."

Again the dog rumbled, deep in its chest, but it was in the bright eyes that Paul read a meaning. He nodded. "You must go," he said, "Your place is with the hunt. It was more than happenstance that drew me here. I will stay tonight and deal with tomorrow when it comes."

A moment longer the grey dog stayed facing him; then, with another low growl, it moved past, leaving the path to the cottage open. As the dog went by, Paul saw the number of its scars again, more clearly, and his heart was sore.

He turned. The dog had done the same. He remembered their last farewell, and the howl that had gone forth from the heart of the Godwood.

He said, "What can I say to you? I have sworn to kill the wolf when next we meet."

The dog lifted its head.

Paul whispered, "It may have been a rash promise, but if I am dead, who can tax me with it? You drove him back. He is mine to kill, if I can."

The grey dog came back toward him to where he still crouched, on the path. The dog, who was the Companion in every world, licked him gently on his face before it turned again to go.

Paul was crying, whose dry eyes had sent him to the Summer Tree. "Farewell," he said, but softly. "And go lightly. There is some brightness allowed. Even for you. The morning will offer light."

He watched the dog go up the slope down which he had come and then disappear past the curve around which Kevin, too, had gone.

At length he rose and, taking the reins of the horse,

unlatched the gate and walked over to the barn. He put his horse in an empty stall.

Closing the barn and then the gate, he walked through the yard to the back door of the cottage and stepped up on the porch. Before knocking he looked up: stars and moon overhead, a few fast-moving wisps of cloud scudding southward with the wind. Nothing else to be seen. They were up there, he knew, nine horsemen in the sky. Eight of them were kings, but the one on the white horse was a child.

He knocked and, so as not to frighten her, called softly, "It is a friend. You will know me."

She opened it quickly this time, surprising him. Her eyes were hollowed. She clutched a robe about herself. She said, "I thought someone might come. I left a light."

"Thank you," said Paul.

"Come in. He is asleep, finally. Please be quiet."

Paul stepped inside. She moved to take his coat and saw he wasn't wearing one. Her eyes widened.

"I have some power," he said. "If you will let me, I thought I'd stay the night."

She said, "He is gone, then?" A voice far past tears. It was worse, somehow.

Paul nodded. "What can I say? Do you want to know?"

She had courage; she did want to know. He told her, softly, so as not to wake the child. After he had done, she said only, "It is a cold fate for one with so warm a heart."

Paul tried. "He will ride now through all the worlds of the Tapestry. He may never die."

She was a young woman still, but not her eyes that night. "A cold fate," she repeated, rocking in the chair before the fire.

In the silence he heard the child turn in its bed behind the drawn curtain. He looked over.

"He was up very late," Vae murmured. "Waiting. He did a thing this afternoon—he traced a flower in the snow. They used to do it together, as children will, but this one Dari did alone, after Finn left. And . . . he colored it."

"What do you mean?"

"Just that. I don't know how, but he tinted the snow to color his flower. You'll see in the morning."

"I probably marred it just now, crossing the yard."

"Probably," she said. "There is little left of the night, but I think I will try to sleep. You look very tired, too."

He shrugged.

"There is only Finn's bed," she said. "I'm sorry."

He rose. "That will suit me very well."

A short while later, in the dark, he heard two things. The first was the sound of a mother crying for her child, and the second was the wind outside growing in strength in the hours before dawn.

The calling came. It woke Dari, as it always did. At first it felt like a dream again but he rubbed his eyes and knew he was awake, though very tired. He listened, and it seemed to him that there was something new this time. They were crying for him to come out with them, as they always did, but the voices in the wind were naming him by another name.

He was cold, though, and if he was cold in his bed, he would die outside in the wind. Little boys couldn't go out into that wind. He was very cold. Rubbing his eyes drowsily, he slid into his slippers and voyaged across the floor to crawl into bed with Finn.

But it wasn't Finn who was there. A dark figure rose up in Finn's own bed and said to him, "Yes, Darien, what can I do?"

Dari was frightened but he didn't want to wake his mother so he didn't cry. He padded back to his own bed, which was even colder now, and lay wide awake, wanting Finn, not understanding how Finn, who was supposed to love him, could have left him all alone. After a while he felt his eyes change color; he could always feel it inside. They had changed when he did the flower, and now they did so again, and he lay there hearing the wind voices more clearly than he ever had before.

# PART III
## Dun Maura

# Chapter 10

In the morning a shining company left Paras Derval by the eastern gate, led by two Kings. And with them were the children of Kings, Diarmuid dan Ailell, Levon dan Ivor, and Sharra dal Shalhassan; and there were also Matt Sören, who had been a King, and Arthur Pendragon, the Warrior, cursed to be a King forever without rest; and there were many great and high ones beside, and five hundred men of Brennin and Cathal.

Grey was the morning under grey clouds from the north, but bright was the mood of Aileron the High King, freed at last from powerless planning within his walls. And his exhilaration at being released to act ran through the mingled armies like a thread of gold.

He wanted to set a swift pace, for there were things to be done in Morvran that night, but scarcely had the company cleared the outskirts of the town when he was forced to raise his hand and bring them to a stop.

On the snow-clad slope north of the cleared road a dog barked, sharp and carrying in the cold air. And then as the High King, moved by some instinct, signaled the halt, they heard the dog bark three times more, and every man in that company who knew dogs heard frantic joy in the sound.

Even as they stopped, they saw the grey shape of a hunting dog begin to tumble and dash down through the snow toward them, barking all the while, somersaulting head over tail in its haste.

It was Aileron who saw the light blaze in Arthur's face. The Warrior leaped from his horse down into the road and, at the top of his great voice, cried, *"Cavall!"*

Bracing his legs, he opened wide his arms and was knocked flying, nonetheless, by the wild leap of the dog. Over and over they rolled, the dog yelping in intoxicated delight, the Warrior mock growling in his chest.

All through the company, smiles and then laughter began to blossom like flowers in a stony place.

Heedless of his clothing or his dignity, Arthur played in the road with the dog he had named Cavall, and it was a long time before he stood to face the company. Arthur was breathing hard, but there was a brightness to his eyes in which Kim Ford found some belated dispensation for what she had done on Glastonbury Tor.

"This is," asked Aileron with gentle irony, "your dog?"

With a smile, Arthur acknowledged the tone. But his answer moved them to another place. "He is," he said, "insofar as he is anyone's. He was mine once, a very long time ago, but Cavall fights his own wars now." He looked down at the animal beside him. "And it seems that he has been hurt in those wars."

When the dog stood still, they could see the network of scars and unevenly regenerated fur that covered its body. They were terrible to look at.

"I can tell you whence those came." Loren Silvercloak moved his mount to stand beside those of the Kings. "He battled Galadan, the Wolflord, in Mörnirwood to save the life of the one who became the Twiceborn."

Arthur lifted his head. "The battle foretold? Macha and Nemain's?"

"Yes," Kim said, moving forward in her turn.

Arthur's eyes swung to her. "The Wolflord is the one who seeks the annihilation of this world?"

"He is," she replied. "Because of Lisen of the Wood, who rejected him for Amairgen."

"I care not for the reason," Arthur said, a coldness in his voice. "These are his wolves we go to hunt?"

"They are," she said.

He turned to Aileron. "My lord King, I had a reason to hunt before this: to forget a grief. There is a second reason now. Is there room in your hunting pack for another dog?"

"There is pride of place," Aileron replied. "Will you lead us now?"

"Cavall will," said Arthur, mounting as he spoke. Without a backward glance, the grey dog broke into a run.

Ruana chanted the kanior for Ciroa, but not properly. It had not been proper for Taieri either, but to the chant he again added the coda asking forgiveness for this. He was very weak and knew he had not the strength to rise and perform the bloodless rites that were at the heart of the true kanior. Iraima was chanting with him, for which he gave thanks, but Ikatere had fallen silent in the night and lay breathing heavily in his alcove. Ruana knew he was near his end, and grieved, for Ikatere had been golden in friendship.

They were burning Ciroa at the mouth of the cave, and the smoke came in, and the smell of charred flesh. Ruana coughed and broke the rhythm of the kanior. Iraima kept it, though, or else he would have had to start again: there was a coda for failing the bloodless rites, but not for breaking the chant.

After, he rested a little time and then, alone, began the thin chants again: the warnsong and the savesong, one after another. His voice was far from what it had been in the days when those of other caves would ask him to come and lead kanior for their dead. He continued, though, regardless: silence would be the last surrendering. Only when he chanted could he hold his mind from wandering. He wasn't even sure how many of them were left in the cave, and he had no idea of what was happening in the other caves. No one had kept a count for many years, and they had been set upon in the dark.

Iraima's sweet voice came back in with him on the third cycle of the warnsong, and then his heart went redgold with grief and love to hear Ikatere chanting deep again with them for a little time. They spoke not, for words were strength, but Ruana shaded his voice to twine about Ikatere's; he knew his friend would understand.

And then, on the sixth cycle through, as the twilight was descending outside where their captors were camped on the slope, Ruana touched another mind with the savesong. He was singing alone again. Gathering what little was left in him, he focused the chant to a clear point, though it cost him dearly, and sent it out as a beam toward the mind he had found.

Then the mind seized hold of the beam he threw and sent back, effortlessly, the sound of laughter, and Ruana plummeted past black, for he knew whom he had found.

*Fool!* he heard, and lancets cut within him. *Did you think I would not blanket you? Where do you think your feeble sounds have gone?*

He was glad he had been chanting alone, that the others need not endure this. He reached inside, wishing again that he had access to hate or rage, though he would have to atone for such a wish. He sent, along the beam the chant had made, *You are Rakoth Maugrim. I name you.*

And was battered in his mind by laughter. *I named myself a long time ago. What power would you find in naming me, fool of a race of fools? Unworthy to be slaves.*

*Cannot be slaves,* Ruana sent. And then: *Sathain.* The mocking name.

Fire bloomed in his mind. Redblack. He wondered if he could have the other kill him. Then he could—

There was laughter again. *You shall have no bloodcurse to send. You shall be lost. Every one of you. And no one will chant kanior for the last. Had you done what I asked, you would have been mighty in Fionavar again. Now I will rip your thread from the Tapestry and wear it about my throat.*

*Not slaves,* Ruana sent, but faintly.

There was laughter. Then the chantbeam snapped.

For a long time Ruana lay in the dark, choking on the smoke of Ciroa's burning, assailed by the smell of flesh and the sounds the unclean ones made as they feasted.

Then, because he had nothing else to offer, no access to more, and because he would not end in silence, Ruana began the chants again, and Iraima was with him, and much-loved Ikatere. Then his heart came from past black toward gold again to hear Tamure's voice. With four they essayed the wide chant. Not in hope it would go as far as it had to go, for they were blanketed by the Unraveller and were very weak. Not to get through to anyone, but so as not to die in silence, not servants, never slaves, though their thread be torn from the Loom and lost forever in the Dark.

Hers, Jennifer understood, was a different fate from Arthur's, though interwoven endlessly. She remembered now. From first sight of his face she had remembered all of it, nor were the stars in his eyes new for her—she had seen them before.

No curse so dark as his had been given her, for no destiny so high, no thread of the Tapestry, had ever been consigned to her name. She was, instead, the agent of his fate, the working out of his bitter grief. She had died; in the abbey at Amesbury she had died—she wondered, now, how she had failed to recognize it by Stonehenge. She had had her rest, her gift of death, and she knew not how many times she had come back to tear him apart, for the children and for love.

She had no idea, remembering only that first life of all, when she had been Guinevere, daughter of Leodegrance, and had ridden to wed in Camelot, now lost and thought to be a dream.

A dream it had been, but more than that, as well. She had come to Camelot from her father's halls, and there she had done what she had done, and loved as she had loved, and broken a dream and died.

She had only fallen in love twice in her life, with the two shining men of her world. Nor was the second less golden than the first. He was not, whatever might have been said afterward. And the two men had loved each other, too, making all the angles equal, shaped most perfectly for grief.

Saddest story of all the long tales told.

But, she told herself, it would not unfold again this time, not in Fionavar. *He is not here,* she had said, and known, for in this if nowhere else she had knowledge. There was no third one walking here, with the easy, envied stride, the hands she had loved. *I have been maimed but will not, at least, betray,* she had said, while a shower of starlight fell.

And she would not. It was all changed here, profoundly changed. Rakoth Maugrim had set his shadow between the two of them, across the Weaver's casting on the Loom, and everything was marred. No less a grief, more, even, for her, who had seen the unlight of Starkadh, but if she could not cross to love, she would not shatter him as she had before.

She would stay where she was. Surrounded by the grey-robed priestesses in the grey tone-on-tone of where her soul had come, she would walk among the women in the sanctuary while Arthur went to war against the Dark for love of her, for loss of her, and for the children too.

Which led her back, as she paced the quiet curving halls of the Temple, to thoughts of Darien. And to these, too, she seemed to have become reconciled. Paul's doing. Paul, whom she had never understood, but trusted now. She had done what she had done, and they would see where the path led.

Last night, Jaelle had told her about Finn, and they had sat together. She had grieved a little for that boy among the strewn cold stars. Then Kevin had come knocking, very late, had offered blood as all men were bound to do, and then had come to them to say that Paul was with Darien and so it was all right, insofar as it could ever be all right.

Jaelle had left them, after that. Jennifer had said good-bye to Kevin, who was riding east in the morning. There was nothing she could offer in response to the troubled intensity of his gaze, but her new gentleness could speak to the sadness she had always seen in him.

Then, in the morning, Jaelle too had gone, leaving her to walk in the quiet Temple, more serene than she could have ever dreamed herself becoming, until from a recessed alcove near the dome she heard the sound of someone crying desperately.

There was no door to the alcove and so, passing by, she looked and then stopped, seeing that it was Leila. She was going to move on, for the grief was naked and she knew the girl was proud, but Leila looked up from the bench where she sat.

"I'm sorry," said Jennifer. "Can I do anything, or shall I go?"

The girl she remembered from the ta'kiena looked at her with tears brimming in her eyes. "No one can do anything," she said. "I've lost the only man I'll ever love!"

For all her sympathy and mild serenity, Jennifer had to work hard not to smile. Leila's voice was so laden with the weighty despair of adolescence it took her back to the traumas of her own teenage years.

On the other hand, she'd never lost anyone the way this girl had just lost Finn, or been tuned to anyone the way Leila and Finn had been. The impulse to smile passed. "I'm sorry," she said again. "You have a reason to weep. Will it help to hear that time does make it easier?"

As if she had scarcely heard, the girl murmured, "At midwinter full of moon, half a year from now, they will ask me if I wish to be consecrated to these robes. I will accept. I will never love another man."

She was only a child, but in the voice Jennifer heard a profound resolution.

It moved her. "You are very young," she said. "Do not let grief turn you so quickly away from love."

The girl looked up at that. *"And who are you to talk?"* Leila said.

"That is unfair," said Jennifer after a shocked silence.

The tears were glistening on Leila's cheeks. "Maybe," she said. "But how often have you loved, yourself? Have you not waited all your days for him? And now that Arthur is here you are afraid."

She had been Guinevere and was capable of dealing with this. There was too much color in anger, so she said gently, "Is this how it seems to you?"

Leila hadn't expected that tone. "Yes," she said, but not defiantly.

"You are a wise child," said Jennifer, "and perhaps not only a child. You are not wholly wrong, but you must not presume to judge me, Leila. There are greater griefs and lesser, and I am trying to find the lesser."

"Lesser grief," Leila repeated. "Where is joy?"

"Not here," said Jennifer.

"But why?" It was a hurt child asking.

She surprised herself by answering, "Because I broke him once, long ago. And because I was broken here last spring. He is condemned to joylessness and war, and I cannot cross, Leila. Even if I did, I would smash him in the end. I always do."

"Must it be repeated?"

"Over and over," she said. The long tale. "Until he is granted release."

"Then grant it," said Leila simply. "How shall he be redeemed if not in pain? What else will ever do it? Grant him release."

And with that, all the old sorrow seemed to have come back after all. She could not stay it. There was brightly colored pain in all the hues of guilt and grief, and colored, also, was the memory of love, love and desire, and—

"It is not mine to grant!" she cried. *"I loved them both!"*

It echoed. They were near to the dome and the sound reverberated. Leila's eyes opened very wide. "I'm sorry," she said. "I'm sorry!" And she ran forward to bury her head against Jennifer's breast, having voyaged into deeper seas than she knew.

Reflexively stroking the fair hair, Jennifer saw that her hands were trembling. It was the girl who cried, though, and she who gave comfort. Once, in the other time, she had been in the convent garden at Amesbury when a messenger had come, toward sunset. After, as the first stars came out, she had comforted the other women as they came to her in the garden, weeping at the word of Arthur dead.

It was very cold. The lake was frozen. As they passed north of it under the shadow of the wood, Loren wondered if he would have to remind the King of the tradition. Once more, though, Aileron surprised him. As they came up to the bridge over the Latham, the mage saw him signal a halt. Without a backward glance, the King held in his mount until

Jaelle moved past him on a pale grey horse. Arthur called his dog to heel. Then the High Priestess went forward to lead them over the bridge and into Gwen Ystrat.

The river was frozen too. The wood sheltered them somewhat from the wind, but under the piled grey clouds of late afternoon the land lay grim and mournful. There was a corresponding bleakness in the heart of Loren Silvercloak as, for the first time in his days, he passed over into the province of the Mother.

They crossed the second bridge, over the Kharn, where it, too, flowed into Lake Leinan. The road curved south, away from the wood where the wolves were. The hunters were gazing backward over their shoulders at the winter trees. Loren's own thoughts were elsewhere, though. Against his will he turned and looked to the east. In the distance lay the mountains of the Carnevon Range, icy and impassible save through Khath Meigol, where the ghosts of the Paraiko were. They were beautiful, the mountains, but he tore his gaze from them and focused closer in, to a place not two hours ride away, just over the nearest ridge of hills.

It was hard to tell against the dark grey of the sky, but he thought he saw a drift of smoke rising from Dun Maura.

"Loren," Matt said suddenly, "I think we forgot something. Because of the snow." Loren turned to his source. The Dwarf was never happy on a horse, but there was a grimness in his face that went beyond that. It was in Brock's eyes too, on the far side of Matt.

"What is it?"

"Maidaladan," said the Dwarf. "Midsummer's Eve falls tomorrow night."

An oath escaped from the mage. And a moment after, inwardly, he sent forth a heartfelt prayer to the Weaver at the Loom, a prayer that Gereint of the Dalrei, who had wanted to meet them here, knew what he was doing.

Matt's one eye was focused beyond him now, and Loren swung back as well to look east again. Smoke, or shadings in the clouds? He couldn't tell.

Then, in that moment, he felt the first stirrings of desire. He was braced by his training to resist, but after a few seconds he knew that not even the skylore followers of Amairgen would be able to deny the power of Dana in Gwen Ystrat, not on the night before Maidaladan.

The company followed the High Priestess through Morvran amid the blowing snow. There were people in the streets. They bowed but did not cheer. It was not a day for cheering. Beyond the town they came to the precincts of the Temple, and Loren saw the Mormae waiting there, in red, all nine of them. Behind and to one side stood Ivor of the Dalrei, and the old blind shaman, Gereint; farther yet to the side, with relief in their faces, were Teyrnon and Barak. Seeing the two of them, he felt some easing of his own disquiet.

In front of everyone stood a woman well over six feet tall, broad-shouldered and grey-haired, with her back straight and her head imperiously high. She, too, was clad in red, and Loren knew that this had to be Audiart.

"Bright the hour of your return, First of the Mother," she said with cool formality. Her voice was deep for a woman. Jaelle was in front of them and Loren couldn't see her eyes. Even in the overcast afternoon her red hair gleamed. She wore a silver circlet about her head. Audiart did not.

He had time to see these things, for Jaelle made no reply to the other woman. A bird flew suddenly from the Temple wall behind the nine Mormae, its wings loud in the stillness.

Then Jaelle delicately withdrew a booted foot from the stirrups of her saddle and extended it toward Audiart.

Even at a distance, Loren could see the other pale, and there came a low murmuring from the Mormae. For an instant Audiart was motionless, her eyes on Jaelle's face; then she stepped forward with two long strides and, cupping her hands beside the horse of the High Priestess, helped her dismount.

"Continue," Jaelle murmured and, turning her back, walked through the gates of the Temple to the red-clad Mormae. One by one, Loren saw, they knelt for her blessing. Not one of them, he judged, was less than twice her age. Power on power, he thought, knowing there was more to come.

Audiart was speaking again. "Be welcome, Warrior," she said. There was some diffidence in her tone, but she did not kneel. "There is a welcome in Gwen Ystrat for one who was rowed by three Queens to Avalon."

Gravely, and in silence, Arthur nodded.

Audiart hesitated a moment, as if hoping for more. Then she turned, without hurrying, to Aileron, whose bearded features had remained impassive as he waited. "You are here and it is well," she said. "Long years have passed since last a King of Brennin came to Gwen Ystrat for Midsummer's Eve."

She had pitched her voice to carry, and Loren heard sudden whisperings among the horsemen. He also saw that Aileron hadn't realized what day it was either. It was time to act.

The mage moved up beside the High King. He said, and loudly, "I have no doubt the rites of the Goddess will proceed as they always do. We are not concerned with them. You requested aid of the High King, and he has come to give that aid. There will be a wolf hunt in Leinanwood tomorrow." He paused, staring her down, feeling the old anger rise in him. "We are here for a second reason as well, with the countenance and support of the High Priestess. I want it understood that the rituals of Maidaladan are not to interfere with either of the two things we have come to do."

"Is a mage to give commands in Gwen Ystrat?" she asked, in a voice meant to chill.

"The High King does." With time to recover, Aileron was bluntly compelling. "And as Warden of my province of Gwen Ystrat, you are charged by me now to ensure that things come to pass as my First Mage has commanded you."

She would, Loren knew, want revenge for that.

Before Audiart could speak, though, the sound of high thin laughter came drifting to them. Loren looked over to see Gereint swaying back and forth in the snow as he cackled with merriment.

"Oh, young one," the shaman cried, "are you still so fierce in your passions? Come! It has been a long time since I felt your face."

It was a moment before Loren realized that Gereint was speaking to him. With a ruefulness that took him back more than forty years, he dismounted from his horse.

The instant he touched the ground he felt another, deeper, surge of physical desire. He couldn't entirely mask it, and he saw Audiart's mouth go thin with satisfaction. He mastered an impulse to say something very crude to her. Instead, he strode over to where the Dalrei stood and embraced Ivor as an old friend.

"Brightly met, Aven," he said. "Revor would be proud."

Stocky Ivor smiled. "Not so proud as Amairgen of you, First Mage."

Loren shook his head. "Not yet," he said soberly. "Not until the last First Mage is dead and I have cursed his bones."

"So fierce!" Gereint said again, as he'd half expected.

"Have done, old man," Loren replied, but low, so no one but Ivor could hear. "Unless you can say you would not join my curse."

This time Gereint did not laugh. The sightless sockets of his eyes turned to Loren, and he ran gnarled fingers over the mage's face. He had to step close to do so, so what he said was whispered.

"If my heart's hate could kill, Metran would be dead past the Cauldron's reviving. I taught him too, do not forget."

"I remember," the mage murmured, feeling the other's hands gliding over his face. "Why are we here, Gereint? Before Maidaladan?"

The shaman lowered his hands. To the rear, Loren heard orders being shouted as the hunters were dispersed to the lodgings assigned them in the village. Teyrnon had come up, with his round, soft face and sharp intelligence.

"I felt lazy," Gereint said tormentingly. "It was cold and Paras Derval was far away." Neither mage spoke nor laughed, nor did Ivor. After a moment the shaman said, in a deeper voice, "You named two things, young one: the wolves and our own quest. But you know as well as I, and should not have had to ask, that the Goddess works by threes."

Neither Loren nor Teyrnon said a word. Neither of them looked to the east.

The ring was quiet, which was a blessing. She was still deeply drained by the work of the night before. She wasn't sure if she could have dealt with fire again so soon, and she had been expecting it from the moment they crossed the first bridge. There was power all around her here, she could feel it, even through the green shield of the vellin on her wrist which guarded her from magic.

Then, when prepossessing Audiart spoke of Midsummer, the part of Kim that was Ysanne, and shared her knowledge, understood where the power was coming from.

Nothing to be done though. Not by her, in this place. Dun Maura had nothing to do with a Seer's power, nor with the Baelrath either. When the company began to break up— she saw Kevin ride back into Morvran with Brock and two of Diarmuid's men—Kim followed Jaelle and the mages to the Temple.

Just inside the arched entranceway, a priestess stood with a curved, glinting dagger, and an acolyte in brown, trembling a little, held a bowl for her.

Kim saw Loren hesitate, even as Gereint extended his arm for the blade to cut. She knew how hard this would be for the mage. For any follower of the skylore, this blood offering would be tainted with darkest overtones. But Ysanne had told her a thing once, in the cottage by the lake, and Kim laid a hand on the mage's shoulder. "Raederth spent a night here, I think you know," she said.

There was, even now, a sorrow in saying this. Raederth, as First Mage, had been the one who'd seen the young Ysanne among the Mormae in this place. He had known her for a Seer and taken her away, and they had loved each other until he died—slain by a treacherous King.

The lines of Loren's features softened. "It is true," he said. "And so I should be able to, I suppose. Do you think I could stroll about and find an acolyte to share my bed tonight?"

She looked at him more closely and saw the strain she had

missed. "Maidaladan," she murmured. "Is it taking you hard?"

"Hard enough," he said shortly, before stepping forward after Gereint to offer his mageblood to Dana, like any other man.

Deep in thought, Kim walked past the priestess with the blade and came to one of the entrances to the sunken dome. There was an axe, double-edged, mounted in a block of wood behind the altar. She stayed in the entrance looking at it until one of the women came to show her to her chamber.


Old friends, thought Ivor. If there was a single bright thread in the weaving of war it was this: that sometimes paths crossed again, as of warp and weft, that had not done so for years and would not have done, save in darkness. It was good, even in times like these, to sit with Loren Silvercloak, to hear Teyrnon's reflective voice, Barak's laughter, Matt Sören's carefully weighed thoughts. Good, too, to see men and women of whom he'd long heard but never met: Shalhassan of Cathal and his daughter, fair as the rumors had her; Jaelle the High Priestess, as beautiful as Sharra, and as proud; Aileron, the new High King, who had been a boy when Loren had brought him to spend a fortnight among the tribe of Dalrei. A silent child, Ivor remembered him as being, and very good at everything. He was a taciturn King now, it seemed, and said to still be very good at everything.

There was a new element too, another fruit of war: among these high ones, he, Ivor of the Dalrei, now moved as an equal. Not merely one of the nine chieftains on the Plain, but a Lord, first Aven since Revor himself. It was a very hard thing to compass. Leith had taken to calling him Aven around the home, and only half in teasing, Ivor knew. He could see her pride, though the Plain would wash to sea before his wife would speak of such a thing.

Thinking of Leith led his mind to another thought. Riding south into Gwen Ystrat, feeling the sudden hammer of desire in his loins, he had begun to understand what Maidaladan meant and to be grateful to Gereint, yet again, for telling him to bring his wife. It would be wild in Morvran tomorrow night, and he was not entirely pleased that Liane had come south with them. Still, in these matters the unwed women of the Dalrei took directions from no man. And Liane, Ivor thought ruefully, took direction in precious few other matters as well. Leith said it was his fault. It probably was.

His wife would be waiting in the chambers given them here in the Temple. That was for afterward. For now there was a task to be done under the dome, amid the smell of incense burning.

In that place were gathered the last two mages in Brennin, with their sources; the oldest shaman of the Plain, and by far the most powerful; the white-haired Seer of the High Kingdom; and the High Priestess of Dana in Fionavar—these seven were now to move through the shadows of space and time to try to unlock a door: the door behind which lay the source of winter winds and ice on Midsummer's Eve.

Seven to voyage and four to bear witness: the Kings of Brennin and Cathal, the Aven of the Dalrei, and the last one in the room was Arthur Pendragon, the Warrior, who alone of all men in that place had not been made to offer blood.

"Hold!" Jaelle had said to the priestess by the doorway, and Ivor shivered a little, remembering her voice. "Not that one. He has walked with Dana in Avalon." And the grey-robed woman had lowered her knife to let Arthur pass.

Eventually to come, as had Ivor and the others, to this sunken chamber under the dome. It was Gereint's doing, the Aven thought, torn between pride and apprehension. Because of the shaman they were in this place, and it was the shaman who spoke first among that company. Though not as Ivor had expected.

"Seer of Brennin," Gereint said, "we are gathered to do your bidding."

So it came back to her. Even in this place it came back, as had so much else of late. Once, and not a long time ago, she would have doubted it, wondered why. Asked within, if not aloud, who she was that these gathered powers should defer to her. What was she, the inner voice would have cried, that this should be so?

Not any more. With only a faint, far corner of her mind to mourn the loss of innocence, Kim accepted Gereint's deference as being properly due to the only true Seer in the room. She would have taken control if he had not offered it. They were in Gwen Ystrat, which was the Goddess's, and so Jaelle's, but the journey they were now to take fell within Kimberly's province, not any of the others', and if there was danger it was hers to face for them.

Deeply conscious of Ysanne and of her own white hair, she said, "Once before, I had Loren and Jaelle with me—when I pulled Jennifer out from Starkadh." It seemed to her the candles on the altar shifted at the naming of that place. "We will do the same thing again, with Teyrnon and Gereint besides. I am going to lock on an image of the winter and try to go behind it, into the mind of the Unraveller, with the vellin stone to shield me, I hope. I will need your support when I do."

"What about the Baelrath?"

It was Jaelle, intense and focused, no bitterness to her now. Not for this. Kim said, "This is a Seer's art and purely so. I do not think the stone will flame."

Jaelle nodded. Teyrnon said, "If you do get behind the image, what then?"

"Can you stay with me?" she asked the two mages.

Loren nodded. "I think so. To shape an artifice, you mean?"

"Yes. Like the castle you showed us before we first came." She turned to the Kings. There were three of them, and a fourth who had been and would always be, but it was to Aileron she spoke. "My lord High King, it will be hard for you to see, but we may all be sightless under the power. If there is anything shaped by the mages, you must mark what it is."

"I will," he said in his steady, uninflected voice. She looked to the shaman.

"Is there more, Gereint?"

"There is always more," he replied. "But I do not know what it is. We may need the ring, though, after all."

"We may," she said curtly. "I cannot compel it." The very memory of its burning gave her pain.

"Of course not," the blind shaman replied. "Lead us. I will not be far behind."

She composed herself. Looked at the others ringed about her. Matt and Barak had their legs braced wide apart, Jaelle had closed her eyes, and now she saw Teyrnon do the same. Her glance met that of Loren Silvercloak.

"We are lost if this fails," he said. "Take us through, Seer."

"Come, then!" she cried and, closing her eyes, began to drop down, and down, through the layers of consciousness. One by one she felt them come into her: Jaelle, tapping the avarlith; the two mages, Loren fierce and passionate, Teyrnon clear and bright; then Gereint, and with him he brought his totem animal, the night-flying keia of the Plain, and this was a gift to her, to all of them—a gift of his secret name.

*Thank you*, she sent; then, encompassing them all, she went forward, as if in a long flat dive, into the waking dream.

It was very dark and cold. Kim fought back fear. She might be lost down here; it could happen. But they were all lost if she failed. Loren had spoken true. In her heart a brilliant anger burned then, a hatred of the Dark so bright she used it to shape an image in the deep, still place to which they had come, the bottom of the pool.

She had not prepared it beforehand, choosing to let the dream render its own truest shape. And so it did. She felt the others registering it, in all their shadings of grief, anger, and hurting love for the thing marred, seeing that clear image of Daniloth defiantly alight, open and undefended amid an alien landscape of ice and snow.

She went into it. Not to the light, though she yearned for it, with all her heart, but straight into the bleak winter that surrounded it. Driving with all her power she reached back for the strength of the others and made of herself an arrow flung from a bow of light hurtling into the shape of winter.

And broke through.

Very black. The image gone. She was spinning. No controlled flight now. She was going into it and very fast and there was nothing to hand, nothing to grab onto, no—

*I'm here.* And Loren was.

*And I.* Jaelle.

*Always.* Brave Teyrnon.

Still dark, though, and going into it so far. No sense of space, of walls, nowhere to reach, not even with the others there. They were not enough. Not for where she had come, so far into the workings of Maugrim. There was so much Dark. She had seen it once before, in and out for Jennifer—but now there was only *in* and so far yet to go.

Then the fifth one was there and spoke.

*The ring.* She heard Gereint as if he were the voice of the keia itself, creature of the night, guardian of the way to the world of the dead.

*I can't!* she flung back, but even as she formed the thought, Kim felt the terrible fire and there was a red illumination in her mind.

And pain. She did not know that she cried aloud in the Temple. Nor did she know how wildly the light was blazing under the dome.

She was burning. Too near, she was. Too far into the web of Dark, too near the heart of power. The flame was all around, and fire does more than illuminate. It burns, and she was inside. She was—

A balm. A cooling breath as of the night breeze through autumn grasses on the Plain. Gereint. Another now: moonlight falling on Calor Diman, the Crystal Lake. And that was Loren, through Matt.

And then a goad: *Come!* Jaelle cried. *We are near to it.*

And Teyrnon's strength, cool in its very essence: *Farther yet, I think, but I am here.*

So on again she went. Forward and down, now, very nearly lost with how far she had to go. There was fire, but they were guarding her; she could endure it, she would; it was wild but not the Dark, which was an end to everything.

No longer an arrow, she made herself a stone and went down. Driven by need, by a passionate longing for Light, she went into the Dark, a red stone falling into the secret heart, the worm-infested caverns of Maugrim's designs. Into this unplace she fell, having cast loose from all moorings save the one along which she could send back, before she died and was lost, a single clear icon for the mages to shape in the domed room so infinitely far.

Too far. It was too deep and she was going so fast. Her being was a blur, a shadow; they could not hold her. One by one she left the others behind. With a despairing cry, Loren, who was the last, felt her slip away.

So there was fire and Rakoth, with no one to stay either one of them. She was alone and lost.

Or she should have been. But even as she plummeted, burning, a new mind came to hers so far down into the Dark she could scarcely believe it was there.

The burning ebbed again. She could exist, she could move through the pain, and she heard then, as if in a memory of a clean mild place, a deep voice singing.

There was darkness between, like a black-winged creature, screening the other from her. She was almost gone. Almost, but not yet. She had been a red arrow, then a stone. Now she made herelf into a sword, red as it had to be. She turned. In this directionless world she somehow turned and, with the last blazing of her heart, she slashed through the curtain, found the other where he lay, and grasped an image to send back. She had to do it alone, for the mages were gone. With her very last power, using fire like love, she threw the vision back, unimaginably far, toward the sanctuary in Gwen Ystrat. Then it was dark.

She was a broken vessel, a reed on which a wind could play if there could be a wind. She was a twinned soul without form. The ring had faded utterly. She had done what she could.

There was someone with her, though, chanting still.

*Who?* she sent, as everything began to leave her.

*Ruana,* he replied. *Save us,* he sent. *Save us.*

And then she understood. And, understanding, knew she could not let go. There was no release for her yet. No directions existed in this place, but from where her body lay his chanting would be north and east.

In Khath Meigol, where the Paraiko had once been.

*We are,* he sent. *We still are. Save us.*

There was no fire left in the ring. With only the slow chanting to guide her in the black, she began the long ascent to what there was of light.

When the Baelrath blazed Ivor closed his eyes, as much against the pain in the Seer's cry as against the surging of red. They had been asked to bear witness, though, and a moment later he forced himself to look again.

It was hard to see in the punishing glow of the Warstone. He could just make them out, the young Seer and the others around her, and he marked the clenched strain on the faces of Matt and Barak. He had a sense of massive striving, of almost shattering effort. Jaelle was trembling now. Gereint looked like some Eridun death mask. Ivor's heart ached for them, journeying so far in such a silent battling.

Even as he thought this, the chamber exploded with echoing voices as, almost simultaneously, Jaelle and Gereint and tall Barak cried aloud in despair and pain. For a moment longer Matt Soren was silent, perspiration pouring down his craggy face; then Loren's source, too, cried out, a deep tearing sound, and fell to the floor.

As he rushed forward with Arthur and Shalhassan to succor them, Ivor heard Loren Silvercloak murmur with numbed tonelessness, "Too far. She went too far. It is over."

Ivor took the weeping Barak in his arms and led him to a bench set into the curving wall. He went back and did the same for Gereint. The shaman was shaking like the last leaf on a tree in an autumn wind. Ivor feared for him.

Aileron the High King had not moved. Nor had he taken his gaze from Kim. The light was still blazing and she was still on her feet. Ivor glanced at her face and then quickly away: her mouth was wide open in a soundless, endless screaming. She looked as if she were being burned alive.

He went back to Gereint, who was breathing in desperate gasps, his wizened face grey, even in the red light. And then, as Ivor knelt beside his shaman, that light exploded anew, so wildly it made the glow from before seem dim. Power pulsed like an unleashed presence all around them. It seemed to Ivor that the Temple shook.

He heard Aileron cry, *"There is an image! Look!"*

Ivor tried. He turned in time to see the Seer fall, in time to see a blurred shaping in the air beside her, but the light was too red, too bright. He was blinded by it, burned. He could not see.

And then it was dark.

Or it seemed that way. There were still torches on the walls, candles burning on the altar stone, but after the crazed illumination of the Baelrath, still raging in his mind's eye, Ivor felt surrounded by darkness. A sense of failure overwhelmed him. Something had happened; somehow, even without the mages, Kim had sent an image back and now she was lying on the floor with the High King standing over her, and Ivor had no idea what she had sent to them with what looked to have been the last effort of her soul. He couldn't see if she was breathing. There was very little he could see.

A shadow moved. Matt Sören rising to his feet.

Someone spoke. "It was too bright," said Shalhassan. "I could not see." There was pain in his voice.

"Nor I," Ivor murmured. Far too late his sight was returning.

"I saw," Aileron said. "But I do not understand."

"It was a Cauldron." Arthur Pendragon's deep voice was quietly sure. "I marked it as well."

"A Cauldron, yes," Loren said. "At Cader Sedat. We know that already."

"But there is no connection," Jaelle protested weakly. She looked close to collapse. "It quickens the newly dead. What does the Cauldron of Khath Meigol have to do with winter?"

What indeed? Ivor thought, and then he heard Gereint. "Young one," the shaman rasped, almost inaudibly, "this is the mages' hour. You have lived to come to this. First Mage of Brennin, *what is he doing with the Cauldron?*"

The mages' hour, Ivor thought. In the Temple of Dana in Gwen Ystrat. The Weaving of the Tapestry was truly past all comprehending.

Oblivious to their beseeching looks, Loren turned slowly to his source. Mage and Dwarf looked at each other as if no one else was in the room, in the world. Even Teyrnon and Barak were watching the other two and waiting. He was holding his breath, Ivor realized, and his palms were damp.

"Do you remember," Loren said suddenly, and in his voice Ivor heard the timbre of power that lay in Gereint's when he spoke for the god, "do you remember the book of Nilsom?"

"Accursed be his name," Matt Sören replied. "I never read it, Loren."

"Nor I," said Teyrnon softly. "Accursed be his name."

"I did," said Loren. "And so did Metran." He paused. *"I know what he is doing and how he is doing it."*

With a gasp, Ivor expelled air from his lungs and drew breath again. All around him he heard others doing the same. In Matt Sören's one eye he saw a gleam of the same pride with which Leith sometimes looked at him. Quietly, the Dwarf said, "I knew you would. We have a battle then?"

"I promised you one a long time ago," the mage replied. He seemed to Ivor to have grown, even as they watched.

"Weaver be praised!" Aileron suddenly exclaimed.

Quickly they all looked over. The High King had crouched and was cradling Kim's head in his arms, and Ivor could see that she was breathing normally again, and there was color in her face.

In a rapt silence they waited. Ivor, close to tears, saw how young her face was under the white hair. He was too easily moved to tears, he knew. Leith had derided it often enough. But surely it was all right now? He saw tears on the face of the High King and even a suspicious brightness in the eyes of dour Shalhassan of Cathal. In such company, he thought, may not a Dalrei weep?

In a little while she opened her eyes. There was pain in their greyness, and a great weariness, but her voice was clear when she spoke.

"I found something," she said. "I tried to send it back. Did I? Was it enough?"

"You did, and it was enough," Aileron replied gruffly.

She smiled with the simplicity of a child. "Good," she said. "Then I will sleep now. I could sleep for days." And she closed her eyes.

# Chapter 11

"Now you know," said Carde with a wink, "why the men of Gwen Ystrat always look so tired!"

Kevin smiled and drained his glass. The tavern was surprisingly uncrowded, given the prevailing energies of the night. It appeared that both Aileron and Shalhassan had given orders. Diarmuid's band, though, as always, seemed to enjoy an immunity from such disciplinary commands.

"That," said Erron to Carde, "is half a truth at best." He raised a hand to summon another flask of Gwen Ystrat wine, then turned to Kevin. "He's teasing you a bit. There's some of this feeling all year long, I'm told, but only some. Tonight's different—or tomorrow is, actually, and it's spilling over into tonight. What we're feeling now comes only at Maidaladan."

The innkeeper brought over their wine. Upstairs they heard a door open, and a moment later Coll leaned over the railing. "Who's next?" he said with a grin.

"Go ahead," Carde said. "I'll keep the wine cool for you."

Kevin shook his head. "I'll pass," he said as Coll came clumping down the stairs.

Carde raised an eyebrow. "No second offers," he said. "I'm not being that generous tonight, not with so few women about."

Kevin laughed. "Enjoy," he said, raising the glass Erron had filled for him.

Coll slipped into Carde's seat. He poured himself a glass, drained it in a gulp, then fixed Kevin with a surprisingly acute glance. "Are you nervous about tomorrow?" he asked softly, so it wouldn't go beyond their table.

"A little," Kevin said. It was the easiest thing to say, and after a moment he realized that it gave him an out. "Actually," he murmured, "more than a little. I don't think I'm in a party mood tonight." He stood up. "I think I'll turn in, as a matter of fact."

Erron's voice ws sympathetic. "It's not a bad idea, Kevin. Tomorrow night's the real thing, anyhow. What we're feeling now is going to be ten times stronger. With a wolf hunt under your belt, you'll be ready to bed a priestess or three."

"They come out?" Kevin asked, arrested for a moment.

"Only night of the year," Erron said. "Part of the rites of Liadon." He smiled wryly. "The only good part."

Kevin returned the smile. "I'll wait for tomorrow, then. See you in the morning." He clapped Coll on the shoulder, pulled on his coat and gloves, and walked out the door into the bitter chill of the night.

It is bad, he was thinking, when you have to lie to friends. But the reality was too difficult, too alienating, and it was private, too. Let them think he was apprehensive about the hunt; that was better than the truth.

The truth was that nothing of the desire that every other man in the company was feeling had even touched him. None of it. Only from the talk all around had he even grasped that something unusual was happening. Whatever supercharged eroticism was associated with Midsummer's Eve in this place—so much of it that even the priestesses of the Goddess came out from the Temple to make love—whatever was happening wasn't bothering to include him.

The wind was unholy. Worse even than a December holiday he'd spent once on the prairies. It scythed like a blade under his coat. He wasn't going to be able to stay out long. Nothing could. How, Kevin thought, did you fight an enemy who could do this? He had sworn revenge for Jennifer, he remembered, and his mouth twisted with bitter irony. Such bravado that had been. First of all, there wasn't even a war in which to fight—Rakoth Maugrim was breaking them with a hammer of wind and ice. Second, and this truth had been coiling within him since they had arrived from Stonehenge, he wouldn't be much good for anything even if, somehow, they ended the winter and there was a war. The memory of his useless flailing about during the battle on the Plain three nights ago was still raw.

He had moved past jealousy—hadn't lingered long there anyhow—it wasn't really a part of his nature. He was used to being able to *do* something, though. He no longer envied Paul or Kim their dark, burdensome powers—Kim's grief by Pendaran Wood the night before and Paul's loneliness had wiped that away, leaving a kind of pity.

He didn't want their roles or Dave's axe-wielding strength, and no sane person would want any part of what fate Jennifer had found. All he wanted was to *matter*, to have some way, however slight, of effectuating the heartfelt vow he had sworn.

Two, actually. He had done it twice. Once in the Great Hall when Brendel had brought word of the lios alfar dead and Jennifer taken away. Then a second time, when Kim had brought them home and he looked down at what had been done to a woman he loved and then forced himself not to look away, that the scalding image might always be there if courage ever flagged in him.

It was still there, that image, and—he searched himself for this—he was not lacking in courage. He had no fear of tomorrow's hunt, whatever the others might think, only a bitterly honest awareness that he was just along for the ride.

And this, for Kevin Laine, was the hardest thing in any world to handle. What he seemed to be, here in Fionavar, was utterly impotent. Again his mouth crooked bitterly in the cold, for this description was especially accurate now. Every man in Gwen Ystrat was feeling the pull of the Goddess. Every man but him, for whom, all his adult days, the workings of desire had been a deep, enduring constant, known only to the women who had shared a night with him.

If love and desire belonged to the Goddess, it seemed that even she was leaving him. What did that leave?

He shook his head—too much self-pity there. What was left was still Kevin Laine, who was known to be bright and accomplished, a star in law school and one in the making, everyone said, when he got to the courts. He had respect and friendship and he had been loved, more than once. His, a woman had told him years ago, was a face made for good fortune. A curious phrase; he had remembered it.

There was, he told himself, no room for maudlin self-pity in a curriculum vitae like that.

On the other hand, all the glitter of his accomplishments lay squarely within his own world. How could he glory in mock trial triumphs any more? How set his sights on legal excellence after what he had seen here? What could possibly have meaning at home once he had watched Rangat hurl a burning hand into the sky and heard the Unraveller's laughter on the north wind?

Very little, next to nothing. In fact, one thing only, but he did have that one thing, and with the pang of his heart that always came when he hadn't done so for a while, Kevin thought of his father.

*"Fur gezunter heit, und cum gezunter heit,"* Sol Laine had said in Yiddish, when Kevin had told him he had to fly to London on ten hours' notice. *Go safely, and come safely.* Nothing more. In this lay a boundless trust. If Kevin had wanted to tell, Kevin would have explained the trip. If Kevin did not explain, he had a reason and a right.

"Oh, Abba," he murmured aloud in the cruel night. And in the country of the Mother his word for father became a talisman of sorts that carried him in from the slash of wind to the house Diarmuid had been given in Morvran.

There were prerogatives of royalty. Only Coll and Kevin and Brock were sharing the place with the Prince. Coll was in the tavern, and the Dwarf was asleep, and Diarmuid was God knows where.

With a mild amusement registering at the thoughts of Diarmuid tomorrow night, and the deeper easing that thoughts of his father always gave to him, Kevin went to bed. He had a dream but it was elusive and he had forgotten it by morning.

The hunt started with the sunrise. The sky was a bright blue overhead, and the early rays of sunlight glittered on the snow. It was milder too, Dave thought, as if somehow the fact of midsummer was registering. Among the hunters there was an electric energy one could almost see. The erotic surges that had begun when they had first entered Gwen Ystrat were even deeper now. Dave had never felt anything like it in his life, and they said the priestesses would come out to them tonight. It made him weak just to think of it.

He forced his mind back to the morning's work. He had wanted to hunt with the small contingent of the Dalrei, but horses weren't going to be much use in the wood and Aileron had asked the Riders to join the bowmen, who were to ring the forest and cut down any wolves that tried to flee. Dave saw Diarmuid's big lieutenant, Coll, unsling an enormous bow and ride over the bridge to the northwest with Torc and Levon.

It left an opening for him, he supposed, and somewhat reluctantly he walked over with his axe to where Kevin Laine stood joking with two other members of the Prince's band. There was a rumor going about that they had gotten an early start on the midsummer festival last night, defying the orders of the two Kings. Dave couldn't say he was impressed. It was one thing to carouse in town, another to be partying on the eve of battle.

On the other hand, none of them seemed the worse for it this morning, and he didn't really know anyone else to join up with so he awkwardly planted himself by the Prince and waited to be noticed. Diarmuid was rapidly scanning his brother's written instructions. When he finished, he looked up, noting Dave's presence with his disconcertingly blue gaze.

"Room for one more?" Dave asked.

He was prepared for a jibe but the Prince said only, "Of course. I've seen you fight, remember?" He raised his voice very slightly, and the fifty or so men around him quieted. "Gather round, children, and I'll tell you a story. My brother has outdone himself in preparing this. Here is what we are to do."

Despite the frivolous tone, his words were crisp. Behind the Prince, Dave could see the eidolath, the honor guard of Cathal, riding quickly off to the northeast behind Shalhassan. Nearby, Aileron himself was addressing another cluster of men, and, past him, Arthur was doing the same. It was going to be a pincer movement, he gathered, with the two hosts moving together from southwest and northeast.

The archers, about two hundred of them, were to ring the wood. The Cathalians were already along the line of the Kharn River, on the eastern edge, and across the northern boundary as far as the Latham. The bowmen of Brennin were posted from the Latham as well, in the north and then, at intervals, around to the south and west. The thinner copses east of the Kharn had already been checked and found empty, Diarmuid explained. The wolves were within the circle of Leinanwood itself and, if all went according to design, would soon be within the circle of the armies. The dogs were to be set loose to drive the wolves toward the forest center.

"Unless the perfidious wolves have the temerity to disobey the High King's plans, we should meet Shalhassan's forces by the Latham in mid-wood with the wolves between us. If they aren't," Diarmuid concluded, "we blame anyone and everything except the plan. Any questions?"

"Where are the mages?" asked Kevin Laine. He always had questions, Dave thought. One of those. Couldn't just get on with it.

But Diarmuid answered seriously. "We were going to have them. But something happened last night in the Temple. The sources are completely drained. Swords and arrows are all we can use this morning."

And axes, Dave thought grimly. Didn't need anything more. It was cleaner this way with the magic kept out of it. There were no more questions, and no time for more; Aileron had begun moving his company forward. Diarmuid, neat-footed and quick, led them across the Latham bridge to the left flank, and Dave saw Arthur's company take the right.

They were on the southwestern edge of the wood, on the strip of land between forest and frozen lake. Around to the west and north Dave could see the archers, bows drawn, sitting on their horses where the wood thinned out.

Then Aileron signaled Arthur, and Dave saw the Warrior speak to his dog. With a howl, the grey dog exploded forward into Leinanwood and the hunting pack sprang after him. Dave heard faint answering sounds from the northern side as the other half of the pack was released. A moment the men waited; then the High King stepped forward, and they entered the wood.

It grew darker very suddenly, for even without leaves the trees were thick enough to screen the sun. They were moving northwest, before beginning their wide sweep back to the east, so Diarmuid's flank, their own, was in the lead. Abruptly Dave became aware of the smell of wolf, sharp and unmistakable. All around them the dogs were barking, but not urgently. His axe carried at the ready, with its thong looped around his wrist, Dave strode with Kevin Laine on his left and the Dwarf named Brock, bearing an axe of his own, on his right, behind the figure of Diarmuid.

Then, off to their right, Cavall gave tongue again, so loudly that even someone who had never hunted before knew what the sound meant.

"Turn!" Aileron cried from behind them. "Spread out and turn, toward the river!"

Dave's sense of direction was hopelessly gone by then, but he pointed his nose where Diarmuid went and, with quickening heart, set off to find the wolves.

They were found first.

Before they reached the river or the men of Cathal, the black and grey and brindle shapes were upon them. Scorning to be hunted, the giant wolves surged to the attack, and even as he swung the axe in a killing stroke, Dave heard the sounds of battle to the east as well. The men of Cathal had their own fight.

He had no more time to think. Swerving down and to his right, he dodged the fanged leap of a black beast. He felt claws shred his coat. No time to look back; there was another coming. He killed it with a chopping backhand slash, then had to duck, almost to his knees, as another leaped for his face. It was the last clear moment he remembered.

The battle became a chaotic melee as they twisted through the trees, pursuing and pursued. Within his breast Dave felt a surge of the obliterating fury that seemed to be his in battle, and he waded forward through snow red with blood, his axe rising and falling. In front of him all the time he saw the Prince, elegantly lethal with a sword, and heard Diarmuid singing as he killed.

He had no conception of time, could not have said how long it was before they broke through, he and the Prince, with Brock just behind. In front of him he could see the figures of the Cathalians across the frozen river. There were wolves to the right, though, engaging the center of the Brennin ranks and Arthur's flank as well. Dave turned to go to their aid.

"*Wait!*" Diarmuid laid a hand on his arm. "Watch."

Kevin Laine came up beside them, bleeding from a gash on his arm. Dave turned to watch the last of the battle on their side of the Latham.

Not far off, Arthur Pendragon, with grey Cavall by his side, was wreaking controlled destruction among the wolves. Dave had a sudden unexpected sense of how many times the Warrior had swung that blade he carried, and in how many wars.

But it wasn't Arthur whom Diarmuid was watching. Following the Prince's gaze, Dave saw, and Kevin beside him, the same thing Kimberly had seen a year before on a twilit path west of Paras Derval.

Aileron dan Ailell with a sword.

Dave had seen Levon fight, and Torc; he had watched Diarmuid's insouciant deadliness and, just now, Arthur's flawless swordplay with never a motion wasted; he even knew how he battled in his own right, fueled by a rising tide of rage. But Aileron fought the way an eagle flew, or an eltor ran on the summer Plain.

It had ended on the other side. Shalhassan, bloody but triumphant, led his men down to the frozen waters of the Latham, and so they saw as well.

Seven wolves remained. Without a word spoken, they were left for the High King. Six were black, Dave saw, and one was grey, and they attacked in a rush from three sides.

He saw how the grey one died and two of the black, but he never knew what motion of the sword killed the other four.

It was very nearly silent in the wood after that. Dave heard scattered coughing on both sides of the river; a dog barked once, nervously; a man not far away swore softly at the pain of a wound he'd taken. Dave never took his eyes from the High King. Kneeling in the trampled snow, Aileron carefully wiped his blade clean before rising to sheath it. He glanced fleetingly at his brother, then turned, with an expression almost shy, to Arthur Pendragon.

Who said, in a voice of wonder, "Only one man I ever saw could do what you just did."

Aileron's voice was low but steady. "I am not him," he said. "I am not part of it."

"No," said Arthur. "You are not part of it."

After another moment, Aileron turned to the river. "Brightly woven, men of Cathal. A small blow only have we given the Dark this morning, but better that we have given it than otherwise. There are people who will sleep easier tonight for our work in this wood."

Shalhassan of Cathal was splotched in blood from shoulder to boot and there were bloody smears in the forked plaits of his beard, but, kingly still, he nodded grave agreement. "Shall we sound the maron to end the hunt?" Aileron asked formally.

"Do so," Shalhassan said. "All five notes, for there are six of us dead on this side of the river."

"As many here," said Arthur. "If it please you, High King, Cavall can give tongue for both triumph and loss."

Aileron nodded. Arthur spoke to the dog.

Grey Cavall walked to an open space by the riverbank where the snow was neither trampled down nor red with wolf or dog or human blood. In a white place among the bare trees he lifted his head.

But the growl he gave was no sound of triumph nor yet of loss.

Dave would never be sure which caused him to turn, the dog's snarled warning or the trembling of the earth. Faster than thought he spun.

There was an instant—less than that, a scintilla of time in

the space between seconds—and in it he had a flash of memory. Another wood: Pendaran. Flidais, the gnomelike creature with his eerie chants. And one of them: *Beware the boar, beware the swan, the salt sea bore her body on.*

Beware the boar.

He had never seen a creature like the one that rumbled now from the trees. It had to be eight hundred pounds, at least, with savage curving tusks and enraged eyes, and it was an albino, white as the snow all around them.

Kevin Laine, directly in its path, with only a sword and a wounded shoulder, wasn't going to be able to dodge it, and he hadn't a hope in hell of stopping the rush of that thing.

He had turned to face it. Bravely, but too late, and armed with too little. Even as the bizarre memory of Flidais exploded and he heard Diarmuid's cry of warning, Dave took two quick steps, let go of his axe, and launched himself in a lunatic, weaponless dive.

He had the angle, sort of. He hit the boar with a flying tackle on the near side shoulder, and he put every ounce of his weight and strength into it.

He was bounced like a Ping-Pong ball from a wall. He felt himself flying, had time to realize it, before he crashed, pinwheeling, into the trees.

"Kevin!" he screamed and tried, unwisely, to stand. The world rocked. He put a hand to his forehead and it came away covered with blood. There was blood in his eyes; he couldn't see. There was screaming, though, and a snarling dog, and something had happened to his head. There was someone on the ground and people running everywhere, then a person was with him, then another. He tried to rise again. They pushed him back. They were talking to him. He didn't understand.

"Kevin?" he tried to ask. He couldn't form the name. Blood got in his mouth. He turned to cough and fainted dead away from the pain.


It hadn't actually been bravery, or foolish bravado either— there had been no time for such complex things. He'd been at the back and heard a grunt and a trampling sound, so he'd been turning, even before the dog barked and the earth began to shake under the charge of the white boar.

In the half second he'd had, Kevin had thought it was going for Diarmuid and so he yelped to get its attention. Unnecessary, that, for the boar was coming for him all the way.

Strange how much time there seemed to be when there was no time at all. *At least somebody wants me,* was the first hilarious thought that cut in and out of his mind. But he was quick, he'd always been quick, even if he didn't know how to use a sword. He had no place to run and no way on earth of killing this monster. So, as the boar thundered up, grunting insanely and already beginning to raise its tusks to disembowel him, Kevin, timing it with coolest precision, jumped up in a forward somersault, to put his hands on the stinking white fur of the boar's huge back and flip over it like a Minoan bull dancer, to land in the soft snow.

In theory, anyway.

Theory and reality began their radical bifurcation around the axis formed by the flying figure of Dave Martyniuk at precisely the point where his shoulder crashed into that of the boar.

He moved it maybe two inches, all told. Which was just enough to cause Kevin's injured right arm to slip as he reached for the hold that would let him flip. He never got it. He was lying sprawled on top of the boar, with every molecule of usable air cannonballed out of his lungs, when some last primitive mechanism of his mind screamed *roll,* and his body obeyed.

Enough so that the tusk of the animal in its vicious, ripping thrust tore through the outer flesh of his groin and not up and through it to kill. He did his somersault in the end and came down, unlike Dave, in snow.

There was a lot of pain, though, in a very bad place and there were droplets of his blood all over the snow like red flowers.

It was Brock who turned the boar away from him and Diarmuid who planted the first sword. Eventually there were a number of swords; he saw it all, but it was impossible to tell who struck the killing blow.

They were very gentle when it came time to move him and it would have been rude, almost, to scream, so he gripped the branches of his makeshisft stretcher until he thought his hands had torn through the wood, and he didn't scream.

Tried one joke as Diarmuid's face, unnaturally white, loomed up. "If it's a choice between me and the baby," he mumbled, "save the baby." Diar didn't laugh. Kevin wondered if he'd gotten the joke, wondered where Paul was, who would have. Didn't scream.

Didn't pass out until one of the stretcher bearers stumbled over a branch as they left the forest.

When Kevin came to, he saw that Martyniuk was in the next bed, watching him. Had a huge blood-stained bandage around his head. Didn't look too well, himself.

"You're okay," Dave said. "Everything intact."

He wanted to be funny but the relief was too deep for that. He closed his eyes and took a breath. There was surprisingly little pain. When he opened his eyes he saw that there were a number of others in the room: Diar and Coll and Levon. Torc, too, and Erron. Friends. He and Dave were in the front room of the Prince's quarters, in beds moved close to the fire.

"I am okay," he confirmed. Turned to Dave. "You?"

"Fine. Don't know why, though."

"The mages were here," Diarmuid said. "Both of them. They each healed one of you. It took awhile."

Kevin remembered something. "Wait a minute. How? I thought—"

"—that the sources were drained," Diarmuid finished. His eyes were sober. "They were, but we had little choice. They're resting now in the Temple, both Matt and Barak. They'll be all right, Loren says." The Prince smiled slowly. "They won't be around for Maidaladan, though. You'll have to make it up to them. Somehow."

Everyone laughed. Kevin saw Dave looking at him. "Tell me," the big man said slowly, "did I save your life or almost get you killed?"

"We'll go with the first," Kevin said. "But it's a good thing you don't like me much, because if you did, you would have hit that pig with a real tackle instead of faking it. In which case—"

"Hey!" Dave exclaimed. "Hey! That's not . . . that isn't . . ." He stopped because everyone was laughing. He would remember the line, though, for later. Kevin had a way of doing that to him.

"Speaking of pigs," Levon said, helping Dave out, "We're roasting that boar for dinner tonight. You should be able to smell it."

After a moment and some trial sniffs, Kevin could. "That," he said from the heart, "was one big pig."

Diarmuid was grinning. "If you can make it to dinner," he said, "we've already arranged to save the best part for you."

"No!" Kevin moaned, knowing what was coming.

"Yes indeed, I thought you might like from the boar what it almost had from you."

There was a great deal of encouragement and loud laughter, fueled as much, Kevin realized belatedly, by inner excitement as by anything else. It was Maidaladan, Midsummer's Eve, and it showed in every other man in the room. He got up, aware that there was a certain kind of miracle in his doing so. He was bandaged, but he could move and so, it seemed, could Dave. In the big man Kevin read the same scarcely controlled excitement that flared in all the others. Everyone but him. But now there was something nagging at him from somewhere very deep, and it seemed to be important. Not a memory, something else. . . .

There was a lot of laughter and a rough, boisterous humor all around. He went with it, enjoying the camaraderie. When they entered the Morvran meeting house—a dining hall for the night—spontaneous applause burst forth from the companies of Brennin and Cathal, and he realized they were cheering for him and Dave.

They sat with Diarmuid's men and the two young Dalrei. Before dinner formally began, Diarmuid, true to his word, rose from his seat at the high table, bearing a platter ceremoniously before him, and came to Kevin's side.

Amid the gathering hilarity and to the rhythm of five

hundred hungry men banging their fists on the long wooden tables, Kevin reminded himself that such things were said to be a delicacy. With a full glass of wine to hand, he stood up, bowed to Diarmuid, and ate the testicles of the boar that had almost killed him.

Not bad, actually, all things considered.

"Any more?" he asked loudly and got his laugh for the night. Even from Dave Martyniuk, which took some doing.

Aileron made a short speech and so did Shalhassan, both of them too wise to try to say much, given the mood in the hall. Besides, Kevin thought, the Kings must be feeling it too. The serving girls—daughters of the villagers, he gathered—were giggling and dodging already. They didn't seem to mind, though. He wondered what Maidaladan did to the women: to Jaelle and Sharra, even to that battleship Audiart, up at the high table. It was going to be wild later, when the priestesses came out.

There were windows high on all four sides. Amid the pandemonium, Kevin watched it growing dark outside. There was too much noise, too much febrile excitement, for anyone to mark his unwonted quiet.

He was the only one in the hall to see the moon when it first shone through the eastern windows. It was full and this was Midsummer's Eve, and the thing at the edge of his mind was pushing harder now, straining toward a shape. Quietly he rose and went out, not the first to leave. Even in the cold, there were couples clinched heedlessly close outside the banquet hall.

He moved past them, his wound aching a little now, and stood in the middle of the icy street looking up and east at the moon. And in that moment awareness stirred within him, at last, and took a shape. Not desire, but whatever the thing was that lay behind desire.

"It isn't a night to be alone," a voice from just behind him said. He turned to look at Liane. There was a shyness in her eyes.

"Hello," he said. "I didn't see you at the banquet."

"I didn't come. I was sitting with Gereint."

"How is he?" He began to walk, and she fell in stride

beside him on the wide street. Other couples, laughing, running to warmth, passed them on all sides. It was very bright, with the moonlight on the snow.

"Well enough. He isn't happy, though, not the way the others are."

He glanced over at her and then, because it seemed right, took her hand. She wasn't wearing gloves either, and her fingers were cold.

"Why isn't he happy?" A random burst of laughter came from a window nearby, and a candle went out.

"He doesn't think we can do it."

"Do what?"

"Stop the winter. It seems they found out that Metran is making it—I didn't understand how—from the spiraling place, Cader Sedat, out at sea."

A quiet stretch of road. Inside himself Kevin felt a deeper quiet gathering, and suddenly he was afraid. "They can't go there," he said softly.

Her dark eyes were somber. "Not in winter. They can't sail. They can't end the winter while the winter lasts."

It seemed to Kevin, then, that he had a vision of his past, of chasing an elusive dream, waking or asleep, down all the nights of his life. The pieces were falling into place. There was a stillness in his soul. He said, "You told me, the time we were together, that I carried Dun Maura within me."

She stopped abruptly in the road and turned to him.

"I remember," she said.

"Well," he said, "there's something strange happening. I'm not feeling anything of what's hitting everyone else tonight. I'm feeling something else."

Her eyes were very wide in the moonlight. "The boar," she whispered. "You were marked by the boar."

That too. Slowly he nodded. It was coming together. The boar. The moon. Midsummer. The winter they could not end. It had, in fact, come together. From within the quiet, Kevin finally understood.

"You had better leave me," he said, as gently as he could.

It took a moment before he realized that she was crying. He hadn't expected that.

"Liadon?" she asked. Which was the name.

"Yes," he said. "It looks as if. You had better leave me."

She was very young, and he thought she might refuse. He underestimated her, though. With the back of her hand she wiped away her tears. Then, rising on tiptoe, she kissed him on the lips and walked away in the direction from which they had come, toward the lights.

He watched her go. Then he turned and went to the place where the stables were. He found his horse. As he was saddling it, he heard bells ring from the Temple and his movements slowed for a moment. The priestesses of Dana would be coming out.

He finished with the saddle and mounted up. He walked the horse quietly up the lane and stopped in the shadows where it joined the road from Morvran to the Temple. Looking north, he could see them coming, and a moment later he watched the priestesses go by. Some were running and some walked. They all wore long grey cloaks against the cold and they all had their hair unbound and loose down their backs, and all the women seemed to shine a little in the full moonlight. They went past and, turning his head to the left, he saw the men coming out to meet them from the town, and the moon was very bright and it shone on the snow and ice, and on all the men and women in the road as they came together.

In a very little while the street was empty again and then the bells were silent. There were cries and laughter not very far away, but he carried his own deep quiet now, and he set his horse toward the east and began to ride.

Kim woke late in the afternoon. She was in the room they had given her, and Jaelle was sitting quietly beside the bed.

Kim sat up a little and stretched her arms. "Did I sleep all day?" she asked.

Jaelle smiled, which was unexpected. "You were entitled."

"How long have you been watching me?"

"Not long. We've been checking on all of you periodically."

"All of us? Who else?"

"Gereint. The two sources."

Kim pushed herself into a sitting position. "Are you all right?"

Jaelle nodded. "None of us went so far as you. The sources were recovering, until they were drained again."

Kim asked with her eyes, and the red-haired Priestess told her about the hunt and then the boar. "No lasting damage to any of them," she finished, "though Kevin came very close."

Kim shook her head. "I'm glad I didn't see it." She drew a long breath. "Aileron told me that I did send something back. What was it, Jaelle?"

"The Cauldron," the other woman replied, and then, as Kim waited: "The mage says Metran is making the winter with it from Cader Sedat, out at sea."

There was a silence as Kim absorbed this. When it sunk in, all she felt was despair. "Then I did no good at all! We can't do anything about it. We can't get there in winter!"

"Nicely planned, wasn't it?" Jaelle murmured with a dryness that did not mask her own fear.

"What do we do?"

Jaelle stirred. "Not much, tonight. Don't you feel it?"

And with the question, Kim realized she did. "I thought it was just an aftermath," she murmured.

The Priestess shook her head. "Maidaladan. It reaches us later than the men, and more as restlessness than desire, I think, but it is almost sundown, and Midsummer's Eve."

Kim looked at her. "Will you go out?"

Jaelle rose abruptly and took a few paces toward the far wall. Kim thought she'd given offense, but after a moment the tall Priestess turned back to her. "Sorry," she said, surprising Kim for the second time. "An old response. I will go to the banquet but come back afterward. The grey-robed ones must go into the streets tonight, to any man who wants them. The red Mormae never go, though that is custom and not law." She hesitated. "The High Priestess wears white and is not allowed to be part of Maidaladan or to have a man at any other time."

"Is there a reason?" Kim asked.

"You should know it," Jaelle said flatly.

And reaching within, to the place of her second soul, Kim did. "I see," she said quietly. "Is it difficult?"

For a moment Jaelle did not answer. Then she said, "I went from the brown of acolyte straight to the red and then the white."

"Never grey." Kim remembered something. "Neither was Ysanne." And then, as the other stiffened, she asked, "Do you hate her so much? Because she went with Raederth?:

She didn't expect an answer, but it was a strange afternoon, and Jaelle said, "I did once. It is harder now. Perhaps all the hate in me has gone north."

There was a long silence. Jaelle broke it awkwardly.

"I wanted to say . . . you did a very great thing last night, whatever comes of it."

For only the briefest moment Kim hesitated; then she said, "I had help. I'm only going to tell you and Loren, and Aileron, I think, because I'm not sure what will come of it and I want to go carefully."

"What help?" Jaelle said.

"The Paraiko," Kim replied. "The Giants are still alive and under siege in Khath Meigol."

Jaelle sat down quite suddenly. "Dana, Mother of us all!" she breathed. "What do we do?"

Kim shook her head. "I'm not sure. We talk. But not tonight, I guess. As you said, I don't think anything important will happen tonight."

Jaelle's mouth twitched. "Tell that to the ones in grey who have been waiting a year for this."

Kim smiled. "I suppose. You know what I mean. We'll have to talk about Darien, too."

Jaelle said, "Pwyll is with him now."

"I know. I guess he had to go, but I wish he were here."

Jaelle rose again. "I'm going to have to leave. It will be starting soon. I am glad to see you better."

"Thank you," Kim said. "For everything. I may look in on Gereint and the sources. Just to say hello. Where are they?"

Again Jaelle colored. "We put them in beds in the chambers I use. We thought it would be quiet there—not all the priestesses go out if there are men in the Temple."

In spite of everything, Kim had to giggle. "Jaelle," she said, "you've got the only three harmless men in Gwen Ystrat sleeping in your rooms tonight!"

After a second she heard the High Priestess laugh, for the first time she could remember.

When she was alone, for all her good intentions, she fell asleep again. No dreams, no workings of power, just the deep sleep of one who had overtaxed her soul and knew there was more to come.

The bells woke her. She heard the rustle of long robes in the hallway, the quick steps of a great many women, whispers and breathless laughter. After a while it was quiet again.

She lay in bed, wide awake now, thinking of many things. Eventually, because it was Maidaladan, her thoughts went back to an incident from the day before, and, after weighing it and lying still a while longer, she rose, washed her face, and put on her own long robe with nothing underneath.

She went along the curving hallway and listened at a door where a dim light yet showed. It was Midsummer's Eve, in Gwen Ystrat. She knocked, and when he opened it, she stepped inside.

"It is not a night to be alone," she said, looking up at him.

"Are you sure?" he asked, showing the strain.

"I am," she said. Her mouth crooked. "Unless you'd prefer to go in search of that acolyte?"

He made no reply. Only came forward. She lifted her head for his kiss. Then she felt him unclasp her gown and as it fell she was lifted in Loren Silvercloak's strong arms and carried to his bed on Midsummer's Eve.

She was finally beginning to get a sense of what he might do, Sharra thought, of the forms his quest for diversion took. She had been a diversion herself a year ago, but that one had cost him a knife wound and very nearly his life. From her seat at the high table of the banquet hall she watched, a half smile on her lips, as Diarmuid rose and carried the steaming testicles of the boar to the one who had been gored. Miming a servant's gestures, he presented the platter to Kevin.

She remembered that one: he had taken the same leap as she the year before, from the musicians' gallery in Paras Derval, though for a very different reason. He too was handsome, fair as Diarmuid was, though his eyes were brown. There was a sadness in them too, Sharra thought. Nor was she the first woman to see this.

Sadness or no, Kevin made some remark that convulsed those around him. Diarmuid was laughing as he returned to his seat between her father and the High Priestess, on the far side of Aileron. Briefly, he glanced at her as he sat down, and expressionlessly she looked away. They had not spoken since the sunlit afternoon he had so effortlessly mastered all of them. Tonight, though, was Maidaladan, and she was sure enough of him to expect an overture.

As the banquet proceeded—boar meat from the morning and eltor brought down from the Plain by the Dalrei contingent—the tone of the evening grew wilder. She was curious, certainly not afraid, and there was an unsettling disquiet within her as well. When the bells rang, she understood, the priestesses would be coming out. She herself, her father had made clear, would be in the Temple well before that. Already, Arthur Pendragon and Ivor, the Aven of the Dalrei, who had talked entertainingly on either side of her all evening, had gone back to the Temple. Or she assumed that was where they had gone.

There were, therefore, empty seats beside her in the increasingly unruly hall. She could see Shalhassan begin to stir restively. This was not a mood for the Supreme Lord of Cathal. She wondered, fleetingly, if her father was feeling the same upwelling of desire that was becoming more and more obvious in all the other men in the room. He must be, she supposed, and suppressed a smile—it was a difficult thing to envisage Shalhassan at the mercy of his passions.

And in that instant, surprising her despite everything, Diarmuid was next to her. He did not sit. There would be a great many glances turned to them. Leaning on the back of the chair Arthur had been sitting in, he said, in a tone of mildest pleasantry, something that completely disconcerted her. A moment later, with a polite nod of his head, he moved away and, passing down the long room with a laugh or a jibe every few strides, out into the night.

She was her father's daughter, and not even Shalhassan, looking over with an appraising glance, was able to read even a hint of her inner turmoil.

She had expected him to come to her tonight, expected the proposition he would make. For him to murmur as he had just done, "Later," and no more was very much what she had thought he'd do. It fit his style, the indolent insouciance.

What didn't fit, what had unnerved her so much, was that he had made it a question, a quiet request, and had looked for a reply from her. She had no idea what her eyes had told him, or what—and this was worse—she had wanted them to tell.

A few moments later her father rose and, halfway down the room, so did Bashrai. An honor guard, creditably disciplined, escorted the Supreme Lord and Princess of Cathal back to the Temple. At the doorway, Shalhassan, with a gracious gesture if not an actual smile, dismissed them for the night.

She had no servants of her own here; Jaelle had assigned one of the priestesses to look after her. As she entered her room, Sharra saw the woman turning down her bed by the light of the moon that slanted through the curtained window. The priestess was robed and hooded already for the winter outside. Sharra could guess why.

"Will they ring the bells soon?" she asked.

"Very soon, my lady," the woman whispered, and Sharra heard a straining note in her low voice. This, too, unsettled her.

She sat down in the one chair, playing with the single gem she wore about her neck. With quick, almost impatient movements, the priestess finished with the bed.

"Is there more, my lady? Because, if not . . . I'm sorry, but—but it is only tonight . . ." Her voice trembled.

"No," Sharra said kindly. "I will be fine. Just . . . open the window for me before you go."

"The window?" The priestess registered dismay. "Oh, my lady, no! Not for you, surely. You must understand, it will be very wild tonight, and the men of the village have been known to . . ."

She fixed the woman with her most repressive stare. It was hard, though, to quell a hooded priestess of Dana in Gwen Ystrat. "I do not think any men of the village will venture here," she said, "and I am used to sleeping with a window open, even in winter." Very deliberately, she turned her back and began removing her jewelry. Her hands were steady, but she could feel her heart racing at the implication of what she had done.

If he laughed when he entered, or mocked her, she would scream, she decided. And let him deal with the consequences. She heard the catch of the window spring open and a cold breeze blew into the room.

Then she heard the bells, and the priestess behind her drew a ragged breath.

"Thank you," said Sharra, laying her necklace on the table. "I suppose that is your sign."

"The window was, actually," said Diarmuid.

Her dagger was drawn before she finished turning.

He had tossed back the hood and stood regarding her tranquilly. "Remind me to tell you some day about the other time I did this sort of thing. It's a good story. Have you noticed," he added, making conversation, "How tall some of these priestesses are? It was a lucky—"

"Are you trying to earn my hate?" She hurled it at him as if the words were her blade.

He stopped. "Never that," he said, though easily still. "There is no approach to this room from outside for one man by himself, and I chose not to confide in anyone. I had no other way of coming here alone."

"What made you assume you could? How much presumption—"

"Sharra. Have done with that tone. I didn't assume. If you hadn't had the window opened I would have walked out when the bells rang."

"I—" She stopped. There was nothing to say.

"Will you do something for me?" He stepped forward. Instinctively she raised her blade, and at that, for the first time, he smiled. "Yes," he said, "you can cut me. For obvious reasons I offered no blood when I came in. I don't like being in here on Maidaladan without observing the rites. If Dana can affect me the way she is tonight, she deserves propitiation. There's a bowl beside you."

And rolling up the sleeves of his robe and the blue shirt he wore beneath, he extended his wrist to her.

"I am no priestess," she said.

"Tonight, I think, all women are. Do this for me, Sharra."

So, for the second time, her dagger cut into him as she took hold of his wrist and drew a line across the underside. The bright blood welled, and she caught it in the bowl. He had a square of Seresh lace in his pocket, and wordlessly he passed it to her. She laid down the bowl and knife and bound the cut she had made.

"Twice now," he murmured, echoing her own thought. "Will there be a third?"

"You invite it."

He stepped away at that, toward the window. They were on the east side and there was moonlight. There was also, she realized, a long drop below as the ground fell sharply away from the smooth Temple walls. He had clasped his hands loosely on the window ledge and stood looking out. She sat down on the one chair by her bed. When he spoke it was quietly, still, but no longer lightly. "I must be taken for what I am, Sharra. I will never move to the measured gait." He looked at her. "Otherwise I would be High King of Brennin now, and Aileron would be dead. You were there."

She had been. It had been his choice; no one in the Hall that day was likely to forget. She remained silent, her hands in her lap. He said, "When you leaped from the gallery I thought I saw a bird of prey descending for a kill. Later, when you doused me with water as I climbed the walls, I thought I saw a woman with a sense of how to play. I saw both things again in Paras Derval five days ago. Sharra, I did not come here to bed you."

A disbelieving laugh escaped her.

He had turned to look at her. There was moonlight on his face. "It is true. I realized yesterday that I don't like the passion of Maidaladan. I prefer my own. And yours. I did not come to bed you, but to say what I have said."

Her hands were gripping each other very tightly. She mocked him, though, and her voice was cool. "Indeed," she said. "And I gather you came to Larai Rigal last spring just to see the gardens?"

He hadn't moved, but his voice seemed to have come very near, somehow, and it was rougher. "One flower only," said Diarmuid. "I found more than I went to find."

She should be saying something, dealing back to him one of his own deflating, sardonic jibes, but her mouth had gone dry and she could not speak.

And now he did move forward, a half step only, but it took him out of the light. Straining to see in the shadows, Sharra heard him say, carefully and masking now—at last—a tension of his own, "Princess, these are evil times, for war imposes its own constraints and this war may mean an ending to all that we have known. Notwithstanding this, if you will allow, I would court you as formally as ever a Princess of Cathal has been courted, and I will say to your father tomorrow what I say to you tonight."

He paused. There seemed to be moonlight all through the room suddenly, and she was trembling in every limb.

"Sharra," he said, *the sun rises in your eyes.*"

So many men had proposed to her with these, the formal words of love. So many men, but none had ever made her weep. She wanted to rise but did not trust her legs. He was still a distance away. Formally, he had said. Would speak to her father in the morning. And she had heard the rawness in his voice.

It was still there. He said, "If I have startled you, I am sorry for it. This is one thing I am not versed in doing. I will leave you now. I will not speak to Shalhassan unless and until you give me leave."

He moved to the doorway. And then it came to her—he could not see her face where she sat in the shadows, and because she had not spoken. . . .

She did rise then and, uttering the words through and over a cresting wave in her heart, said shyly, but not without a thread of laughter, "Could we not pretend it was not Maidaladan? To see where our own inadequate desire carried us?"

A sound escaped him as he spun.

She moved sideways into the light so he could see her face. She said, "Whom else should I ever love?"

Then he was beside her, and above, and his mouth was on her tears, her eyes, her own mouth, and the full moon of midsummer was upon them as a shower of white light, for all the dark around and all the dark to come.

It was cold in the open but not so very bad tonight, and there was a shining light on the snow and the hills. Overhead the brighter stars gleamed frostily down, but the dimmer ones were lost in the moonlight, for the full moon was high.

Kevin rode at a steady pace toward the east, and gradually the horse began to climb. There was no real path, not among the snow, but the ascent was easy enough and the drifts weren't deep.

The hills ran north and south, and it wasn't long before he crested a high ridge and paused to look down. In the distance the mountains glittered in the silvery light, remote and enchanting. He wasn't going so far.

A shadow moved among the snow and ice to his right and Kevin swung over quickly to look, aware that he was weaponless and alone in a wide night.

It wasn't a wolf.

The grey dog moved slowly, gravely, to stand in front of the horse. It was a beautiful animal for all the brutal scars, and Kevin's heart went out to it. A moment they were thus, a tableau on the hilltop among the snow and the low sweeping sigh of the wind.

Kevin said, "Will you lead me there?"

A moment longer Cavall looked up, as if questioning or needing reassurance from the lone rider on the lone horse.

Kevin understood. "I *am* afraid," he said. "I will not lie to you. There is a strong feeling in me, though, the more so now, since you are here. I would go to Dun Maura. Will you show me the way?"

A swirl of wind moved the snow on the hilltop. When it passed Cavall had turned and was trotting down the slope to the east. For a moment Kevin looked back. There were lights behind him in Morvran and in the Temple, and dimly, if he listened, he could hear shouts and laughter. He twitched the reins and the horse moved forward after the dog, and on the downhill side the lights and noise were lost.

It wouldn't be very far, he knew. For perhaps an hour Cavall led him down out of the hills, winding east and a little north. Horse and man and dog were the only moving things among a winter landscape of evergreens piled with snow, and the molded, silvered forms of the tummocks and gullies. His breath frosted in the night air, and the only sounds were the movements of his horse and the sighing of the wind, softer now since they had come down from the high places.

Then the dog stopped and turned to look back at him again. He had to search for several moments before he saw the cave. They were directly in front of it. There were bushes and overhanging vines over the entrance, and the opening was smaller than he'd thought it would be—more a fissure, really. A slantwise path led from it down into what seemed to be the last of the low hills. If the moonlight had not been so bright he wouldn't have seen it at all.

His hands weren't entirely steady. He look a number of slow, deep breaths and felt his heart's hard beating ease. He swung down off the horse and stood beside Cavall in the snow. He looked at the cave. He was very much afraid.

Drawing another breath, he turned back to the horse. He stroked its nose, his head close, feeling the warmth. Then he took the reins and turned the horse around to face the hills and the town beyond. "Go now," he said, and slapped it on the rump.

A little surprised at how easy it was, he watched the stallion canter off, following its own clear track. He could see it a long way in the clear light before the path they had taken curved south around a slope. For a few seconds more he stood gazing west at the place where it had disappeared.

"Well," he said, turning away, "here goes." The dog was sitting in the snow, watching him with its liquid eyes. So much sadness there. He had an impulse to embrace it, but the dog wasn't his, they had shared nothing, and he would not presume. He made a gesture with his hand, a silly one really, and, saying nothing more, walked into Dun Maura.

This time he didn't look back. There would be only Cavall to see, and the dog would be watching him, motionless in the moonlit snow. Kevin parted the ferns and stepped through the bushes into the cave.

Immediately it was dark. He hadn't brought any sort of light, so he had to wait for his eyes to adjust. As he waited, he became aware of how warm it suddenly was. He removed his coat and dropped it by the entrance, though a little out of the way. After a moment's hesitation he did the same with the beautifully woven vest Diarmuid had given him. His heart jumped at a quick flapping sound outside, but it was only a bird. Once it called, then twice, a long, thin, quavering note. Then, a moment later, it called a third time, a half-tone deeper, and not so long. With a hand on the right side wall, Kevin began moving forward.

It was a smooth path, and the downward slope was gentle. With his hands outstretched, he could feel the walls on either side. He had a sense that the roof of the cave was high, but it was truly dark and he couldn't see.

His heart seemed to have slowed and his palms were dry, though there was a dampness to the rough walls. The blackness was the hard thing, but he knew, as much as he had ever known anything, that he had not come so far only to trip and break his neck on a dark path.

He went on for a long time, how long he didn't know. Twice the walls came very close together, forcing him to turn sideways to pass through. Once something flying in the dark passed very near him, and he ducked belatedly with a primitive fear. This passed, though, it all passed. Eventually the corridor bent sharply right, and down, and in the distance Kevin saw a glow of light.

It was warm. He undid another button of his shirt and then, on impulse, took it off. He looked up. Even with the new light, the roof of the cave was so high it was lost in the shadows. The path widened now, and there were steps. He counted, for no good reason. The twenty-seventh was the last; it took him out of the path to the edge of a huge round chamber that glowed with an orange light from no source he could see.

He stopped on the threshold, instinctively, and as he did so the hair rose up on the back of his neck and he felt the first pulse—not a surge yet, though he knew it would come—of power in that most holy place, and in him the form the power took was, at last, desire.

*"Bright your hair and bright your blood,"* he heard. He spun to his right.

He hadn't seen her, and wouldn't have had she not spoken. Barely three feet away from him there was a crude stone seat carved roughly into the rock face. On it, bent almost double with age, sat a withered, decrepit old crone. Her long stringy hair hung in unkempt yellow-grey whorls down her back and on either side of her narrow face. With knobbed hands, as deformed as her spine, she worked ceaselessly away at a shapeless knitting. When she saw him startle she laughed, opening wide her toothless mouth with a high, wheezing sound. Her eyes, he guessed, had once been blue, but they were milky and rheumy now, dimmed by cataracts.

Her gown would long ago have been white, but now it was stained and soiled an indeterminate shade and torn in many places. Through one tear he saw the slack fall of a shrunken breast.

Slowly, with uttermost deference, Kevin bowed to her, guardian of the threshold in this place. She was laughing still when he rose. Spittle rolled down her chin.

"It is Maidaladan tonight," he said.

Gradually she quieted, looking up at him from the low stone seat, her back so bent she had to twist her neck sideways to do so. "It is," she said. "The Night of the Beloved Son. It is seven hundred years now since last a man came calling on Midsummer's Eve." She pointed with one of her needles, and Kevin looked on the ground beside her to see crumbled bones and a skull.

"I did not let him pass," the crone whispered, and laughed.

He swallowed and fought back fear. "How long," he stammered, "how long have you been here?"

"*Fool!*" she cried, so loudly he jumped. *Foolfoolfoolfool* reverberated in the chamber, and high above he heard the bats. "*Do you think I am alive?*"

*Alivealivealivealive*, he heard, and then heard only his own breathing. He watched the crone lay her knitting down beside the bones at her feet. When she looked up at him again she held only one needle only, long and sharp and dark, and it was trained on his heart. She chanted, clearly but soft, so there was no echo:

> *"Bright your hair and bright your blood,*
> *Yellow and red for the Mother.*
> *Give me your name, Beloved,*
> *Your true name, and no other."*

In the moment before he answered, Kevin Laine had time to remember a great many things, some with sorrow and some with love. He drew himself up before her; there was a power in him, an upsurge of desire; he too could make the echoes ring in Dun Maura.

"*Liadon!*" he cried, and in the resounding of it, the burgeoning strength within himself, he felt a breath, a touch, as of wind across his face.

Slowly the crone lowered the needle.

"It is so," she whispered. "Pass."

He did not move. His heart was beating rapidly now, though not with fear any more. "There is a wishing in me," he said.

"There always is," the crone replied.

Kevin said, "Bright my hair and bright my blood. I offered blood once, in Paras Derval, but that was far from here, and not tonight."

He waited and for the first time saw a change in her eyes. They seemed to clear, to move back toward their lost blue; it may have been a trick of the orange light on the stone seat, but he thought he saw her straighten where she sat.

With the same needle she pointed, inward, to the chamber. Not far away, almost on the threshold still, Kevin saw the elements of offering. No brightly polished dagger here, no exquisitely crafted bowl to catch the falling gift. This was the oldest place, the hearth. There was a rock rising up, a little past the height of his chest, from the cave floor, and it came to no level, rounded peak, but to a long jagged crest. Beside the rock was a stone bowl, little more than a cup. It had had two handles once, but one had broken off. There was no design on it, no potter's glaze; it was rough, barely functional, and Kevin could not even hazard a guess how old it was.

"Pass," the crone repeated.

He went to the rock and picked up the bowl, carefully. It was very heavy to his hand. Again he paused, and again a great many things came back to him from far away, like lights on a distance shore, or lights of a town seen at night from a winter hill.

He was very sure. With a smooth, unhurried motion, he bent over the rock and laid his cheek open on the jagged crest. Even as he felt the pain and caught the welling blood, he heard an ululating wail from behind him, a wild sound of joy and grief in one rising and falling cry as he came into his power.

He turned. The crone had risen. Her eyes were very blue, her gown was white, her hair was white as snow, her fingers long and slender. Her teeth were white, her lips were red, and a red flush was in her cheeks, as well, and he knew it for desire.

He said, "There is a wish in my heart."

She laughed. A gentle laugh, indulgent, tender, a mother's laugh over the cradle of her child.

"Beloved," she said. "Oh, be welcome again, Liadon. Beloved Son. . . . Maidaladan. She will love you, she will." And the Guardian of the Threshold, old still but no longer a crone, laid a finger on his still flowing wound, and he felt the skin close to her touch and the bleeding stop.

She rose up on her toes and kissed him full on the lips. Desire broke over him like a wave in a high wind. She said,

"Twelve hundred years have passed since I claimed my due from a sacrifice come freely."

There were tears in her eyes.

"Go now," she said. "Midnight is upon us, Liadon. You know where to go; you remember. Pour the bowl and the wish of your heart, Beloved. She will be there. For you she will come as swiftly as she did when the first boar marked the first of all her lovers." With her long fingers she was disrobing him even as she spoke.

Desire, power, crest of the wave. He was the force behind the wave and the foam where it broke. Wordlessly, he turned, remembering the way, and crossing the wide chamber, bearing his blood in a stone bowl, he came to its farthest point. To the very brink of the chasm.

Naked as he had been in the womb, he stood over it. And now he did not let his mind go back to the lost things from before; instead, he turned his whole being to the one wish of his heart, the one gift he sought of her in return, and he poured out the brimming cup of his blood into the dark chasm, to summon Dana from the earth on Midsummer's Eve.

In the chamber behind him the glow died utterly. In the absolute black he waited and there was so much power in him, so much longing. The longing of all his days brought to a point, to this point, this crevasse. Dun Maura. Maid-aladan. His heart's desire. The boar. The blood. The dog in the snow outside. Full moon. All the nights, all the traveling through all the nights of love. And now.

And now she had come, and it was more than anything could be, more than all. She was, and she was there for him in the dark, suspended in the air above the chasm.

"Liadon," she whispered, and the throaty desire in the sound set him on fire. Then to crown it, and shape it, for she loved him and would love him, she whispered again, and she said, "Kevin," and then, *"Oh, come!"*

And he leaped.

She was there and her arms were around him in the dark as she claimed him for her own. It seemed to him as if they floated for a moment, and then the long falling began. Her legs twined about his, he reached and found her breasts. He caressed her hips, her thighs, felt her open like a flower to his touch, felt himself wild, rampant, entered her. They fell. There was no light, there were no walls. Her mouth made sounds as she kissed him. He thrust and heard her moan, he heard his own harsh breathing, felt the storm gathering, the power, knew this was the destination of his days, heard Dana say his name, all his names in all the worlds, felt himself explode deep into her, with the fire of his seed. With her own transfiguring ecstasy she flared alight; she was incandescent with what he had done to her, and by the light of her desire he saw the earth coming up to gather him, and he knew he had come home, to the end of journeying. End of longing, with the ground rushing now to meet, the walls streaming by; no regret, much love, power, a certain hope, spent desire, and only the one sorrow for which to grieve in the last half second, as the final earth came up to meet him.

*Abba*, he thought, incongruously. And met.

In the Temple, Jaelle woke. She sat bolt upright in bed and waited. A moment later the sound came again, and this time she was awake and there could be no mistake. Not for this, and not tonight. She was High Priestess, she wore white and was untouched, because there had to be one so tuned to the Mother that if the cry went up it would be heard. Again it came to her, the sound she had never thought to hear, a cry not uttered for longer than anyone living knew. Oh, the ritual had been done, had been enacted every morning after Maidaladan since the first Temple was raised in Gwen Ystrat. But the lamenting of the priestesses at sunrise was one thing, it was a symbol, a remembering.

The voice in her mind was infinitely otherwise. Its mourning was for no symbolic loss, but for the Beloved Son. Jaelle rose, aware that she was trembling, still not quite believing what she heard. But the sound was high and compelling, laden with timeless grief, and she was High Priestess and understood what had come to pass.

There were three men sleeping in the front room of her chambers. None of them stirred as she passed through. She did not go into the corridor. Instead she came to another, smaller doorway and, barefoot in the cold, walked quickly down a dark narrow hallway and opened another door at the end of it.

She came out under the dome, behind the altar and the axe. There she paused. The voice was loud within her, though, urgent and exultant, even in its grief, and it carried her with it.

She was High Priestess. It was the night of Maidaladan, and, impossibly, the sacrifice had come to pass. She laid both hands on the axe that only the High Priestess could lift. She took it from its rest, and swinging around, she brought it crashing down on the altar. Hugely, the sound reverberated. Only when it ended did she lift her own voice in the words that echoed within her being.

"*Rahod hedai Liadon!*" Jaelle cried. "Liadon has died again!" She wept. She grieved with all her heart. And she knew every priestess in Fionavar had heard her. She was High Priestess.

They were awakening now, all those in the Temple. They were coming from their sleep. They saw her there, her robe torn, blood on her face, the axe lifted from its rest.

"*Rahod hedai Liadon!*" Jaelle cried again, feeling it rise within her, demanding utterance. The Mormae were all there now; she saw them begin to tear their own robes, to rend their faces in a wildness of grief and she heard them lift their voices to lament as she had done.

There was an acolyte beside her, weeping. She carried Jaelle's cloak and boots. In haste, the High Priestess put them on. She moved to lead them away, all of them, east, to where it had come to pass. There were men in the room now, the two mages, the Kings; there was fear in their eyes. They stepped aside to let her pass. There was a woman who did not.

"Jaelle," said Kim. "Who is it?"

She hardly broke her stride. "I do not know. Come!" She went outside. There were lights being lit all over Morvran and down the long street leading from the town she saw the priestesses running toward her. Her horse had been brought. She mounted up and, without waiting for anyone, she set off for Dun Maura.

They all followed. Two on a horse, in many cases, as the soldiers bore with them the priestesses who had leaped, crying, from their beds. It was midsummer and the dawn would come early. There was already a grey light when they came up to the cave and saw the dog.

Arthur dismounted and walked over to Cavall. For a moment he gazed into the eyes of his dog, then he straightened and looked at the cave. At the entrance Jaelle knelt among the red flowers now blooming amid the snow, and there were tears streaming down her face.

The sun came up.

"Who?" asked Loren Silvercloak. "Who was it?"

There were a great many people there by then. They looked around at each other in the first of the morning light.

Kim Ford closed her eyes.

All around them the priestesses of Dana began, raggedly at first, but then in harmony, to sing their lament for the dead Liadon.

"Look!" said Shalhassan of Cathal. "The snow is melting!"

Everyone looked but Kim. Everyone saw.

*Oh, my darling man,* thought Kimberly. There was a murmur surging toward a roar. Awe and disbelief. The beginnings of a desperate joy. The priestesses were wailing in their grief and ecstasy. The sun was shining on the melting snow.

"Where's Kevin?" said Diarmuid sharply.

*Where, oh, where? Oh, my darling.*

# PART IV

## Cader Sedat

# Chapter 12

Oldest of three brothers, Paul Schafer had a general sense of how to deal with children. But a general sense wasn't going to be much good here, not with this child. Dari was his problem for the morning, because Vae had her own griefs to deal with: a child's loss to mourn and an almost impossible letter to write to North Keep.

He'd promised to see that the letter got there, and then he had taken Dari outside to play. Or, actually, just to walk in the snow because the boy—he looked to be seven or eight now, Paul judged—wasn't in a mood to play and didn't really trust Paul anyhow.

Reaching back fifteen years to a memory of his brothers, Paul talked. He didn't push Dari to say or do anything, didn't offer to toss him or carry him; he just talked, and not as one talks to a child.

He told Dari about his own world and about Loren Silvercloak, the mage who could go back and forth between the worlds. He talked about the war, about why Shahar, Dari's father, had to be away, and about how many mothers and children had had their men go away to war because of the Dark.

"Finn wasn't a man, though," said Dari. His first words that morning.

They were in the woods, following a winding trail. Off to the left Paul could see glimpses of the lake, the only unfrozen lake, he guessed, in Fionavar. He looked down at the child, weighing his words.

"Some boys," he said, "become like men sooner than others. Finn was like that."

Dari, in a blue coat and scarf, and mittens and boots, looked gravely up at him. His eyes were very blue. After a long moment he seemed to come to a decision. He said, "I can make a flower in the snow."

"I know," said Paul, smiling. "With a stick. Your mother told me you made one yesterday."

"I don't need a stick," Darien said. Turning away, he gestured toward the untrodden snow on the path ahead of them. The gesture of his hand in the air was duplicated in the snow. Paul saw the outline of a flower take shape.

He also saw something else.

"That's . . . very good," he said, as evenly as he could, while bells of alarm were going off in his head. Darien didn't turn. With another movement, not a tracing this time, simply a spreading of his fingers, he colored the flower he'd made. It was blue-green where the petals were, and red at the center.

Red, like Darien's eyes, when he made it.

"That's very good," Paul managed to say again. He cleared his throat: "Shall we go home for lunch?"

They had walked a long way and, going back, Dari got tired and asked to be carried. Paul swung him up on his shoulders and jogged and bounced him part of the way. Dari laughed for the first time. It was a nice laugh, a child's.

After Vae had given him lunch, Dari napped for most of the afternoon. He was quiet in the evening too. At dinnertime, Vae, without asking, set three places. She, too, said very little; her eyes were red-rimmed, but Paul didn't see her weep. After, when the sun set, she lit the candles and built up the fire. Paul put the child to bed and made him laugh again with shadow figures on the wall before he pulled the curtains around the bed.

Then he told Vae what he had decided to do, and after a while she began to talk, softly, about Finn. He listened, saying nothing. Eventually he understood something—it took too long, he was still slow with this one thing—and he moved closer and took her in his arms. She stopped talking, then, and lowered her head simply to weep.

He spent a second night in Finn's bed. Dari didn't come to

him this time. Paul lay awake, listening to the north wind whistle down the valley.

In the morning, after breakfast, he took Dari down to the lake. They stood on the shore, and he taught the child how to skip flat stones across the water. It was a delaying action, but he was still apprehensive and uncertain about his decision of the night before. When he'd finally fallen asleep, he'd dreamt about Darien's flower, and the red at its center had become an eye in the dream, and Paul had been afraid and unable to look at it.

The child's eyes were blue now, by the water, and he seemed quietly intent on learning how to skip a stone. It was almost possible to convince oneself that he was just a boy and would remain so. Almost possible. Paul bent low. "Like this," he said, and made a stone skip five times across the lake. Straightening, he watched the child run to look for more stones to throw. Then, lifting his glance, he saw a silver-haired figure ride around the bend in the road from Paras Derval.

"Hello," said Brendel as he came up. And, then, dismounting, "Hello, little one. There's a stone just beside you and a good one, I think."

The lios alfar stood, facing Paul, and his eyes were sober and knowing.

"Kevin told you?" Paul asked.

Brendel nodded. "He said you would be angry, but not very."

Paul's mouth twitched. "He knows me too well."

Brendel smiled, but his tell-tale eyes were violet. "He said something else. He said there seemed to be a choice of Light or Dark involved and that, perhaps, the lios alfar should be here."

For a moment, Paul was silent. Then he said, "He's the cleverest of all of us, you know. I never thought of that."

To the east, in Gwen Ystrat, the men of Brennin and Cathal were entering Leinanwood and a white boar was rousing itself from a very long sleep.

Behind Brendel, Dari tried, not very successfully, to skip

a stone. Glancing at him, the lios said softly, "What did you want to do?"

"Take him to the Summer Tree," Paul replied.

Brendel went very still. "Power before the choice?" he asked.

Dari skipped a stone three times and laughed. "Very good," Paul told him automatically, and then, to Brendel, "He cannot choose as a child, and I'm afraid he has power already." He told Brendel about the flower. Dari had run a few steps along the shore, looking for another stone.

The lios alfar was as a quiescent silver flame amid the snow. His face was grave; it was ageless and beautiful. When Paul was done, he said, "Can we gamble so, with the World-loom at risk?"

And Paul replied, "For whatever reason, Rakoth did not want him to live. Jennifer says Darien is random."

Brendel shook his head. "What does that mean? I am afraid, Pwyll, very greatly afraid."

They could hear Dari laughing as he hunted for skipping stones. Paul said, "No one who has ever lived, surely, can ever have been so poised between Light and Dark." And then, as Brendel made no reply, he said again, hearing the doubt and the hope, both, in his own voice, "Rakoth did not want him to live."

"For whatever reason," Brendel repeated.

It was mild by the lake. The waters were ruffled but not choppy. Dari skipped a stone five times and turned, smiling, to see if Paul had been watching him. They both had.

"Weaver lend us light," Brendel said.

"Well done, little one," said Paul. "Shall we show Brendel our path through the woods?"

"Finn's path," said Dari and set off, leading them.

From within the cottage Vae watched them go. Paul, she saw, was dark, and the lios alfar's hair gleamed silver in the light, but Darien was golden as he went into the trees.

Paul had always been planning to come back alone with a question to ask, but it seemed to have worked out otherwise.

As they came to the place where the trees of the lake copse

began to merge with the darker ones of the forest, Dari slowed, uncertainly. Gracefully, Brendel swept forward and swung him lightly up to his shoulders. In silence, then, Paul walked past both of them as once he had walked past three men at night, and near to this place. Carrying his head very high, feeling the throb of power already, he came into the Godwood for the second time.

It was daylight, and winter, but it was dark in Mörnirwood among the ancient trees, and Paul found himself vibrating inwardly like a tuning fork. There were memories. He heard Brendel behind him, talking to the child, but they seemed very distant. What was close were the images: Ailell, the old High King, playing chess by candlelight; Kevin singing "Rachel's Song"; this wood at night; music; Galadan and the dog; then a red full moon on new moon night, the mist, the God, and rain.

He came to the place where the trees formed a double row, and this, too, he remembered. There was no snow on the path, nor would there be, he knew; not so near the Tree. There was no music this time, and for all the shadows it was not night, but the power was there, it was always there, and he was part of it. Behind him, Brendel and the boy were silent now, and in silence Paul led them around a curve in the twin line of trees and into the glade of the Summer Tree. Which was as it had been, the night they bound him upon it.

There was dappled light. The sun was high and it shone down on the glade. He remembered how it had burned him a year ago, merciless in a blank, cloudless sky.

He put away his memories.

He said, "Cernan, I would speak with you," and heard Brendel draw a shocked breath. He did not turn. Long moments passed. Then from behind a screen of trees surrounding the glade a god came forward.

He was very tall, long of limb and tanned a chestnut brown. He wore no clothing at all. His eyes were brown like those of a stag, and lightly he moved, like a stag, and the horns on his head, seven-tined, were those of a stag as well. There was a wildness to him, and an infinite majesty, and when he spoke there was that in his voice which evoked all the dark forests, untamed.

"I am not to be summoned so," he said, and it seemed as though the light in the glade had gone dim.

"By me you are," said Paul calmly. "In this place."

Even as he spoke there came a muted roll of thunder. Brendel was just behind him. He was aware of the child, alert and unafraid, walking now about the perimeter of the glade.

"You were to have died," Cernan said. Stern and even cruel he looked. "I bowed to honor the manner of your death."

"Even so," said Paul. There was thunder again. The air seemed tangibly charged with power. It crackled. The sun shone, but far off, as if through a haze. "Even so," Paul repeated. "But I am alive and returned hither to this place."

Thunder again, and then an ominous silence.

"What would you, then?" Cernan said.

Paul said in his own voice, "You know who the child is?"

"I know he is of the andain," said Cernan of the Beasts. "And so he belongs to Galadan, to my son."

Galadan," Paul said harshly, "belongs to me. When next we meet, which will be the third time."

Again a silence. The horned god took a step forward. "My son is very strong," he said. "Stronger than us, for we may not intervene." He paused. And then, with a new note in his voice, said, "He was not always as he is."

So much pain, Paul thought. Even in this. Then he heard, bitter and implacable, the voice of Brendel: "He killed Ra-Termaine at Andarien. Would you have us pity him?"

"He is my son," said Cernan.

Paul stirred. So much darkness around him with no raven voices to guide. He said, still doubting, still afraid, "We need you, Woodlord. Your counsel and your power. The child has come into his strength, and it is red. There is a choice of Light we all must make, but his is gravest of all, I fear, and he is but a child." After a pause, he said it: "He is Rakoth's child, Cernan."

There was a silence. "Why?" the god whispered in dismay. "Why was he allowed to live?"

Paul became aware of murmuring among the trees. He remembered it. He said, "To make the choice. The most important choice in all the worlds. But not as a child; his power has come too soon." He heard Brendel breathing beside him.

"It is only as a child," Cernan said, "that he can be controlled."

Paul shook his head. "There is no controlling him, nor could there ever be. Woodlord, he is a battlefield and must be old enough to know it!" Saying the words, he felt them ring true. There was no thunder, but a strange, anticipatory pulsing ran within him. He said, "Cernan, can you take him through to his maturity?"

Cernan of the Beasts lifted his mighty head, and for the first time something in him daunted Paul. The god opened his mouth to speak—

They never heard what he meant to say.

From the far side of the glade there came a flash of light, blinding almost, in the charged dimness of that place.

"Weaver at the Loom!" Brendel cried.

"*Not quite,*" said Darien.

He came out from behind the Summer Tree, and he was no longer a child. Naked as Cernan, he stood, but fair-haired as he had been from birth, and not so tall as was the god. He was about the height, Paul realized, with a numbing apprehension, that Finn had been, and looked to be the same age as well.

"Dari . . ." he began, but the nickname didn't fit any more, it didn't apply to this golden presence in the glade. He tried again. "Darien, this is what I brought you for, but how did you do it alone?"

He was answered with a laugh that turned apprehension to terror. "You forgot something," said Darien. "You all did. Such a simple thing as winter led you to forget. We are in an oak grove and Midsummer's Eve is coming on! With such power to draw upon, why should I need the horned god to come into my power?"

"Not your power," Paul replied as steadily as he could, watching Darien's eyes, which were still blue. "Your maturity. You are old enough now to know why. You have a choice to make."

"*Shall I go ask my father,*" Darien cried, "*what to do?*"

And with a gesture he torched the trees around the glade into a circle of fire, red like the red flash of his eyes.

Paul staggered back, feeling the rush of heat as he had not felt the cold. He heard Cernan cry out, but before the god could act, Brendel stepped forward.

"No," he said. "Put out the fire and hear me before you go." There was a music in his voice, bells in a high place of light. "Only once," Brendel said quietly, and Darien moved a hand.

The fire died. The trees were untouched. Illusion, Paul realized. It had been an illusion. He still felt the fading heat on his skin, though, and in the place of his own power he felt a helplessness.

Ethereal, almost luminous, Brendel faced the child of Rakoth. "You heard us name your father," he said, "but you do not know your mother's name, and you have her hair and her hands. More than that: your father's eyes are red, your mother's green. Your eyes are blue, Darien. You are not bound to any destiny. No one born, ever, has had so pure a choice of Light or Dark."

"It is so," came Cernan's deep voice from the trees.

Paul couldn't see Brendel's eyes, but Darien's were blue again and he was beautiful. No longer a child but young, still, with a beardless open face, and so very great a power.

"If the choice is pure," said Darien, "should I not hear my father as well as you? If only to be fair?" He laughed then, at something he saw in Brendel's face.

"Darien," said Paul quietly, "you have been loved. What did Finn tell you about the choice?"

It was a gamble. Another one, for he didn't know if Finn would have said anything at all.

A gamble, and he seemed to have lost. "He left," said Darien, a spasm of pain raking across his face. *"He left!"* the boy cried again. He gestured with a hand—a hand like Jennifer's—and disappeared.

There was silence, then a sound of something rushing from the glade.

"Why," said Cernan of the Beasts again—the god who had mocked Maugrim long ago and named him Sathain—"why was he allowed to live?"

Paul looked at him, then at the suddenly frail-seeming lios alfar. He clenched his fists. "To choose!" he cried with a certain desperation. Reaching within, to the throb of power, he sought confirmation and found none.

Together, Paul and Brendel left the glade and then the Godwood. It had been a long walk there; it seemed even longer going back. The sun was westering behind them when they came again to the cottage. Three had gone out in the morning, but Vae saw only two return.

She let them in, and the lios alfar bowed to her and then kissed her cheek, which was unexpected. She had never seen one of them before. Once, it would have thrilled her beyond measure. Once. They sat down wearily in the two chairs by the fire, and she made an herbal tea while they told her what had come to pass.

"It was for nothing then," she said when the tale was done. "It was worse than nothing, all we did, if he has gone over to his father. I thought love might count for more."

Neither of them answered her, which was answer enough. Paul threw more wood on the fire. He felt bruised by the day's events. "There is no need for you to stay here now," he said. "Shall we take you back to the city in the morning?"

Slowly, she nodded. And then, as the loneliness hit home, said tremulously, "It will be an empty house. Cannot Shahar come home to serve in Paras Derval?"

"He can," said Paul quietly. "Oh, Vae, I am so sorry. I will see that he comes home."

She did weep, then, for a little while. She hadn't wanted to. But Finn had gone impossibly far, and Dari now as well, and Shahar had been away for so long.

They stayed the night. By the light of candles and the fire, they helped her gather the few belongings she had brought to the cottage. When it grew late they let the fire die, and the lios slept in Dari's bed and Paul in Finn's again. They were to leave at first light.

They woke before that, though. It was Brendel who stirred and the other two, in shallow sleep, heard him rise. It was still night, perhaps two hours before dawn.

"What is it?" Paul asked.

"I am not sure," the lios replied. "Something."

They dressed, all three of them, and walked out toward the lake. The full moon was low now but very bright. The wind had shifted to the south, blowing toward them from over the water. The stars overhead and west were dimmed by the moon. They shone brighter, Paul saw, in the east.

Then, still looking east, he lowered his glance. Unable to speak, he touched Brendel and Vae and then pointed.

All along the hills, clearly visible in the light of the moon, the snow was starting to melt.

He hadn't gone far, nor been invisible for long—it wasn't a thing he could sustain. He heard the god go off in the guise of a stag and then the other two, walking slowly, in silence. He had an impulse to follow but he remained where he was among the trees. Later, when everyone had gone, Darien rose and left as well.

There was something, like a fist or a stone, buried in his chest. It hurt. He wasn't used to this body, the one he had accelerated himself into. He wasn't used to knowing who his father was either. He knew the first discomfort would pass, suspected the second would. Wasn't sure how he felt about that, or about anything. He was naked, but he wasn't cold. He was deeply angry at everyone. He was beginning to guess how strong he was.

There was a place—Finn had found it—north of the cottage and high up on the highest of the hills. In summer it would have been an easy climb, Finn had said. Darien had never known a summer. When Finn took him, the drifts had been up to Dari's chest and Finn had carried him much of the way.

He wasn't Dari any more. That name was another thing lost, another fragment gone away. He stood in front of the small cave on the hill slope. It sheltered him from the wind, though he didn't need shelter. From here you could see the towers of the palace of Paras Derval, though not the town.

You could also look down, as it grew dark, on the lights in

the cottage by the lake. His eyes were very good. He could see figures moving behind the drawn curtains. He watched them. After a while, he did begin to feel cold. It had all happened very fast. He couldn't quite fit into this body or deal with the older mind he now had. He was still half in Dari's shape, in the blue winter coat and mittens. He still wanted to be carried down and be put to bed.

It was hard not to cry, looking at the lights, and harder when the lights went out. He was alone then with only moonlight and the snow and the voices again in the wind. He didn't cry, though, he moved back toward anger instead. *Why was he allowed to live?* Cernan had said. None of them wanted him, not even Finn, who had gone away.

It was cold and he was hungry. On the thought, he flashed red and made himself into an owl. He flew for an hour and found three night rodents near the wood. He flew back to the cave. It was warmer as a bird and he fell asleep in that shape.

When the wind shifted he woke, because with the coming of the south wind the voices had ceased. They had been clear and alluring but now they stopped.

He had become Darien again while he slept. Stepping from the cave, he looked all around him at the melting snow. Later, in the morning light, he watched his mother leave, riding off with the lios and the man.

He tried to make himself into a bird again but he couldn't. He wasn't strong enough to do it so soon. He walked down the slope to the cottage. He went inside. She had left Finn's clothes and his own. He looked at the small things he had worn; then he put on some of Finn's clothing and went away.

# Chapter 13

"And so, in the middle of the banquet that night, Kevin walked out. Liane saw him on the street and she says"— Dave fought for control—" she says he was very sure, and that he looked . . . he looked . . ."

Paul turned his back on them all and walked to the window. They were in the Temple in Paras Derval: Jennifer's rooms. He had come to tell her about Darien. She had listened, remote and regal, virtually untouched. It had moved him almost to anger. But then they had heard sounds outside and people at the door, and Dave Martyniuk and Jaelle herself had come in and told them what had happened to make the winter end.

It was twilight. Outside the snow was nearly gone. No flooding, no dangerous rising of rivers or lakes. If the Goddess could do this, she could do it harmlessly. And she could do this thing because of the sacrifice. Liadon, the beloved son, who was . . . who was Kevin, of course.

There was a great difficulty in his throat, and his eyes were stinging. He wouldn't look back at the others. To himself and to the twilight he said:

> "Love do you remember
> My name? I was lost
> In summer turned winter
> Made bitter by frost.
> And when June comes December
> The heart pays the cost."

Kevin's own words from a year before. "Rachel's Song," he had called it. But now—now everything had been changed, the metaphor made achingly real. So completely so, he couldn't even grasp how such a thing could come to pass.

There was a great deal happening, much too fast, and Paul wasn't sure if he could move past it. He wasn't sure at all. His heart couldn't move so fast. *There will come a tomorrow when you weep for me,* Kevin had sung a year ago. He'd been singing of Rachel, for whom Paul had not yet cried. Singing of Rachel, not himself.

Even so.

It was very quiet behind him, and he wondered if they had gone. But then he heard Jaelle's voice. Cold, cold Priestess. But she wasn't now, it seemed. She said, "He could not have done this, not have been found worthy, had he not been traveling toward the Goddess all his life. I don't know if this is of aid to you, but I offer it as true."

He wiped his eyes and turned back. In time to see Jennifer, who had been composed to hear of Darien and tautly silent as Dave spoke, now rise at Jaelle's words, a white grief in her face, her mouth open, eyes blazing with naked pain, and Paul realized that if she was opening now to this, she was open to everything. He bitterly regretted his moment of anger. He took a step toward her, but even as he did, she made a choking sound and fled.

Dave stood to follow, awkward sorrow investing his square features. Someone in the hallway moved to block the way.

"Let her go," said Leila. "This was necessary."

"Oh, shut up!" Paul raged. An urge to strike this ever-present, ever-placid child rose fiercely within him.

"Leila," said Jaelle wearily, "close the door and go away." The girl did so.

Paul sank into a chair, uncaring, for once, that Jaelle should see him as less than strong. What did such things matter now? *They shall not grow old, as we that are left. . . .*

"Where's Loren?" he asked abruptly.

"In town," Dave said. "So's Teyrnon. There's a meeting in the palace tomorrow. It seems . . . it seems Kim and the others did find out what was causing the winter."

"What was it?" Paul asked tiredly.

"Metran," Jaelle said. "From Cader Sedat. Loren wants to go after him, to the island where Amairgen died."

He sighed. So much happening. His heart wasn't going to be able to keep up. *At the going down of the sun and in the morning . . .*

"Is Kim in the palace? Is she okay?" It suddenly seemed strange to him that she hadn't come here to Jennifer.

He read it in their faces before either of them spoke.

"No!" he exclaimed. "Not her too!"

"No, no, no," Dave rushed to say. "No, she's all right. She's just . . . not here." He turned helplessly to Jaelle.

Quietly, the High Priestess explained what Kimberly had said about the Giants, and then told him what the Seer had decided to do. He had to admire the control in Jaelle's voice, the cool lucidity. When she was done he said nothing. He couldn't think of anything to say. His mind didn't seem to be working very well.

Dave cleared his throat. "We should go," the big man said. Paul registered, for the first time, the bandage on his head. He should inquire, he knew, but he was so tired.

"Go ahead," Paul murmured. He wasn't quite sure if he could stand up, even if he wanted to. "I'll catch up."

Dave turned to leave but paused in the doorway. "I wish . . ." he began. He swallowed. "I wish a lot of things." He went out. Jaelle did not.

He didn't want to be alone with her. It was no time to have to cope with that. He would have to go, after all.

She said, "You asked me once if there could be a sharing of burdens between us and I said no." He looked up. "I am wiser now," she said, unsmiling, "and the burdens are heavier. I learned something a year ago from you, and from Kevin again two nights ago. Is it too late to say I was wrong?"

He wasn't ready for this, he hadn't been ready for any of what seemed to be happening. He was composed of grief and bitterness in equal measure. *As we that are left . . .*

"I'm so pleased we've been of use to you," he said. "You must try me on a better day." He saw her head snap back.

He pushed himself up and left the room so she would not see him weep.

In the domed place, as he passed, the priestesses were wailing a lament. He hardly heard. The voice in his mind was Kevin Laine's from a year ago in a lament of his own:

> *"The breaking of waves on a long shore,*
> *In the grey morning the slow fall of rain,*
> *Oh, love, remember, remember me."*

He walked out into the fading light. His eyes were misted, and he could not see that all along the Temple slope the green grass had returned and there were flowers.

Her dreams were myriad, and Kevin rode through all of them. Fair and witty, effortlessly clever, but not laughing. Not now. Kim saw his face as it must have been when he followed the dog to Dun Maura.

It seemed to her a heartbreaking thing that she could not remember the last words he had said to her. On the swift ride to Gwen Ystrat he had ridden up to tell her what Paul had done and of his own decision to let Brendel know about Darien. She had listened and approved; briefly smiled at his wry prediction of Paul's likely response.

She had been preoccupied, though, already moving in her mind toward the dark journey that lay ahead in Morvran. He must have sensed this, she realized later, for after a moment he'd touched her lightly on the arm, said something in a mild tone, and dropped back to rejoin Diarmuid's men.

It wouldn't have been anything consequential—a pleasantry, a gentle bit of teasing—but now he was gone and she hadn't heard the last thing he'd ever said to her.

She half woke from the hard dreams. She was in the King's House in Morvran. She couldn't possibly have stayed another night in the sanctuary. With Jaelle gone, with the armies returned to Paras Derval, the Temple was Audiart's again, and the triumph in the eyes of that woman was more than Kim could bear.

Of course they had won something. The snow was melting everywhere—in the morning it would be gone and she, too, would set forth, though not to Paras Derval. There had been a victory, a showing forth of Dana's power to balk the designs of the Dark. The power had been paid for, though, bought with blood, and more. There were red flowers growing everywhere. They were Kevin's, and he was gone.

Her window was open and the night breeze was fresh and mild with the promise of spring. A spring such as never before, burgeoning almost overnight. Not a gift, though. Bought and paid for, every flower, every blade of grass.

From the room next door she heard Gereint's breathing. It was slow and even, not ragged as before. He would be all right in the morning, which meant that Ivor, too, could depart. The Aven could ill afford to linger, for with the winter ending the Plain lay open again to the north.

Was everything the Goddess did double-edged? She knew the answer to that. Knew also that, this once, the question was unfair because they had so desperately needed this spring. She wasn't minded to be fair, though. Not yet. She turned over in bed and fell asleep, to dream again. But not of Kevin this time, though his flowers were there.

She was the Seer of Brennin, dreamer of the dream. For the second time in three nights she saw the vision that was sending her away from everyone she knew. It had come to her two nights ago, in Loren's bed, after a lovemaking they would each remember with gratitude. She had been inside this dream when Jaelle's voice, mourning the death of Liadon, had awakened them.

Now it came again, twisting, as such images always did, along the timeloops of the Tapestry. There was smoke from burning fires and half-seen figures beyond. There were caves, but not like Dun Maura: these were deep and wide, and high up in the mountains. Then the image blurred, time slipped through the lattice of her vision. She saw herself—this was later—and there were fresh lacerations scoring her face and arms. No blood, though, for some reason, no blood. A fire. A chanting all around. And then the Baelrath flamed and, as in the dream of Stonehenge, she was almost shattered by the pain she knew it would bring. Worse, even, this was. Something monstrous and unforgivable. So immense a blazing to so vast a consequence that even after all that had come to pass her mind cried out in the dream the racking question she thought had been left behind: *Who was she that she should do this thing?*

To which there was no answer. Only sunlight streaming in through the window and innumerable birds singing in the light of spring.

She rose up, though not immediately. The aching of her heart cut hard against the flourish of that dawn, and she had to wait for it to ease. She walked outside. Her companion was waiting, with both horses saddled and ready. She had been planning to go alone, at first, but the mages and Jaelle—united for once—had joined Aileron in forbidding this. They had wanted her to have a company of men, but this, in turn, she had refused. What she was doing had to do with repaying a debt and not really with the war, she told them. She hadn't told them the other thing.

She'd accepted one companion because, in part, she wasn't sure of the way. They'd had to be content with that. "I told you from the beginning," she'd said to Aileron. "I don't follow orders very well." No one had laughed or even smiled. Not surprisingly. She hadn't been smiling herself. Kevin was dead, and all the roads were parting. The Weaver alone knew if they would come together again.

And there was another parting now. Ivor's guard led out the blind shaman, Gereint, toward where the Aven waited with his wife and daughter. Liane, Kim saw, was red-eyed, still. So many smaller griefs there were within the larger ones.

Gereint, in his uncanny way, stopped right in front of her. She accepted the sightless touch of his mind. He was weak, she saw, but not finished yet.

"Not yet," he said aloud. "I'll be fine when I've had a haunch of eltor meat on the grass under the stars."

Impulsively, Kim stepped forward and kissed him on the cheek. "I wish I could join you," she said.

His bony hand gripped her shoulder. "I wish you could too, dreamer. I am glad to have stood with you before I died."

"We may do so again," she said.

He made no reply to that. Only gripped her shoulder more tightly and, stepping nearer, whispered, so only she could hear, "I saw the Circlet of Lisen last night, but not who was wearing it." The last phrase was almost an apology.

She drew a breath and said, "That was Ysanne's to see, and so it is mine. Go easy, Gereint, back to your Plain. You will have tasks enough waiting there. You cannot be everything to all of us."

"Nor can you," he said. "You shall have my thoughts."

And because of who he was, she said, "No. You won't want to share what I think I'm about to do. Send them west, Gereint. The war is Loren's now, and Matt's, I think. In the place where Amairgen died."

She let him reach into her, to see the twin shadows of her dream. "Oh, child," he murmured and, taking her two hands between his own, raised them to his lips and kissed them both. Then he walked away as if weighted by more than years.

Kim turned around to where her companion waited patiently. The grass was green, the birds sang everywhere. The sun was well above the Carnevon Range. She looked up, shielding her eyes against the light.

"Are we ready?" she asked.

"We are," said Brock of Banir Tal.

She mounted up and fell into stride beside his horse for the long ride to Khath Meigol.

*Traveling toward the Goddess all his life,* Jaelle had said of Kevin, and, alone of those in the room, Jennifer had truly understood. Not even the High Priestess could know how deeply true that was. Hearing the words, Jennifer felt suddenly as if every nerve within her had been stripped of its sheath and laid open.

All the nights, she saw now with terrible clarity. All the nights she had lain beside him after the arc of lovemaking was done, watching Kevin struggle to come back from so far. The one uncontrolled thing in him she had never understood, had feared. His was a descent, a downward spiral into passion, that her soul could not track. So many nights she'd lain awake, looking at the simplified beauty of his face as he slept.

She understood now, finally.

And so there was a last sleepless night for her shaped by Kevin Laine. She was awake when the birdsong began outside the Temple, and she had parted her curtains to watch the morning come. The breeze was fresh with the scents of spring, and there were leaves budding on all the trees. Colors, a great many colors in the world again, after the black branches and white snow of winter. There was green once more, so bright and alive it was stronger, at last, than the green unlight of Starkadh. As her eyes looked out on the spring, Jennifer's heart, which was Guinevere's, began to look out as well. Nor was this the least of Kevin's legacies.

There came a knocking at her door. She opened it to see Matt Sören with a walking stick in one hand and flowers in the other.

"It is spring," he said, "and these are the first flowers. Loren is meeting in the palace with a great many people. I thought you might come with me to Aideen's grave."

As they walked around the lower town and then struck a path to the west, she was remembering the story he had told her so long ago. Or not really as long as it seemed. The story of Nilsom, the mage who had turned evil, and of Aideen, his source, who had loved him: the only woman since Lisen to be source to a mage. It was Aideen who had saved Brennin, saved the Summer Tree, from Nilsom and the mad High King, Vailerth. She had refused to be source for her mage at the end. Had denied her strength to him and then killed herself.

Matt had told her the tale in the Great Hall at Paras Derval. Before she went riding and found the lios alfar. Before Galadan had, in turn, found her and given her to the swan.

Westward, they walked now, through the miracle of this spring, and everywhere Jennifer looked there was life returning to the land. She heard crickets, the drone of bees, saw a scarlet-winged bird take wing from an apple tree, and then a brown rabbit dart from a clump of shrubbery. She saw Matt drinking it in as well with his one eye, as if slaking a long thirst. In silence they walked amid the sounds of hope until, at the edge of the forest, Matt finally stopped.

Every year, he had told her, the Council of Mages would curse Nilsom at midwinter when they met. And every year, as well, they would curse Aideen—who had broken the profoundest law of their Order when she betrayed her mage—even though it had been to save Brennin from destruction, and the Tree that lay within this wood.

And every spring, Matt had said, he and Loren would bring the first flowers to this grave.

It was almost invisible. One had to know the place. A mound of earth, no stone, the trees at the edge of Mörnir-wood for shade. Sorrow and peace together came over Jennifer as she saw Matt kneel and lay his flowers on the mound.

Sorrow and peace, and then she saw that the Dwarf was weeping, and her own tears came at last from the heart that spring had unlocked. For Aideen she wept, and bright Kevin gone; for Darien she cried, and the choice he had to make; for Laesha and Drance, slain when she was taken; for all the living, too, faced with the terror of the Dark, faced with war and the hatred of Maugrim, born into the time of his return.

And finally, finally by Aideen's grave in Kevin's spring, she wept for herself and for Arthur.

It lasted a long time. Matt did not rise, nor did he look up until, at length, she stopped.

"There is heart's ease in this place," he said.

"Ease?" she said. A weary little laugh. "With so many tears between the two of us?"

"The only way, sometimes," he replied. "Do you not feel it, though?"

After a moment she smiled as she had not done for a very long time. He rose from near the grave. He looked at her and said, "You will leave the Temple now?"

She did not reply. Slowly the smile faded. She said, "Is this why you brought me here?"

222

His dark eye never wavered from her face, but there was a certain diffidence in his voice. "I know only a few things," said Matt Sören, "but these I know truly. I know that I have seen stars shining in the depths of the Warrior's eyes. I know that he is cursed, and not allowed to die. I know, because you told me, what was done to you. And I know, because I see it now, that you are not allowing yourself to live. Jennifer, of the two fates, it seems to me the worse."

Gravely, she regarded him, her golden hair stirred by the wind. She lifted a hand to push it back from her face. "Do you know," she said, so quietly he had to strain to hear, "how much grief there was when I was Guinevere?"

"I think I do. There is always grief. It is joy that is the rarest thing," said the onetime King of Dwarves.

To this she made no reply. It was a Queen of Sorrows who stood with him by the Godwood, and for all the earnest certitude of his words, Matt knew a moment of doubt. Almost to himself, for reassurance, he murmured, "There can be no hope for anything in a living death."

She heard. Her gaze came back to him. "Oh, Matt," she said. "Oh, Matt, for what should I hope? He has been cursed to this. I am the agent of the Weaver's will. For what should I hope?"

Her voice went to his heart like a blade. But the Dwarf drew himself up to his fullest height and said the thing he had brought her there to say, and there was no doubt in him for this.

"Never believe it!" Matt Sören cried. "We are not slaves to the Loom. Nor are you only Guinevere—you are Jennifer now, as well. You bring your own history to this hour, everything you have lived. You bring Kevin here within you, and you bring Rakoth, whom you survived. You are here, and whole, and each thing you have endured has made you stronger. It need not be now as it has been before!"

She heard him. She nodded slowly. She turned and walked with him back to Paras Derval through the profligate bestowing of that morning. He was not wrong, for the Dwarves were wise in such things.

Nevertheless.

Nevertheless, even as they walked, her mind was turning back to another morning in another spring. Almost as bright as this, though not so long awaited.

There had been cherry trees in blossom all around when she had stood by Arthur's side to see Lancelot first ride into Camelot.

Hidden among the trees on the slopes north of them, a figure watched their return as he had watched them walking to the grave. He was lonely, and minded to go down to them, but he didn't know who they were and, since Cernan's words, he was deeply mistrustful of everyone. He stayed where he was.

Darien thought the woman was very beautiful, though.

"He is still there," said Loren, "and he still has the Cauldron. It may take him time to put it to another use, but if we give him that time, he will. Aileron, unless you forbid me, I will leave to take ship from Taerlindel in the morning."

Tense sound rippled through the Council Chamber. Paul saw the High King's brow knitted with concern. Slowly, Aileron shook his head. "Loren," he said, "everything you say is true, and the gods know how dearly I want Metran dead. But how can I send you to Cader Sedat when we don't even know how to find it?"

"Let me sail," the mage said stonily. "I will find it."

"Loren, we don't even know if Amairgen did. All we know is that he died!"

"He was sourceless," Loren replied. "Lisen stayed behind. He had his knowledge but not his power. I am less wise, far, but Matt will be with me."

"Silvercloak, there were other mages on Amairgen's ship. Three of them, with their sources. None came back." It was Jaelle, Paul saw. She glittered that morning, more coldly formidable than ever before. If there was an ascendency that day, it was hers, for Dana had acted and the winter was over.

224

They were not going to be allowed to forget it. Even so, he felt sorry for his last words yesterday evening. Hers had been a gesture unlikely to be repeated.

"It is true," Aileron was saying. "Loren, how can I let you go? Where will we be if you die? Lisen saw a death ship from her tower—what mariner could I ask to sail another?"

"This one." They all turned to the door in astonishment. Coll took two steps forward from his post beside Shain and said clearly, "The High King will know I am from Taerlindel. Before Prince Diarmuid took me from that place to serve in his company, I had spent all my life at sea. If Loren wants a mariner, I will be his man, and my mother's father has a ship I built with him. It will take us there with fifty men."

There was a silence. Into which there dropped, like a stone in a pool, the voice of Arthur Pendragon.

"Has your ship a name?" he asked.

Coll flushed suddenly, as if conscious for the first time of where he was. "None that will mean anything," he stammered. "It is a name in no language I know, but my mother's father said it was a ship's name in his family far back. We called it *Prydwen*, my lord."

Arthur's face went very still. Slowly the Warrior nodded, then he turned from Coll to Aileron. "My lord High King," he said, "I have kept my peace for fear of intruding myself between you and your First Mage. I can tell you, though, that if your concern is only for finding Cader Sedat—we called it Caer Sidi once, and Caer Rigor, but it is the same place—I have been there and know where it is. This may be why I was brought to you."

"What is it, then?" asked Shalhassan of Cathal. "What is Cader Sedat?"

"A place of death," said Arthur. "But you knew that much already."

It was very quiet in the room.

"It will be guarded," Aileron said. "There will be death waiting at sea, as well."

*Thought, Memory.* Paul rose. "There will be," he said as

they turned to look at him. "But I think I can deal with that."

It didn't take very long, after that. With a sense of grim purpose, the company followed Aileron and Shalhassan from the room when the council ended.

Paul waited by the doorway. Brendel walked past with a worried expression but did not stop. Dave, too, looked at him as he went out with Levon and Torc.

"We'll talk later," Paul said. Dave would be going north to the Dalrei, he knew. If there was war while *Prydwen* sailed, it would surely begin on the Plain.

Niavin of Seresh and Mabon of Rhoden went by, deep in talk, and then Jaelle walked out, head held very high, and would not meet his glance—all ice again, now that spring had returned. It wasn't for her that he was waiting, though. Eventually the room had emptied, save for one man.

He and Arthur looked at each other. "I have a question," said Paul. The Warrior lifted his head. "When you were there last, how many of you survived?"

"Seven," said Arthur softly. "Only seven."

Paul nodded. It was as if he remembered this. One of the ravens had spoken. Arthur came up to him.

"Between us?" he said, in the deep voice.

"Between us," said Paul. Together they walked from the Council Chamber and down the corridors. There were pages and soldiers running past them in all directions now—the palace was aflame with war fever. They were quiet, though, the two of them, as they walked in stride through the turmoil.

Outside Arthur's room they stopped. Paul said, very low so it would not be overheard, "You said this might be what you were summoned for. A while ago you said you never saw the end of things." He left it at that.

For a long moment Arthur was silent, then he nodded once. "It is a place of death," he said for the second time and, after a hesitation, added, "It would not displease me as events have gone."

Paul opened his mouth to say something, then thought

better of it. He turned, instead, and walked down the corridor to where his own room was. His and Kevin's, until two days ago. Behind him, he heard Arthur opening his door.

Jennifer saw the door open, had time to draw a breath, and then he was in the room, bringing with him all the summer stars.

"Oh, my love," she said and her voice broke, after all. "I need you to forgive me for so much. I am afraid—"

She had space for nothing more. A deep sound came from within his chest, and in three strides Arthur was across the room and on his knees, his head buried in the folds of the dress she wore, and over and over again he was saying her name.

Her hands were cradling him to her, running through his hair, the grey amid the brown. She tried to speak, could not. Could scarcely breathe. She lifted his face that she might look at him and saw the tears of bitter longing pouring down. "Oh, my love," she gasped and, lowering her head, she tried to kiss them all away. She found his mouth with her own, blindly, as if they were both blind and lost without the other. She was trembling as with fever. She could hardly stand. He rose and gathered her to him and, after so long, her head was on his chest again, and she could feel his arms around her and could hear the strong beat of his heart, which had been her home.

"Oh, Guinevere," she heard him say after a space of time. "My need is great."

"And mine," she replied, feeling the last dark webs of Starkadh tear asunder so that she stood open to desire. "Oh, please," she said. "Oh, please, my love." And he took her to his bed, across which a slant of sunlight fell, and they rose above their doom for part of an afternoon.

After, he told her where it was he had to go and she felt all the griefs of the worlds return to rest in her. She was clear, though; she had spun free from Rakoth, and she was stronger for every single thing she had survived, as Matt had said. She rose up and stood in the sunlight of the room, clad only in her hair, and said, "You must come back to me. What I told you before is true: there is no Lancelot here. It has changed, Arthur. Only the two of us are here now, only us."

In the slant of sun she watched the stars sliding through his eyes. The summer stars, whence he had come. Slowly he shook his head, and she ached for his age and his weariness.

"It cannot be so," he said. "I killed the children, Guinevere."

She could find nothing at all to say. In the silence she could almost hear the patient, inexorable shuttling of the Loom.

Saddest story of all the long tales told.

# Chapter 14

In the morning came Arthur and Guinevere together out of Paras Derval to the great square before the palace gates. Two companies were gathered there, one to ride north, the other west to the sea, and there was not a heart among all those assembled that did not lift to see the two of them together.

Dave Martyniuk, waiting behind Levon for the signal to ride, looked past the five hundred men Aileron had given them to lead to the Plain, and he gazed at Jennifer with a memory flaring in his mind.

The very first evening: when Loren had told the five of them who he really was, and Dave, disbelieving and hostile, had stormed toward the door. To be stopped by Jennifer saying his name. And then, as he had turned, by a majesty he saw in her face. He could not have named it then, nor did he have words for it now, but he saw the same thing in her this morning and it was not transitory or ephemeral.

She left Arthur's side and walked, clad in a gown green as her eyes, green as the grass, to where he stood. Something of irresolution must have showed in his face, because as she came near he heard her laugh and say, "If you so much as start to bow or anything like that, Dave, I'll beat you up. I swear I will."

It was good to hear her laugh. He checked the bow he had, in fact, been about to offer and, instead, surprised them both by bending to kiss her cheek.

"Thank you," she said and took his hand in hers.

He smiled down on her and, for once, didn't feel awkward or uncouth.

Paul Schafer came up to join them, and with her other hand Jennifer claimed one of his. The three of them stood, linked so, for a moment.

"Well," said Dave.

Paul looked soberly at him. "You're going right into it, you know."

"I know," Dave replied. "But if I have a place in this, I think it's with the Dalrei. It . . . won't be any easier where you're heading." They were silent amid the bustle and clatter of the square. Then Dave turned to Jennifer. "I've been thinking about something," he said. "Way back, when Kim took you out of . . . that place, Kevin did something. You won't remember, you were unconscious then, but he swore vengeance for what had been done to you."

"I remember," said Paul.

"Well," Dave went on, "he must have wondered how he would ever do it, but . . . I'm thinking that he found a way."

There was sunshine pouring down from a sky laced with scattered billows of clouds. Men in shirt sleeves walked all around them.

"He did more," said Jennifer, her eyes bright. "He got me all the way out. He finished what Kim started."

"Damn," said Paul gently. "I thought it was my charm." Remembered words, not his own.

Tears, laughter, and they parted.

Sharra watched the Aven's handsome son lead five hundred men away to the north. Standing with her father near the chariots, she saw Jennifer and Paul walk back to join the company that would soon be riding west. Shalhassan was going with them as far as Seresh. With the snow melted, there was urgent need now for his additional troops and he wanted to give his own orders in Cynan.

Aileron was already up on his black horse, and she saw Loren the mage mount up as well. Her heart was beating very fast.

Diarmuid had come to her again last night by way of her window. He had brought her a flower. She had not thrown water at him, this time, and had been at pains to point that out. He professed gratitude and later, in a different voice, a great deal more.

Then he had said, "I am going to a difficult place, my dear. To do a difficult thing. It may be wiser if I speak to your father if we . . . after we return. I would not have you bound to me while I am—"

She had covered his mouth with her hand and then, turning in bed as if to kiss him, moved the hand away and bit his lower lip instead.

"Coward!" she said. "I *knew* you were afraid. You promised me a formal wooing and I am holding you to it."

"Formal it is, then," he said. "You want an Intercedent, as well?"

"Of course!" she said. And then, because she was crying, and couldn't pretend any more, she said, "I was bound to you from Larai Rigal, Diar."

He kissed her, gently and then with passion, and then his mouth began to travel her and eventually she lost track of time and place.

"Formally," he'd said again, afterward. In a certain tone.

And now, in the morning light, amid the busy square, a figure suddenly pushed through the gathered crowd and began a purposeful walk toward her father. Sharra felt herself going red. She closed her eyes for a moment, wishing desperately that she had bit him harder, much, much harder. And in a different place. Then, in spite of herself, she began to giggle.

Formally, he had promised. Even to the Interceder who was to speak for him, after the old fashion. He had also warned her in Gwen Ystrat that he would never move to the measured gait, he would always have to play.

And so Tegid of Rhoden was his Intercedent.

The fat man—he was truly enormous—was blessedly sober. He had even trimmed his eccentric beard and donned a decent outfit in russet tones for his august mission. His round red face very serious, Tegid stopped directly in front

*231*

of her father. His progress had been noted and marked by shouts and laughter. Now Tegid waited patiently for a modicum of silence. He absentmindedly scratched his behind, then remembered where he was and crossed his arms quickly on his chest.

Shalhassan regarded him with a mild, expressionless curiosity. Which became a wince a moment later as Tegid boomed out his title.

"Supreme Lord of Cathal," Tegid repeated, a little more softly, for his mighty lungs had shaped a silence all around with that first shout, "have I your attendant ear?"

"You have," her father said with grave courtesy.

"Then I am bid to tell you that I am sent here by a lord of infinite nobility, whose virtues I could number until the moon rose and set and rose again. I am sent to say to you, in this place and among the people here gathered in concourse, that the sun rises in your daughter's eyes."

There was a roar of astonishment.

"And who," asked Shalhassan, still courteously, "is the lord of infinite nobility?"

"A figure of speech, that," said Diarmuid, emerging from the crowd to their left. "And the moon business was his own idea. But he *is* my Intercedent and the heart of his message is true, and from my own heart. I would wed your daughter, Shalhassan."

The noise in the square was quite uncontrollable now. It was hard to hear anything. Sharra saw her father turn slowly to her, a question in his eyes, and something else that it took her a moment to recognize as tenderness.

She nodded once. And with her lips shaped a "Yes," for him to see.

The noise peaked and then slowly faded as Shalhassan waited beside his chariot, grave and unmoving. He looked at Diarmuid, whose own expression was sober now. He looked back at her.

He smiled. He *smiled*.

"Praise be to the Weaver and all the gods!" said Shalhassan of Cathal. "Finally she's done something adult!" And striding forward, he embraced Diarmuid as a son, in the manner of the ritual.

So it was amid laughter and joy that that company set forth to ride to Taerlindel, where a ship lay waiting to bear fifty men to a place of death.

Diarmuid's men, of course. It hadn't even been a subject of discussion. It had been assumed, automatic. If Coll was sailing the ship, then Diarmuid was commanding it and the men of South Keep were going to Cader Sedat.

Riding alone near the back of the party, Paul saw them, laughing and lighthearted, singing, even, at the promise of action. He looked at Coll and red Averren, the lieutenants; at Carde and greying Rothe and lean, agile Erron; at the other forty the Prince had named. He wondered if they knew what they were going to; he wondered if he knew, himself.

Up at the front, Diarmuid glanced back to check on the company, and Paul met his blue gaze for a moment. He didn't move forward, though, and Diarmuid didn't drop back. Kevin's absence was a hollow place within his chest. He felt quite alone. Thinking of Kim, far away and riding east, made it even worse.

Shalhassan left them in the afternoon at Seresh. He would be ferried across to Cynan, almost immediately. The mild, beneficent sunshine was a constant reminder of the need for haste.

They turned north on the highway to Rhoden. A number of people were coming to see them off: Aileron, of course, and Na-Brendel of Daniloth. Sharra was coming as well; she would return to Paras Derval with Aileron and wait for her father there. Teyrnon and Barak, he saw, were deep in conversation with Loren and Matt. Only the latter two were sailing; the younger mage would stay with the King. They were spreading themselves very thin, Paul thought.

They didn't really have much choice.

Not far ahead he saw Tegid bouncing along in one of the Cathalian war chariots, and for a moment he smiled at the sight. Shalhassan had proved human, after all, and he had a sense of humor. Beyond the fat man rode Jaelle, also alone. He thought briefly of catching up to her. He didn't, though—he had too much to think about without trying to apologize to the Priestess. He could guess how she'd respond. A bit of a surprise, her coming, though: the provinces of Dana came to an end at the sea.

Which led him to thoughts of whose provinces began and of his statement to the Council the morning before. "I think I can deal with that," he'd said, in the quiet tones of the Twiceborn. Quiet, yes, but very, very rash. And they would be counting on him now.

Reflecting this, his features carefully unrevealing, Paul saw that they were turning west again, off the highway onto a smaller road. They had had the rich grainlands of the Seresh hinterland on their right until now, but, as they turned, the land began to drop slowly down in unfolding ridges. He saw sheep and goats and another grazing animal he couldn't recognize and then, before he saw it, he heard the sea.

They came to Taerlindel late in the day and the sun had led them there. It was out over the sea. The breeze was salt and fresh and the tide was in, the white-capped waves rolling up to the line of sandy beaches stretching away to the south toward Seresh and the Saeren mouth.

In front of them lay the harbor of Taerlindel, northward facing, sheltered by a promontory from the wind and surf. There were small fishing boats bobbing at anchor, a few larger ones, and one ship, painted gold and red, that would be *Prydwen*.

Once, Loren had told him, a fleet had anchored here. But the last war with Cathal had decimated the navies of both countries, and after the truce no ships had been built to replace them. And with Andarien a wasteland for a thousand years there was no longer any need, the mage had explained, to sail to Linden Bay.

A number of houses ringed the harbor and a few more ran back away from the sea into the sloping hills. The town was very beautiful in the late afternoon light. He only gave it a brief glance, though, before he stopped his horse to let the last of the party pass him by. On the road above Taerlindel his gaze went out, as far as it might, over the grey-green sea.

They had let the light flare again from Atronel the past three nights, to celebrate and honor the spring returned. Now, toward evening of this fourth day, Leyse of the Swan Mark walked, in white for the white swan, Lauriel, beside the luminous figure of Ra-Tenniel, and they were alone by Celyn Lake gathering sylvain, red and silver.

Within the woven shadows of Daniloth, shadows that twisted time into channels unknown for all save the lios, it had never been winter. Lathen Mistweaver's mighty spell had been proof against the cold. For too long, though, had the lios gazed out from the shifting, blurred borders of the Shadowland to see snow sweeping across the Plain and the barren desolation of Andarien. A lonely, vulnerable island of muted color had they been, in a world of white malevolence.

No longer. Ever bold, Ra-Tenniel took the long, slim hand of Leyse—and, for once, she let him do so—and led her past the muting of Lathen's shadows, out into the open spaces where the river ran into Celyn Lake.

In the sunset it was a place of enchantment and serenity. There were willows growing by the riverbank and aum trees in early leaf. In the young grass he spread his cloak, green as a vellin stone, and she sat down with him upon it, her arms full of sylvain. Her eyes were a soft gold like the setting sun, her hair burnished bronze by its rays.

He looked from her to the sun, to the aum tree overhead, and the gentle flow of the river below them. Never far from sadness, in the way of the lios, he lifted his voice in a lament, amid the evening drone of bees and the liquescent splash of water over stone, for the ravaging of Andarien a thousand years ago.

Gravely she listened, laden with flowers, as he sang the long ballad of long-ago grief. The sun went down. In the twilight a light breeze stirred the leaves over their heads when, at length, he ended. In the west, above the place where the sun had set, gleamed a single star, the one named long ago for Lauriel, slain by black Avaia at the Bael Rangat. For a long time they watched it; then they turned to go, back into the Shadowland from where the stars were dim.

One glance Ra-Tenniel threw back over his shoulder at Andarien. And then he stopped and turned, and he looked again with the long sight of the lios alfar.

Ever, from the beginning, had the impatience of his hate marked Rakoth's designs. The winter now past had been a departure, terrifying in its implications of purposed, unhurried destruction.

But the winter was over now and, looking north with eyes whose color shifted swiftly through to violet, Ra-Tenniel, Lord of the lios alfar, saw a dark horde moving through the ruin of Andarien. Not toward them, though. Even as Leyse turned to watch with him, the army of Rakoth swung eastward. Eastward, around Celyn, to come down through Gwynir.

And to the Plain.

Had he waited until dark, Rakoth might have sent them forth quite unseen for a full night's riding. He had not waited, and Ra-Tenniel offered a quick prayer. Swiftly he and Leyse returned to Atronel. They did not send their light on high that night, not with an army of the Dark abroad in the land. Instead they gathered together all the high ones of the Marks on the mound at Atronel. As the King had expected, it was fierce Galen who said at once that she would ride to Celidon. Again, as expected, Lydan, however cautious he might be, would not let his twin ride alone. They rose to go when Ra-Tenniel gave leave. He raised a hand to stop them, though.

"You will have to make speed," he said. "Very great speed. Take the raithen. It is time the golden and silver horses of Daniloth were seen again in Fionavar." Galen's eyes went blue, and a moment later so did those of her brother. Then they left to ride.

With the aid of those who remained, Ra-Tenniel made the summonglass come to urgent warning so that the glass in the High King's chambers in Paras Derval might leap to life as well.

It was not their fault that the High King was in Taerlindel that night and would not return to word of the summonglass afire until the afternoon of the following day.

He couldn't sleep. Very late at night Paul rose up and walked from Coll's mother's house down to the harbor. The moon, falling from full, was high. It laid a silver track along the sea. The tide was going out and the sand ran a long way toward the promontory. The wind had shifted around to the north. It was cool, he knew, but he still seemed to be immune to the cold, natural or unnatural. It was one of the few things that marked what he was. That, and the ravens, and the tacit, waiting presence in his pulse.

*Prydwen* rode easily at anchor. They had loaded her up in the last light of evening and Coll's grandfather had pronounced her ready to sail. In the moonlight the gold paint on her hull looked silver and the furled white sails gleamed.

It was very quiet. He walked back along the wooden dock and, other than the soft slap of the sea against the boats, his boots made the only sound. There were no lights shining in Taerlindel. Overhead the stars seemed very bright, even in the moonlight.

Leaving the harbor, he walked along the stone jetty until it ended. He passed the last house of the town. There was a track that curved up and east for a way, following the indentation of the bay. It was bright enough to follow and he did. After two hundred paces or so the track crested and then started down and north, and in a little while he came to sand again and a long beach open to the sea.

The surge and sigh of the waves was louder here. Almost, he heard something in them, but almost wouldn't be enough. He took off his boots and stockings and, leaving them on the sand, went forward. The sand was wet where the tide had washed back. The waves glowed a phosphorescent silver. He felt the ocean wash over his feet. It would be cold, he knew, but he didn't feel it. He went a little farther out and then stopped, ankle deep only, to be present but not to presume. He stood very still, trying, though not knowing how, even now, to marshal whatever he was. He listened. Heard nothing but the low sound of the sea.

And then, within himself, he felt a surging in his blood. He wet his lips. He waited; it came again. The third time he thought he had the rhythm, which was not that of the sea because it did not come from the sea. He looked up at the stars but not back at the land. *Mörnir*, he prayed.

"Liranan!" he cried as the fourth surge came and he heard the crash of thunder in his own voice.

With the fifth surge, he cried the name again, and a last time when the sixth pulse roared within him. At the seventh surging of his blood, though, Paul was silent and he waited.

Far out at sea he saw a white wave cresting higher than any of the others that were running in to meet the tide. When it met the long retreating surf, when it crashed, high and glittering, he heard a voice cry, "Catch me if you can!" and in his mind he dove after the god of the sea.

It was not dark or cold. Lights seemed everywhere, palely hued—it was as if he moved amid constellations of sunken stars.

Something flashed: a silver fish. He followed and it doubled back to lose him. He cut back as well, between the water stars. There was coral below, green and blue, pink, orange, shades of gold. The silver fish slipped under an arch of it, and when Paul came through, it was gone.

He waited. Felt another pulse.

"Liranan!" he called and felt thunder rock the deep. When the echoes rolled away he saw the fish again, larger now, with rainbow colors of the coral stippling its sides. It fled and he followed.

Down it went and he with it. They plunged past massive, lurking menaces in the lower depths where the sea stars were dim and colors lost.

Up it shot as if hurtling back to light. Past the sunken stars it went and broke water in a moonlit leap; from the beach, ankle deep in the tide, Paul saw it flash and fall.

And then it ran. No twisting now. On a straight course out to sea, the sea god fled the thunder voice. And was followed. They went so far beyond the memory of land that Paul thought he heard a thread of singing in the waves. He was afraid, for he guessed what he was hearing. He did not call again. He saw the silver fish ahead of him. He thought of all the dead and the living in their need, and he caught Liranan far out at sea and touched him with a finger of his mind.

"Caught you!" he said aloud, breathless on the beach where he had not moved at all. "Come," he gasped, "and let me speak with you, brother mine."

And then the god took his true form, and he rose up in the silvered sea and strode, shimmering with falling water, to the beach. As he came near, Paul saw that the falling water was as a robe to Liranan, to clothe his majesty, and the colors of the sea stars and the coral fell through it ceaselessly.

"You have named me as a brother," said the god in a voice that hissed like waves through and over rocks. His beard was long and white. His eyes were the same color as the moon. He said, "How do you so presume? Name yourself!"

"You know my name," said Paul. The inner surge had died away. He spoke in his own voice. "You know my name, Sealord, else you would not have come to my call."

"Not so. I heard my father's voice. Now I do not. Who are you who can speak with the thunder of Mörnir?"

And Paul stepped forward with the retreating tide, and he looked full into the face of the sea god, and he said, "I am Pwyll Twiceborn, Lord of the Summer Tree," and Liranan made the sea waves to crash around them both.

"I had heard tell of this," the sea god said. "Now I understand." He was very tall. It was hard to discern if the sliding waters of his robe were falling into the sea about his feet, or rising from the sea, or the both at once. He was beautiful, and terrible, and stern. "What would you, then?" he said.

And Paul replied, "We sail for Cader Sedat in the morning."

A sound came from the god like a wave striking a high rock. Then he was silent, looking down at Paul in the bright moonlight. After a long time he said, "It is a guarded place, brother." There was a thread of sorrow in his voice. Paul had heard it in the sea before.

He said, "Can the guarding prevail over you?"

"I do not know," said Liranan. "But I am barred from acting on the Tapestry. All the gods are. Twiceborn, you must know that this is so."

"Not if you are summoned."

There was silence again, save for the endless murmur of the tide washing out and the waves.

"You are in Brennin now," said the god, "and near to the wood of your power. You will be far out at sea then, mortal brother. How will you compel me?"

Paul said, "We have no choice but to sail. The Cauldron of Khath Meigol is at Cader Sedat."

"You cannot bind a god in his own element, Twiceborn." The voice was proud but not cold. Almost sorrowful.

Paul moved his hands in a gesture Kevin Laine would have known. "I will have to try," he said.

A moment longer Liranan regarded him, then he said something very low. It mingled with the sigh of the waves and Paul could not hear what the god had said. Before he could ask, Liranan had raised an arm, the colors weaving in his water robe. He spread his fingers out over Paul's head and then was gone.

Paul felt a sprinkling of sea spray in his face and hair; then, looking down, he saw that he was barefoot on the sand, no longer in the sea. Time had passed. The moon was low now, over in the west. Along its silver track he saw a silver fish break water once and go down to swim between the sea stars and the colors of the coral.

When he turned to go back he stumbled, and only then did he realize how tired he was. The sand seemed to go on for a long way. Twice he almost fell. After the second time he stopped and stood breathing deeply for a time without moving. He felt lightheaded, as if he had been breathing air too rich. He had a distant recollection of the song he had heard far out at sea.

He shook his head and walked back to where he'd left his boots. He knelt down to put them on but then sat on the sand, his arms resting on his knees, his head lowered between them. The song was slowly fading and he could feel his breathing gradually coming back to normal, though not his strength.

He saw a shadow fall alongside his own on the sand.

Without looking up, he said acidly, "You must enjoy seeing me like this. You seem to cultivate the opportunities."

"You are shivering," Jaelle said matter-of-factly. He felt her cloak settle over his shoulders. It bore the scent of her.

"I'm not cold," he said. But, looking at his hands, he saw that they were trembling.

She moved from beside him and he looked up at her. There was a circlet on her brow, holding her hair back in the wind. The moon touched her cheekbones, but the green eyes were shadowed. She said, "I saw the two of you in a light that did not come from the moon. Pwyll, whatever else you are, you are mortal, and that was not a shining wherein we can live."

He said nothing.

After a moment she went on. "You told me long ago, when I took you from the Tree, that we were human before we were anything else."

He roused himself and looked up again. "You said I was wrong."

"You were, then."

In the stillness the waves seemed very far away, but they did not cease. He said, "I was going to apologize to you on the way here. You seem to always catch me at a hard time."

"Oh, Pwyll. How could there be an easy time?" She sounded older, suddenly. He listened for mockery and heard none.

"I don't know," he admitted. And then, "Jaelle, if we don't come back from this voyage, you had better tell Aileron and Teyrnon about Darien. Jennifer won't want to, but I don't see that you'll have any choice. They'll have to be prepared for him."

She moved a little, and now he could see her eyes. She had given him her cloak and so was clad only in a long sleeping gown. The wind blew from off the sea. He rose and placed the cloak over her shoulders and did up the clasp at her throat.

Looking at her, at her fierce beauty rendered so grave by what she had seen, he remembered something and, aware that she had access to knowledge of her own, he asked, "Jaelle, when do the lios hear their song?"

"When they are ready to sail," she replied. "Usually it is weariness that leads them away."

Behind him he could still hear the slow withdrawing of the tide. "What do they do?"

"Build a ship in Daniloth and set sail west at night."

"Where? An island?"

She shook her head. "It is not in Fionavar. When one of the lios alfar sails far enough to the west, he crosses to another world. One shaped by the Weaver for them alone. For what purpose, I know not, nor, I believe, do they."

Paul was silent.

"Why do you ask?" she said.

He hesitated. The old mistrust, from the first time ever they spoke together, when she had taken him down from the Tree. After a moment, though, meeting her gaze, he said, "I heard a song just now, far out at sea where I chased the god."

She closed her eyes. Moonlight made a marble statue of her, pale and austere. She said, "Dana has no sway at sea. I know not what this might mean." She opened her eyes again.

"Nor I," he said.

"Pwyll," she asked, "can this be done? Can you get to Cader Sedat?"

"I'm not sure," he said truthfully. "Or even if we can do anything if we do get there. I know Loren is right, though. We have to try."

"You know I would come if I could—"

"I do know," Paul said. "You will have enough, and more, to deal with here. Pity the ones like Jennifer and Sharra, who can only wait and love, and hope that that counts for something beyond pain."

She opened her mouth as if to speak, but changed her mind and was silent. Unbidden, the words of a ballad came to him and, almost under his breath, he offered them to the night breeze and the sea:

> *"What is a woman that you forsake her,*
> *And the hearth-fire and the home-acre,*
> *To go with the old grey Widow-maker?"*

"Weaver forfend," Jaelle said, and turned away.

He followed her along the narrow track to Taerlindel. On their right, as they went, the moon sank into the sea and they came back into a town lit only by the stars.

When the sun rose, the company made ready to set sail in *Prydwen.* Aileron the High King went aboard and bade farewell to his First Mage, to Paul Schafer and Arthur Pendragon, to the men of South Keep who would man that ship, and to Coll of Taerlindel who would sail her.

Last of all he faced his brother. With grave eyes they looked at each other: Aileron's so brown they were almost black, Diarmuid's bluer than the sky overhead.

Watching from the dock, unmindful of her tears, Sharra saw Diarmuid speak and then nod his head. Then she saw him move forward and kiss his brother on the cheek. A moment later Aileron spun about and came down the ramp. There was no expression at all in his face. She hated him a little.

*Prydwen's* sails were unfurled and they filled. The ramp was drawn up. The wind blew from the south and east: they could run with it.

Na-Brendel of Daniloth stood beside the High King and his guard. There were three women there as well, watching as the ship cast loose and began to slip away. One woman was a Princess, one a High Priestess; beside them, though, stood one who had been a Queen, and Brendel could not look away from her.

Jennifer's eyes were clear and bright as she gazed after the ship and at the man who stood in its stern gazing back at her. Strength and pride she was sending out to him, Brendel knew, and he watched her stand thus until *Prydwen* was a white dot only at the place where sea and sky came together.

Only then did she turn to the High King, only then did sorrow come back into her face. And something more than that.

"Can you spare a guard for me?" she said. "I would go to Lisen's Tower."

There was compassion in Aileron's eyes as if he, too, had heard what Brendel heard: the circles of time coming around again, a pattern shaping on the Loom.

"Oh, my dear," said Jaelle in a strange voice.

"The Anor Lisen has stood empty a thousand years," Aileron said gently. "Pendaran is not a place where we may safely go."

"They will not harm me there," Jennifer said with calm certitude. "Someone should watch for them from that place."

He had been meaning to go home to Daniloth. It had been too long since he had trod the mound of Atronel.

"I will take you there and stay with you," Brendel said, shouldering a different destiny.

# Chapter 15

Over and above everything else, Ivor thought, there were Tabor and Gereint.

The Aven was riding a wide circle about the gathered camps. He had returned from Gwen Ystrat the evening before. Two slow days' riding it had been, but Gereint had not been able to sustain a faster pace.

Today was his first chance to inspect the camps, and he was guardedly pleased with this one thing at least. Pending a report from Levon—expected back that night—as to the Council's decision in Paras Derval, Ivor's own plan was to leave the women and children with a guard in the sheltered curve of land east of the Latham. The eltor were already starting north, but enough would linger to ensure sufficient hunting.

The rest of the Dalrei he proposed to lead north very soon, to take up a position by the Adein River. When the High King and Shalhassan of Cathal joined them, the combined forces might venture farther north. The Dalrei alone could not. But neither could they wait here, for Maugrim might well come down very soon and Ivor had no intention of yielding Celidon while he lived. Unless there was a massive attack, he thought, they could hold the line of the Adein alone.

He reached the northernmost of the camps and waved a greeting to Tulger of the eighth tribe, his friend. He didn't slow to talk, though; he had things to think about.

Tabor and Gereint.

He had looked closely at his younger son yesterday on

their return. Tabor had smiled and hugged him and said everything he ought to say. Even allowing for the long winter he was unnaturally pale, his skin so white it was almost translucent. The Aven had tried to tell himself that it was his usual oversensitivity to his children that was misleading him, but then, at night in bed, Leith had told him she was worried and Ivor's heart had skipped a beat.

His wife would have sooner bitten off her tongue than trouble him in such a way, without cause.

So this morning, early, he'd gone walking along the river with his younger son in the freshness of the spring, over the green grass of their Plain. The Latham ice had melted in a night. The river ran, sparkling and cold, out of the mountains; it was a bright blue in the sunlight. Ivor had felt his spirits lift, in spite of all his cares, just to see and be a part of this returning life.

"Father," Tabor had said before Ivor had even asked him anything, "I can't do anything about it."

Ivor's momentary pleasure had sluiced away. He'd turned to the boy. Fifteen, Tabor was. No more than that, and he was small-boned and so pale, now, he looked even younger. Ivor said nothing. He waited.

Tabor said, "She carries me with her. When we fly, and especially this last time, when we killed. It is different in the sky, Father. I don't know how many times I can come back."

"You must try not to ride her, then," Ivor had said painfully. He was remembering the night at the edge of Pendaran Wood, when he watched Tabor and the winged creature of his dreaming wheel between the stars and the Plain.

"I know," Tabor had said by the river. "But we are at war, Father. How can I not ride?"

Gruffly, Ivor had said, "We are at war and I am Aven of the Dalrei. You are one of the Riders I command. You must let me decide how best to use such strength as we have."

"Yes, Father," Tabor had said.

*Double-edged,* Ivor thought now, looping back south along the western bank of the Latham toward where Cullion's fourth tribe was quartered. Every gift the Goddess gave was double-edged. He tried, not very successfully, not to feel bitter about it. The glorious winged creature with its shining silver horn was as mighty a weapon of war as anything they had, and the price of using it, he now saw, was going to be losing his youngest child.

Cullion, sharp-faced and soft-eyed, came riding out to intercept him, and Ivor was forced to stop and wait. Cullion was young to be Chieftain of a tribe but he was steady and alert, and Ivor trusted him more than most of them.

"Aven," Cullion said now without preamble, "when do we leave? Should I order a hunt or not?"

"Hold off for today," the Aven said. "Cechtar did well yesterday. Come down to us if you need a few eltor."

"I will. And what about—"

"An auberei should reach you soon. There's a Council tonight in our camp. I've left it until late because I'm hoping Levon will be back with news from Paras Derval."

"Good. Aven, I've been pushing my shaman since the snow started melting—"

"Don't push him," Ivor said automatically.

"—but he's offered nothing at all. What about Gereint?"

"Nothing," said Ivor and rode on.

He had not been young when they blinded him. He had been next in line, waiting at Celidon for years, before word had come with the auberei that Colynas, shaman to Banor and the third tribe, was dead.

He was old now, and the blinding had been a long time ago, but he remembered it with utter clarity. Nor was that surprising: the torches and the stars and the circling men of Banor's tribe were the last things Gereint had ever seen.

It had been a rich life, he thought; more full than he could have dreamed. If it had ended before Rangat had gone up in fire, he would have said he'd lived and died a happy man.

From the time he'd been marked by the Oldest at Celidon, where the first tribe always stayed, Gereint's destiny had been different from that of all the other young men just called to their fast.

For one thing, he'd left Celidon. Only the marked ones of

the first tribe did that. He'd learned to be a hunter, for the shaman had to know of the hunt and the eltor. He had traveled from tribe to tribe, spending a season with each, for the shaman had to know of the ways of all the tribes, never knowing which tribe he was to join, which Chieftain to serve. He had lain with women, too, in all the nine tribes, to sprinkle his marked seed across the Plain. He had no idea how many children he'd fathered in those waiting years; he did remember certain nights very well. He'd had years of it, seasons of traveling and seasons at Celidon with the parchments of the Law, and the other fragments that were not Law but which the shamans had to know.

He'd thought he'd had enough time, more than most of the shamans had, and he had begun it all by seeing a keia for his totem which had marked him inwardly, even among the marked.

He'd thought he was ready when the blinding came. Ready for the change, though not the pain. You were never ready for the pain: you came to your power through that agony, and there was no preparing for it.

He'd recognized what followed, though, and had welcomed the inner sight as one greets a lover long sought. He'd served Banor well for more than twenty years, though there had always been a distance between them.

Never with Ivor. No distance at all, and friendship, founded on respect, at first, and then something beyond. To fail the Chieftain of the third tribe, who was now Aven of all the Dalrei, would tear Gereint apart.

It was doing so now.

But he had, now that it had come down to war between the powers, no real choice. Two days ago, in Gwen Ystrat, the girl had told him not to track her where she went. Look west, she'd said, and opened her mind, to show him both what she was journeying to and what she'd seen of Loren's quest. The first had caused him pain such as he had not known since they blinded him. The second had revealed to him where his own burden lay, and his utterly unexpected inadequacy.

Long years he'd had, before he lost his eyes, to find a

truer sight. Long years to travel up and down the Plain, to look at the things of the visible world and learn their nature. He had thought he'd done it well, and nothing until now had led him to change his mind. Nothing, until now. But now he knew wherein he had failed.

He had never seen the sea.

How could a Dalrei, however wise, ever dream that this one thing might undermine the deepest challenge of his days? It was Cernan of the Beasts whom the Dalrei knew, and Green Ceinwen. The god who left his place in Pendaran to run with the eltor on the Plain, and the hunting goddess who was sister to him. What did the Riders know of sea-born Liranan?

There would be a ship sailing west, the girl had shown him that. And seeing the image in her mind, Gereint had understood another thing, something beyond what even the Seer of Brennin knew. He had never seen the sea, but he had to find that ship wherever it might be among the waves.

And so he closed himself. He left the Aven bereft of any guidance he might have to offer. A bad time, the worst, but he truly had no choice. He told Ivor what he was going to do, but not where or why. He let the living force that kept his aged body still alive dwindle to a single inner spark. Then, sitting down cross-legged on the mat in the shaman's house of the camp beside the Latham, he sent that spark voyaging far, far from its home.

When the turmoil and frenzy overtook the camps later that night, he never knew of them. They moved his body the next day in the midst of chaos—he'd told Ivor he could be moved—but he was oblivious to that. By then, he had passed beyond Pendaran.

He had seen the Wood. He could place and focus himself by his memory of the forest and the contours of its emanations in his mind. He'd sensed the dark, unforgiving hostility of the Wood and then something else. He had been passing over the Anor Lisen, of which he knew. There was a light on in the Tower, but that, of course, he didn't realize. He did apprehend a presence there, and he had an instant to wonder.

Only an instant, because then he was past the end of land and out over the waves and he knew a helpless, spinning panic. He had no shape to give to this, no memory, scarcely a name to compass it. Impossibly, there seemed to be stars both above and below. Old and frail, blind in the night, Gereint bade his spirit leave the land he'd always known, for the incalculable vastness of the unseen, unimaginable, the dark and roiling sea.

"You cannot," said Mabon of Rhoden, catching up to them, "drive five hundred men all day without rest."

His tone was mild. Aileron had made clear that Levon was leading this company, and Mabon hadn't demurred at all. Dave saw Levon grin sheepishly, though. "I know," he said to the Duke. "I've been meaning to stop. It's just that as we get closer . . ."

The Duke of Rhoden smiled. "I understand. I feel like that whenever I'm riding home." Mabon, Dave had decided, was all right. The Duke was past his best years and carried more weight than he needed to, but he hadn't had any trouble keeping up and had gone to sleep in his blanket on the grass the night before like an old campaigner.

Levon was shaking his head, upset with himself. When they reached an elevation in the rolling prairie he raised a hand for a halt. Dave heard heartfelt murmurs of relief running through the company behind him.

He was grateful for the rest himself. He hadn't been born to the saddle like Levon and Torc, or even these horsemen from the northern reaches of Brennin, and he'd been doing an awful lot of riding the past few days.

He swung down and stretched his legs. Did a few deep knee bends, touched his toes, swung his arms in circles. He caught a look from Torc and grinned. He didn't mind teasing from the dark Dalrei; Torc was a brother. He did a few push-ups right beside the cloth that Torc was covering with food. He heard the other man snort with suppressed laughter.

Dave flopped over on his back, thought about sit-ups, and

decided to eat instead. He took a dried strip of eltor meat and a roll of Brennin bread. He smeared them both with the mustardy sauce the Dalrei loved and lay back, chewing happily.

It was spring. Birds wheeled overhead and the breeze from the southeast was mild and cool. The grass tickled his nose and he sat up to grab a wedge of cheese. Torc was lying back as well, his eyes closed. He could fall asleep in twenty seconds. In fact, Dave realized, he just had.

It was almost impossible to believe that all of this had been covered with snow and exposed to an icy wind only five days ago. Thinking about that, Dave thought about Kevin and felt his restful mood slipping away like wind through his fingers. His mind began to turn from the open sky and the wide grasslands to darker places. Especially that one dark place where Kevin Laine had gone: the cave in Gwen Ystrat with the snow beginning to melt outside. He remembered the red flowers, the grey dog, and he would die remembering the wailing of the priestesses.

He sat up again. Torc stirred but did not wake. Overhead the sun was bright and warming. It was a good day to be alive, and Dave forced his mind away from its recollections. He knew, from bitter experience with his family, how unstable he became when he went too far with emotions like those that were stirring now.

He couldn't afford it. Maybe, just maybe, if there could come a space of time with leisure to work things through, he might sit down for a day or two and figure out why he had cried for Kevin Laine as he had not for anyone since he was a child.

Not now, though. That was perilous territory for him, Dave knew. He put Kevin, with some sorrow, in the same place he put his father—not forgotten, quite, but not to be addressed—and walked over to where Levon was sitting with the Duke of Rhoden.

"Restless?" Levon asked, looking up with a smile.

Dave hunkered down on his calves. "Torc isn't," he said with a backward jerk of his head.

Mabon chuckled. "I'm glad at least one of you is showing

normal responses. I thought you were minded to ride straight through to the Latham."

Levon shook his head. "I would have needed a rest. Torc might have done it, though. He isn't tired, just smarter than we are."

"Do you know," said Mabon, "I think you are right." And he turned over on his back, spread a square of lace across his eyes, and was snoring within a minute.

Levon grinned and gestured with his head. He and Dave rose and walked a little away from the others.

"How much farther?" Dave asked. He turned through a full circle: in all directions he could see nothing but the Plain.

"We'll be there tonight," Levon replied. "We may see the outposts before dark. We lost a bit of time yesterday with Mabon's business in North Keep. I suppose that's why I was pushing."

The Duke had been forced to delay them in order to convey a series of instructions to the North Keep garrison from Aileron. He'd also had orders of his own to be carried down the road to Rhoden. Dave had been impressed with Mabon's unflappable efficiency—it was a quality, he'd been told, upon which men of Rhoden prided themselves. Those from Seresh, he gathered, were rather more excitable.

He said, "I slowed us up there, too. I'm sorry."

"I'd been meaning to ask. What was that about?"

"A favor for Paul. Aileron ordered it. Do you remember the boy who came when we summoned Owein?"

Levon nodded. "I am not likely to forget."

"Paul wanted his father posted back to Paras Derval, and there was a letter. I said I'd find him. It took a while." Dave remembered standing awkwardly by as Shahar wept for what had happened to his son. He'd tried to think of something to say and failed, naturally. There were, he supposed, some things he'd never be able to handle properly.

"Did he remind you of Tabor?" Levon asked suddenly. "That boy?"

"A little," Dave said, after thinking about it.

Levon shook his head. "More than a little, for me. I think I'd like to get moving."

They turned back. Torc, Dave saw, was on his feet. Levon gestured, and the dark Dalrei put fingers to his mouth and whistled piercingly. The company began preparing to ride. Dave reached his horse, mounted up, and jogged to the front where Levon and Mabon waited.

The men of Brennin were in place and mounted very fast. Aileron had sent them men who knew what they were doing. Torc came up and nodded. Levon gave him a smile and raised his hand to wave them forward.

"Mörnir!" the Duke of Rhoden exclaimed.

Dave saw a shadow. He smelled something rotting.

He heard an arrow sing. But by that time he was flying through the air, knocked cleanly from his horse by Mabon's leap. The Duke fell with him on the grass. *This*, thought Dave absurdly, *is what Kevin did to Coll.*

Then he saw what the black swan had done to his horse. Amid the stench of putrescence and the sickly sweet smell of blood, he fought to hold down his midday meal.

Avaia was already far above them, wheeling north. Dave's brown stallion had had its back broken with the shattering force of the swan's descent. Her claws had shredded it into strips of meat. The horse's head had been ripped almost completely off. Blood fountained from the neck.

Levon had been knocked from his mount as well by the buffeting of the giant wings. Amid the screams of terrified horses and the shouts of men, he hurried over. Torc was gazing after the swan, his bow held in white fingers. Dave saw that they were shaking: he'd never seen Torc like that before.

He found that his legs would work and he stood up. Mabon of Rhoden rose slowly, red-faced; he'd had the wind knocked out of his lungs.

No one said a word for a moment. Avaia was out of sight already. Flidais, Dave was thinking, as he tried to control his pulse. *Beware the boar, beware the swan.* . . .

"You saved my life," he said.

"I know," said Mabon quietly. No affectation. "I was looking to check the sun and I saw her diving."

"Did you hit her?" Levon asked Torc.

Torc shook his head. "Her wing, maybe. Maybe."

It had been so sudden, so terrifyingly brutal an attack. The sky was empty again, the wind blew gentle as before over the waving grasses. There was a dead horse beside them, though, its intestines oozing out, and a lingering odor of corruption that did not come from the horse.

"Why?" Dave asked. "Why me?"

Levon's brown eyes were moving from shock to a grave knowledge. "One thing, only, I can think of," he said. "She risked a great deal diving like that. She would have had to sense something and to have decided that there was a great deal to gain." He gestured.

Dave put his hand to his side and touched the curving shape of Owein's Horn.

Often, in his own world, it had come to pass that opposing players in a basketball game would single out Dave Martyniuk as the most dangerous player on his team. He would be treated to special attention: double coverage, verbal needling, frequently some less than legal intimidation. As he got older, and better at the game, it happened with increasing regularity.

It never ever worked.

"Let's bury this horse," Dave said now, in a voice so grim it startled even the two Dalrei. "Give me a saddle for one of the others and let's get moving, Levon!" He stepped forward and retrieved his axe from the ruins of his saddle. There was blood all over it. Painstakingly, he wiped it clean until the head shone when he held it to the light.

They buried the horse; they gave him a saddle and another mount.

They rode.

Ivor was in the shaman's house at sunset when they brought him word.

He had come at the end of the day to look in on his friend and had remained, helpless and appalled by what he read in Gereint's face. The shaman's body was placid and unmoving on his mat, but his mouth was twisted with a soundless terror and even the dark sockets of his eyes offered testimony of a terrible voyaging. Aching and afraid for the aged shaman, Ivor stayed, as if by bearing witness he could ease Gereint's journey in some inchoate way. The old one was lost, Ivor realized, and with all his heart he longed to call him home.

Instead, he watched.

Then Cechtar came. "Levon is coming in," he said from the doorway. "He has brought the Duke of Rhoden and five hundred men. And there is something else, Aven."

Ivor turned.

The big Rider's face was working strangely. "Two others have come from the north. Aven . . . they are the lios alfar and—oh, come see what they ride!"

He had never seen the lios. Of all the Dalrei living, only Levon and Torc had done so. And Levon was back, too, with five hundred of the High King's men. With a quickening heart, Ivor rose. He cast one lingering glance at Gereint, then went out.

Levon was bringing his men in from the southwest; squinting, he could see them against the setting sun. In the open space before him, though, waiting quietly, were two of the lios alfar mounted up on raithen, and Ivor had never in his days thought to see either.

The lios were silver-haired, both, slim, with the elongated fingers and wide-set, changeable eyes of which he'd heard. Nothing he'd ever heard could prepare him, though, for their elusive, humbling beauty and, even motionless, their grace.

For all that, it was the raithen that claimed Ivor's speechless gaze. The Dalrei were horsemen and lived to ride. The raithen of Daniloth were to horses as the gods were to men, and there were two of them before him now.

They were golden as the setting sun all through their bodies, but the head and tail and the four feet of each of them were silver, like the not-yet-risen moon. Their eyes were fiercely blue and shining with intelligence, and Ivor loved them on the instant with all his soul. And knew that every Dalrei there did the same.

A wave of pure happiness went through him for a moment. And then was dashed to pieces when the lios spoke to tell of an army of the Dark sweeping even now across the northern Plain.

"We warned them at Celidon," the woman said. "Lydan and I will ride now toward Brennin. We alerted the High King with the summonglass last night. He should be on the Plain by now, heading for Daniloth. We will cut him off. Where do you want him to ride?"

Ivor found his voice amid the sudden babble of sound. "To Adein," he said crsiply. "We will try to beat the Dark Ones to the river and hold them there for the High King. Can we make it?"

"If you go now and very fast you might," said the one called Lydan. "Galen and I will ride to Aileron"

"Wait!" Ivor cried. "You must rest. Surely the raithen must. If you have come all the way from Daniloth . . ."

The lios had to be brother and sister, so alike were they. They shook their heads. "They have had a thousand years to rest," said Galen. "Both of these were at the Bael Rangat. They have not run free since."

Ivor's mouth fell open. He closed it.

"How many do you have?" he heard Cechtar breathe.

"These two and three others. They do not breed since the war against Maugrim. Too many of them died. Something changed in them. When these five are gone, no raithen will ever outpace the wind again." Lydan's voice was a chord of loss.

Ivor gazed at the raithen with a bitter sorrow. "Go then," he said. "Unleash them. Bright be the moon for you, and know we will not forget."

As one, the lios raised open hands in salute. Then they turned the raithen, spoke to them, and the Dalrai saw two comets, golden and silver, take flight across the darkening Plain.

In Paras Derval, Aileron the High King had just returned from Taerlindel. On the road back, he had been met with word of the summonglass alight. He was just then giving orders for an army to ride. They had too far to go, though. Much too far.

On the Plain, Levon came up to his father. Mabon of Rhoden stood behind him.

Ivor said to the Duke, "You have been riding two days. I cannot ask your men to come. Will you guard our women and children?"

"You can ask anything you must ask," said Mabon quietly. "Can you do without five hundred men?"

Ivor hesitated.

"No," said a woman's voice. "No, we cannot. Take them all, Aven. We must not lose Celidon!"

Ivor looked at his wife and saw the resolution in her face. "We cannot lose our women, either," he said. "Our children."

"Five hundred will not save us." It was Liane, standing beside her mother. "If they defeat you, five hundred will mean nothing at all. Take everyone, Father."

She was not wrong, he knew. But how could he leave them so utterly exposed? A thought came to him. He quailed before it for a moment, but then the Aven said, "Tabor."

"Yes, Father," his youngest child replied, stepping forward.

"If I take everyone, can you guard the camps? The two of you?"

He heard Leith draw a breath. He grieved for her, for every one of them.

"Yes, Father," said Tabor, pale as moonlight. Ivor stepped close and looked into his son's eyes. So much distance already.

"Weaver hold you dear," he murmured. "Hold all of you." He turned back to the Duke of Rhoden. "We ride in an hour," he said. "We will not stop before the Adein, unless we meet an army. Go with Cechtar—your men will need fresh horses." He gave orders to Levon and others to the gathered auberei, who were already mounted up to carry word to the other tribes. The camp exploded all around him.

He found a moment to look at Leith and took infinite solace from the calm in her eyes. They did not speak. It had all been said, at one time or another, between the two of them.

It was, in fact, less than an hour before he laced his fingers in her hair and bent in the saddle to kiss her good-bye. Her eyes were dry, her face quiet and strong, and so, too, was his. He might weep too easily for joy or domestic sorrow, or love, but it was the Aven of the Dalrei, first since Revor was given the Plain, who now sat his horse in the darkness. There was death in his heart, and bitter hate, and fiercest, coldest resolution.

They would need torches until the moon rose. He sent the auberei forward with fire to lead the way. His older son was at his side and the Duke of Rhoden and the seven Chieftains, all but the Oldest one at Celidon, where they had to go. Behind them, mounted and waiting, were five hundred men of Brennin and every single Rider of the Plain save one. He forbade himself to think of the one. He saw Davor and Torc and recognized the glitter in the dark man's eyes.

He rose up in his saddle. "In the name of Light," he cried, "to Celidon!"

"To Celidon!" they roared with one voice.

Ivor turned his horse to the north. Ahead, the auberei were watching. He nodded once.

They rode.

Tabor deferred quietly to the gathered shamans, who in turn deferred to his mother. In the morning, following the Aven's instructions, they set about moving across the river to the last camp in the very corner of the Plain, where the land began to rise toward the mountains. The river would offer some slight defense, and the mountains a place to hide if it came to that.

It went quickly, with few tears, even from the very young ones. Tabor asked two of the older boys to help him with

Gereint, but they were frightened by the shaman's face and he couldn't really blame them. He made the hammock himself, then got his sister to carry Gereint with him. They forded the river on foot at a shallow place. Gereint showed no awareness of them at all. Liane did well, and he told her so. She thanked him. After she had gone, he stayed a while with the shaman in the dark house where they had set him down. He thought about his praising Liane, and her thanking him, and of how much had changed.

Later, he went to check with his mother. There were no problems. By early afternoon they were all in the new camp. It was crowded, but with the men gone there was enough room in a camp built for four tribes. It was painfully quiet. The children weren't laughing, Tabor realized.

From the slopes of the mountain east of the camp a pair of keen eyes had been watching them all morning. And now, as the woman and children of the Dalrei uneasily settled in to their new camp, all their thoughts far away, in the north by Celidon, the watcher began to laugh. His laughter went on for a long time, quite unheard, save by the wild creatures of the mountains who did not understand or care. Soon enough—there was plenty of time—the watcher rose and started back east, carrying word. He was still laughing.

It was Kim's turn to lead. They had been switching after every rest period since they had left the horses behind and begun to climb. This was their fourth day, the third in the mountains. It wasn't too bad yet, here in the pass. Brock had said that the next day would be hardest, and then they would be close to Khath Meigol.

He hadn't asked anything about what would happen then.

In spite of herself, she was deeply grateful for his companionship and as deeply admiring of the stoic way in which he was leading her to a place more haunted than any other in Fionavar. He had believed her, though, had trusted her when she said that the ghosts of the Paraiko were not roaming with their bloodcurse in the mountain pass.

The Paraiko themselves were there. In their caves. Alive. And, in some way she still hadn't seen, being held.

She looked back. Brock was trudging sturdily along just behind, carrying most of their gear: one fight she'd lost. The Dwarves were even more stubborn than the Fords, it seemed.

"Break time," she called down. "Looks like a flat ledge where the trail bends up there." Brock grunted agreement.

She scrambled up; had to use her hands a couple of times, but it really wasn't too hard. She'd been right, there was a flat plateau there, even bigger than she'd guessed. A perfect place to stop and rest.

Unfortunately, it was occupied.

She was grabbed and muzzled before she could scream a warning. All unsuspecting, Brock followed her up and within seconds they were both disarmed, she of her dagger, he of his axe, and tied quite securely.

They were forced to sit in the middle of the plateau as the large level space gradually filled with their captors.

After a little while another figure leaped up from the trail along which they'd been climbing. He was a big man with a matted black beard. He was bald, and had a green tattooed design etched into his forehead and his cheeks. It showed beneath the beard as well. He took a moment to register their presence, then he laughed.

No one else had made a sound. There were perhaps fifty figures surrounding them. The bald, tattooed man walked commandingly into the center and stood over Kim and Brock. For a moment he looked down at them. Then he drew back a booted foot and viciously kicked the Dwarf in the side of the head. Brock crumpled, blood pouring from his scalp.

Kim drew breath to scream, and he kicked her in the side. In agony, retching for air, she heard him laugh again.

"Do you know," the bald man asked his companions in a gutteral voice, "what the Dalrei have done down below?"

Kim closed her eyes. She wondered how many of her ribs were broken. If Brock was dead.

*Save us,* she heard within her mind. The slow chanting. *Oh, save us.*

There had been a time when Dave hadn't regarded any of this as his concern at all. That had changed, long ago, and not because of any abstract awareness of the interwoven threads of all the worlds. It had been Ivor and Liane, his memories of them as he'd ridden south to Paras Derval a year ago. After the terror of the Mountain, it had been the presence of Levon and Torc beside him, and then it had been battle by Llewenmere, when men he knew had died—slain by loathsome creatures he could not help but hate. There had been brothers found in Pendaran Wood and, finally, there had been Jennifer and what had been done to her.

It was his war now too.

He'd always been an athlete and had prided himself on that as much as surviving the rigors of law school. He'd never let himself get out of shape and, in the season after their return home when they waited to go back to Fionavar—for Loren to come for them, or Kim to have her long-sought dream—he had worked his body harder than ever before. He'd had an idea of what might lie ahead. Dave was in better physical condition than at any point in his life.

And he had never ached so much in every muscle and bone, or been more brutally exhausted. At any point in his life.

They had ridden through the night, by torchlight until the moon rose and then by its shining. He had been in the saddle from Paras Derval the two days before that, too, riding at speed. But that speed, for which Mabon had gently chided Levon, was as nothing compared to the headlong night ride of the Dalrei, north behind their Aven.

He'd wondered about the horses during the night and even more now as the sun rose on their right—wondered

*261*

how long they could sustain this killing speed. They did, though, they kept it up, pounding over the grass without rest. They were not raithen, but every one of the horses had been bred and trained and loved by the Dalrei on this open prairie, and this was their finest hour in a thousand years. Dave stroked the streaming mane of the stallion he now rode and felt a great vein pulsing in its neck. It was a black horse—like Aileron's. Who, Dave prayed, silently, was riding his own black not far behind them now, alerted by the lios alfar.

It was Levon who made his father stop before the sun climbed overhead. Who ordered them all to stretch and eat. To walk their horses and let them drink of the waters of Rienna by Cynmere, where they had come. Men falling down with utter fatigue could not fight a battle. On the other hand, they had to win the race to Celidon and to Adein, if they could. Dave chewed some meat and bread, drank from the cold waters of the river, did his knee bends and flexes, and was back up in the saddle before the rest time was done. So too, he saw, was every other man in the army.

They rode.

It would be the stuff of legend and of song if any generations came after them, to tell old stories and sing them. Sing the ride of Ivor, who rode to Celidon with the Dalrei behind him through a wild night and a day to meet the army of the Dark and to battle them on the Plain in the name of Light.

Dave let the black have its head as he had for the whole journey. He felt the churning power of its strides, unflagging even now, despite the weight it bore, and he drew grimmer resolution yet from the heart of the horse that carried him.

He was close behind the Aven and the Chieftains when they saw the lone auberei come streaking toward them. The sun was over to the west now, starting down. Ahead of them the single auberei stopped, then expertly turned his horse and began racing along with them in stride with Ivor's grey.

"Where are they?" the Aven screamed.

"Coming to the river, even now!"

Dave drew a breath. Rakoth's army had not reached Celidon.

262

"Will we beat them there?" he heard Ivor cry.

"I don't know!" the auberei replied despairingly.

Dave saw Ivor rise up in his saddle, then. *In the name of Light!* the Aven roared and urged his horse forward. Somehow, they all did. Somehow the horses increased their speed. Dave saw Ivor's grey hurtle past the auberei who were leading them and he threw the black after it, feeling the horse respond with a courage that humbled him. A blurred thunder on the Plain they were, akin to the great swifts of the eltor themselves.

He saw Celidon whip by on their right. Had an impression of standing stones much like Stonehenge, though not fallen, not fallen yet. He glimpsed, beyond the stones, the great camp at mid-Plain, this heart of the Dalrei's home for twelve hundred years. Then they were past, and flying, flying to the river in the waning of the afternoon and, seeing Torc, beside him, loosen his sword, Dave drew his axe at last from where it hung by his saddle. He caught Torc's eye; their glances held for a second. He looked ahead for Levon and saw him, sword drawn, looking back at them as he rode.

They cleared a rise in the land. He saw the Adein sparkle in the sun. He saw the svart alfar, hideous green creatures he knew, and larger dun-colored ones as well. They were beginning to wade across the river. Only beginning. Ivor had come in time. A thing to be sung forever, if there should be anyone to sing.

For there were very, very many foes coming to them. The Plain north of Adein was dark with the vastness of Rakoth's army. Their harsh cries rang in the air: alarm at the sight of the Dalrei and then high, mocking triumph at how few there were.

His axe held ready, Dave raced down behind Ivor. His heart lurched to see the ranks of the svart alfar part to make way for urgach mounted upon slaug, and there were hundred of them, hundreds upon hundreds, among thousands upon thousands of the svart alfar.

He thought about death. Then, briefly, of his parents and his brother, who might never know. He thought about Kevin and Jennifer, of the two brothers with him now, of the slaughter by Llewenmere a year ago. He saw the leader of the urgach, the largest of them all, saw that it was clad mockingly in white, and with his heart and soul he hated it.

"Revor!" he cried with all the Dalrei, and, "Ivor!" with all of them. Then he reached the Adein, weariness gone, blood frenzy rising like a flood, and there was war.

They did not cross the river; it was the only feature of the level grasslands that gave them any edge at all. The svart alfar were small, even the dun-colored ones, and unmounted; they had to wade across Adein and up its banks into the swords of the Dalrei. Dave saw Torc sheath his blade and draw his bow, and soon the arrows of the Riders were flying over the river to wreak death on the other side. Only in passing did he grasp this, for he was in the midst of chaos and spurting blood, wheeling the black horse along the bank, hammering the axe down again and again, scything, chopping, once stabbing a svart with it when there was no room to swing. He felt the svart's breastbone crack under his thrust.

He tried to stay close to Levon and Ivor, but the ground was slippery with blood and river water, and then a cluster of the urgach came between on the terrifying, six-legged slaug, and he was suddenly fighting for sheer survival.

They were being forced back from the river; they could not stand and fight level with the urgach. The Adein was running red with blood now in the waning light, and there were so many svart alfar dead and dying in the stream that the living ones were crossing over the bodies of the dead behind the urgach and the slaug.

By Dave's side, Torc was fighting with a sword again. A tall warrior from North Keep was next to him, and desperately the three of them tried to hold close to the river, knowing how they would be overrun if they fell back too far. An urgach crashed up to Dave. He smelt the fetid breath of the horned slaug; the black horse wheeled sideways without command. The heavy sword of the urgach whistled past Dave's head, and, before it could come back, Dave leaned forward and with all his strength buried the axe in the ugly, hairy head. He jerked it free and lashed a backhand blow at the slaug even as the urgach slid like a tree to the bloodied ground.

A kill, but even as he drew breath, he saw another of the huge creatures angling for him, and he knew he could not keep this up, he could not hold this line. Torc, too, had killed and was desperately turning to face another slaug-mounted foe. The svarts were crossing the river now in numbers, and with a sickness in his heart, Dave saw how many were yet to come, and that they were using knives and short swords to cut open the Riders' horses from below.

Incoherently, he screamed, and as his battle rage rose up again, he kicked the black horse to meet the first oncoming slaug. He was in close too fast for the startled urgach to swing its sword. With his left hand Dave raked savagely at its eyes, and as it howled, he killed it with a short swing of the axe.

"Davor!" he heard. A warning too late. He felt pain lance through his left side and, looking down, saw that a svart had stabbed him from below. Torc killed it. Dave pulled the dagger free from his ribs, gasping. Blood followed. There was another urgach coming toward him, and two more beyond Torc. The North Keep man was down. They were almost alone near the river—the Dalrei were falling back; even the Aven was withdrawing. Dave looked at Torc, saw a deep gash on the other's face, and read bitterest despair in his eyes.

Then, from over the river, north where the Dark was, he heard the sound of singing, high and clear. Dave turned as the urgach hesitated and, looking, caught his breath in joy and wonder.

Over the Plain from the north and west the lios alfar were riding to war. Bright and glorious they were, behind their Lord, whose hair shone golden in the light, and they sang as they came out from the Shadowland at last.

Swift were their horses, passing swift their blades, fierce was the fire in the hearts of the Children of Light. Into the ranks of the svarts they rode, sharp and glittering, and the foot soldiers of the Dark screamed with hate and fear to see them come.

The urgach were all on the south bank now. The terrible giant in white roared a command, and a number of them turned back north, trampling scores of the svart alfar, living and dead, as they did.

Shouting with relief, ignoring the flowering pain in his side, Dave hastened to follow, to kill the urgach as they withdrew, to claim the riverbank again. Then, by the water, he heard Torc say, "Oh, Cernan. No!" And looking up into the sky he felt joy turn to ashes in his mouth.

Overhead, like a moving cloud of death, Avaia descended, and with her, grey and black, darkening the sky, came at least three hundred of her brood. The swans of Maugrim came down from the unrelenting heavens and the lios alfar were blotted by darkness and began to die.

The urgach in white screamed again, this time in brutal triumph, and the slaug turned a second time, leaving the lios to the swans and the emboldened svarts, and the Dalrei were beleaguered again by overmastering numbers.

Hacking his way east toward where Ivor—still riding, still wielding his blade—had also regained the river, Dave saw Barth and Navon fighting side by side near the Aven. Then he saw the huge leader of the urgach come up to them and a warning shout tore from his raw throat. The babies in the wood, Torc's babies and his own, the ones they had guarded together. The sword of the giant urgach crashed in an arc that seemed to bruise the very air. It cut through Barth's neck as through a flower stem, and Dave saw the boy's head fly free and blood fountain before it fell into the trampled mud by Adein. The same sword stroke descending sliced heavily, brutally, into Navon's side, and he saw the boy slide from his horse even as he heard a terrifying sound.

He realized that he had made the sound. His own side was sticky with blood. He saw Torc, wild-eyed with hate, surge past him toward the urgach in white. He tried to keep up. Three svarts barred his way. He killed two with his axe and heard the other's head crack open under the hooves of his black horse.

He glanced north and saw the lios battling Avaia and the swans. There were not enough. There had never been enough. They had come out from Daniloth because they would not stand by and watch the Dalrei die. And now they were dying too.

"Oh, Cernan," he heard someone say, in despair. Cechtar's voice. "This hour knows our name!"

Dave followed the big Rider's glance to the east. And saw. The wolves were coming. Both north and south of the river. And leading them was a giant animal, black with a splash of silver between his ears, and he knew from what he had been told that this was Galadan of the andain, lieutenant to Maugrim. It was true. The hour knew their name.

He heard his name. From within.

Not the summoning of death as the Dalrei believed; not the call of the final hour. Absurdly, the inner voice he heard sounded like Kevin Laine's. *Dave,* he heard again. *You idiot. Do it now!*

And on the thought, he reached down and, bringing Owein's Horn to his lips, he sounded it then with all the strength that was left in him.

It was Light again, the sound, and the Dark could not hear it. Even so, they slowed in their advance. His head was tilted back as he blew. He saw Avaia watching him; saw her wheel suddenly aloft. He listened to the sound he made and it was not the same as before. Not moonlight on snow or water, nor sunrise, nor candles by a hearth. This was the noon sun flashing from a sword, it was the red light of a burning fire, it was the torches they had carried on the ride last night, it was the cold hard glitter of the stars.

And from between the stars, Owein came. And the Wild Hunt was with him, hurtling down from far above the swans, and every one of the shadowy kings had a drawn, upraised sword, and so too did the child who led them.

Into the phalanx of Avaia's brood they flew, smoke on flying horses, shadowy death in the darkening sky, and nothing in the air could withstand them, and they killed. Dave saw Avaia leave her sons and daughters to their doom and flash away north in flight. He heard the wild laughter of the kings he had unleashed, and he saw them circle one by one over him and raise swords in salute.

Then the swans were all dead or flying away and the Hunt descended on Fionavar for the first time in so many thousand years. Galadan's wolves were fleeing and the svart alfar and the urgach upon slaug, and Dave saw the shadowy kings wheel above them, killing at will, and there were tears pouring down his begrimed face.

Then he saw the Hunt split in two as four went with the child who had been Finn in wild, airborne pursuit of the army of the Dark. The other kings, and Owein was one of them, stayed by Adein, and in the evening light *they began to kill the lios and the Dalrei, one by one.*

Dave Martyniuk screamed. He leaped from his horse.

He began to run along the riverbank. "No!" he roared. "No, no, oh, no! Please!" He stumbled and fell in the mud. A body moved under him. He heard the unleashed laughter of the Hunt. He looked up. He saw Owein, grey like smoke on his black, shadowy horse, loom above Levon dan Ivor, who stood before his father, and he heard Owein laugh again for purest joy. He tried to rise; felt something give way in his side.

Heard a half-remembered voice above all the noise cry, "Sky King, sheath your sword! I put my will upon you!" Then he fell back, bleeding and brokenhearted in the filthy mud, and heard no more.

He woke to moonlight. He was clean and clothed. He rose. There was no pain. He felt his side and, through the shirt he wore, traced the line of a healed scar. Slowly, he looked around. He was on a mound in the Plain. Away to the north, half a mile perhaps, he saw the river glitter silver in the moonlight. He did not remember the mound, or passing this place. There were lights off to the east: Celidon. No sounds in the night, no movement by the river.

He put a hand to his hip.

"I have not taken it back," he heard her say. He turned to the west where she was, and when he had turned, he knelt, and bowed his head.

"Look at me," she said, and he did.

She was in green, as before, by the pool in Faelinn Grove. There was an illumination in her face, but muted, so he could look upon her. There were a bow and a quiver on her back, and in her hand she held out Owein's Horn.

He was afraid, and he said, "Goddess, how should I ever summon them again?"

Ceinwen smiled. She said, "Not ever, unless someone stronger than the Hunt is there to master them. I should not have done what I did, and I will pay for it. We are not to act on the Tapestry. But you had the horn from me, though for a lesser purpose, and I could not stand by and see Owein unchecked."

He swallowed. She was very beautiful, very tall above him, very bright. "How may a goddess be made to pay?" he asked.

She laughed. He remembered it. She said, "Red Nemain will find a way, and Macha will, if she does not. Never fear."

Memory was coming back. And, with it, a desperate pain.

"They were killing everyone," he stammered. "All of us."

"Of course they were," Green Ceinwen said, shining on the mound. "How should you expect the wildest magic to tamely serve your will?"

"So many dead," he said. His heart was sore with it.

"I have gathered them," Ceinwen said, not ungently. And Dave suddenly understood whence this mound had come, and what it was.

"Levon?" he asked, afraid. "The Aven?"

"Not all need die," she said. She had said that to him before. "I have put the living to sleep by the river. They sleep in Celidon as well, although the lights burn. They will rise in the morning, though, carrying their wounds."

"I do not," he said, with difficulty.

"I know," she said. "I did not want you to."

He rose. He knew she wanted him to rise. They stood on the mound in the clear moonlight. She shone for him softly, like the moon. She came forward and kissed him upon the lips. She motioned with a hand, and he was blinded, almost, by the sudden glory of her nakedness. She touched him. Trembling, he raised a hand toward her hair. She made a sound. Touched him again.

Then he lay down with a goddess, in the green, green of the grass.

# Chapter 16

At midafternoon on the second day, Paul caught a certain glance from Diarmuid and he rose. Together they went to the stern of the ship, where Arthur stood with his dog. Around them the men of South Keep manned *Prydwen* with easy efficiency, and Coll, at the helm, held their course hard on west. Due west, Arthur had instructed, and told Coll he would let him know when time came to turn, and where. It was to an island not on any map that they were sailing.

Nor were they sure what lay waiting there. Which was why the three of them, with Cavall padding lightly alongside on the dark planks of the deck, now walked together to the prow where two figures stood together as they had stood every waking hour since *Prydwen* had set sail.

"Loren," Diarmuid said quietly.

The mage slowly turned from staring at the sea. Matt looked around as well.

"Loren, we must talk," the Prince went on, quietly still, but not without authority.

The mage stared at them for a long moment; then he said, his voice rasping, "I know. You understand that I break our Law if I tell you?"

"I do," said Diarmuid. "But we must know what he is doing, Loren. And how. Your Council's Law must not serve the Dark."

Matt, his face impassive, turned back to look out at sea. Loren remained facing the three of them. He said, "Metran is using the Cauldron to revive the svart alfar on Cader Sedat when they die."

Arthur nodded. "But what is killing them?"

"He is," said Loren Silvercloak.

They waited. Matt's gaze was fixed out over the water, but Paul saw how his hands gripped the railing of the ship.

Loren said, "Know you, that in the Book of Nilsom—"

"Accursed be his name," Matt Sören said.

"—in that Book," Loren continued, "is written a monstrous way in which a mage can have the strength of more than his one source."

No one spoke. Paul felt the wind as the sun slipped behind a cloud.

"Metran is using Denbarra as a conduit," Loren said, controlling his voice. "A conduit for the energy of the svart alfar."

"Why are they dying?" Paul asked.

"Because he is draining them to death."

Diarmuid nodded. "And the dead ones are revived with the Cauldron? Over and over again. Is that how he made the winter? How he was strong enough?"

"Yes," said Loren simply.

There was a silence. *Prydwen* rode through a calm sea.

"He will have others with him to do this?" Arthur said.

"He will have to," the mage replied. "The ones used to source him will be incapable of moving."

"Denbarra," Paul said. "Is he so evil? Why is he doing this?"

Matt whipped around. "Because a source does not betray his mage!" They all heard the bitterness.

Loren laid a hand on the Dwarf's shoulder. "Easy," he said. "I don't think he can now, in any case. We shall see, if we get there."

*If we get there.* Diarmuid strolled thoughtfully away to talk with Coll at the helm. A moment later, Arthur and Cavall went back to their place at the stern.

"Can he make the winter again?" Paul asked Loren.

"I think so. He can do almost anything he wants with so much power."

The two of them turned to lean on the railing on either side of Matt. They gazed out at the empty sea.

"I took flowers to Aideen's grave," the Dwarf said, after a moment. "With Jennifer."

Loren looked at him. "I don't think Denbarra has her choice," he repeated after a moment.

"In the beginning he did," the Dwarf growled.

"Were I Metran, what would you have done?"

"Cut your heart out!" Matt Sören said.

Loren looked at his source, a smile beginning to play about his mouth. "Would you?" he asked.

For a long time Matt glared back at him. Then he grimaced and shook his head. He turned once more to the sea. Paul felt something ease in his heart. Not to lightness, but toward acceptance and resignation. He wasn't sure why he found strength in the Dwarf's admission, but he did, and he knew he had need of that strength, with greater need yet to come.

He'd been sleeping badly since Kevin died, so Paul had volunteered to take one of the pre-dawn watches. It was a time to think and remember. The only sounds were the creaking of the ship and the slap of waves in the darkness below. Overhead, *Prydwen's* three sails were full, and they were running easily with the wind. There were four other watchmen stationed around the deck, and red-haired Averren was at the helm.

With no one near him, it was a very private time, almost a peaceful one. He went with his memories. Kevin's death would never be less than a grief, nor would it ever be less than a thing of wonder, of glory, even. So many people died in war, so many had died already in this one, but none had dealt such a blow to the Dark as they passed over into Night. And none, he thought, ever would. *Rahod hedai Liadon*, the priestesses had moaned in the Temple at Paras Derval, while outside the green grass was coming back in a night. Already, through the net of sorrow that wrapped his heart, Paul could feel a light beginning to shine. Let Rakoth Maugrim fear, and everyone in Fionavar—even cold Jaelle—acknowledge what Kevin had wrought, what his soul had been equal to.

And yet, he thought, to be fair, Jaelle had acknowledged it to him twice. He shook his head. The High Priestess with her emerald eyes was more than he could deal with now. He thought of Rachel and remembered music. Her music, and then Kev's, in the tavern. They would share it now, forever, in him. A difficult realization, that.

"Am I intruding?"

Paul glanced back and, after a moment, shook his head. "Night thoughts," he said.

"I couldn't sleep," Coll murmured, and moved up to the railing. "Thought I might be of some use up top, but it's a quiet night and Averren knows his business."

Paul smiled again. Listened to the easy sound of the ship and the sea. "It's a strange hour," he said. "I like it, actually. I've never been to sea before."

"I grew up on ships," Coll said quietly. "This feels like coming home."

"Why did you leave, then?"

"Diar asked me to," the big man said simply. Paul waited and, after a moment, Coll clasped his hands loosely over the rail and went on. "My mother worked in the tavern at Taerlindel. I never knew who my father was. All the mariners brought me up, it sometimes seemed. Taught me what they knew. My first memories are of being held up to steer a ship when I was too small to reach the tiller on my own."

His voice was deep and low. Paul remembered the one other time the two of them had talked alone at night. About the Summer Tree. How many years ago it seemed.

Coll said, "I was seventeen when Diarmuid and Aileron first came to spend a summer at Taerlindel. I was older than both of them and minded to despise the royal brats. But Aileron . . . did everything impossibly quickly and impossibly well, and Diar . . ." He paused. A remembering smile played over his face.

"And Diar did everything his own way, and equally well, and he beat me in a fight outside my mother's father's house. Then, to apologize, he disguised us both and took me to the tavern where my mother worked. I wasn't allowed in there, you see. Even my mother didn't know me that night—they thought I'd come from Paras Derval with one of the court women."

"Women?" Paul asked.

"Diar was the girl. He was young, remember." They laughed softly in the dark. "I was wondering about him, just a little; then he got two of the town girls to walk with us on the beach beyond the track."

"I know it," said Paul.

Coll glanced at him. "They came because they thought Diarmuid was a woman and I was a lord from Paras Derval. We spent three hours on the beach. I'd never laughed so hard in my life as I did when he took off his skirt to swim and I saw their faces."

They were both smiling. Paul was beginning to understand something, though not yet something else.

"Later, when his mother died, he was made Warden of the South Marches—I think they wanted him out of Paras Derval as much as anything else. He was even wilder in those days. Younger, and he'd loved the Queen, too. He came to Taerlindel and asked me to be his Second, and I went."

The moon was west, as if leading them on. Paul said, looking at it, "He's been lucky to have you. For ballast. And Sharra now, too. I think she's a match for him."

Coll nodded. "I think so. He loves her. He loves very strongly."

Paul absorbed that, and after a moment it began to clear up the one puzzle he hadn't quite understood.

He looked over at Coll. He could make out the square, honest face and the large many-times-broken nose. He said, "The one other night we talked alone, you said to me that had you any power you would curse Aileron. You weren't even supposed to name him, then. Do you remember?"

"Of course I do," said Coll clamly. Around them the quiet sounds of the ship seemed only to deepen the night stillness.

"Is it because he took all the father's love?"

Coll looked at him, still calm. "In part," he said. "You were good at guessing things from the start, I remember. But there is another thing, and you should be able to guess that too."

Paul thought about it. "Well—" he began.

The sound of singing came to them over the water.

"Listen!" cried Averren, quite unnecessarily.

They all listened, the seven men awake on *Prydwen*. The singing was coming from ahead of them and off to starboard.

Averren moved the tiller over that they might come nearer to it. Elusive and faint was that sound, thin and beautiful. Like a fragile web it spun out of the dark toward them, woven of sweet sadness and allure. There were a great many voices twined together in it.

Paul had heard that song before. "We're in trouble," he said.

Coll's head whipped around. "What?"

The monster's head broke water off the starboard bow. Up and up it went, towering over *Prydwen*'s masts. The moon lit its gigantic flat head: the lidless eyes, the gaping, carnivorous jaws, the mottled grey-green slimy skin. *Prydwen* grated on something. Averren grappled with the helm and Coll hurried to aid him. One of the watchmen screamed a warning.

Paul caught a glimpse in the uncertain moonlight of something white, like a horn, between the monster's terrible eyes. He still heard the singing, clear, heartachingly beautiful. A sick premonition swept over him. He turned instinctively. On the other side of *Prydwen* the monster's tail had curved and it was raised, blotting the southern sky, to smash down on them!

*Raven wings.* He knew.

"Soulmonger!" Paul screamed. "Loren, make a shield!"

He saw the huge tail reach its full height. Saw it coming down with the force of malignant death, to crush them out of life. Then saw it smash brutally into nothing but air. *Prydwen* bounced like a toy with the shock of it, but the mage's shield held. Loren came running up on deck, Diarmuid and Arthur supporting Matt Sören. Paul glimpsed the racking strain in the Dwarf's face and then deliberately cut himself off from all sensation. There was no time to waste. He reached within for the pulse of Mörnir.

And found it, desperately faint, thin as starlight beside the moon. Which is what, in a way, it was. He was too far. Liranan had spoken true. How could he compel the sea god in the sea?

He tried. Felt the third pulse beat in him and cried with the fourth, "Liranan!"

He sensed, rather than saw, the effortless eluding of the

god. Despair threatened to drown him. He dove, within his mind, as he had done on the beach. He heard the singing everywhere and then, far down and far away, the voice of Liranan: "I am sorry, brother. Truly sorry."

He tried again. Put all his soul into the summoning. As if from undersea he saw the shadow of *Prydwen* above, and he apprehended the full magnitude of the monster that guarded Cader Sedat. Soulmonger, he thought again. Rage rose overwhelmingly in him, he channeled all its blind force into his call. He felt himself breaking with the desperate strain. It was not enough.

"I told you it would be so," he heard the sea god say. Far off he saw a silver fish eluding through dark water. There were no sea stars. Overhead, *Prydwen* bounced wildly again, and he knew Loren had somehow blocked a second crashing of the monster's tail. Not a third, he thought. He cannot block a third.

And in his mind a voice spoke: *Then there must not be a third. Twiceborn, this is Gereint. Summon now, through me. I am rooted in the land.*

Paul linked with the blind shaman he had never seen. Power surged within him, the godpulse of Mörnir beating fiercer than his own. Underwater in his mind, he stretched a hand downward through the ocean dark. He felt an explosion of his power, grounded on the Plain in Gereint. He felt it crest. Overhead, the vast tail was rising again. "Liranan!" Paul cried for the last time. On the deck of *Prydwen* they heard it like the voice of thunder.

And the sea god came.

Paul felt it as a rising of the sea. He heard the god cry out for joy at being allowed to act. He felt the bond with Gereint going, then; before he could speak again, or send any thought at all, the shaman's mind was gone from his. How far, Paul thought. How far he came. And how far back he has to go.

Then he was on the ship again and seeing with his own eyes, tenuously in the moonlight, how the Soulmonger of Maugrim battled Liranan, god of the sea. And all the while the singing never stopped.

Loren had dropped the protective shield. Matt was lying

on the deck. Coll, at the helm, fought to steer *Prydwen* through the troughs and ridges shaped by the titans on their starboard bow. Paul saw a man fly overboard as the ship bucked like a horse in the foaming sea.

The god was fighting in his own form, in his shining water robe, and he could fly up like a wave flew, he could make a whirlpool of the sea below, and he did both those things.

By means of a power Paul could scarcely grasp, a hole suddenly formed in the sea. *Prydwen* bounced and rocked, her timbers screaming, on the very lip of it. He saw the vortex whirling faster and faster, and as its wildness grew he saw that even the vast bulk of the Soulmonger was no proof against the weight of the roused sea.

The monster was going down. The battle would be in the deep, and Paul knew this was for their sake. He watched the god, luminous and shimmering, hang suspended on a high wave overhead as he shaped the sucking whirlpool to draw the other undersea.

The Soulmonger's slimy scum-encrusted head came down. It was almost as large as the ship, Paul saw. He saw the huge lidless eyes up close, the man-sized teeth bared in fury.

He saw Diarmuid dan Ailell leap from *Prydwen*'s deck to land on the flat plane of the monster's head. He heard Coll cry out. The singing was all around them, even through the roaring of the sea. With disbelieving eyes, he saw the Prince slip, scramble for footing, then lurch over to stand between the eyes of Soulmonger and, with one mighty pull, tear free the white horn from its head.

The pull overbalanced him. Paul saw the monster going down, the seas closing over it. As he fell, Diarmuid turned and leaped, twisting, toward *Prydwen*.

To catch, one-handed, the rope Arthur Pendragon had sent flying out to him.

They reeled him aboard against the pull of the closing sea. Paul turned just in time to see Liranan let fall the wave on which he'd hung and plummet down after the creature he was now allowed to fight because he had been summoned and compelled.

The singing stopped.

A thousand years, Paul thought, heartsick. Since first Rakoth had used Cader Sedat in the Bael Rangat. For a thousand years the Soulmonger had lurked in the ocean deeps, unable to be opposed. Invincibly vast.

Paul was on his knees, weeping for the captured souls. For the voices of all the bright lios alfar who had set sail to their song, to find a world shaped by the Weaver for them alone.

Not one of them would have gotten there, he now knew. For a thousand years the lios had set forth, singly and in pairs, over a moonless sea.

To meet the Soulmonger of Maugrim. And become its voice.

*Most hated by the Dark, for their name was Light.*

A long while he wept, whose dry eyes had brought so much pain once and then, later, had been rain. After a time he became aware that there was a kind of light shining and he looked up. He was very weak, but Coll was on one side of him and Diarmuid, limping a little, was on the other.

All the men of *Prydwen*—including Matt, he saw—were gathered at the starboard side. They made way for him in respectful silence. Passing to the rail, Paul saw Liranan standing on the surface of the sea, and the shining came from the moonlight caught and enhanced in the million droplets of his water robe.

He and the god looked at each other; then Liranan spoke aloud. "He is dead."

A murmur rose and fell along the length of the ship.

Paul thought of the singing and the bright lios in their small boats. A thousand years of setting sail to the high, sweet summons of their song. A thousand years, and none of them had known.

He said coldly, "Ceinwen gave a horn. You could have warned them."

The sea god shook his head. "I could not," he said. "We were enjoined when first the Unraveller came into Fionavar that we might not interfere of our own will. Green Ceinwen will have answer to make ere long, and for more than the gift of a horn, but I will not transgress against the Weaver's will." He paused. "Even so, it has been a bitter grief. He is dead, brother. I did not think you could summon me. Sea stars will shine here again because of you."

Paul said, "I had help."

After another moment, Liranan, as Cernan had done long ago, bowed to him. Then the god disappeared into the darkness of the sea.

Paul looked at Loren. He saw the tracks of tears on the mage's face. "You know?" he asked. Loren nodded jerkily.

"What?" said Diarmuid.

They had to be told. Paul said, over the grief, "The singing was the lios alfar. The ones who sailed. They never got farther west than here, since the Bael Rangat. Not one of them." *Brendel,* he was thinking. *How will I tell Brendel?*

He heard the men of South Keep. Their helpless rage. It was Diarmuid he watched.

"What did you go for?" he asked the Prince.

"Yes, what?" Loren repeated.

Diarmuid turned to the mage. "You didn't see?" He released Paul's arm and limped over to the steps leading up to the tiller. He came back with something that glittered white in the moonlight. He held it out to the mage.

"Oh," said Matt Sören.

Loren said nothing. It was in his face.

"My lord First Mage of Brennin," Diarmuid said, holding his emotion rigidly in check. "Will you accept as a gift from me a thing of greatest worth? This is the staff of Amairgen Whitebranch that Lisen made for him so long ago."

Paul clenched his hands. So many levels of sorrow. It seemed that someone else hadn't made it past this point either. Now they knew what had happened to the first and greatest of the mages.

Loren took the staff and held it sideways, cradled in both his hands. For all its years in the sea, the white wood was unworn and unsullied, and Paul knew there was a power in it.

"Wield it, Silvercloak!" he heard Diarmuid say. "Take revenge for him, for all the dead. Let his staff be used at Cader Sedat. For this did I bring it back."

Loren's fingers closed tightly around the wood.

"Be it so," was all he said, but the sound of doom was in his voice.

"Be it so now, then," said a deeper voice. They turned. "The wind has shifted," Arthur said.

"North," said Coll after a second.

Arthur looked only at Loren. "We reach Cader Sedat by sailing due north into a north wind. Can you do this, mage?"

Loren and Matt turned to each other as Paul had seen them do before. They exchanged an intensely private glance, unhurried, as if they had all the time in the world. Matt was desperately weary, he knew, and Loren had to be, as well, but he also knew it wasn't going to matter.

He saw the mage look up at Coll. He saw the bleakness of his smile. "Man your ship," he heard Loren say, "and point her to the north."

They hadn't noticed the dawn coming on. But as Coll and the men of South Keep sprang to obey, the sun leaped up behind them out of the sea.

Then it was on their right, as Coll of Taerlindel grappled his ship over straight into the strong north wind. Loren had gone below. When he reappeared he was clad in the cloak of shifting silver hues that gave him his name. Tall and stern, his hour begun at last, his and Matt's, he strode to *Prydwen's* prow and he carried the staff of Amairgen Whitebranch. Beside him, equally stern, equally proud, walked Matt Sören, who had once been King under Banir Lök and had forsaken that destiny for the one that led him to this place.

"*Cenolan!*" Loren cried. He extended the staff straight out in front of him. "*Sed amairgen, sed remagan, den sedath iren!*" He hurled the words out over the waves, and power surged through them like a greater wave. Paul heard a roar of sound, a rushing of winds as if from all the corners of the sea. They flowed around *Prydwen* as Liranan's whirlpool had spun past her sides and, after a chaotic, swirling moment Paul saw that they were sailing on a hushed and windless sea, utterly calm, like glass, while on either side of them the wild winds raged.

And ahead, not very far at all, lit by the morning sun, lay

an island with a castle high upon it, and the island was slowly revolving in the glassy sea. The windows of the castle were begrimed and smeared and so, too, were its walls.

"It shone once," Arthur said quietly.

From the very highest point of the castle a black plume of smoke was rising, straight as a rod, into the sky. The island was rocky and bare of vegetation.

"It was green once," Arthur said. "Cavall!"

The dog was growling and straining forward, his teeth bared. He quieted when Arthur spoke.

Loren never moved. He held the staff rigidly before him.

There were no guards. Soulmonger had been guard enough. When they came close, the spinning of the island stopped. Paul guessed that they were spinning with it now, but he had no idea where they were. It was not Fionavar, though, that much he understood.

Coll ordered the anchors cast overboard.

Loren lowered his arm. He looked at Matt. The Dwarf nodded once, then found a place to sit. They rode at anchor in the windless sea just offshore from Cader Sedat.

"All right," said Loren Silvercloak. "Diarmuid, Arthur, I don't care how you do it, but this is what I need."

*It is a place of death,* Arthur had said to him. As they came near, Paul realized that it had been meant literally. There was a tomblike feel to the castle. The very doors—four of them, Arthur said—were set within the slopes of the grey mound from which Cader Sedat rose. The walls climbed high, but the entranceway went down into the earth.

They stood before one of these great iron doors, and for once Paul saw Diarmuid hesitate. Loren and Matt had gone another way to another door. There were no guards to be seen. The deep silence was unsettling. Nothing lived near that place, Paul saw, and was afraid.

"The door will open," said Arthur quietly. "Getting out again was the hard thing, last time."

Diarmuid smiled then. He seemed about to say something, but instead he went forward and pushed on the door of Cader Sedat. It opened soundlessly. He stepped aside and, with a gesture, motioned Arthur to lead them. The Warrior drew a sword and went in. Forty of them followed him out of the sunlight into the dark.

It was very cold; even Paul felt it. This chill went beyond the protection of Mörnir, and he was not proof against it. The dead, Paul thought, and then had another thought: this was the center, where they were, everything spiraled around this island. Wherever it was. In whatever world.

The corridors were dusty. Spiderwebs tangled them as they walked. There were branching hallways everywhere, and most of them led down. It was very dark, and Paul could see nothing along those corridors. Their own path led upward, on a slowly rising slant, and after what seemed a long time they rounded a corner and, not far off, saw a glow of greenish light.

Very close to them, not five feet away, another corridor branched left, and up. From it, running, came a svart alfar.

The svart had time to see them. Time to open his mouth. No time to scream. Six arrows ripped into him. He threw up his arms and died.

Flat out, without thought, Paul dived. A guess, a glimpse. With one desperate hand outstretched he caught the flask the svart had carried before it could smash on the floor. He rolled as he landed, as silently as he could. They waited. A moment later Arthur nodded. No alarm had been raised.

Paul scrambled to his feet and walked back to the others. Wordlessly, Diarmuid handed back his sword.

"Sorry," Paul murmured. He had tossed it without warning when he leaped.

"I will bleed to death," Diamuid whispered, holding up the scratched hand with which he'd made the catch. "What was he carrying?"

Paul handed over the flask. Diarmuid unstoppered it and sniffed at the neck. He lifted his head, mock astonishment visible even in the wan green light.

"By the river blood of Lisen," said the Prince softly. "South Keep wine!" And he raised the flask and took a long drink. "Anyone else?" he asked politely.

There were, predictably, no takers, but even Arthur allowed himself a smile.

282

Diarmuid's expression changed. "Well done, Pwyll," he said crisply. "Carde, get the body out of the hallway. My lord Arthur, shall we go look at a renegade mage?"

In the shadows Paul thought he saw starlight flash for a moment in the Warrior's eyes. He looked at Cavall, remembering something. In silence, he followed the two leaders down the last corridor. Near the end they dropped to their knees and crawled. Diarmuid made room for him, and Paul wriggled along on his belly and came up to the doorway beside the Prince. They lay there, the three of them, with the South Keep men behind, and looked out over a scene shaped to appal.

Five steps led down from the arched doorway where they were. There were a number of other entrances to the huge chamber below. The roof was so high it was lost in darkness. The floor was illuminated, though: there were torches set around the walls, burning with the eerie green light they had seen from the corridor. The doorway they had reached was about midway along the Great Hall of Cader Sedat. At the head of the chamber, on a dais, stood Metran, once First Mage of Brennin, and beside him was the Cauldron of Khath Meigol over a roaring fire.

It was huge. The Giants had made it, Paul remembered, and he would have been able to guess had he not known. It was black, as best as he could tell in the light, and there were words engraved on the outer rim of it, stained and coated with grime. At least fifteen svart alfar stood on a raised platform around it, and they were handling a net into which, one by one, others of their kind were laid and dropped, lifeless, into the boiling Cauldron.

It was hard to see in the green light, but Paul strained his eyes and watched as one of the ugly creatures was withdrawn from the water. Carefully, the others swung him away from the steaming mouth of the Cauldron and then they stood him up.

And Paul saw the one who had been dead a moment ago walk stumblingly, with others helping him, to stand behind another man.

Denbarra, source to Metran. And looking at the slack-jawed, drooling figure of the source, Paul understood what

Loren had meant when he said Denbarra would have no choice in the matter any more.

There were well over a hundred svart alfar behind him, mindlessly draining their lives to feed Metran's power, as Denbarra mindlessly served as a conduit for them. Even as they watched, Paul saw two of the svarts drop where they stood. He saw them collected instantly by others, not part of the power web, and carried toward the Cauldron, and he saw others still, being led back from it to stand behind Denbarra.

A loathing rose up in him. Fighting for control, he looked at last squarely on the mage who had made the winter Kevin had died to end.

A stumbling, senile, straggly bearded figure Metran had seemed when they first arrived. A sham, all of it, a seamless, undetected sham to mask pure treachery. The man before them now stood in complete control amid the green lights and black Cauldron smoke. Paul saw that he didn't look old any more. He was slowly chanting words over the pages of a book.

He hadn't known he carried so much rage within himself.

Impotent rage, it seemed.

"We can't do it," he heard Diarmuid snarl as he grasped the same truth himself.

"This is what I need," Loren had said as *Prydwen* rode at anchor beside the island.

In a way it hadn't been much at all, and in another way it was everything. But then, Paul remembered thinking, they had not come here expecting to return.

Metran would be doing two things, Loren had explained with a terseness alien to him. He would be pouring the vast preponderance of his enhanced power into building another assault on Fionavar. But some of his strength he would be holding back to form a shield around himself and his sources and the Cauldron. They need not expect to find many guards at all, if indeed there were any, because Metran's shield—as Loren's own, that had blocked the Soulmonger— would be guard enough.

In order for Loren to have any hope of smashing the

Cauldron, they had to get Metran to lower that shield. And there was only one thought that occurred to any of them—they would have to battle the svarts. Not those being used as sources, but the ones, and there would have to be a great many, who were there as support.

If they could create enough chaos and panic among the svarts, Metran might just be moved to turn his defensive shield into an attacking pulse leveled at the South Keep invaders.

"And when he does that," Loren said grimly, "if I time it right and he doesn't know I'm with you, Matt and I may have a chance at the Cauldron."

No one said anything about what would happen when Metran's might, augmented by the svart alfar and the inherent power of Cader Sedat, hit the South Keep men.

There was, really, nothing to say. This was what they had come to do.

And they couldn't do it. With the wily caution of years of secret scheming, Metran had forestalled even this desperate stratagem. There *were* no support svart alfar they could attack. They could see the shield, a shimmering as of summer heat rising from fallow fields. It covered the entire front of the Hall, *and all the svart alfar were behind it.* Only an occasional runner, like the winebearer they had killed, would make a darting foray out from the Hall. And they couldn't mount a threat against so few. They couldn't do anything. If they charged down onto the floor, the svarts would have a laughing time picking them off with arrows from behind the shield. Metran wouldn't even have to look up from his book.

Frantically, Paul scanned the Hall, saw Diarmuid doing the same. To have come so far, for Kevin to have died to let them come, for Gereint to have hurled his very soul to them—and for this, for nothing! There were no doors behind the screen, no windows over the dais whereon the Cauldron stood, and Metran, and all the svart alfar.

"The wall?" he murmured hopelessly. "In through the back wall?"

"Five feet thick," Diamuid said. "And he'll have shielded

it, anyway." Paul had never seen him look as now he did. He supposed he appeared the same way himself. He felt sick. He saw that he was shaking.

He heard from just behind them Cavall whimper once, very softly.

His sudden memory from the dark corridor came back. Quickly he looked past Diarmuid. Lying prone beyond the Prince, gazing back at Paul, was Arthur. Who said, a whisper of sound, "I think this *is* what Kim brought me for. I never see the end, in any case." There was something unbearable in his face. Paul heard Diarmuid draw a sharp breath and he watched Arthur move back from the entrance so he could rise without being seen. Paul and the Prince followed.

The Warrior crouched before his dog. Cavall had known, Paul realized. His own rage was gone. He hurt instead, as he had not since he'd seen the grey dog's eyes under the Summer Tree.

Arthur had his hands in the scarred fur of the dog's ruff. They looked at each other, man and dog; Paul found he could not watch. Looking away, he heard Arthur say, "Farewell, my gallant joy. You would come with me, I know, but it may not be. You will be needed yet, great heart. There . . . may yet come a day when we need not part."

Paul still could not look at them. There was something difficult in his throat. It was hard to breathe, around the ache of it. He heard Arthur rise. He saw him lay a broad hand on Diarmuid's shoulder.

"Weaver grant you rest," Diarmuid said. Nothing more. But he was crying. Arthur turned to Paul. The summer stars were in his eyes. Paul did not weep. He had been on the Tree, had been warned by Arthur himself that this might happen. He held out both his hands and felt them clasped.

"What shall I say?" he asked. "If I have the chance?"

Arthur looked at him. There was so much grey in the brown hair and beard. "Tell her . . ." He stopped, then slowly shook his head. "No. She knows already everything that ever could be told."

Paul nodded and was crying, after all. Despite everything. What preparation was adequate to this? He felt his hands released into the cold again. The stars turned away. He saw Arthur draw his sword in the corridor and then go down the five steps alone into the Hall.

The one prize that might draw the killing force of Metran's power.

He went quickly and was most of the way to the dais before he stopped. Scrambling back with Diarmuid to watch, Paul saw that Metran and the svarts were so absorbed they hadn't even seen him.

"Slave of the Dark, hear me!" cried Arthur Pendragon in the great voice that had been heard in so many of the worlds. It reverberated through Cader Sedat. The svart alfar shouted in alarm. Paul saw Metran's head snap up, but he also saw that the mage was unafraid.

He gave Arthur an unhurried scrutiny from beneath his white eyebrows and bony forehead. And, Paul thought bitterly, from behind the safety of his shield.

"I intend to hear you," Metran said tranquilly. "Before you die you will tell me who you are and how you came here."

"Speak not lightly of dying in this place," Arthur said. "You are among the great of all the worlds here. And they can be awakened. As for my name: know that I am Arthur Pendragon, son of Uther, King of Britain. I am the Warrior Condemned, summoned here to battle you, *and I cannot die!*"

Only an arrow, Paul thought fearfully. An arrow could kill him now. But the svart alfar were gibbering in panic, and even Metran's gaze seemed less secure.

"Our books of lore," he said, "tell a different tale."

"Doubtless," Arthur replied. "But before you run to them, know this: I command you now to quit this place on the hour or I shall go down and wake the dead in their wrath to drive you into the sea!"

Metran's eyes wavered indecisively. He came slowly from behind the high table. He hesitated, then said, sharp and brittle in the huge room, "It is told you can be killed. Over and over, you have been killed. I will offer your head before the throne in Starkadh!"

He raised one arm high over his head. There came a low sound from Cavall. Arthur's head was lifted, waiting. *This is it,* Paul thought, and he prayed.

Then Metran lowered his hand slowly and began, brutally, to laugh.

It lasted a time time, corrosive, contemptuous. *He's an actor,* Paul remembered, wincing under the laceration of that mockery. *He fooled them all for so long.*

"Loren, Loren, Loren," Metran finally gasped, overcome by his own amusement. "Just because you are a fool must you take me for one? Come and tell me how you eluded the Soulmonger, then let me put you out of pain." His laughter ended. There was a bleak malevolence in his face.

From the far side of the Hall, Paul heard Loren's voice. "Metran, you had a father, but I will not trouble his rest by giving your full name. Know that the Council of the Mages has ordered your death, and so, too, has the High King of Brennin. You have been cursed in Council and are now to die. Know also that we did not elude the Soulmonger. We slew him."

"Hah!" Metran barked. "Will you bluster still, Silvercloak?"

"I never did," said Loren and, with Matt, he stepped into the green light of the Great Hall. "Behold the staff of Amairgen for proof!" And he held the Whitebranch high.

At that, Metran stepped back and Paul saw real dismay on his face. But for a moment only.

"Brightly woven, then!" said Metran sarcastically. "A feat to be sung! And for reward now, I will allow you to stand here and watch, Loren. Watch helplessly, you and whoever you coerced into this voyage, while I move a rain of death from Eridu, where it has been falling for three days now, over the mountains into the High Kingdom."

"In the name of the Weaver," Diarmuid said, horrified, as Metran deliberately turned his back on Loren and returned to his table by the Cauldron. Once more the svart alfar resumed their cycling of the living and dead. Through it all Denbarra stood, his eyes staring at nothing, his mouth open, slack and soundless.

"Look," Paul said.

Matt was talking urgently to Loren. They saw the mage stand irresolute a moment, looking at the Dwarf; then Matt said something more and Loren nodded once.

He turned back to the dais and, raising the staff of Amairgen, pointed it at the Cauldron. Metran glanced up at him and smiled. Loren spoke a word, then another. When he spoke the third, a bolt of silver light leaped from the staff, dazzling all of them.

The stones of Cader Sedat shook. Paul opened his eyes. He saw Metran struggling to his feet. He felt the castle trembling still. He saw the vast Cauldron of Khath Meigol sway and rock on its base above the fire.

Then he saw it settle back again as it had been.

The shield had held. He turned and watched Matt slowly rising from the ground. Even from a distance he could see the Dwarf trembling with what that power surge had taken from him. And, abruptly, he remembered that Matt had sourced a shield against the Soulmonger that same day, and then a steering of all the worlds' winds away from them as they sailed to the island. He couldn't begin to comprehend what the Dwarf was enduring. What words were there, what thoughts even, in the face of a thing like this? And how did you deal with the fact that it wasn't enough?

Shaken but unhurt, Metran stepped forward again. "You have bought the death you came for now," he said with no trace of idle play in him any more. "When you are dead, I can begin shaping the death rain again; it makes no matter in the end. I shall grind your bones to powder and lay your skull by my bed, Loren Silvercloak, servant of Ailell." And he closed the book on the table and began gesturing in a gathering motion with his arms.

He was bringing in his power, Paul realized. He was going to use it all on Loren and Matt. This was the end, then. And if that was so—

Paul leaped from the entranceway, down the stairs, and ran across the floor to Matt's side. He dropped to his knees there.

"A shoulder might help," he said. "Lean on me."

Without a word, Matt did so, and, from above, Paul felt Loren touch him once in a gesture of farewell. Then he saw the Whitebranch lifted again, to point squarely at Metran, who stood now between them and the Cauldron. He watched Metran level a long finger straight at the three of them.

Then both mages spoke together and the Great Hall shook to its foundations as two bolts of power exploded toward each other. One was silver, like the moon, like the cloak Loren wore, and the other was the baleful green of the lights in that place; they met midway between the mages, and where they met a fire leaped to flame in the air.

Paul heard Matt Sören fight to control his breathing. Above him, he glimpsed Loren's rigid arm holding the staff, straining to channel the power the Dwarf was feeding him. And on the dais he saw Metran, sourced by so very many of the svart alfar, bend the same power that had made winter in midsummer directly down on them. Easily, effortlessly.

He felt Matt begin to tremble. The Dwarf leaned more heavily on his arm. He had nothing to offer them. Only a shoulder. Only pity. Only love.

Crackling savagely, the two beams of power locked into each other as the castle continued to shake under their unleashed force. They held and held, the silver and the green, held each other flaming in the air while worlds hung in the balance. So long it went on, Paul had an illusion that time had stopped. He helped up the Dwarf—both arms around him now—and prayed with all his soul to what he knew of Light.

Then he saw that none of it was enough. Not courage, wisdom, prayer, necessity. Not one against so many. Slowly, with brutal clarity, the silver thrust of power was being pushed back toward them. Inch by bitter, fighting inch Paul saw Loren forced to give way. He heard the mage's breathing now, ragged and shallow. He looked up and saw sweat pouring in rivulets down Loren's face. Beside him, Matt was still on his feet, still fighting, though his whole body shook now as with a lethal fever.

A shoulder. Pity. Love. What else could he give them here

at the end? And with whom else would he rather die than these two?

Matt Sören spoke. With an effort so total it almost shattered Paul's heart, the Dwarf forced sounds out of his chest. "Loren," he gasped, his face contorted with strain. "Loren . . . do now!"

The green surge of Metran's might leaped half a foot nearer to them. Paul could feel the fire now. Loren was silent. His breathing rasped horribly.

"Loren," Matt mumbled again. "I have lived for this. Do it now." The Dwarf's one eye was closed. He trembled continuously. Paul closed his own eyes, and held Matt as tightly as he could.

"Matt," he heard the mage say. "Oh, Matt." The name, nothing more.

Then the Dwarf spoke to Paul and he said, "Thank you, my friend. You had better move back now." And grieving, grieving, Paul did so. Looking up, he saw Loren's face distort with wildest hate. He heard the mage cry out then, tapping into his uttermost power, sourced in Matt Sören the Dwarf, channeled through the Whitebranch of Amairgen, and the very heart and soul of Loren Silvercloak were in that cry and in the blast that followed it.

There came a flash of obliterating light. The very island rocked this time, and with that shaking of Cader Sedat a tremor rolled through every one of the Weaver's worlds.

Metran screamed, high and short, as if cut off. Stones shook loose from the walls over their heads. Paul saw Matt fall to the ground, saw Loren drop beside him. Then, looking up toward the dais, he saw the Cauldron of Khath Meigol crack asunder with a sound like a mountain shattering.

The shield was down. He knew Metran was dead. Knew someone else was, too. He saw the svart alfar, bred to kill, beginning to run with swords and knives toward them, and, crying aloud, he rose up and drew his own sword to guard those who had done what they had done.

The svarts never reached him. They were met by forty men of Brennin, led by Diarmuid dan Ailell, and the soldiers of South Keep cut a swath of sheer fury through the ranks of the Dark. Paul charged into the battle, wielding a sword with love running high in his heart like a tide—love, and the need to hammer through grief.

There were many svarts and they were a long time in the killing, but they killed them all. Eventually Paul found himself, bleeding from a number of minor wounds, standing with Diarmuid and Coll in one of the passageways leading back to the Great Hall. There was nowhere else to go, so they went back there.

In the entrance they paused and looked out over the carnage wrought in that place. They were near to the dais and walked up to it. Metran lay flung on his back, his face shattered, his body disfigured by hideous burns. Near him lay Denbarra. The source had been babbling through the fight, with the staring eyes of the hopelessly mad, until Diarmuid had put a sword through his heart and left him near his mage.

Not far from them, still smoldering, lay the thousand, thousand fragments of the Cauldron of Khath Meigol, shattered. Like a heart, thought Paul, and turned to walk the other way. He had to step over and around the dead svart alfar and the stones of the walls and ceiling dislodged in the final cataclysm. It was very quiet now. The green lights were gone. Diarmuid's men were lighting torches around the Hall. By their glow Paul saw, as he came near, a figure on his knees rocking slowly back and forth amid the devastation with a dark head cradled in his lap.

*I have lived for this,* Matt Sören had said; and had made his mage go into him for killing, uttermost power. And had died.

Looking down in silence, Paul saw then in the Dwarf's face, dead, a thing he had never seen in it, living: Matt Sören smiled amid the ruin of Cader Sedat, not the grimace they had learned to know but the true smile of one who has had what he most desired.

A thousand, thousand fragments, like a heart. Paul looked at Loren.

He touched the kneeling man, once, as the mage had

292

touched him before; then he walked away. Looking back, he saw that Loren had cast his cloak over his face.

He saw Arthur with Diarmuid and went over to them. The torches were lit now, all around the Hall. Arthur said, "We have time, all the time we need to take. Let us leave him for a while."

Together the three of them walked with Cavall down the dark, moldering corridors of Cader Sedat. It was damp and cold. A chill, sourceless wind seemed to be blowing among the crumbling stones.

"You spoke of the dead?" Paul murmured.

"I did," said Arthur. "Spiral Castle holds, below the level of the sea, the mightiest of the dead in all the worlds." They turned. Another darker corridor.

"You spoke of waking them," Paul said.

Arthur shook his head. "I cannot. I was trying to frighten him. They can only be wakened by name and, when last here, I was very young and I did not know—" He stopped, then, and stood utterly still.

*No!* Paul thought. *It is enough. It has been enough, surely.*

He opened his mouth to speak but found he could not. The Warrior took a slow breath, as if drawing it from his long past, from the core of his being. Then he nodded, once only, and with effort, as if moving his head against a weight of worlds.

"Come," was all he said. Paul looked at Diarmuid, and in the darkness he saw the same stiff apprehension in the Prince's face. They followed Arthur and the dog.

This time they went down. The corridor Arthur took sloped sharply, and they had to use the walls to keep their balance. The stones were clammy to the touch. There was light now, though, a faint phosphorescence of the corridor itself. Diarmuid's white tunic gleamed in it.

They became aware of a steady pounding noise beyond the walls.

"The sea," Arthur said quietly, and then stopped before a door Paul had not seen. The Warrior turned to the two of them. "You may prefer to wait out here," he said.

There was a silence.

Paul shook his head. "I have tasted death," he said.

Diarmuid smiled, a brief flash of his old smile. "One of us in there," he said, "had best be normal, don't you think?"

So they left the dog by the door and passed within, amid the incessant pounding of the sea on the walls.

There were fewer than Paul had thought there would be. It was not an overly large chamber. The floor was stone and without adornment. In the center stood a single pillar, and upon it one candle burned with a white flame that did not waver. The walls gleamed palely. Set around the room in alcoves dimly lit by the candle and the phosphorescence of the walls were perhaps twenty bodies lying on beds of stone. Only that many, Paul thought, from all the dead in all the worlds. Almost he walked over to look upon them, to see the faces of the chosen great, but a diffidence overtook him, a sense of intruding upon their rest. Then he felt Diarmuid's hand on his arm, and he saw that Arthur was standing in front of one of the alcoves and that his hands were covering his face.

"It is enough!" Paul cried aloud and moved to Arthur's side.

In front of them, as if asleep, save that he did not breathe, lay a man of more than middle height. His hair was black, his cheeks shaven. His eyes were closed, but wide-set under a high forehead. His mouth and chin were firm, and his hands, Paul saw, clasped the hilt of a sword and were very beautiful. He looked to have been a lord among men, and if he was lying in this place, Paul knew, he had been.

He also knew who this was.

"My lord Arthur," said Diarmuid painfully, "you do not have to do this. It is neither written nor compelled."

Arthur lowered his hands. His gaze never left the face of the man who lay on the stone.

"He will be needed," he said. "He cannot but be needed. I should have known it was too soon for me to die."

"You are willing your own grief," Paul whispered.

Arthur turned to him at that, and his eyes were compassionate. "It was willed long ago."

Looking on Arthur Pendragon's face in that moment, Paul saw a purer nobility than he had ever seen in his days. More, even, than in Liranan, or Cernan of the Beasts. Here was the quintessence, and everything in him cried out against the doom that lay behind this monstrous choice.

Diarmuid, he saw, had turned away.

"*Lancelot!*" said Arthur to the figure on the bed of stone.

His eyes were brown. He was taller than Paul had first thought. His voice was mild and low and unexpectedly gentle. The other surprising thing was the dog. Paul had thought Cavall's loyalty would make him hostile, but instead he'd come up to the dark-haired man with a quiet sound of joy. Lancelot had knelt to stroke the torn grey fur, and Paul could see him register the presence of the scars. Then he had walked in silence between Paul and Diarmuid back up to the living world.

He had only spoken at the very beginning. After he had first risen to the Warrior's command. Risen, as if, truly, he had only been asleep and not dead so very, very long.

Arthur had said, "Be welcome. We are at war against the Dark in Fionavar, which is the first world of all. I have been summoned, and so now are you."

And Lancelot had replied with courtesy and sorrow, "Why have you done this, my lord, to the three of us?"

Arthur had closed his eyes at that. Then opened them and said, "Because there are more at risk than the three of us. I will see if I can have us fight in different companies."

And Lancelot had answered mildly, "Arthur, you know I will not fight save under you and by your side."

At which point Arthur had turned on his heel to walk away, and Diarmuid and Paul had named themselves and, with Lancelot, had followed the Warrior back from the place of the dead amid the pounding of the sea.

Loren had risen. His cloak lay covering the body of Matt Sören. The mage, his face numb with weariness and shock, listened as Diarmuid and Arthur made plans for their departure. He hardly acknowledged Lancelot's presence, though the men of South Keep were whispering among each other with awe.

It was, Paul gathered, still daylight outside. Not long after noon, in fact. It seemed to him as if they had been on the island forever. In a way, he supposed, a part of him would always be on this island. Too much had happened here. They were going to be leaving almost immediately, it appeared. No one was minded to spend a night in this place.

Loren turned. Paul saw him walk over to one of the torches. He stood there with the pages of a book in his hand, feeding them one by one to the flame. Paul went over to him. Loren's face was streaked with the tracks of tears and sweat, running down through the soot and grime stirred up when the last bolt fell. Matt's last, Paul thought. And Loren's too. His source was dead. He wasn't a mage any more.

"The Book of Nilsom," said the man who had bade them cross with him so long ago. He gave Paul a number of pages. Together they stood, reaching up in turn to set each page alight.

It took a long time and they did it carefully. Somehow eased by the shared, simple task, Paul watched the last leaf burn; then he and Loren turned back to the others.

Who were staring, all of them, at one place in the Hall.

There were over forty men in that place but Paul couldn't hear any of them breathe. He walked toward Lancelot through the ring of men, saw the pure, unyielding will in his eyes, watched the color begin to drain from his face, and he began to grasp the magnitude of this man who was trying to surmount, by sheerest resolution, the movement of the wheel of time and the shuttling of the Loom. They stood very close; he saw it all.

Beside him, Loren made a strangled sound and a gesture of denial. Paul heard the flap of wings. Even here. *Thought, Memory.*

"Loren, wait!" he said. "He did it once before. And this is Cader Sedat."

Slowly, the mage advanced, and Paul with him, to stand a little nearer yet. A little nearer to the place where Lancelot du Lac, newly wakened from his own death, knelt on the stone floor with the hands of Matt Sören between his own, and held up to his brow.

And because they were closer than the others, he and Loren were the first to see the Dwarf begin to breathe.

Paul could never remember what it was he shouted. He knew that the cry that went up from the men of Brennin dislodged yet more stones from the walls of Cader Sedat. Loren dropped to his knees, his face alight, on the other side of the Dwarf from Lancelot. The dark-haired man was white but composed, and they saw Matt's breathing become slowly steadier.

And then the Dwarf looked up at them.

He gazed at Loren for a long time, then turned to Lancelot. He glanced at his hands clasped in the other's, still, and Paul could see him grasp what had happened. Matt looked up at their hovering, torchlit faces. His mouth twitched in a remembered way.

"What happened to my other eye?" Matt Sören said to Lancelot, and they all laughed and wept for joy.

It was because of where they were, Lancelot explained, and because he was so newly wakened from death himself, and because Matt had suffered no killing wound, only a draining of his life force. And, he added in his courteous, diffident way, because he had done this once before at Camelot.

Matt nodded slowly. He was already on his feet. They clustered close to him, unwilling to leave him alone, to have any distance come between. Loren's tired face glowed. It eased the heart to look on him.

"Well," said Diarmuid, "now that we have our mage and source back, shall we sail?"

There was a chorus of agreement.

"We should," said Loren. "But you should know that Teyrnon is now the only mage in Fionavar."

"What?" It was the Dwarf.

Loren smiled sadly. "Reach for me, my friend."

Slowly they saw Matt's face drain of color.

"Easy," Loren cautioned. "Be easy." He turned to the others. "Let no one grieve. When Matt died our link was broken and I ceased to be a mage. Bringing him back could not reforge what had been severed." There was a silence.

"Oh, Loren," Matt said faintly.

Loren wheeled on him and there was a fire in his eyes. "Hear me!" He spun again and looked at the company. "I was a man before I was a mage. I hated the Dark as a child and I do so now, and I can wield a sword!" He turned back to Matt and his voice deepened. "You left your destiny once to link it with my own and it led you far from home, my friend. Now, it seems, the circle is closing. Will you accept me? Am I a fit companion for the rightful King of Dwarves, who must go back now to Calor Diman to reclaim his Crown?"

And they were humbled and abashed at what blazed forth from Loren in that moment, as he knelt on the stones before Matt.

They had gathered what there was to gather, and had begun to leave the Hall. So much had happened. Every one of them was bone-weary and stumbling with it. So much. Paul thought he could sleep for days.

He and Arthur seemed to be the last ones. The others were walking up the corridor already. There would be light outside. He marveled at that. Here there were only the torches, and the smoldering embers of the fire that had burned beneath the Cauldron of Khath Meigol.

He saw that Arthur had paused in the doorway for a last look back. Paul turned as well. And realized that they were not the last of the party, after all. Amid the wreckage of that shattered place a dark-haired figure stood, looking up at the two of them.

Or, not really the two of them. He saw Arthur and Lancelot gaze at each other and something so deep he could never have tried to name it passed between the two of them. Then Arthur spoke, and there was sorrow in his voice and there was love. "Oh, Lance, come," he said. "She will be waiting for you."

*Here ends THE WANDERING FIRE,*
*the second book of*
*THE FIONAVAR TAPESTRY*